FINDING DANDI

Hell Yeah! Book 9 - Cajun Style

SABLE HUNTER

Copyright © 2013
Sable Hunter
All rights reserved.
www.sablehunter.com

ISBN-13: 978-1484810750
ISBN-10: 1484810759

Six brothers. One Dynasty—
TEBOW RANCH.
Meet the McCoy brothers and their friends— men who love as hard as they play.

Texas Cowboys – nothing hotter.
HELL YEAH!

Take a moment to check out Sable's current and upcoming projects.

Visit her on:
Website: http://www.sablehunter.com
Facebook: https://www.facebook.com/authorsablehunter
Email: sablehunter@rocketmail.com

Check out all of Sable's books on Amazon
http://www.amazon.com/author/sablehunter

Cover and Technical Advising by Added Touches
http://www.addedtouches.com

CONTENTS

PROLOGUE

Meet Lucas Dane Wagner

Lucas at Work

"I am here to help you, Lana. There is no reason you can't enjoy your sex life." Leaning back in his leather chair, he studied the pretty blonde woman sitting in front of him, folding and refolding the hem of her skirt. She was so nervous; there was no need to be.

"My husband is getting very put out with me. I love his touch, but it's a vicious circle. The harder I try to please him, the more frustrated I become. He wants me to have an orgasm, and I just can't. I'm so afraid he's going to divorce me." She began to cry.

This was a sad story Lucas had heard too often. Couples would experience one setback, maybe premature ejaculation or a failure to climax. This disappointment would lead to another episode, and soon the expectation to fail would spiral out of control. "Lana, your husband loves you. He told me so. Let's get him in here, I have some suggestions for you both that I think will help, I promise."

He pressed the call button for his secretary and asked her to send Gary Peters in to join his wife. In a few seconds the tall, sandy-haired male came in, looking extremely uncomfortable. No matter how advanced or progressive society became, people always hesitated to discuss or confess their sexual short-comings. Especially men. "Sit, please." He motioned toward the other large wing-back chair in front of his desk.

Lucas loved sex – he craved it. Bringing a woman to orgasm was the crowning joy in his life. His chosen field of work was meant to help other people learn the satisfaction and fulfillment that only sexual intimacy can bring.

"Hi, Honey," Lana touched her husband's hand. He smiled back. Lucas smiled, too. He could help these people.

"Okay, I want to set your minds at ease. We can fix this. You two are very fortunate. There is an abundance of love and desire in

i

your relationship, all we have to do is get you to relax and let it happen."

"We try . . ." Lana began, but Lucas held up his hand.

"This is what I want you to do tonight." They both looked at him, anxiously. "I want you to have a relaxing dinner and remind yourself why you fell in love. Laugh together, remember your wedding, or the first time you met. Hold hands on the couch. Gary, give your wife a back rub. Treat one another with respect and flirt a little bit."

"That doesn't sound too hard, but will it work?" Lana cut her eyes at her husband, as if asking him to back up her concern. Unfortunately, most people wanted him to prescribe a pill for what ailed them instead of admitting that the problem was one that required a change in behavior or attitude.

"I'm not finished," he assured them. "When you get ready to go to bed, I want you to try this – Gary you sit up in the bed, leaning back against the headboard. Spread your legs and let Lana sit in between them with her back against your front." He knew the more specific his instructions, the more inclined they would be to follow them.

"What?" Lana flushed pink and put her hands over her warm cheeks.

"It's okay, Darling," Gary touched her arm. "We need to try."

"I know, I'm just embarrassed."

"Don't be," Lucas sympathized. "This is a common problem, and what I'm asking you to do will work. Gary, Lana's only role during this exercise is to feel pleasure. And your only role is to give pleasure." He smiled at the young couple. "Of course, Gary is a man, Lana. Giving you pleasure is going to be a bigger turn-on than anything he has ever experienced."

"God, that sounds good," Gary groaned and Lana blushed anew.

Lucas continued with his directions. "While Lana is relaxing against you, Gary, what I want you to do, is to begin to touch her. Rub her shoulders and arms. Kiss her neck, put your hands on her breasts and massage them. Take her nipples between your fingers and play with them."

"Hell," Gary groaned. Even Lana leaned forward, hanging on his every word.

"Lana, you turn your head and seek his lips. If something feels good, let him know. Whimpers and moans of pleasure, compliments to one another — all of these things will fuel your desire."

"Sounds like it." Gary agreed.

"When Lana is unable to be still in your arms, you'll know she is aroused. Slip your hand between her legs and massage her vulva. Rub her clit around and around — don't worry about trying to penetrate her, just focus on making her feel wonderful." He left it there. If it worked like he thought it would, Lana would be brought to orgasm and beg her husband to make love to her.

"We'll try it now!" Gary stood up and held out his hand. He was anxious to get home, and from the bloom in Lana's cheeks — she was anxious to join him. Lucas watched them leave, wishing he had someone waiting at home for him. One day, one day he would.

Pushing up from his chair, he went to the window and looked out at the bustling scene. The view from his office was downtown Little Rock. From where he stood, he could see a panorama of the city - the Clinton Presidential Library, the River Market District and the scenic Arkansas River. The whole area was a happening place full of trendy restaurants, museums, art galleries and expensive boutiques. This town had been good to him, but it was almost time to move on. After graduating from Tulane University in New Orleans, he had performed his residency here at the illustrious Anderson Clinic, renowned for its groundbreaking work in psychiatric care and intimacy issues. But his residency was over. It was time for him to make his mark in the world.

Lucas was pleased with his progress. So far, his life was on schedule. He had many people to thank for that, one man in particular - Dr. Fredrich Solomon. Dr. Solomon had been his favorite professor, and soon would be his business associate, hopefully. If the creek didn't rise and hell didn't freeze over, everything was on track for him to be offered a partnership. The only thing holding it up was his meeting with the board on Valentine's Day, just over two weeks away. They were so impressed with him that they were flying in from various parts of the country to interview him here in Little Rock. Not many young doctors were afforded such an honor.

Dr. Solomon had been his mentor and his inspiration. Lucas had tried to live his life based on his wise friend's words and example. One lecture had really hit home. "Most people are complicated. They war with themselves. Their hearts and minds are torn in two different directions. Some struggle with who they are and who they wish they were. Others battle disappointment in what they have become and who they used to be. Very few people are simple and straight forward. We all harbor natures we have to tame or tendencies we have to control. I am not necessarily speaking of something as radical as a Jekyll/Hyde syndrome; I'm speaking of the ordinary, everyday task of being the master of our fate and the captain of our soul. Only you can decide who you are and what you want to accomplish in this world. Only you can conquer your demons and move forward in the direction you wish to go."

He had agreed with every word his mentor said, for he was two people. The first Lucas was the dedicated, determined doctor-to-be. His dream was to be a viable, needed part of a community where he could hold his head up and walk among his neighbors, peers and patients knowing that he was someone they could respect and depend upon.

Turning from the window, he walked to the coffeepot, pouring himself a strong cup of rich brew. The second Lucas was more complicated, he was vulnerable. A scene from his childhood raised its ugly head. "Keep your filthy hands off of me," his mother had screamed at his poor father. "I'll go where I please, with whom I please. I'll sleep where I want to and with who I want to, and you and this worrisome brat can like it or lump it."

Lucas had neither liked it nor lumped it; he had suffered through it and vowed before God in heaven that his life would be different.

Everyone's past molds their future. Lucas was no different. Returning to his desk, he opened a drawer, and took out a worn picture of himself and his parents. It was not a formal portrait; there had never been money or opportunity for his small family to visit a real photographer. This casual shot had been taken by his grandmother one Christmas. The man and the woman who tried to smile for the camera only managed to look miserable; and he, sitting between them, had known how unhappy they were. Children always knew. In this photo, he had been seven years old.

Lucas threw the image down on his desk. Memories of coming home to an empty house every day came flooding back. There would be nothing to eat in the refrigerator except ketchup and bread, and he'd have to pick up the liquor bottles and dirty dishes off the kitchen table so he'd have a place to eat his meal and do his homework.

He remembered the arguments and the fights his parents had. He remembered the neighbors standing on their porches to listen and watch the spectacle of Della and Wayne Wagner as they hurled insults and accusations at one another. Sometimes their battles would be played out in the front yard. When they had warred with one another, they hadn't cared who heard or how their child was affected. Sadly, the accusations they threw at one another were true. His mother was blatantly unfaithful to her husband and his father drank himself to death because of it.

She hadn't even tried to hide her infidelity, strange men would bring her home night after night and several times he and his dad would be called to come pick her up from strip clubs or bars when she would be stranded and drunk, too broke to call a cab home.

Lucas had survived. He had even thrived, but he had made the decision early that his life would be different. Respectability, stability and tradition would define his world. Never would he allow a child of his to wonder when his mother was coming home or have to defend her reputation to his friends or classmates. His family would be cherished and adored. To make that happen, Lucas intended to marry the perfect woman – a woman who would put home and hearth above all else, a woman with high morals, whose greatest ambition in life was to make a haven for him and their children.

"Lucas, your three o'clock is here." The voice over the intercom was welcome. He enjoyed his job. In a few moments, he was joined by a young man seeking his help for inadequacy issues, and he was determined to give it.

Meet Dandi Lyn Alexander

Dandi at Fifteen

"You are going to have a wonderful life, Dandi." Miss Etta led the way through the thick pine trees at the back of her property. "I just wish I was going to be around to see it."

"Don't say that, Miss Etta," she followed along behind the tall grey-haired woman who had been her salvation. "I need you, I'll always need you." Beneath their feet the straw and leaves were so thick that Dandi had to jump through it at times. Cockle-burrs stuck to the legs of her jeans. How Miss Etta managed to glide through the underbrush without even getting a twig stuck in her frilly purple sundress was a mystery.

"Look," the older lady pointed at a small hill, deftly changing the subject. Her days were numbered, but she still had some time left to spend with Dandi. "Do you know what that is?"

"No," Dandi never doubted that it was more than it appeared to be, Miss Etta's world was full of knowledge and wonder. She covered her eyes with her hand, shading them from the bright afternoon sun.

"It's a Native American burial mound – right here, on my property. There are three of them," she pointed out more small hills in the distance. Her proper, soft voice was filled with pride. Miss Etta had a hint of a southern drawl, but it was tempered by decades of exposure to other cultures, dealing with varied people in cities around the world. "I've contacted the government and the Forest Service. I would like for an archaeologist to come and investigate this area."

Dandi was fascinated. She walked slowly around the gentle rise. "Are people buried here? Really?" Visions of chiefs in war, colorful bonnets and squaws tending fires outside their wigwams sprung from her imagination.

"Perhaps," Miss Etta's voice changed. She was going into story mode. Dandi loved it when Miss Etta taught her things. "There are many theories concerning these mounds. Some feel they were part of rituals, others think they were sanctuaries. We don't really know, and they can't be disturbed without being destroyed. I want them preserved and recognized."

As they walked together, Dandi spotted a small arrowhead. "May I pick it up?"

"Yes," she was given permission, so she reached down to get it and handed it to the other woman. "This would have been used to hunt birds, perhaps by a child no older than you."

"Did girls hunt also?"

"Sometimes, I think. These people would have done whatever was necessary for their survival. Let's sit and imagine what their life might have been like. Take out your sketch pad and draw what your instinct tells you." Dandi took her bright orange backpack off and drew out her precious paper and pencils. Plopping down beside her friend who sat on a stump worn smooth by time and wind, Dandi drew her knees up and steadied the pad. As Miss Etta talked, she drew. "This land was populated by Native Americas as far back as 2900 B.C., almost four thousand years ago. Soon, I will take you over to Poverty Point near Vicksburg and let you climb the Bird Mound. But for now, picture the families — hunting, fishing, making pottery and laughing as they cooked around the campfires. These were real people, who loved and lived and bore children and died — right here."

That day, Dandi decided she wanted to be an archaeologist when she grew up. Dancing and painting were wonderful hobbies and she enjoyed trying to do what Miss Etta taught her, but discovering the past and learning about people and places long gone struck a chord in her that nothing else had ever done.

When she was out and about with her friend like this, Dandi could forget what her home life was like. Since her father had passed away, her world had crumbled. Her mom had worked so hard — leaving Dandi alone most of the time. And when she had remarried, a whole new set of problems had emerged. She had even been forced to give up her dear father's last name, LeBlanc and take her new stepfather's name — Alexander. She hated it.

Home wasn't safe for Dandi anymore.

So, she clung to Miss Etta. Every day she escaped into worlds that she would have never known if not for this gracious woman who shared her time and life with Dandi. Ballet, modern dance, art, music — Dandi was like a sponge, absorbing everything she was offered. Most of all, she absorbed the love.

"Remember, Dandi," her mentor patted the ground beside her, and she scooted closer to the older lady who was kind to the young, gangly teenager. "No matter what the years bring, you will know what you are capable of accomplishing. You are talented, more so than any young woman I have ever worked with." Her words brought warmth to Dandi's cheeks. Miss Etta was classy, a retired professor who still longed to impart tidbits of wisdom to those who would listen. "One day, you'll have a family and a man who loves you. There is nothing in this world that is not within your grasp. My wish for you is this: always remember who you are and always remember you have great value. Never let anyone make you feel less important than you are. You are an amazing girl. You, Dandi Alexander are worthy to be loved."

As Miss Etta spoke her tender words of encouragement, Dandi dreamed about what her life would be like. She wanted to make a difference in this world, and she wanted to be loved. Surely, that was not too much to ask.

CHAPTER ONE

"It's your choice; you can go to jail or strip in my club."

Dandi hugged herself tightly, her body was covered with goose bumps and very few of them were due to the icy cold that seeped through the cracks in the window behind Romero's paper strewn desk. For a moment she stared at the window, it looked as hopeless as she felt - the glass had been painted a dirty tan to keep people from seeing into the building. She wanted to cry, but she refused to give these idiots the satisfaction. "I didn't steal your damn money."

"The evidence says otherwise," drawled Officer Cahill, who was so overweight that just walking across the room winded him. He grinned at Tony Romero, who was lounging back in the oversize chair, his feet up on the rickety desk. Some women would probably consider Romero good-looking, but Dandi thought he was disgusting – slick and arrogant. His swarthy complexion and close-cropped dark hair reminded her of the typical villain in every gangster movie she had ever seen, and here she was living out the familiar plot-line in full cinematic color.

Dandi's skin crawled as she felt Romero's gaze slither across her body. The near-to-nothing sequined blue uniform he required the waitresses to wear left little to the imagination, consisting only of a halter top and short-shorts. Could stripping be much worse? Still, the idea of baring her body to every leering Tom, Dick or Harry that slunk into Club Tonga made her sick. "Your evidence was planted." With more courage than she felt, she raised her head and stared the crook in the eye.

Romero didn't comment upon her accusation, instead he turned to Cahill and lifted one eyebrow. Cahill was on Romero's payroll, she knew it and so did everyone else who came into the club. Now, he did Romero's talking for him. "Do you want to explain that to a judge? We know you have a record."

Knowing when she was beat, Dandi dropped her head and closed her eyes. Why did life have to be so hard? Nervously she rubbed her hand over the small tattoo on the back of her neck. Just knowing the tiny phoenix was there usually gave her strength. She had risen from the ashes more than once, but this obstacle appeared to be insurmountable.

"It's your call, Alexander," Romero snarled Dandi's last name as if it tasted bad. "If you'd rather go down to the station with Officer Cahill instead of stripping for me to pay off your debt, I understand. You've been a good waitress until you decided to pocket what belonged to me. If we hadn't searched your locker, you'd still be stealing me blind."

Romero's grin and wink directed at Cahill told Dandi how much he enjoyed manipulating her. Still, she couldn't help but fight back. "You have the money. What debt would I be working off, exactly?" Her heart ached with the knowledge that she couldn't allow herself to be arrested; the judge wouldn't be as lenient the second time. No amount of explaining had convinced anyone she was innocent of shoplifting. Jewel had been the one with the sticky fingers. One of her ex-roommates had been trying to filch a cheap watch at the department store. When the security guard became suspicious, Jewel slipped it into Dandi's pocket and Dandi had paid the price. There had been a fine and three months of probation for a ten dollar watch that she had no desire to buy, much less steal.

"Don't sass us, Sweetheart," big, bulky Cahill stepped into her space, grabbing her roughly by the arm. "Put your hands behind your back. I'll enjoy escorting you downtown. We might even stop along the way; it would give us a little time to get better acquainted."

"Don't call me sweetheart, and you're the last person I would want to touch me," his vile breath tickled her face and caused the bile to rise in her throat. Dandi wanted to scream, but what good would it do? If only she hadn't felt relaxed enough to dance yesterday, she'd still be carting beers and dodging drunks who tried to pinch her bottom – not ideal, but she was making enough to buy the insulin she needed with a little left over for food and her share of the tiny apartment.

The impromptu performance had been so innocent. Tonga's DJ had come in early to reorganize and clean out his play-list. Jeff was a nice guy, at least he had been kind to Dandi. They had been chatting while she wiped down the tables and refilled the salt and pepper shakers. He had been playing random songs, when one came on that had swept Dandi back in time, back to when she had been safe and loved.

"After All" told of lovers who were given a second chance. Even though it was a sappy tune, it had caught her imagination. A lifetime ago, she had been her dad's Angel, he had told her so. Later Miss Etta had taught her to move with the ebb and flow of the music, letting her body immerse itself in the emotions that flooded her soul. Her dad had loved to watch her dance. When the singer crooned the part about two angels who'd been rescued from the fall, tears had clouded her eyes – and Dandi had stepped out and began a routine that she hadn't attempted in years. One of the other girls had fetched Romero to see the young cocktail waitress as she moved about the club, lost in her own memories.

Dandi had always been able to lose herself in music. Now, standing here before Romero, she was afraid she might lose herself all together. There was no way she could afford to go to jail, she might not survive. Steeling her resolve for the inevitable, she relented, "I'll dance, but I won't strip."

"You'll do as you're told, you little bitch." Romero's voice was low and smooth, yet with a sharp edge that made her cringe. "Get ready. You'll perform tonight. I have just the costume for you. I know you'll be amateurish, but your body is perfect enough to hold their interest until you learn the ropes. Head over to the girl's dressing room and I'll have Minnie bring the dress to you. Jane will show you some moves. And dance to that same song – it'll bring some class to the joint. I liked it."

Before Dandi could turn to leave, Cahill pushed her hair over her shoulder, his fat, stubby fingers lingering on her skin. She jerked back, not wanting his attention. "Why you dirty, little . . ." The off-duty police officer pulled back his fist back to hit her, but Romero grabbed his arm.

"No bruises on the face, if you want to punish her, there are other ways."

"What ways?"

While they bickered, Dandi rushed from Romero's office and ran down the narrow, dark hall. She didn't want to wait around and find out how they could hurt her – she'd rather not think about it. Temptation was strong to just slip out the front door and keep on running. The thought made her hesitate in front of the door as she stared at the exit sign; it looked like the gateway to freedom to her. Could she get away and disappear? How far could she get? They'd hunt for her, but perhaps she could leave town.

"Don't even think about it," Romero whispered in her ear and she jumped, obviously guilty. He ran a hard finger up her side, marking every rib. "You'll never get away from me, I own you. I own lots of people."

"No, you are wrong. You'll never own me." God, he gave her the creeps. The other girls whispered about what went on here: drugs, prostitution, even organized crime. Just last night Dandi had heard Romero and Cahill arguing. Something was going down. Romero was being threatened by someone more powerful and dirtier than he was. God, she wished she had never come to this place. How had her life become such a nightmare?

"We'll see about that. You need money for your drugs, don't you?" With a firm grip, he took her by the elbow and guided her behind the stage, pushing her forward.

Yes, she needed the insulin. Until she could find another way to make enough money, he had her over a barrel.

The voices of the other strippers could be heard clearly as they readied themselves for the evening's performances. "Act glad to be one of the girls," he pinched the tender flesh of her upper arm, "none of that uppity shit."

"I don't act uppity," she defended herself, in vain. Romero gave her another sharp pinch and shoved her through the door into a harshly lit room that smelled of strong perfume and hair spray. Four women in various states of undress stopped what they were doing to see what their boss was up to. "Girls, Miss. Alexander will be joining you on stage. See that she knows how it works around here."

He left without a backward glance and one by one the women sized her up. Dandi felt like a bug under a microscope. Liza smiled tentatively. She was the youngest, a slim redhead with a dusting of freckles over her arms and shoulders. It wasn't pleasant to think about, but Liza might be a year or two younger than she was and Dandi had just turned nineteen. Underage girls working in a place like this was wrong, but she knew it happened.

"So, Miss High and Mighty is going to strip?" Taking two steps forward, another woman named Patty ended up right in her face. With one hand, she swiped bleached blonde hair over her shoulder while the other hand rested on a sharply cocked hip. Her fingernails were long and obviously acrylic. Everything about her was sharp – including her nose, but Dandi was sure that no man's gaze made it any higher than her silicon enhanced bust line. It was hard to tell Patty's age; perhaps she was in her early to mid-twenties. The blonde was the most popular dancer and never let any of the other girls forget it.

Dandi knew 'dancer' was not the best term for what she'd be doing, but she refused to think of it any other way.

Patty chewed a piece of gum, vigorously. "All I can say is that you best stay out of my way. I have my favorite customers and if I see you coming on to them, I'll jump your ass."

She didn't make back at the bimbo, it would serve no purpose. Dandi had never considered herself to be better than anyone, she simply had been raised to be respectable, polite and kind – a good girl. Telling Patty that she had no desire to horn in on her pet customers seemed like a waste of breath. Instead, she stepped to one side and walked toward the vacant dressing table which was covered with assorted stage make-up. This was a fiasco, she didn't know squat about making herself up like a showgirl.

Only – she didn't make it to her destination. "Don't walk away from me!" Patty jerked her backwards.

"What do you want from me?" she shouted, losing her temper. It had been a rough day.

"We saw you dance yesterday. What did you call all of that swooping and jumping around you did? That's not how you strip! Why Romero is so crazy for you to perform is a mystery to me." With a calculated, nasty move, Patty stepped forward and ground her high-heel shoe right on top of Dandi's foot. With a whimper, she almost went to her knees.

"Hey, leave her alone." Jane came to stand by Dandi. "You know how Romero is controlling her - the same way he's controlling Liza. They didn't ask to be here, not like we did."

Jane was older, but she had a good heart. Not as attractive as she probably used to be, Jane didn't pull in the tips the other girls did. Dandi felt sorry for her. Even she knew women became trapped in this lifestyle and when they grew too old for it, there was nowhere to go.

Stepping back from Patty, she lifted her sore foot off the floor and put it protectively behind the calf of her other leg. "Thank you, Jane." She appreciated the support, but Dandi could fight her own battles. "The dance I was performing was a mix of modern dance and ballet, not that you'd know about something so cultured."

"Did you just insult me, you little bitch?" Patty raised one hand, claws extended.

"All right, all right, that's enough. We've got a show to put on." Carla was jaded, but she was realistic. Not quite as old as Jane, the curvaceous woman had been around the block. "Liza, you're up first tonight, and Dandi - you'll go third after me. What are you wearing?"

A knock on the door answered Carla's question. Ancient Minnie came in with a filmy white garment that looked more like a peignoir set than a stripper's costume.

"Ooooh that's pretty," Liza reached for it. "I want to wear it!"

"Nope, this is for the newbie. Romero calls it his angel costume. Angel – that's what he is going to bill you as, Angel Baby. Jeff is out there hunting every song he can find that mentions an angel." Minnie handed the gown over to Dandi, who took it reluctantly.

She didn't feel like an angel, unless it was one with a broken wing. Looking around at the assorted group, she tried to think of a way out of this mess, but there wasn't one. "I really don't want to do this," she said out loud, so caught up in her own misery she hadn't realized she spoke.

"I don't think you have a choice. Try the costume on, it's not so bad." Minnie urged. "I might have to make some adjustments." When Dandi stalled, Minnie gave her a nudge toward the screen in the far corner. "Step back there, if you're shy."

Shy? Heck yes, she was shy. No man had ever seen her naked, other than a doctor, and the thought of pulling her clothes off in front of a room full of horny old men chilled her to the bone. "What do I wear under this?" she examined the way the dress was made. "It has no back."

"Pasties!" Minnie held out her hand which contained two round, filmy pieces of fabric. "Romero said you could wear them till you got used to being nekkid."

"We call them breast petals," Liza offered. "I wore them for a while. It helped."

"Here's a C-string for your hoo-hoo." Minnie placed a poor excuse for a pair of bottoms in her hand. It was just a string, like she said, the scrap of cloth made a thong look like a tablecloth. Despite her pitiful situation, Dandi had to smile at the elderly woman who seemed so at ease with the seamy side of life.

Sweet Mother of God, if her Dad could see her now, he would roll over in his grave. 'Forgive me, Papa,' she thought. Pulling off her clothes, she fitted the strange items on her body. The 'petals' were affixed with a gum adhesive and barely covered her puffy areolas.

"You've got a nice rack, Girly."

Dandi jumped, realizing Minnie was behind the screen with her. "Could I have some privacy?"

An odd, old cackle erupted from her cracked lips. "I'm the least of your worries. In a while, you'll be just a piece of meat wiggling around in front of sex-starved males."

"Great", she whispered, slipping the white costume over her head. The filmy material settled down over her curves like it had been created just for her.

"Wow," Jane peeked around the corner. "You do look like an angel. Turn around." It wasn't that she thought she was better than the other women, but Dandi didn't know how they could live this way. She felt her heart sink at the idea of being leered at, or possibly touched. As she stood there watching Minnie demonstrate how the Velcro sections worked on the skirt, she wondered how she would make it through the night.

As the minutes crept by, Dandi applied a smattering of make-up, but Carla insisted that she add more. "Stage make-up has to be more dramatic. The lights wash out the color." By the time she was through, Dandi thought she looked like a clown - or a harlot. Her eyes were huge, her cheekbones stood out prominently. The only lipstick in her meager collection was pale pink, but now her lips were dark red. Dandi didn't even recognize the reflection staring back at her from the mirror.

"Liza, your regular John is at the bar. He wants to talk to you." Cahill called from the doorway. "You girls better speed it up, ten minutes to show time. And boy, do we have a randy crowd!"

"Shit!" Liza threw a jar of face cream against the wall. "I hate when he touches me!"

The hopeless look on the other woman's face and the reality of her words slid over Dandi's heart like a sheet of ice. God! So, it was true. "You turn tricks?" Her voice sounded small, even to herself.

Patty wiggled her tube top, adjusting her ample breasts. "We all do, and you will, too."

"No, I won't!" she was adamant, but a sick feeling of dread permeated her chest.

From that moment on, Dandi began to search for a way out. She would perform, but she wouldn't dance naked, and she would not sell her body. Period.

The rest of that first evening passed in a daze. Jane showed her a simple routine, how to move her body seductively and remove clothing at the same time. When it was her turn to mount the stage, Dandi's whole body shook with pure fear. A film of sweat covered her skin. The stage lights were so hot, and she felt so exposed. Frozen, she stood and stared out into the crowd. Even though her breasts and lower body were covered, it was painfully obvious every man was undressing her with their eyes. Several men approached the stage, and she backed up with unease. Only Romero's glare from the other side of the footlights kept her from fleeing. How could she do this?

Desperately, she let her eyes rove the room, seeking a friend, but there was none to be found. Cahill stood by the door, thumping his nightstick in his hand. Closing her eyes, she sought calm. When the familiar music began to play, she separated herself from reality, letting her mind wander back in time. Dandi wasn't in the Tonga Club; she was at Etta's house, performing for her old friend.

Self-preservation allowed her to shut out the audience; her eyes didn't register the lustful looks, nor did her ears comprehend the lewd comments. Only the music was important and how her body responded to the emotions the song invoked. So, she danced – swayed, moved with longing – her spirit was carried away on the wings of lost dreams and happier days that had long since slipped through her fingers.

*****

Romero growled his displeasure. "Bitch, give the customers what they want! Strip!" he barked, but she ignored him. Only the reactions of the customers stopped him from snatching her by the hair and hauling her off the stage. Many were rubbing their crotches; the little innocent was turning them on. But it was their hypnotized expressions, their intent focus on the woman that gave him pause. Almost as a single entity, every male in the room either moved forward or leaned closer. They all wanted her – each and every one of them.

'And you shall have her', Romero promised, silently. Dollar signs were bouncing around in his head. The little ballerina would be his next cash cow. Before the week was out, he'd have her baring every inch of that toned little body on stage and spreading her legs in the back room. And he'd be one of the first to sample her pussy. Just like the others in the room, his cock was hard for Dandi Alexander.

*****

After the performance, Dandi was chastised for her routine. Romero insisted that Jane work with her some more, showing her how to seductively remove a little of her clothing at a time. Biting the inside of her cheek, she gyrated and wiggled her hips – thrust out her breasts and held her hands above her head, moving in ways that were totally unfamiliar to her. The girls also taught her how to use the pole, how to slide up and down it suggestively. If she had a man of her own, one who loved her, Dandi would have performed for him, knowing she was cherished and protected. But this – this was obscene to her.

Cahill and Romero watched from the sidelines, smirking and pointing. Little did they know, but she had no intention of using this knowledge any more than she had to. Several times, they called out instructions – "Shake your ass! Rub your nipples!" Dandi didn't argue, instead she gritted her teeth and half-heartedly complied, biding her time.

When the club closed in the wee hours of the morning, she was horrified to learn that she still had no freedom. Instead of being allowed to return to her apartment, Romero insisted she stay at the club. Dandi was in a near panic! Evidently, she was a prisoner. Cahill and the other bouncers took turns watching the door of the shabby, broom-size closet where she was to spend her off-hours. Even after the doors were locked for the night, someone stood guard to insure she didn't make a break for it.

Pacing the floor like a caged animal, Dandi's eyes were drawn to the double bed that dominated the room, and the more she stared at it, the more her throat closed. It was hard to breathe. She had enough sense to know why the bed was a double and not a twin. This was where she was expected to entertain 'johns.'

There wasn't a shower for her to use, so she wiped off in the small sink in the corner of the room. The only toilet was the public one at the end of the hall, and all they gave her to wear to bed was a club T-shirt. Sleep was a long time coming, and her dreams were fraught with eerie music and faces that faded in an out, laughing at her.

The next day wasn't any easier. Cahill escorted her to the office of her apartment building and spoke privately with the owner. Before she knew it, she was out of her lease and out of her apartment. The three girls whom Dandi lived with in the meager space just watched her gather her things. They didn't ask questions, nor did they try to intervene to help her. All Cahill allowed her to take was what would fit in one suitcase, so she filled it with clothes and the small locked box that contained a few papers and things that belonged to her mother. The rest of her things, he said, could be divided among the roommates or given to goodwill.

On the way back to Club Tonga, Cahill made an awkward pass at her, but she fended him off. "If I didn't have to work at the station tonight, I wouldn't let you get away with being so proper, Angel Baby. You owe me."

"How do you figure that I owe you anything?" She couldn't believe his audacity.

"Romero is paying me extra to keep an eye on you. He has big plans for his new star."

"Like what?"

"You'll see," he promised her with a wink. "Some of Romero's investors are interested in you. Who knows? You may be on your way to Vegas. There's a lot of opportunities for high class, uh, dancers out in Vegas."

Dandi's heart ached. She didn't really understand what he was saying, but it couldn't be good. Her hopes for a normal life, a home and children were growing dimmer and dimmer. Leaning her head on the car glass, she day-dreamed about the man she might one day marry if her life ever turned around again. It seemed to her she would recognize him at first sight, there would be a connection. If he was her soul-mate, she would feel it the moment he walked through the door. Dandi had no idea what he would look like – looks weren't the important thing. He would be strong and kind, that's what she clung to.

Even in her pitiful circumstances, she refused to give up on the idea. Always she glanced at strangers, even searching the crowd at Tonga, looking for him. It wasn't that she expected a knight-in-shining armor to rescue her like Richard Gere did Julia Roberts in Pretty Woman, but she did fantasize about someone to run to when the storms of life threatened to pull her asunder.

When they arrived back at the club, Cahill escorted her back to her room. As she shut the door in his face, it was as if she were shutting the door to her former life. Her future loomed ahead of her like the iceberg in front of the Titanic. If she didn't change her course soon, Romero would be her pimp and she would be his whore.

That night, when it came time for her to strip - she danced, removing just a few of the scarves attached to her skirt - that was all. The music was different, but her resolve was the same. As she gave herself over to the song, Dandi escaped her garish cage and soared in her imagination. As she swept past the edge of the stage, a hand reached out and grasped one of the scarves; it came loose and floated away. Quickly she moved aside, but another hand reached out and another – and soon her legs were bare and all that covered her modesty was a tiny strip of fabric. As the music pulsed around her, shame pierced through Dandi like butcher knives. Dollar bills flew to the floor at her feet, but she stepped over them and ran down the steps to the frail haven of her small room.

Short was her solitude, however, because Romero insisted she perform an encore. Dandi had begged for the rest of her costume to be returned to her, but he denied her request. So this time when she performed, her skin remained flushed with disgrace. No matter how much she tried, there was no retreating into fantasy. With each step, each bow – each circle she made – Dandi was firmly rooted in the lewd world she now inhabited, displaying her body to strangers. By the time her set was over, she could no longer see the crowd for the tears in her eyes.

They say the more you do distasteful things, the easier they become. But for Dandi this rule did not hold true. Her third day as an exotic dancer was the worst. In spite of Romero's warnings, she had donned her full costume and made a practice of staying toward the back of the stage, a safe distance from any overzealous patron who would yank at her clothing. When she had finished, retreating to her sanctuary, he had followed – barging in without knocking, for she had no lock on the door to protect herself.

"Didn't I tell you what was going to happen?" Before she knew it, Romero had slapped her twice. "How dare you defy me? Do you think you're special? Do you think you don't have to follow my orders? You are a stripper, Slut! You will strip, completely, or I'll make you wish you had never been born!"

Dandi lost it, "Don't touch me!" She fought back, lunging at him, going for his eyes with her fingernails. If she'd had her knife in hand, she would have plunged it into his chest.

"Bitch! Get her off of me!"

The bartender and one of the bouncers came rushing down the hall to his aid. It was definitely overkill, because Dandi's strength was no match for even one of the men, much less both. "Take her to my office," Romero ordered.

Dandi knew she was in trouble, and she was right.

"Get me the cane," he snarled.

Now she knew what Romero had meant about the 'other ways' she could be made to suffer. "If you won't strip, this will be the price you pay. I will whip you every day that you do not obey me. Do you understand?"

"Won't this mark her up, Boss?"

"I know how to do this; I can make her scream without breaking the skin too much. She'll look like a pain junkie." Cahill held her still and Romero caned her back and bottom. Dandi screamed and fought, which made him hit her harder. No one came to help.

Later in the bed, Dandi curled into a little knot, arms wrapped around her middle. It hurt too much to lie on her back. In a while, she'd get up and wipe some of the blood away. The pain from the beating had dulled to a hot, raw throb, but the pain in her heart nearly took her breath away. She couldn't help but wonder how many days it would be till Romero forced her to sell her body. It was coming, she knew it was.

The next day, Dandi squirmed and whimpered as Minnie covered the bloody whelps and stripes with body make-up. "Why did you do this to yourself, Girl? Don't you know you can't win against these goons?" The old woman's sympathy was evident, but what she suggested went against everything Dandi believed in. She would not give in. She would not give up; she would fight until she could fight no more.

One day bled into the next. Like a robot, she fulfilled her assigned times to dance. Mechanically, she would walk to and from the stage, isolating herself within a bubble of oblivion – ignoring the jibes and the suggestive remarks, not feeling the touches or even the pinches. There were times when she feared for her sanity, because the safety of her dream world was far more preferable than the cruel confines of her reality. Only when the music played and she danced could she slip the bonds of her torment and fly among the stars.

As time passed, she discovered Minnie had been right – she couldn't win. Succumbing to pressure, Dandi danced more suggestively, wore skimpier costumes, used the stripper pole - but she refused, adamantly, to dance completely nude. For this rebellion, she paid dearly in beatings and near starvation. If she hadn't hid her insulin under a loose board in the closet, Romero would have confiscated it and used her need for the medicine to control her. She knew this because she had caught Cahill rummaging through her things, and he had been dumb enough to tell her why. At times, Dandi feared for her life. Romero was involved with dangerous people; people who had no qualms about making those who caused them trouble disappear.

One night as she dressed for her last set, Carla came up to her, handing her the skirt of the white costume that Dandi hated with every bone in her body. If she ever walked away from this place, she swore she would never wear white again. Romero had furnished her other costumes – some silver, some black, some gold, but he preferred to see her in white. "You're famous," Carla drawled.

"Famous? What do you mean?"

"Patty is going to be livid. Some guy filmed you dancing; it's on the internet. You, Angel Baby, are a YouTube sensation with several million views. Heck, who knows? You may turn out to be more popular than 'Gangnam Style.'"

"Great, that's all I need." Dandi wasn't thrilled.

"At first, Romero was angry. He was yelling about banning cameras and phones. But the crowds have picked up the last few days, the phone has been ringing off the wall, and he even got a phone call from one of the major television stations wanting to interview the both of you. Didn't you realize the place was jumping last night? The number almost doubled our usual Friday night crowd."

"I haven't noticed. What's so special about how I dance?"

"Because you dance, Silly," Carla laughed. "The rest of us just wiggle and gyrate while you put on a performance worthy of Broadway – or so the video said."

"Damn," she sighed. "I was hoping to get fired."

"No chance of that," Carla sidestepped to allow Jane room to look in the mirror. "You're Romero's favorite. It's only a matter of time before you're the Queen Bee around here. There's a photographer coming tonight to take pictures of you, Romero is commissioning posters! Someone said you were mentioned on TMZ!"

Dandi closed her eyes – "No, I don't want any of that. I just want out of here."

Jane patted her shoulder. "Just count your blessings; at least you're not hooking, yet."

"Don't speak so soon, I heard Romero talking. Dandi's going to be auctioned off – soon – sold to the highest bidder. What do you think about that?" Patty's viper voice delivered the information like she was handing out the winning prize.

Dandi felt as if a death sentence had been handed down. Times had been hard for her since she had run away from home, but even loneliness and fast-food minimum wages had been heaven compared to this concentration camp. If only she hadn't gotten sick.

There had to be a way out, she just had to find it. Wiping the tears from her eyes, Dandi vowed she would escape at the first opportunity. She would run as if her life depended on it – and it just might.

CHAPTER TWO

Lucas Dane Wagner parked his silver Dodge Charger in the crowded front lot of the gentleman's club on East Texas Avenue. Damn, he felt too old for a bachelor party. Too many resident hours had taken their toll. Between work and classes, he'd had little to no time for sleep, much less anything else. If Tim hadn't been a good friend, he would have begged off. Thank goodness, it was coming to an end. In two weeks he'd have a job - he was counting on it.

Club Tonga seemed to be a typical looking strip joint. He had hoped the get-together would be held at one of the nicer Shreveport hotels. They could have had a dancer visit the party, but the guys had insisted it be here, at this particular club where Angel Baby danced. "Angel Baby, what a name." Why Tim and the others were so taken with this exotic dancer was a mystery to him. He couldn't wait to see what was so special about her, if anything.

"How much?"

He turned to see a balding older man approach a young red-headed woman. Her answer wasn't loud enough for him to hear, but she took the man by the arm and led him back into the club. A deal had been made.

Lucas certainly didn't have any hang-ups about sex. It was his business. Despite his history with his mother, he understood that places like Tonga served a purpose; he had no problem with men seeking female companionship nor with women who enjoyed the company of men. What he regretted was those who suffered from addictions that kept them from leading normal lives, men or women who neglected their families and the opportunity for a fulfilling relationship to imbibe in the intoxicating world of the flesh trade. The flip side of the coin was the women who got caught up in the whirlpool of sex, drugs, and the men who would take advantage of them. Yes, Lucas understood the dynamics; he just didn't intend to ever let himself get embroiled in the lifestyle.

"I'm in love! Did you see the ass on that girl?"

Lucas had to smile. He wasn't expecting to buy a lap dance tonight, but he damn sure didn't have a rule against looking. This was his vacation, such as it was. Tonight, he was in northern

Louisiana, a place that he had spent many happy days. Shreveport wasn't his idea of a vacation destination, but his visit had accomplished two important things. He was able to make Tim's bachelor party and he had also been able to meet with his mentor who had traveled from Atlanta to have dinner with him. The discussions they shared had proved fruitful. Dr. Solomon had given him some additional tips to impress the partners. The older man assured him, again, that the partners had reviewed his work and if nothing untoward happened, an offer would be extended for him to start his own practice under the umbrella of the Solomon Group. Nothing could please Lucas more; this would be the culmination of his dream. On the fourteenth of February he'd find out for sure, but until then he planned on walking the straight and narrow. His future was too important. Nothing could come before his work, proving himself meant everything.

A thump and a yelp broke his concentration. Someone had stumbled into the Charger – drunk most likely. "Damn, might as well go in and join the party." Locking the car, he made his way across the cracked pavement to the metal building that seemed to expand and contract with the waves of loud music. God, a person could happily go deaf in a place such as this. He shoved his hands in his pockets, seeking to warm his fingers. He should have brought a warmer coat. The news said a severe Arctic front was moving in from the north. Lucas intended to wish the groom well, share a drink and hit the road back to Arkansas.

When he stepped aside for two inebriated men to venture out into the night, he could smell smoke, liquor and the stale sweat of over-stimulated males. Once inside, the interior of Club Tonga held no surprises - dim lighting, free-flowing liquor and scantily clad women. He smiled, letting his gaze travel over a statuesque blonde with tits that wouldn't quit. Damn! It had been too long! Lucas needed sex, and lately he had been on a starvation diet.

Standing still to let his eyes adjust, he scanned the crowd looking for Tim or any of the others. Ah! There they were, up near the front. He could see Ralph, Tracy, Jerry and John – all sharing a table and all with their eyes focused on the stage. In fact, everyone was focused on the stage. Other than the music, there was a hushed silence in the air – very few jeers, almost no catcalls. In fact, the expressions on the men's faces could be defined as beatified awe. Confused, Lucas glanced up at the stage to see what was causing the audience to behave so strangely.

And then he knew. Just like the other men, he stared at a vision in white. The woman was beautiful in ways that seemed alien to the setting where she displayed her charms. Her body was perfect, curves in all the right places, yet she was graceful and elegant. Pirouettes and fluid movements flowed into an arabesque. Her long dark hair cascaded over fragile shoulders and down her back. Lucas wanted to touch, to hold - to protect.

Mesmerized, he watched the darling Little Dancer move across the stage en pointe. Her face was delectable, every feature kissable. He felt he could stare at her until the world ended and never tire of the view. What was such a treasure doing in a place like this? The stripping she did was minimal – very few moves which could be termed risqué, instead she poured her heart into the dance, seemingly unmindful of her surroundings.

"Strip, Bitch!" a man called from near the edge of the stage. "I'm not going to pay you to be just a damn prima donna!"

"Leave her be," an older customer slurred. "I like it."

"I wanna see her tits!" another shouted.

"Yea! Let's see your ass! You've kept us standing here with our tongues hanging out for weeks!"

The ice was broken and cries for the young woman to 'take it off – take it all off!' sounded across the room. Lucas watched her stumble as she became aware of what they were saying. A look of panic crossed her delicate features. This woman didn't belong here. Lucas knew that without a shadow of a doubt. In fact, he had the oddest suspicion that she belonged with him. Shaking his head, he tried to disabuse himself of the strange notion, but it didn't work – the feeling just wouldn't go away.

*****

Dandi felt so alone. Right now, if someone offered money for her, Romero would sell her like a slice of pie. She needed this to be over - now. Nervously, she scanned the audience. Every face seemed to belong to a ravager, every movement was menacing. Men in suits, men in t-shirts – old men, young men – all of them feasted on her with their eyes. She felt their gapes and stares like licks on her skin.

There was nowhere to turn, no one to run to . . . until her attention was captured by one man – one large, mountain of a man who covered the ground he stood on and looked capable of defeating any enemy who threatened him or what he cherished. Now, this was a hero.

He stared straight into her eyes. The look on his face was different than the others – he watched her, but it was a proprietary look, not a lewd one. Oh, how she wished he was there for her. An urge to propel her body off the stage and into his arms threatened to overwhelm her.

Walking up behind Tim, Lucas placed a hand on his buddy's shoulder, but his eyes never left the woman. He wanted her – pure and simple.

"Hey, Luc! Isn't she something?" Tim lolled his head back and gave him a silly grin; clearly the party had begun without him.

"Yes, she is." He agreed as he shook hands with other friends and members of Tim's wedding party. The dancer was everything he had been told, and more. Truth be known, Lucas was having a hard time concentrating on anything but her.

"I'm getting married."

Focusing on his friend for a moment, he realized Tim was already three sheets to the wind. "Yes, I know. This is your big send-off before you enter the bonds of holy matrimony. How much have you had to drink, Buddy?"

"Too much! Ha!"

"I'll ask the waitress for a cup of coffee." He motioned to a petite doll with a pixie hair-cut. "A coffee, please."

She winked at him, looking down at his package. "I'm available later, if you're looking for a good time."

"Thanks, Doll." He winked back, knowing she didn't have what it took to capture his interest. The music rolled to a climax and Lucas turned back to the stage. He held his breath as the angel in white finished her dance with a move that took her to the floor in a poignant, graceful bow. Oddly, she hadn't stripped to bare skin the way he expected. Not a lot of bills were thrown to the stage, either, but she ignored what was there, stepping over them as if they were fallen leaves.

Lucas was perplexed at her behavior, but angered at those around her. The dark, angry man grabbed her elbow and wrenched her off the dais, and as he did a big fellow with baseball glove sized hands reached out and pulled at her other arm. She made a sound of pain and protest as she was yanked around. There was no way he could let this pass. "Enough! Take your hands off of her!" he yelled as he made his way to the stage. Pushing his way in between the girl and her aggressors, Lucas found himself met with angry stares and barely checked violence. It wouldn't take much to start a brawl, if they were brave enough.

The angel looked at him with big eyes, as if he were her only salvation. "Thank you," she mouthed. And though he tried to stymie the thought, all he could think about was what other things those beautiful lips might be able to do.

"You want her, Viking? That could be arranged. All my girls are for sale for the right price." This came from the man who had been yelling instructions and threats.

"No, Romero! I never agreed to anything other than dancing," the angel protested, struggling when the idiot reached around Lucas to grab her again.

If she was being forced that changed everything. He was infuriated. He wanted the other man's hands off of her – right now. "Let the girl go." He enunciated each syllable slowly.

Before the ass could respond, two bouncers came up to flank Romero. "I think you should return to your party, Sir," was their smooth suggestion, but the words were said with a savage expression on their faces – letting him know that they would love to have an excuse to take the argument outside.

"Only if the lady tells me she doesn't need my help."

Romero laughed, "There are no ladies here, Viking." With a grip that would bruise a big man, he pressed harshly on the Angel's arm. "Get your ass in the back. If you bring someone else into our business, they'll only get hurt. Do you want that?"

"I'm not afraid of these assholes," Lucas directed the comment toward her, but when he had stopped playing stare down with the two bouncers, she was gone.

"Go back to your party, Caveman, or get off my property." The acidic threat didn't bother Lucas. He was torn between demanding to be taken to her, and biding his time to see what happened.

Several tense moments passed, finally Lucas backed away. Right now, he didn't know what her story was. Something didn't feel right. He'd keep his eyes open for her the rest of the night and see what happened.

A busty little hostess in a pink bikini escorted them to a semi-private area where they could still see the girls dancing, but enjoy a bit more privacy. Hot wings, sub sandwiches, boiled shrimp - all were laid out in abundance.

"Did you see that stripper?" Ralph exclaimed. "She was one hot little piece of ass."

"Man, I sure would like me some of that," Tracy echoed the sentiment. Bottles of beer were passed around and one chubby dark-haired waitress jumped and squealed as her ass was slapped.

An odd feeling of agitation came over Lucas; he didn't like to hear them talking about the Angel that way. It didn't make any sense, he knew. He had just met her and she was as far from meeting the criteria he had set for his ideal woman as the east is from the west. But right now, that didn't really seem to matter.

*****

Alone in her room, Dandi literally shook with nerves. Each time she performed, it got worse. Every instinct she possessed told her time was running out. She picked up the small knife hidden under her pillow. Selma, one of her first roommates, had insisted she buy this knife and learn how to use it. Just holding it made her feel better, but it would be precious little help if push came to shove. Could she use it if she had too? Maybe. But all she really wanted to do was find the big man who had been willing to stand up for her. She didn't know him. Could she trust him?

A knock on the door made her jump. With trepidation, she opened the door just a crack. It was Jane. "I gotta talk to you."

"What's wrong?"

Jane put an arm around her, and even though they were alone, she whispered in Dandi's ear. "I just overheard Romero talking. He's setting up some action for you tonight."

"Action?"

"Tricks, Johns – he's putting you to work tonight, setting up some kind of bidding war." The older stripper's face was solemn with sympathy,

Panic seared through Dandi's chest. She had hoped Carla was mistaken, "What can I do?"

"You need to get out of here," Jane urged. "I don't know how, but you need to leave." She squeezed Dandi's shoulder. "I know this isn't the life you want, you aren't made for this hell. Get out before Romero ruins your life. I'll cover for you as long as I can."

"Thanks," she hugged the woman back and closed the door behind her. Getting out had been her plan, but she had hoped to have more time to prepare.

*****

"Are you sure you want to get married and leave all of this?" Jerry asked while he raised his glass in a toast to two more of Tim's friends who were a bit late arriving.

"Who says I'm leaving anything? Lois will come here with me. She's a good sport."

"Ha! Women are never good sports about strippers," John spoke with a knowing tone in his voice.

"Angel Baby would be worth any trouble. Damn, I would love to tap that." Ralph had a beer in each hand and his foot in his mouth. Tim's best man was getting on Lucas's nerves.

"Hell, Doc!" Ralph got right in his face. "All this shit should be right up your alley, ain't you studying to be a sex doctor?"

Some people could get drunk faster than others. Lucas started not to answer him, but changed his mind. Idiots needed to be informed when at all possible. "I'm a psychiatrist specializing in intimacy issues, sexual and otherwise."

"Aren't you gonna have sex with your patients?" A guffaw sent a stream of beer down Ralph's beard.

"No, that's what a sexual surrogate does – not a psychiatrist." He refused to try and explain any farther.

"Hey, Buddy," he leaned near his college roommate. "Since I'm not going to be at the wedding, I wanted to give you and Lois your gift now." Handing Tim two airline tickets and a packet of information, he said, "Congratulations, the honeymoon is on me. A week in Hawaii for two, first class all the way. " He knew first year residents could barely afford rent, much less an expensive wedding. The gift had set him back, but his new job was just around the corner.

"Thank you, Man." Tim hugged his friend. "We've had some wild times, haven't we?"

"Yes, we have." And still having them, the old crew was living it up. Several were being singled out by strippers. Lucas noticed a blonde openly rub Tracy's crotch while she pushed her tits right into his face.

"Hey, everyone," Tim yelled right in Lucas's ear and he winced, backing up a bit. "Lucas just gave Lois and me a tropical honeymoon!" He waved the gift high in the air.

Cheers went up at Tim's announcement.

"I can't top that, but I'll buy you a lap dance. Just take your pick," John waved his hand toward the girls who were making their way around the room.

Lucas knew strippers solicited lap dances. The women made a good portion of their income from personal one-on-one contact with the customers. To be honest, he loved to be teased during sex, but he preferred a lap dance to be an appetizer and not the main course. Tonight, he might make an exception - if the right woman asked him.

He hadn't come to Club Tonga for anything other than to show his respect to Tim. But the idea of the Little Dancer gyrating in his lap made his cock swell to bursting and thoughts of travel played a distant second fiddle.

"Look, here she comes." Ralph punched John. "I bet she asks me. Who could resist this face?" They guffawed like college boys.

He didn't have to look around to know who they were talking about. Turning, he saw her. She came through the crowd looking like a perfect gazelle moving through a herd of wildebeest. A feeling of relief swept over him. She was okay.

Dandi only saw him. The Viking. Her hero – maybe. The other girls had been staring at him, making lewd comments. They all wanted in his pants. One had said that he looked like some actor but Dandi couldn't place the name. It would come to her, sooner or later. He certainly looked like a god to her. Rubbing her palms on her dress, she tried to calm down, knowing she was about to do something she had never expected to do. She was going to ask a stranger for help. Taking a deep breath, she steadied herself – looking up into his handsome face. "Would you come with me, please? I need to talk to you, privately."

"Yes." He didn't even hesitate.

"Privately! We know what that means!"

Lucas swung on Ralph, "I've heard all out of you that I can stand."

"Sorry."

Turning back to the Angel, he saw her chest expand and contract – those beautiful breasts rising and falling with each breath. She was nervous. God, she was totally adorable, an intriguing mix of sensuality and innocence. The Little Dancer was like no stripper he had ever known.

Lucas let his gaze rove over her, hungrily. She was petite, maybe five-foot-four. Dressed in a backless black outfit, she looked like pure sin. Her hair hung like an ebony waterfall of lush ringlets. What would it be like to bury his face in all of that softness, feel the strands gently move across his naked skin, let his fingers massage her scalp? Damn!

Her body was a perfect hour-glass with flared hips and luscious tits; he could see the outline of melt-in-your-mouth nipples bumping up against material sheer enough to torture him. Mercy! He was unbelievably turned on. Just the idea of her hands on him had his blood surging through his veins like lava.

"Would you come with me?" She held out her hand and he took it, tossing a head nod to his friends who groaned behind him – all wishing they were in his shoes. If he didn't see them anymore tonight, it wouldn't bother him a bit. He'd much rather sample this little doll's treasures.

Angel Baby led him through the crowd, pulling him along behind her like she was pulling a little red wagon. She didn't have to tug hard; he was going with her very willingly. Several men stared at him with undisguised envy. And he didn't blame them a bit. When they neared the bar, a customer stopped her and asked for a photo.

She glanced at him apologetically. "Excuse me, please."

"Certainly, I'll be waiting." She was so polite. He took a good long look at her legs – smooth, tanned and toned – dancer's legs. Lucas could almost feel them wrapped around his waist as he slammed into her with powerful strokes – her little heels would dig into his ass and she would leave rake marks on his back.

He stood by patiently while she conferred with another of the ladies, accepting a hug. Then she patiently posed with another customer while his friend took their picture. He noticed that she moved the man's hand when it got too close to her breast.

Lucas almost intervened.

Dandi was tired of the pictures and the interviews and the attention, she was anxious to return to her hero. When she turned back to him, it was to watch a tall, skinny man slipping the Viking's wallet out of his back pants pocket. "Stop! He's taking your wallet!" she cried. The pick-pocket jerked it out and Dandi didn't even hesitate – she hated thieves! She grasped him by the arm before he could take off.

It all happened fast, Lucas heard the little dancer yell at the same time he felt a bump against his back. He wheeled around, but the little thing was fast - she had already launched herself at the thief, holding his arm. The man didn't let go of his wallet, before Lucas could move the three or four feet to take care of it, the bastard knocked her flying with a hard backhand to the face. Lucas was stunned and infuriated. "Dammit! Big mistake, Asshole!"

Lucas lunged through the air and tackled the guy to the ground. Every once in a while his footballs days came in handy. "Why don't you try to hit me, Bastard? Or do you just get off hitting fragile little girls?" He flipped the idiot over and pulled his hands back in a hold designed to painfully subdue. One of the bouncers came to relieve Lucas of his burden. He grabbed his wallet and pocketed it, knowing full well the police would not be called. Now – where was she?

Several people had gathered around his little champion, but he elbowed his way to her side. "Are you okay?" Without delay, he pulled her close and moved her hand away from her face so he could see the damage. Her lip had been cut open and a dark spot was already forming on her cheek. "I'm so sorry, Honey. You should have just let the idiot get away. I'd have handled it." Right there in front of the whole club, he bent to tenderly kiss the pain away.

Dandi wasn't going to cry, but she did want to be held more than anything. The thought of stepping into his arms seemed magical, but she didn't want to do it in front of Romero or any of the girls. What she had in mind required a certain amount of subtlety, "I'm okay. It doesn't hurt. Can we go talk now?" She pulled out of his arms. It was hard to do.

"I have a few things to say to you, too." Talk – he wanted more than talking. "What's your name, Angel?" Lucas asked as he walked next to her. This time he would shield her instead of trailing along behind. Gawkers watched their every move, but she seemed withdrawn and unaware, like something was bearing on her mind. Seeing a waitress walk by with a glass of ice, he stopped her and took it. She didn't argue, just smiled.

"Dandi, my name's Dandi."

"Dandi," he felt the name caress his tongue. "I like it, it's beautiful. My name is Lucas."

They walked to the very back and down a narrow hall to what appeared to be a storage room. As soon as they were inside the door, she surprised the hell out of him. Stepping right up against him, she stood on tiptoe and kissed his cheek. The kiss was very chaste, but sweet enough to melt his heart.

"What was that for?"

"For the ice and for defending me. No one has stood up for me in a long, long time. Thank you." With that simple explanation, she backed away.

"Well, its damn time someone stood up for you. Besides, I'd say you returned the favor by helping me get my wallet back. Come here, I want to see your face. Hand me something soft, we need to get some ice on that bruise."

"I'll be fine. I've been bruised before." At his stern look, she went to her drawer and took out a soft pair of underwear.

Was the fact she had been bruised before supposed to make him feel better?

"I'm sure you would have caught him anyway." Blushing, she handed the pale pink panties to him.

"Probably, but I still think you're the sweetest, bravest woman I've ever met." He rubbed his thumb across the hurt place wishing he could take her pain away. "Though she be but little, she is fierce."

"Shakespeare, A Midsummer's Night Dream," She responded to his kindness, coming to him until their bodies touched. He was so warm. Dandi began to tremble. With the lightest of caresses, he brushed her face with the silk covered ice. A tiny gasp slipped from her lips.

"Cold?"

"Yes." And hotter than she'd ever been in her life. He was looking at her lip intently – Dandi wanted to reach out and kiss him so much she ached. Glancing over his shoulder at the clock, she knew Romero would be watching for her, this couldn't take forever. "I have something to ask you." Looking down, she gathered her courage.

God, she was so soft and sweet. He wanted to gather her close and never let her go. Angling his hips back, he concealed the fact that he was rock-hard and ready for a tumble. "I know what you're going to ask. You want to give me a lap dance."

Dandi jerked her head up. Lap dance? God, he wanted a lap dance. "Well. . ." What was she going to do? She had never done this before. Could she even fake it? Heck, she had to try; maybe she could make a trade. "Yes, I want to give you a lap dance."

"Are you sure you feel like it, Baby?" Giving in to his desire, he kissed the corner of her mouth. "You don't have to, although I'd give five years of my life to have you in my arms."

Customers weren't usually allowed to touch during a lap dance – but what went on in a private one, she really had no idea. "I'd like to try. Maybe, I'll be able to please you."

He didn't tell her, but just being in the same room with her pleased him.

Quickly she gathered the portable player already preset with appropriate music, Romero had given it to her several days ago. And the straight back chair, she'd need that. Dandi sat it about three feet from the door so she could use the surface to lean on when she . . . oh my! How was she going to make those moves when she couldn't even bring herself to think them? It was a good thing she had been watching the other girls, or she wouldn't have a clue. Turning on the music, she motioned to the chair. "If you'll sit down, please."

This was so important, she needed to do it right. A zipper – a button – a clasp, Dandi removed her skirt and her top. Underneath, she wore a tiny black bra and a smaller pair of black lace panties.

"Damn" Lucas growled. High, full breasts spilled out over a little scrap of lace. He gripped the edge of the chair to keep from cupping those succulent little melons. And the rest of her – Lord God Almighty – what had he gotten himself into? He should be on his way to Arkansas, but the only place he wanted to be was between her legs. The music filled the room – seductive, raunchy – an erotic beat that made his pulse pound in time with the drum.

Stepping between his legs, she began to move. Like a harem dancer, she put her arms over her head – sensuously. Her breasts thrust up and out and she leaned in – closer, closer – Lucas's mouth watered. "I bet your nipples taste like candy."

He was talking to her, oh no. "Maybe, I'm not sure." She had to concentrate. Dandi thought a second – dang, this was harder than dancing onstage. Mainly because this mattered – he mattered. "Would you like a sample?"

"Hell yeah!"

"If you're a good boy, we'll see." With more bravado than she felt, Dandi moved her hips in a slow, undulating circle. When Lucas swallowed hard, she knew she was doing it right. Turning her back to him, Dandi kept up the wiggle.

She thanked heaven the lights were dim and the heavy stage make-up covered the scars on her back, or at least she hoped they did. Lifting her hair she bared her neck, surprised at how she felt. Sexy. For the first time, Dandi felt moved by what she was doing. Her nipples were tightening and a heat was beginning to build deep inside. She knew it was Lucas himself who caused her reaction; no other man had ever affected her this way.

Lucas was staring, mesmerized. A little tattooed phoenix on her neck caught his attention. "Nice tat." His eyes slid along her back, over her hips and down sleek thighs that were parted just enough for him to see a hint of pink between them. When she bent over and pushed that heart-shaped, epic ass toward him - he groaned. "Can I touch?" He knew the answer would be 'no', but he had to ask.

"Yes."

Yes? His hands heard the answer before his brain did. Lifting from the death grip on the edge of the chair, they made contact with soft, velvet skin. Jesus! It was only his palms that grazed her hip as she moved it sensuously right in front of his face, but it was enough to make his cock rock-hard and leak. The urge to nip her ass came just as she turned around – but the view was even better from the front – he had no complaints.

As she had seen Jane do, Dandi placed her palms on either side of her throat and slowly slid them down over her chest and around each breast, cupping them. She bent over and rubbed the fabric covered nipples against his cheek. She knew this wasn't the smoothest performance, for she was literally shaking. If Dandi hadn't been already turned on, the expression on the Viking's face would have done the trick. His eyes were burning, and she could see his heartbeat at the base of his throat. When he placed a kiss in her cleavage, it was her turn to groan. Quickly, she pulled up before she gave in to the inclination to sit down on his lap and kiss him till he begged for mercy.

Dandi was going on instinct now; all ability to think was quickly going out the window. Sliding her palm down her middle, she touched herself – dipping her fingers between her legs, caressing the fabric right over her clitoris. God! Her body jerked. She was so aroused, and by the look of things – he was too. Lucas was huge!

Lucas almost lost it. His cock was literally throbbing. "I could help you with that." His hands had settled at her waist, his thumbs moving in slow circles on her skin.

"I could use a little help," she admitted breathlessly, and she needed – more. Having seen some of the girls straddle the men, she capitulated to her desire and settled herself on one of his thick thighs. "You don't mind if I sit, do you?" Making rhythmic little moves, she closed her eyes, letting the rough material of his jeans give mind-numbing friction to her aching pussy.

"Hell, no," he growled. "Make yourself at home."

Dandi cupped his face and began rubbing herself back and forth on the hard muscles of his leg. "This feels so good. I've never met a man like you, you make me feel free," she whispered.

He tried to process her words – he really did. But, God! This was like no lap dance Lucas had ever experienced. He wasn't complaining. And when her eyes closed, her thighs gripped his and her delectable mouth formed a perfect 'O' – he realized the little doll was cumming. A rosy flush of excitement colored her chest and neck. This was no fake performance; this was real – and highly contagious.

Seeing Dandi taking pleasure from his body set him off like a Roman candle. Lucas Dane Wagner did something he hadn't done since puberty – he flooded his shorts with cum.

Damn!

It was a few seconds before Dandi could comprehend what they had done. Oh, she had masturbated a few times, but this was so far out of her realm of experience that she, quite frankly didn't know what to do. "Sorry," she started to back up. "I guess I got a little carried away."

"Don't you dare move," Lucas pulled her close. "That was the sexiest damn thing I've ever seen."

Dandi smiled, she disagreed. If anything was sexy – it was him. Resting her cheek against the taut muscles of his wide, hard chest, she let herself relax for a moment while she came down from her orgasm. Dandi could imagine paradise with this man; Lucas would not only make her feel like a desirable woman, he would make her feel like the only woman. What would it be like to learn pleasure from him?

Being in his arms was amazing, she could almost imagine that she belonged there – almost – until he succinctly burst her bubble.

"How much do I owe you?"

CHAPTER THREE

'How much do I owe you?'

The words were like a splash of acid in her face. For a brief time she had forgotten. This wasn't personal. Lucas was a paying customer. Oh, he was different – honorable and heroic, but she needed to remember where she was and how it looked to him. The truth made her heart ache, but that was just the way it was. "You don't owe me anything," she said dismissively.

"What do you mean?" he took her by the chin, forcing her to look at him.

He was going to make this difficult. Dandi tried to act nonchalant. Her emotions were in turmoil. "I can't charge you for the lap dance. It was my first time. I didn't know what I was doing."

"You were perfect. I was blown away." He sounded stunned. "This doesn't make sense."

She couldn't argue with him on that point. "It's okay," she blushed, her hands still on his shoulders. "I didn't expect what happened any more than you did." Why was it so hard to let him go? Still, there was no way she could ask him to take her away now. Even though he had been nice to her, it was evident that he saw her as a woman who could sell herself. Trying to explain everything to him would take too long, and she had no assurance how he'd feel if she did. No, it would be best if she figured this out on her own. "Let's just say it was on the house."

"I want to spend more time with you." What he was asking, Lucas wasn't sure, but he wasn't ready to walk away from her.

"Sorry, I have, uh, something else to do." She needed to leave. Knowing it was time to put some distance between them, she eased off his lap. When she did, she noticed a large wet spot on the front of his jeans. "Oh, my, look at you! Let me get you something to wipe up with."

Lucas looked down. Hell! "Yea, I guess you better." He snorted. "You got me all excited. I haven't done that since I dreamed about Buffy Sue Peters in seventh grade."

"Lucky Buffy Sue." Thankfully, their concern over his appearance seemed to change the topic. Dandi wet a wash cloth and handed it and a towel to him, then politely turned her back.

She could hear him unzipping his pants so he could clean himself. "I'll just pull my shirt out; it will cover up my mess." He laughed again. "People will think I wet myself."

"I'm sure it happens all the time," she was embarrassed to say. "The accident, I mean."

"If you're anywhere around, I'm sure of it." While he was adjusting himself, she redressed and he was able to enjoy the view. Yes, she was just as stunning as he'd first thought – stunning from every angle.

A knock on the door made them both turn. Dandi hoped it wasn't Romero; he might demand to know why she had brought Lucas to her room instead of the VIP area. Heck! What if he presumed she was selling herself and demanded money? Uneasily, she opened the door, but it wasn't Romero.

"Lucas? I hate to disturb you, man. But Tim needs you."

"What's up?" Dandi stepped out of his way and Lucas went to the door. Tracy stood with his back to him, like he was expecting them to be naked. "What's wrong with Tim?"

"He's collapsed. At first we thought he was drunk, but I think there's more wrong than that. We knew you'd know what to do."

Damn! "I gotta go check on him." He took one last long look at Dandi. "I don't feel right leaving you like this." Lucas wasn't psychic by any means, but he felt a connection between them that he wasn't ready to let go of so soon.

Blue eyes sought hers; she wanted to ask him what he meant. Maybe she was making a mistake, maybe he would help her.

"Lucas . . ." Tracy waited, impatiently.

He was needed. "Go, its okay. I hope there's nothing seriously wrong with your friend."

Lucas cursed under his breath. No woman had never gotten under his skin this fast before. Cupping her face, he rubbed a thumb over the velvet skin of her cheek. "Thank you." The words seemed inadequate. "I'll see you before I go. Okay?" As he stared into her big, dark eyes, he saw tears shimmering on the surface. She didn't respond and that worried him. "I enjoyed you."

"I enjoyed you, too." A slight hiccup in her voice told him she was feeling something for him – but what?

"Lucas. . ." Tracy looked scared, so Lucas pulled himself away, leaving the Little Dancer behind. Every step he took away from her caused him something akin to physical pain. As he made his way through the crowd, Lucas saw a sight that unnerved him. A man dressed in a suit had the owner cornered, shaking a folder in his face. Mob. Lucas could smell it a mile away. He didn't like this place, and he liked that Dandi was here even less.

*****

Hurriedly, she began to change clothes. There was no way of knowing how long she had before Romero would come looking for her. Digging under the boards in her closet, she retrieved her lock box, a small wad of bills and her precious supply of insulin – only one package of vials left. No mind, she was getting out of here! She'd figure that problem out down the road. Her hands were shaking so bad she could barely hold anything.

As she jammed her small stash of belonging into the duffle, she couldn't help but think of Lucas. He'd had the kindest, most beautiful eyes she had ever seen. How long had it been since someone had shown such concern for her? When she had looked into his face, it was easy to imagine she'd been waiting for him her whole life. 'Stop it, Dandi,' she lectured herself. There will be time for fairytales later.'

Her heart was hammering. Could she get away? Opening the door, she peeked out. No one was looking. The coast was clear. Shouting from the front told her that a customer may have gotten a little too familiar with a waitress. There was always chaos and conflict of some kind. And then she heard a pop. Was that a gun shot?

Surely not.

It was probably glass breaking. People screamed. God, she hoped no one was hurt. But, now was her chance. Clutching her bag, she headed toward the bathroom, hugging the wall to remain as inconspicuous as possible. What she had on was not the best choice for stealth wear, but she didn't really have a choice. Holding her breath, she pushed on the door, praying that no one else was in the room. Dang, she wished she had time to relieve herself, with the diabetes it seemed she wanted to go all the time. Someone could come in at any moment; there was no time for delay.

Quivering with uncertainty, she went to the window and pushed. God, she hoped it wasn't set with an alarm! Closing her eyes, she lifted. Thankfully, only a mild squeak met her ears and a blast of cold air hit her like a wet blanket. Valentine's Day was just around the corner, so temperatures as low as this were uncommon for Louisiana. Adrenaline pumped through her veins, she was finally taking the steps necessary to save herself and it felt good.

Tossing her bag out, Dandi hoisted herself up, over and out. Her years of dancing and stretching had finally paid off. Now, all she had to do was decide which direction to head. The traffic on East Texas Avenue was heavy for this time of the evening. God it was cold! Dandi literally shook; she wasn't dressed for this at all!

Boom!

A crack of thunder and a blaze of lightning split the sky. Rain began to fall – she thought, but tiny pings began to sound on the steel roof of the club - sleet. A tinge of dismay crept into her mind. She had no car, no coat – nowhere to go and very little money. Was she crazy? She shook her head. It didn't really matter. Anything was preferable to what awaited her if she stayed here at Club Tonga.

Creeping around the corner, what Dandi saw made her freeze in her tracks. Lucas was standing in the parking lot beside his car. She watched him open the driver's side door, get in and start the engine. Everything within her wanted to run to him as hard as she could, but she didn't. Instead she stood still, just in case his headlights moved over her hiding place. He was about to drive out of her world, and the thought made her heart ache.

But - - wait. What was he doing? He cut the engine and got out, making his way back into the club. As far as she could tell, he hadn't locked the door.

A wild, desperate thought struck her. What if she stowed away in his car and just rode as far as he went? He'd never know she was there, and she wouldn't have to bother him with her problems. Dandi had no way of knowing where he was going – but did it matter? She just needed to put some distance between her and Romero as quickly as she could.

It wasn't the best plan, but it was the only one she had.

Creeping as silently as she could, Dandi stayed near the side of the building, making her way to the big car. Riding in a warm vehicle sure would beat walking in this freezing weather. Besides, if she hung around in the neighborhood, there was a chance she could be found by one of the bouncers, or arrested by Cahill at any moment. Unless she could disappear, getting caught was almost a certainty. Romero had too many eyes in this neighborhood.

Feeling the need to hurry, Dandi glanced around, making sure no one was watching. The parking lot was devoid of people. They were all inside, so she made a run for it.

Away from the shelter of the club, the sharp wind almost knocked her down. Reaching the car, she grasped the cold metal, but her fingers were stiff and slipped off the handle, making it pop loudly. She glanced around to see if anyone had taken notice of her, or if Lucas was returning – no, she was alone. Thank God, the car was unlocked. Opening the back driver's side door, she slid in and settled herself in the floorboard, covering her head with an afghan she found on the seat. Niggles of guilt made her stomach feel queasy, but she wouldn't hurt anything and just as soon as he stopped, she'd slip out and he would be none the wiser.

Even though she was in out of the elements, she still shivered; her toes and fingers were like ice. The chill wasn't the only reason she was shaking, Dandi's nerves were dancing like Mexican jumping beans. Embarking with no plan, other than to escape was terrifying.

In the near-dead silence, her breathing sounded deafening. Only the occasional car horn or a distant raised voice penetrated the thick quietude. Dandi waited, trying to calm herself. It seemed like a lifetime passed before she heard approaching footsteps. Her body tensed. Was it Lucas? Yes, the door opened and his considerable weight made the car shift. Would he see her? Could he hear her? For a brief interlude, he was strangely still and Dandi just knew he was peering over the back seat staring at the strange lump on his floorboard. The urge to look up was overwhelming, so she peeked through a fold and saw nothing but the odd pattern of passing car lights on the headliner of the Dodge.

Lucas sighed heavily as if he was resigning himself to a decision. Dandi wondered how his friend had fared. She hoped he was okay. There had been sirens earlier, but in this neighborhood the sounds were commonplace. It was hard for her to tell the difference between an ambulance, a fire truck or a cop car.

Finally, the engine turned over and she felt the car begin to move. Where they were going or how far she had no idea. Whenever he stopped, she would get out and it would be as if she had never been there. Laying her head against the seat where he sat, she tried to ignore the pain in her back. Now wasn't the time to fall apart, she had to be strong.

Gripping the edge of the blanket, she couldn't stop the flood of thoughts from racing through her brain. More than anything, she longed for her life to be different. Even within the chaos of Club Tonga, she realized the connection she had felt with Lucas was extraordinary. She had very little experience, but she knew their attraction had been powerful. Tender feelings and tarnished dreams caused tears to well up in her eyes. She would have given anything in the world to have met him under different circumstances.

Without warning, music filled the car and Dandi jerked with surprise – jazz. She held her breath. Had he felt her movement? No, he began to hum a little. Off-key. Dandi smiled. She found the little imperfection endearing. With relief she let her body relax and her breathing became normal. Before long the rhythm of the road and the warmth of the heater lulled her to sleep.

*****

Lucas couldn't stop worrying. It was a good thing that Tracy had come after him because their friend hadn't been drunk; he had eaten something made with peanuts and had suffered an allergic reaction which had hampered his breathing. Lucas had known he carried an epipen and had been able to help him. The party had ended on a down note, but at least Tim was going to be fine.

His friend wasn't his main concern, however. The Little Dancer's welfare haunted him. He couldn't forget what it felt like to hold her; he couldn't forget her voice, her eyes – God, Lucas wanted her. He wanted her to be safe. Honestly he'd wanted to throw her over his shoulder and carry her out of that damn place. She didn't belong there.

After dealing with Tim, he'd gone to look for her, but she had disappeared. None of the other girls had seen her – or so they said. Even after he had decided it was time to leave – he couldn't. Lucas had gone back one more time to see if he could speak with her. He didn't know exactly what he would have said, but he knew he wanted to see her again. When he had ventured into the back hall near her room, he had run into more than he bargained for.

Romero had shot someone. Lucas had walked around a corner and seen the aftermath. The man who had confronted the club owner lay gasping in a pool of his own blood. Thankfully Lucas hadn't been seen; he had pulled back and stood in the shadows. But what he heard had chilled him to the bone. They had seen Dandi going into the bathroom and assumed she had witnessed the whole thing. Now, they couldn't find her. Romero assumed she had run from him, escaping through a window.

"Find the little bitch, she cannot be allowed to get away. Look for her – whatever it takes. She's on foot, she won't get far." Several men had scattered looking for her. The whole business scared the shit out of Lucas. What had happened to the man or if he would live wasn't his main concern - Dandi was.

With care he left the club, making a phone call to the police. Quickly, he gave all the information he had, and hung up. He had no way of knowing if the man was dead or alive, but there had been a shooting and a helluva lot of blood. And having heard the threat, he also told them he feared a woman known as 'Angel Baby' could be in danger, also. Lucas didn't know if he had done the right thing, but he had to try.

Now, it was time to get out of here while he had the chance. Soon the place would be crawling with cops, and he'd rather be hunting Dandi than answering the same questions over and over. He had done his civic duty. While he'd talked to the 9-1-1 operator, he'd searched behind and under every car – just to be sure. After he had completed the phone call, he had even risked discovery and went back inside the club one more time, trying to find any clue he could about where she might have gone.

To his surprise, someone else seemed to be concerned about the Little Dancer, one of the strippers named Jane. She was the woman he had seen Dandi hug earlier. Lucas had asked her if she had seen Dandi and the woman had looked as if she was about to cry. She said that Dandi was gone and she hoped she never came back. Lucas had told her he was trying to find her, to help her. "Do you know where she might have gone?" She didn't know. "Does she have a cell phone with her?" No, no phone. "Can I trust you?" he had asked, and when the woman had said 'yes', Lucas had given her his card. "If she comes back, would you call me or have her call me?" Jane had agreed.

*****

"He's dead."

Cahill's police radio went off announcing the trouble at Tonga.

Romero was panicking, but he was thinking, "See, I told you she saw me. I had the silencer on; no one heard that shot unless they were right on top of us."

"Shit." Cahill was nervous.

Dispatch could be heard giving details. "Answer it, idiot. You can be first on the scene."

The cop did as he was asked, giving his twenty as being about a block or two away.

"Good thinking."

"We need to ditch that gun, Boss. And you need to get out of here and see if we can get you a plausible alibi figured out."

"I'm outta here, you make yourself indispensable. But remember, you answer to me."

*****

Lucas had driven off the property seconds before the cop cars arrived. He could see them in his rear view mirror as he made the next block. "Now where are you, Dandi?" Wherever she had gone, she was off Club Tonga property. So, he'd take his search to the streets. Turning his windshield wipers up a notch, Lucas stared at the freezing rain, wondering which direction to take. His hope was to find her before those bastards did.

Moving into the middle lane, Lucas began to silently pray. 'Please God, let me see her.' Methodically, he went up and down every block – every side street – searching for a glimpse of the small woman. The sleet was getting a bit heavier, and he had to drive slowly because patches of ice were beginning to form on the highway. Where was she? Where had she gone? She had been afraid, that much he knew. Another thing that bothered him was what Romero had said about her being for sale. How many men had they forced upon her? Fuck! He hit the steering wheel with his palm. Lucas didn't know what terrified him most, the idea that she was being prostituted or the thought that she was out in this storm alone.

"Dandi", he whispered her name, loving the feel of it on his tongue. Lucas could help her, he knew he could. Damn, he should have grabbed hold of her and held on when he had the chance. If he had to, he'd turn this town upside down to find her. Glancing at the clock, he saw it was getting late. Time was slipping away.

Scanning the roadside, he glimpsed down alleyways and yards. If he were her, he'd stay out of sight of the road. Wise on one hand, but what if he missed her too? What was he going to do? A woman on foot would be so vulnerable. God! He hated this! Frustrated, the radio and its happy music began to get on his nerves. Flipping the knob, he turned off the offending noise.

Dang, he was nearing the interstate, she wouldn't have come this far. Preparing to turn around, he slowed the car. Nothing was right, it was too hot and his legs were cramped. First, he adjusted the heater; next he tried adjusting his seat. Rrrrr. Rrrrr. Lucas was surprised to find the automatic controls wouldn't send the driver's seat backward. He tried again. Rrrrr. Clearly, there was something jamming the mechanism or there was something . . . right behind him.

And then he heard it – a very soft, yet unmistakable feminine yawn. Damn! He had a stowaway!

Hope flared in his heart. Could it be? Christ, he had to know. Waiting till there was no one on the road but him, he flipped on one of the overhead lights, turned and took a quick glance over the seat. Hallelujah! Talk about an answer to prayer! Dandi lay right behind him, her head on his back seat. She looked peaceful, warm and entirely snuggable.

Turning back to the road, he couldn't help but make a fist in the air. "Yes!" Suddenly his heart felt lighter and he couldn't wipe the grin off of his face. She was safe! She was with him and they both had a second chance. Pushing a strand of hair out of his eyes, he angled the rearview mirror so he could see into the back seat.

All he needed to do now was get them out of town. His cabin on Pine Ridge was isolated. Lucas didn't think he had been followed, because he had weaved in and out of a dozen side streets and had seen no indication anyone was on his trail.

Now, he wished she would wake up.

Miles clicked by till finally – patience paid off.

Achoo! A sweet little sneeze sounded from the rear.

"Bless you," he responded, matter-of-factly.

"Thank you."

Silence

Lucas wished he had a video camera. The sight of her head slowly appearing – rising from behind the seat until he could see two big, beautiful eyes staring at him was priceless.

"Oops."

"Have a good nap?"

"Yes, I can explain. . ." Dandi spoke slowly.

"Please do," Lucas had no intention of giving her a hard time, but he was so happy, he just had to tease her a bit.

"Are you mad?"

"Mad about you, does that count?"

He was kidding, she knew he was. "Can I come up there with you?"

"Sure, I want you close to me. Let me pull over for you."

"No need." Before he could say Arkansas Razorbacks, she had shimmied her lithe little body over the seat and plopped down right beside him.

"Fasten your seat belt, Love."

"Yes, Sir." She complied sweetly. Her polite little acquiescence made his lust flare.

"Good girl." Lucas was having a hard time keeping his eyes on the road.

"I'm sorry I hitched a ride without asking." The headlights from approaching vehicles made a pleasing pattern of shadows and lights move across her gorgeous face.

"I'm not." And that was no lie. "I'm glad. I was worried about you. I've been looking for you."

"You have?" There was wonder in her voice.

"Hell, yes. I've been driving the streets searching for you. You were in danger and there was no way in hell I was going to walk away and leave you to face it by yourself."

"Danger? What kind of danger? Do you mean Romero bringing men to my room?"

Men to her room? Shit. He didn't want to think about that. "No, that's not what I meant." Lucas realized she had no idea what had gone on. "Romero shot a man, and someone saw you sneaking into the bathroom about that same time. They thought you were a witness. Romero's men, as well as the cops are out hunting for you. And Romero won't give up easily."

"Oh, my Lord." She held a hand to her heart. "I can get myself into a mess without even trying." Then, it dawned on her what he had said. "All the time I was in the back seat, you were looking for me? Why would you do that?"

Why? Good question. He sought an answer. There was no doubt he was sexually drawn to her. Just sitting near to her had him hard and hungry. "I was worried about you." Understatement. Light from a passing car illuminated her perfect face. She was waiting for him to say more. "The idea of something happening to you was totally unacceptable." Even thinking about the possibilities set his teeth on edge.

Her instincts had been right, Lucas was a good man. Dandi's heart felt full and she gave in to an impulse. Unfastening her seat belt, she leaned over and kissed him on the cheek. The big man tensed beneath her lips. She drew back, giving him space. "Thank you, but I didn't see any shooting. All I could think about was getting away from Romero."

"You're welcome. I'd better call the police and tell them you are safe with me." Lucas picked up his phone.

"No, please don't!" She stopped him. "I never wanted to dance on stage, but Romero accused me of stealing money from him. He was blackmailing me." Dandi knew she was talking too fast, but she needed to make him realize why phoning the police wouldn't be a good idea. "Someone planted it in my locker, and my stripping was his price for not pressing charges against me. His right hand man is a dirty cop. I won't have a chance. I'm afraid. I don't want to be arrested." Again. She added, silently.

"You're not going to be arrested," he assured her. "Romero has bigger worries than blackmail right now. He would want you as far from police custody as possible."

"I hope so," she let out a long sigh. "This whole thing has been a nightmare."

"Explain to me more about the blackmailing?." Lucas felt like he had been whomped upside the head with a two-by-four. All he wanted to do was touch her. When she had kissed him on the cheek, his blood pressure had sky-rocketed.

Dandi turned toward him, pulling one leg up under her. "He saw me dance. I was just fooling around while I cleaned off tables and when he approached me about working as a stripper, I refused. But he wouldn't take no for an answer." Dandi told how she had danced to "After All" and how Romero had threatened her.

The more Lucas listened, the angrier he became. "Bastard!" She had been mistreated.

"I couldn't afford to be arrested, not after the shoplifting charge when I was underage." Embarrassed, she told of the time she had been arrested for stealing. "Since my mother died, everything has gone from bad to worse."

"Dandi, don't worry about the arrest threat or the cops. We'll straighten it out later. After all, you didn't see anything." None of it was fair. He knew people went through difficult times, but Dandi seemed to have had more than her share. "I'm so sorry you had to go through all that."

"I took you to my room to ask you to help me, I didn't intend to offer you a lap dance," she confessed.

Slanting her a possessive glance, he declared. "Why didn't you tell me? Don't you know I would have moved heaven and earth to help you? You didn't have to stowaway; I would have carried you out the front door and dared anyone to stop me."

Biting her lower lip, Dandi watched him carefully. Lord, it would be so easy to fall for this man. "I got off track when you asked for the lap dance. I didn't want to disappoint you."

"You didn't, I loved every second of it."

His voice sent tingles of delight racing up and down her skin. "I'm glad."

"So, why didn't you ask me to get you out of there? I was totally and completely at your mercy." The woman was incredible; she had him almost panting with need.

"You asked me how much you owed me."

"Explain." One word conveyed remorse and determination.

"When you defended me, and showed concern when that guy hit me . . ." she looked out the window into the blackness, "I just thought you saw me . . . differently, but when you wanted to pay me, I realized you thought I was no different from the other girls."

"Dandi, look at me."

She did, she couldn't help it. His voice seemed to caress her very soul. In the dim light, she stared at the shadows of his chiseled face, wishing she could see him more clearly.

"I did see you differently. That's why I couldn't rest till I found you."

His answer thrilled Dandi's heart. "I'm just glad I got out before I lost myself."

"I can understand you wanting to leave. You didn't belong there. But if you didn't know about the shooting, why did you decide to run just as the storm of the century hit?" Lucas pointed out the window as big flakes of snow began to replace the sleet.

Dandi let out a long breath, visibly relaxing. "Jane and one of the other girls warned me that Romero had plans to put me to work tonight. If I hadn't left when I did, I'd probably be servicing strange men right now."

Lucas saw her shudder. "Well, you're not. You're with me."

Dandi hugged herself tightly. She hadn't realized how much danger she had actually been in. "You saved me. How will I ever thank you?"

"Having you here, safe and sound is thanks enough."

"Oh." He was her hero, handsome and powerful. Dandi shivered at the thrill of being near him. "Thor, you look like Thor," she said with a smile as it finally dawned on her who he resembled. "You know, the super hero with the big hammer. Or rather you look like the gorgeous actor who plays Thor."

"Ha! Thor, huh?" Yea, and he had the big hammer to prove it. She was adorable. There was no telling what she had been through, and she still could make him smile. "You think I'm gorgeous?" he couldn't help but grin.

"You know you are."

"Not as gorgeous as you," he winked at her. Both grew silent. In spite of their attempt at humor, it was apparent she had narrowly missed disaster.

Finally, Lucas asked. "Well, what's your plan?" It dawned on him she hadn't asked where they were going or even what direction they were heading.

Plan? Oh yea, she needed one of those. A sign on the side of the road told her they weren't in Louisiana anymore, they were in Arkansas. Dandi wished she had more sensible information to offer, but she didn't. A sense of despair washed over her. "When I left the club, I had no plan other than to get as far away as I could, even if it was just across town. I don't know where I'm going or what I'm going to do."

Funny, Lucas couldn't seem to recall the vague image of that perfect woman he had kept on a mental pedestal for these years. All he could see was Dandi. He knew what she could do; she could come home with him. Before he could suggest it, she went on with her explanation.

"I'm very grateful to you. When I climbed into your back seat, I vowed I wouldn't cause you any trouble. I have enough money for a motel. So if you see one, stop. Tomorrow I'll find a shelter where I can stay until the excitement dies down in Shreveport. Perhaps, I can find a job that doesn't involve me removing my clothes," she emphasized with a smile.

"You were going to ask me to just put you out? Alone? Don't you have family?" He didn't intend to raise his voice, but the idea of leaving her at some ratty motel didn't sit well with him at all.

"Lucas, I . . ." she stopped talking. A wave of dizziness made her sway. "Could I turn down the heat a bit?" She was so thirsty, her blood sugar must have hit rock bottom and she didn't even have a piece of peppermint. "I need to stop when you can." It was time for a shot, some water, a bite to eat – and a bathroom.

"Sure, do you need to go to the ladies' room?"

"Yea, I do," among other things.

"Are you okay?" She looked pale.

"I'll be okay, I'm a little hungry."

"When's the last time you ate?"

"I don't know, yesterday, maybe," she barely spoke above a whisper.

"Hell, you should take better care of yourself. I'll get gas while you do what you need to do." He watched her, worriedly. She looked listless.

Thankfully, it wasn't too long before he put on the blinker. She pushed her sweat dampened hair out of her face as he pulled into a convenience store. "Thank you," she picked up her duffle bag when he pulled up to the gas pump.

"Why are you taking that with you?" She wasn't leaving him, not yet, not if he could help it.

"I need to freshen up in the bathroom and take some medicine. Do you want a soda or something?" Dandi put on a brave front; she didn't really want him to see her as weak. There was a distinctive tremble in her voice, but she masked it as best she could.

Good, she wasn't skipping out on him. "Yea, get me one of whatever you're having." He watched her make her way to the door. Was she swaying? "Where's your coat?" he yelled.

"I don't have one," she answered over her shoulder.

"The woman needs a keeper." Good thing he was highly qualified for the job. Shaking his head, Lucas pumped his gas. Like he had considered earlier, the best solution was to convince her to go home with him. He could help her, make sure she was okay. The fact that he was completely in lust with her wasn't a factor. Liar. But, would she do it? Looking up, he saw a car about to back out right on top of her. "Look out, Dandi!" he yelled.

"Hey, watch out lady!"

"Sorry," she moved to one side and allowed the vehicle to back out. "I'm okay," she looked back at Lucas. She really wasn't, but the insulin and food would work fast. She felt sad, it would be so easy to get used to his attention and concern. A neon sign to the left of the store caught her attention. A small, dingy motel sat right next door. Well, that was convenient. A wave of sorrow hit her. She wasn't ready to say goodbye to Lucas.

When she entered the small market, two salesclerks watched her like a hawk. Dandi couldn't figure out why until she realized she still had on her Club Tonga stripper shirt. 'I strip at Tonga' was not the best recommendation one could display across their chest. "Hi," she spoke to them anyway and got a smirk for her trouble. Oh, well. She picked out a couple of sandwiches, some juice, a moon pie for Lucas and two chocolate yoo-hoos. Going to the register, she glanced out the window and saw him hang up the hose, "I'll pay for his gas." It was the least she could do for the ride.

"Seventy-seven dollars and fifty two cents," the cashier said snidely.

"Okay," she used a good chunk of the cash in her purse to pay out. That car had a heck of a tank on it.

"We don't like your sort in our store," the older woman said to Dandi under her breath. "I saw you strip in that video, and we saw you on the news. We know who you are."

The unkind words stung. "I understand. I'm leaving soon, but I need to use your facilities." Before going any further, she opened the juice and took a big drink. The coolness and the sugar content would help. Now, the shot, then get out before she was thrown out.

Lucas was making his way to the door and he was looking right at her. She waved at him and pointed at the bathroom, wanting to get away from the judgmental women as quickly as possible. "I'll be back in a second."

"I think we need to talk," he called out to her. As he walked up to the counter, he could hear the clerks whispering.

"I'll go check," one of them said as she hurried back toward the restroom. What was going on? He didn't have to wonder long, the frizzy haired employee came barreling back to him. "That floozy you're with is in the restroom doing drugs. I saw the needle before she shut the door. We don't allow crap like that in our store."

Her accusative tone angered Lucas, but her suggestion scared him to death. Could Dandi be on something? She had looked pale. God, what had they done to her? He hurried to the back and knocked on the door. "Dandi?"

"I'll be out in a minute," she answered.

"Open the door – now!" Lucas demanded in a loud voice.

"Okay, okay," she muttered. Dang, he must really have to go. Wasn't there a boy's restroom? She opened the door with syringe in hand. "What's wrong?"

"What are you taking?" He looked at the needle. "Damn, Dandi!"

"Taking?" she was confused – and sick. Why did he look so angry? What had she done? Lucas was eying her hand that held the needle as if she were holding a poisonous snake. "Oh," with dismay, she realized he thought she was a junkie. "It's not what you think."

"Give it here," he held out his hand. "These people will call the police on you. You'll end up in jail, anyway. Is that what you want?"

CHAPTER FOUR

With a look of desperate disapproval, he held out his hand for the syringe. "Give it to me."

She did as he asked. "But I need it, Lucas."

"No, you don't. We'll get you help."

"Look," she held up the vial. "It's insulin." Her voice cracked and she stumbled, catching the sink. "Please, just leave. I'll be fine. Thanks for everything." She turned her back on him.

The truth hit Lucas like a wave. She was diabetic. She wasn't a drug addict, she was sick. "Baby, I'm so sorry."

"It doesn't matter." Her voice sounded defeated. "Please leave, I need to use the bathroom before I give myself a shot."

She didn't look at him, and he felt about six inches tall. "No." He wasn't leaving.

"If you're gonna stay in here, turn around." Her voice was weak, but she was determined to get her way. Dandi waited until he did as she asked before she pulled her jeans and panties down to sit on the toilet. "Turn on the water in the sink, please. I don't want you to hear me pee."

"I don't know why you're being so shy. You do remember we made each other cum, just hours ago?"

"This is different." She sighed as if giving up.

"How?" If she thought this was over, she was sadly mistaken.

"Bathroom stuff is worse." He could hear her tearing off the toilet paper and flushing. "I need to wash my hands."

When he faced her again, he could tell she was as weak as dishwater. "Hold on, I've got you." He helped her to the sink. "Where are your testing strips or whatever you use to test your blood sugar?"

"In my duffle bag."

After she rinsed and dried her hands, he helped her back to the toilet, closing the seat so she could sit down. Kneeling, he opened her bag and found the small meter. "Where do you want to check?" She gave him her hand; he took one finger, held the meter to it and took the minute amount of blood. When she didn't even flinch, he kissed the tiny spot and looked up to find her watching him intently. "What?"

"You are a very nice man."

"I don't feel very nice, but thank you." He kissed her hand again, just for good measure.

"And you are very handsome."

Lucas laughed. "You're sicker than I thought. I think you're talking out of your head." It would take but a few seconds for a reading. "Are you hypoglycemic or hyperglycemic?"

"Hypo – low blood sugar."

She was right. Lucas checked, it was very low. "Sixty-five. Let's get some insulin in you. How much?" She told him the dose and he readied the shot. .

"You're good at this."

"I'm good at lots of things," he teased.

"I bet."

His feeble attempt at humor was met by a weak little giggle which went straight to his heart. "Where do you want it?"

"Up here," she pulled down her pants till her upper thigh was bare.

His hand shook as he pressed the needle in. She was so beautiful and so vulnerable. "There. Now let's get you something to eat," without asking, he picked her up.

"I could get used to this," she sighed contentedly, putting her arms around his neck. Lucas held her down toward the floor so she could pick up her bag and small sack of groceries.

"Me too," he admitted, as he maneuvered her around in his arms so he could open the door.

The two nosy women were hovering outside the door and Lucas resented their interference and their attitude. He had hurt Dandi. It was his fault for jumping to conclusions, but these women were getting on his nerves. "You were wrong," he said to them, flatly.

Lucas didn't bother to explain, they weren't worth it. "Sit here," he took her to a small table in the corner. "I'll be back with something for you to eat."

She held up her bag, "I already bought some stuff and I'd rather get going, if that's okay with you."

"I'm here with you. It'll be all right. Did you get fruit? You need fruit." He left her before she could say anything else.

Gathering a banana, a couple of apples and a few other items, Lucas went up to pay for the food and his gas. To his surprise, he was told that Dandi had already paid for the fuel. A tender feeling made his chest ache. She had very little, but she had paid for his gas. He was touched. Over and over again, she was surprising him. When she had thrown herself at that pickpocket to help him, he had lost a piece of his heart.

While Dandi was waiting for Lucas to return, she considered her options. A telephone book was lying on the table and she scanned the yellow pages for a nearby shelter. There wasn't one. She'd probably have to go to Little Rock or to Oklahoma City, or maybe south to New Orleans. Anywhere would do as long as it was a safe distance away from Romero and Shreveport. Twirling a strand of hair around her finger, she sighed.

Thoughts of starting over were hard to process. All she could think about was how much her heart hurt when she had seen the disappointment on Lucas's face. He had just assumed she was doing drugs. What he had said about seeing her differently wasn't true. Her heart sank. What had she expected? His perception of her was still colored by where they had met – at a strip joint where she had been stripping. 'How much do I owe you?' the question still rang in her ears.

"Here eat this; you need the natural sugar."

Lucas spoke behind her, Dandi jumped a little. She took the partially peeled banana from his hand. "Thank you," she sighed and took a big bite. It was so good.

"You bought my gas. Why did you do that?"

"To pay - for you - giving me - a ride," she answered around a mouthful of banana.

Lucas kissed the top of her head, she was so cute.

She swallowed and held up a plastic bottle. "Here's your yoo-hoo, and a moon-pie."

He took her odd idea of a snack. "You didn't owe me for a ride," he chided her as he sat down. "I want to apologize to you, Dandi. You have done nothing to warrant the way I treated you in there. I'm sorry."

She studied the plastic on the sandwich intently. "There's no need for you to apologize." Dandi handed him the ham and swiss and she kept the pimento cheese. "What else could you think? You came to a logical conclusion based on what you knew about me." The sad truth hit her; she would always be lumped in with people like Patty and Romero for as long as anyone knew of her time at Club Tonga. How long did they keep you-tube videos available? Forever? Great.

Her voice was lifeless, like she had given up hope. He had hurt her. "I didn't think – that's the problem. I reacted without knowing the facts. I'm training to be a doctor, I ought to know better."

"A doctor?" Dandi sighed. "I had a suspicion you were perfect, now I know you are. What are you doing dealing with the likes of me?" All of Miss Etta's encouraging words about dreams and self-worth seemed far-away. Being beaten down day after day had taken its toll.

"I'm a lucky son-of-a-bitch is what I am. Any man fortunate enough to spend time with you is damn lucky."

He seemed almost angry. She didn't know what to say, so she just said. "Thank you."

"Let me get you a water, You need liquids." He headed back to the beverage cooler and she followed him with her eyes. Lucas had her head spinning and it had nothing to do with low blood sugar. Since her mom died, her life had been a series of mistakes and missteps; she had taken no time for romance or dating. Sexual attraction was an emotion she had avoided, it had only come out to play when she was alone and fantasizing about the man she would someday love. At the moment, Dandi's mind was having the devil of a time convincing her body and her heart that Lucas was not that man.

She ate slowly while he paid for her water, letting her imagination take over. How she wished she could have a little more time with him. Several women waiting to check out watched him, making no attempt to hide their admiration.

While one clerk waited on Lucas, the other walked boldly up to her - a young, pimply faced woman with bad teeth. "Just as soon as you get that food swallowed, we want you out of here, Missy.

We don't allow whores in our store." She pronounced the w in whore, which did nothing to negate the ugliness of her words.

"I'm not a whore," she said softly.

"All right, that's enough." Lucas had returned and heard enough. "You don't know Dandi, Miss. I'm sick and tired of your sanctimonious bullshit. Either apologize to this lady right now, or I'm going to call the gaming commission for those illegal slot machines you have in your back room." He wouldn't have noticed them if it hadn't been for the squeal of delight emanating from the narrow hall. A woman had run out breathless with excitement over her luck on the penny machine.

A mean hard look passed over the woman's face, but she did as Lucas asked. "I'm sorry."

Lucas couldn't resist a parting shot. "She's leaving, but it's not because of you. Dandi is coming home with me. She doesn't have to fight her battles alone – not anymore."

What was he talking about? Just a minute ago he had been ready to believe she used drugs. Was she dreaming? He quickly gathered their things and escorted her out to the car. She didn't have to be urged; she didn't want to stay around those women any longer than necessary. He helped her in, placed the food in her lap and fastened the seat belt. "How do you feel now?"

"Better." Her heart was tender; she was still reeling from all that had happened.

"Good, those women were idiots." He shut the door and headed around to drive. Lucas was a formidable figure. To have him on her side, even for this brief period, was life-changing.

When he sat down and started the engine, she touched his arm. "Lucas, you don't have to take me anywhere. There's a motel right here." She pointed toward the flashing 'Vacancy' sign.

"Didn't you hear what I said in the store, Dandi?" He picked up a lock of her hair and rubbed it between his fingers. "I want you to come home with me." Lucas knew change was coming to his life. In just a couple of weeks, he'd be moving. Meeting this beautiful woman had not been on his agenda, but the best things in life seldom are. He didn't intend for this magic to slip through his fingers.

Yes, she had heard what he said, but she felt it was his anger at the clerks talking or maybe his guilt for misjudging her. "You want me to stay at your house for a little while?" She had to make sure she understood.

"Yes, I can't leave you here. This motel is a dump." Placing one of his big hands over hers, he stroked the back of it with his thumb. Dandi shivered. "Don't ask me to do that."

Dandi's eyes widened. She wanted so badly to accept, but she didn't know what was going on, not really. "I'd be okay, you know. I've been taking care of myself for a while."

Lucas cocked his head to one side and studied her face intently. "I know, and I could take you to a better motel and give you money and walk away – except for one very important point."

"What's that?"

"I don't want to."

He caressed her face. "I want to protect you – that's a given. But I also can't get what we shared out of my head. What I felt with you was amazing and I want more. I want you."

His stark words made her body grow warm. "Nothing like this has ever happened to me before."

"When you came, your little body trembling in my arms – I can't forget it, I can't forget you."

His words were provocative; Dandi's pussy throbbed in response. She didn't really know what to say. "I've never felt this way before."

Lucas smiled. He was getting to her – good. Now, she'd know how he felt. "Eat your sandwich, you're gonna need it," taking a knife out of his pocket, he cut up an apple, and opened her yoo-hoo. "I'm not so sure all of this chocolate is good for you."

"I'm splurging. Besides, I'm a big girl."

She was amazed to see heat flame in his eyes.

"I'd say you were a woman full grown, ripe and ready for the picking." Then a look of abject horror covered his face. "Aren't you?"

Dandi laughed as she wiped pimento cheese from her lip. "Yes, I'm nineteen."

"Thank God. Let's get out of here." Before backing the car, he adjusted the heat and surveyed the area. Romero still bore heavy on his mind, but the likelihood of them being followed after he had taken such a circuitous route was unlikely.

"Good, I'm ready to go. It's like a new chapter in my life is beginning."

"Yes, a new start," he agreed. Dandi was such a breath of fresh air; it was hard for him to reconcile what she'd been through with the seemingly innocent woman before him. Whatever she'd endured, whatever bad decisions she had made, he didn't believe for a second they were her fault. "Have you been diabetic since childhood?"

"No, I was just diagnosed a few months ago. That's why I went to work at Club Tonga as a waitress. The wages weren't much higher than the burger joints, but the tips made up the difference. One of my roommates worked at another club and convinced me that was what I should do."

Lucas reached into an open bag of lemon drops and took one. "Be a waitress?"

Dandi flushed. "Yes, I never intended to strip. I love to dance," she clarified with an apologetic smile. "My childhood mentor, Miss Etta, taught me ballet and modern dance; I adore moving to the music."

"I could tell." He'd never forget how graceful and amazing she'd looked dancing in that hell-hole.

"What's your last name?" She wanted to know everything about him.

"Wagner, what's yours?"

"Alexander." It was nice to be sharing their personal information. She hoped they shared more. "Lucas Wagner, I like that." Just the sound of his name caused a stab of desire to sizzle in her belly.

"Do you have any family?" He has asked her that before, but she hadn't answered. She'd been sick.

Dandi chewed slowly and swallowed. "I have a cousin, an older male cousin, but I haven't heard from him in years, that's all. I don't even know where he's living now."

She had no family. Dandi was alone. He didn't like it, not at all. Choosing his words carefully, Lucas made his case. "It would be better if you laid low for a week or so. I tell you what, in two weeks I have my final interview for a position that I've been working my ass off for. If I get it, which I'm pretty confident I will, I'll be moving. Why don't you plan on staying with me till then? That will give you time to decide where you're going and what you want to do." He thought it sounded logical.

Oh, a time limit. Her heart sank a little even though her head saw the logic of the plan. "Okay, I guess – if you're sure I won't be in the way."

"No, I have plenty of room." He felt like the weight of the world had been lifted from his shoulders. She'd have time to sort out her affairs, and he'd have time to decide what he was going to do with these unfamiliar feelings in his heart.

Dandi knew there were unanswered questions. What did he want from her? What was she willing to give him? Whatever the answers were, she knew being with Lucas was a thousand times better than being at Romero's mercy. "I have a stipulation."

Lucas laughed. "You have a stipulation?" He wasn't surprised. She was a woman, after all. Whatever she needed to feel comfortable, he'd do.

"Yes, I want to help while I'm with you. I can cook and clean, I want to pay my way."

If she'd asked for diamonds, he would have been less surprised. "Dandi . . ."

"No, I will not take advantage of you. I can be useful – I promise. You're giving me a safe place to be while I decide what I'm going to do next and where I belong. I trust you."

Biting his tongue, he managed to control the impulse to tell her he knew where she belonged, with him. Lucas had no hang ups about sex or enjoying sex with whomever he pleased. But he had to remember his mission. At some point in time, and he didn't know when – Lucas intended to settle down with the right woman. Until that time, he sure as hell didn't intend to remain celibate. He always made sure the woman knew the score, but he'd have to tread lightly with Dandi, she was nothing like the other women he had been with. "I'm glad, Dandi. I wouldn't hurt you for the world." Dandi picked up his hand and held it tight against her abdomen and his heart melted. If she was half as sweet as she seemed to be, he was in big trouble. She might not qualify as his idea of Miss Right, but she was going to turn him inside out before it was over.

"Where are we going? I haven't even thought to ask." She sat up in the seat, holding her back from touching the upholstery. It was sore; she needed to check on it pretty quick.

"West of Little Rock, near Hot Springs." She was still holding his hand, which was fine by him. He could drive one handed, no problem. What was a problem was the way she was petting his hand, rubbing and squeezing it. The innocent affection made his cock grow bigger with every passing second. Lucas smiled to himself – such sweet torture. "Talk to me. Tell me anything."

"Okay. My Dad died when I was young." Dandi opened up, telling him everything about her mother and the years they had spent alone, about the church where she spent so much time and Miss Etta. When she got to the part about her stepfather and stepbrother, her voice dropped to a near whisper. "Sam would corner me in the hall or the bathroom, pinning me against the wall. He would pinch my breasts and try to push his hand between my legs. I would manage to throw the sniveling little bastard off, but my fighting back would only excite him; he said he enjoyed my playing hard to get, calling me his 'spitting kitten.' When I went to Arlon for help, I didn't get any, he just laughed and said 'boys would be boys.'"

"Did you go to the police?"

"No, I ran to my mom's church for help. They didn't believe me. Arlon Alexander was a pillar of the church, a long-time member. When the pastor called Arlon to come pick me up, I just left. Without Mother, home wasn't home anyway."

As Lucas listened, he had become more furious with every word she said. "I'm so sorry." Those three words were so inadequate. If he ever got the chance to meet her stepfather or stepbrother face to face, they'd never abuse a little girl again. "No child should have to make the decision you made."

Little by little they bonded. He told her a bit about his childhood and his goals and dreams, but none of the ugly details. She had seen enough ugliness to last a lifetime.

"What kind of doctor will you be?" she asked with awe.

"I will be a doctor of psychiatry," he clarified. Now was not the time to reveal his specialty; he didn't want to scare her off. "It's my dream to help people cope with the problems life throws at them. People like you. You've been through a lot, both with your step family and at the club. I told you that I wanted to help you, remember?"

His comment hit Dandi like a blow to the sternum. "That's nice," she said slowly. Now, she was confused. Wouldn't you know it? Here she was having visions of a white picket fence and two-point-five children and Lucas possibly saw her as a 'project'. A wave of disappointment made her heart ache. Looking down at his hand, she squeezed it one last time and let it go.

"What's wrong?"

Dandi gave him a sweet smile; he didn't have to know she could have fallen in love with him. That would be her secret. "Nothing is wrong. I accept your offer of help, if you accept mine."

"Deal."

After a while, Dandi slept. Lucas kept an eye on her, the road and the rear-view mirror. Still no sign of being followed, he was convinced they had made a clean getaway. The sun was coming up over the Ozarks before he got to the top of Pine Ridge. Snow had blanketed the entire landscape in white.

Dandi slowly awoke. "This will be like a vacation!" As they drove up the drive-way, she looked in every direction, taking it all in. "It's beautiful." Lucas's home was a magical mountain hide-away, a two-story log home with huge glass windows, big decks and two fireplaces. The yard was a rolling expanse that led down to a stream with rocks big enough to climb on. "I love it." She couldn't wait to get out and explore and play in the snow.

"Thanks, I built most of the house myself. It took years; I came up and worked on it when I could. It was good therapy." Pulling into the garage, he shut the door and helped her out. While he was gathering their things out of the car, Lucas thought to ask. "How much insulin and testing supplies do you have? We may lose electricity and get snowed in. I want to make sure you have enough."

"Hmmmm," Dandi thought. "Enough for about ten days, I'll have to count and be sure."

"Don't hesitate to tell me what you need. I can always take the four-wheeler out of here if need be."

"Thank you." She wasn't used to someone caring about her one way or the other. It was a good feeling. Everything fascinated her, she had to stop and look at his work table full of tools and in the freezer. "If you'll take out this piece of chuck, I'll cook you a roast that will melt in your mouth," she pointed at the large hunk of beef.

Lucas was no fool; he took the roast out and toted it in one hand while he opened the door for her with the other. "Make yourself at home." He set her bag on the kitchen table while he put the roast in the sink to thaw.

Dandi was in a cook's heaven. "What I couldn't do in a kitchen like this." She held her arms out and twirled around. "This place is a dream." She scurried around and touched the double ovens and the microwave and the French refrigerator. "I shall make you a very happy man," she said almost solemnly.

"Damn," Lucas groaned. "I like the sound of that." She was talking about food, but his body had other ideas.

"Can I look around?" She didn't wait for an answer; Angel Baby took off, oohing and aahing over everything. "I love rocking chairs!" she exclaimed and he heard the sound of rocking on the wooden floor. Lord, he had plans for that chair – just thinking of her straddling him – naked and luscious in his arms made his mouth water. Everything was reminding him of sex; he had it bad. But he also had manners; he was a gentleman. This Angel was a guest in his home; he hadn't known her even twenty-four hours, and in spite of his better judgment - he had feelings for her. All of those things forced him to rein in his libido.

He caught up with her in the den as she inspected the fireplace. "We can make s'mores!" she smiled at him with wonder.

"Anything you'd like – that's what we'll do." Hell, he might have to behave, but that didn't stop him from dreaming. He knew what he wanted. Lucas wanted to sink deep inside of her, place his mark on her so that she would never forget what it was like to be with him. Jesus! He had to make himself move. "There's a suite just off this room that I think you'll like. It's almost a private retreat. The room even has its own bath." He showed her around, opened the bathroom door and turned on the light, then turned down the covers of the big bed that was piled high with fluffy pillows.

"It's beautiful," she had to admit. "Where do you sleep?"

"Upstairs."

"Oh."

Did she sound disappointed? It was probably wishful thinking on his part. For a few moments, they were silent. Dandi let out a long sigh, it wasn't a sigh of sadness – rather it was one of contentment.

"Why don't you try and get some sleep? I'm sure you're tired. I'll wake you in a few hours. I could use a rest myself. I think I'll just put a fire in the fireplace and lie back in the recliner."

"Leave the door open, okay? I don't want to be alone."

Lucas almost offered to join her, but he resisted the impulse. "I'll be right here." If he sat in front of the fireplace, he'd be able to see her sleeping in bed.

"Thank you," taking a nap sounded good to Dandi. "I'm so tired; it's been a long, long time since I felt safe."

"You're safe. I'd protect you with my life."

"I believe you." she yawned – the sweetest yawn. He wanted to chunk his good intentions and just crawl into bed with her. If all he got to do was hold her, it'd be more than he could ask for. She went to the bed and crawled in, still in her clothes. Nestling down into the covers, she lay on one side, facing him.

Before shutting her eyes, Dandi smiled at him and he felt as if a wave of heat hit him broadside – a heat that warmed his heart and lit up his world. "Sleep well, Baby. I'll watch over you." He walked away.

*****

Dandi cuddled down into the soft mattress and pulled the covers up to her chin. She had always slept alone, so why was she so lonely? Pretending, she reached out and touched the other side of the bed, imagining Lucas's big warm body lying next to her. What would she do? Taking the other pillow, she hugged it close, trying to visualize how it would feel to snuggle up to him. She would run her hands all over his body and shower him with kisses. Beyond touching and kissing, her imagination had to take over and carry her to places she had never been before.

Dandi had never been particularly curious about men beyond what a normal, sheltered girl would be, but she was intensely curious about Lucas. If she ever had the chance, she would kiss a line down his body from his mouth to his middle – and lower, just like in those romance novels she'd read on Jewel's e-reader. Heat suffused her cheeks. Here she was, a runaway from a strip club, had been only hours or days away from being pushed into selling her body – and she was a veritable innocent.

Dandi's upbringing had been typical Bible-belt. She had been involved in church outings, youth camps, even a program specifically designed to teach young people abstinence and chastity. The program had been called 'True Love Waits.' She had embraced the teachings of the church – to a degree. While her Sunday School teachers and pastor had instilled in her good values, Miss Etta had tempered that religious fervor with common sense. Her mentor had taught Dandi the wisdom of moderation. So she wasn't a virgin because she thought sex was wrong or evil, she was a virgin because she had never met anyone she wanted to share her body with – until now.

Dandi wanted Lucas. What he felt for her, she wasn't certain. He said he wanted her. He said he wanted to protect her. He said he wanted to help her. None of that equaled forever, so she didn't expect it, but finding joy today and however long it lasted would be amazing. So, if she got the opportunity, she would give herself to him.

Even though she was tired, sleep was a long time coming, but when it did, Dandi slept hard.

*****

Being as quiet as he could, Lucas prepared a fire. He stretched out in the recliner and stared through the open door to where Dandi lay. As he watched her sleep, Lucas felt more peaceful than he had in a long time. Thinking back over the last twenty-four hours, he couldn't quite believe all that had happened. Taking his phone from his pocket, he placed a quick call to check on Tim. Speaking softly with Lois, he was relieved to hear that his friend was fine. Saying a quick goodbye to the prospective bride, he realized something unexpected. Lucas was happy for Tim and Lois, but he was also envious. Meeting Dandi had highlighted the undeniable fact that he was lonely. Sometimes the best laid plans were not the easiest to keep.

As the fire crackled and Dandi slept, Lucas tried to relax. Heaven lay between the sheets in his guestroom and he was sitting here alone. How crazy was that? As he lay back, he hungered.

Rubbing his hand over his swollen cock, he prayed for patience. Dandi would be well worth the wait. So, what was he going to do in the meantime?

Suffer.

*****

Dandi woke slowly. Where was she? Opening her eyes, she looked through the open door of the bedroom and could see Lucas sleeping in the recliner. Feeling contented, she stretched – too much. "OW!" Her body jerked with the unexpected pain. God! Where she had been caned still hurt like hell. What if she was getting infected? She had been so tired last night she hadn't taken time to clean the injured area. Bad decision. Didn't she have enough problems without adding blood poisoning to the mix?

"What?" Something had awakened him. Pop! The fire crackled and danced, throwing out cinders onto the rug. Lucas rose, picked up the fireplace shovel and scooped them up before they could leave a burn mark. Another groan from the bedroom caused him to straighten up with alarm. "Dandi? What's wrong?" He rehung the shovel and went to her. She lay on her stomach. Placing a hand on her back, he knelt by her. She was so little.

The little bit of pressure he placed on her skin was agony. Something was wrong. She managed not to scream, but she did whimper.

"Are you hurt?"

"It's nothing."

"Damnit – don't tell me that."

"It's my back."

"Let me see," he pulled at the covers and her shirt. "Damn, I can't get to you. Take it off."

Dandi jerked away from him. The words, 'take it off', had come to stand for all she hated. "No, I'm okay."

"No, you're not. Let me help you, I need to help you."

The magic words seemed to work. She stilled. Lucas stepped over and flipped on the overhead light – immediately struck by her fragile beauty. Leaning over her, he gently picked up the shirt. What he saw horrified him. Stripes marred her beautiful skin. Angry whelps and marks clearly told a sordid story. "Damn, I didn't see this when you danced for me. It was covered up. How did this happen? Who beat you?"

"Romero."

Lucas spoke before he thought. "Did he whip you as part of some BDSM scene?"

Dandi tried to think, what did the letters stand for? Oh, kinky sex. "No. He caned me."

"Fuck!" Lucas swore. "Let's get you out of these clothes." He saw her cut those big doe eyes up at him and it was easy to read the pain. "It's okay; I'll take care of you." She sat up and unbuttoned the shirt. "Have you seen a doctor?"

"No," she whispered. "I cleaned it as best I could, but Minnie kept it covered with stage makeup so I could perform. He whipped me three times, so it never really got a chance to heal."

Dandi crossed her arms over her gorgeous ample breasts. Lucas's hands shook as he pushed her hair off of her back so he could inspect the sore places. "We need to pull your pants off; there are places on your upper hip." He held her arm while she went to her knees and unzipped her jeans, pushing them down past her hips. She sat back down and Lucas pulled them down and off her sleek, shapely legs. Dandi had the most perfect little body he had ever seen, which made the damage done to it even more of a crime. "Lie back down on your tummy while I get what I need to clean you up. I'm afraid it's getting infected."

Her eyes followed him as he moved across the room to the bathroom. She could see him clearly as he began rummaging around in the medicine cabinet. Dandi couldn't help but admire the broad, strong body of her defender. His shoulders were as wide as a bus. He was the kind of man a woman wanted to cling to and lean on. As she studied him, she had to smile - in contrast to his brawn, he had the most beautiful golden hair. It hung almost to his shoulders. So many people in Louisiana had the dark hair of the Creoles, like her own. She wondered if his was as soft to the touch as it looked. But when he returned with a washcloth, soap, rubbing alcohol, and some type of ointment, she felt her whole body draw up into a knot. "It's going to burn." She could hear Lucas chuckle.

Smiling at her child-like fear, he stood beside the bed. "I think the burning is a sign the medicine is working. If it's infected, we're going to have to go get you some antibiotics." Lord Have

Mercy! The sight of her on the bed, flat of her belly with that delectable heart-shaped rear sticking up in the air took his breath away. But she was hurt – so he pushed the lust down and let concern take center stage.

"You're a doctor; don't you have some lying around?"

"I'm not that kind of doctor, unfortunately."

"I wish you were," she mumbled in the pillow.

He began to gently press the cloth to her skin, cleaning away the residual make-up and dried blood. Dammit! How could that monster do something like this to her? "Why do you wish I were a medical doctor? It doesn't take a lot of smarts to spread on a little ointment."

"Because you will analyze me, and try to fix what you think is wrong with me. I'll be Liza Doolittle to your Dr. Henry Higgins. I'm no 'my fair lady' – and this is gonna hurt." She hissed in anticipation of what was about to happen.

"I'll be gentle – promise." If she only knew, psychoanalyzing her was the last thing he wanted to do. Kneeling by her on his knees, his eyes were drawn to that sweet, tongue-traceable indention that ran down her back. Very carefully, he moved a couple of long dark ringlets aside so he could apply the medicine without getting it into her hair. "And as for the other - Baby, you'd never come up short in comparison with anybody."

The statement he had just made ran totally against his life-long assertions. How did he know Dandi wasn't like his mother? He couldn't answer how, but he knew she was as different from Della Wagner as night was from day. Hell, what was going on with him? He couldn't lose focus of his goal, no matter how bad his cock longed to bury deep inside of his Little Dancer. Regardless, he reassured her. "So, don't worry; I will not be probing into your psyche. Do you know why?"

"No. Why?"

"Because therapists shouldn't treat a patient with whom they are intimately involved."

Oh my goodness. "Are we intimately involved?"

"No, but I hope we soon will be. I'm waiting for you to feel better and give me some sign that you want me." Lucas hadn't planned on being quite so forthright with her, but he couldn't help it – if he didn't get her in his arms soon, he was going to go out of his mind.

CHAPTER FIVE

"Oh, you want a sign, hmmm." She wondered what kind of sign he was looking for and where she could find one. Her own absurd thought made her smile. He wanted her enough to wait till she was ready – not many men were than considerate.

"Why did he whip you?" He couldn't imagine a man hitting such a fragile, beautiful woman.

"I wouldn't do as I was told."

"Bastard," with great care, he began to press the wet cloth against her flesh. Instead of trying to help her, someone had been more concerned with just covering up the damage. The son of a bitch that did this to her needed the shit beat out of him. With gentle strokes, he prepared the injured area for treatment. Even though there was discomfort, she was more focused on how he made her feel. She was aware of him as a man, very aware. Staying still while he tended her wounds was almost impossible. She vacillated between wanting to pull away from him and wanting to crawl into his lap like a lost child who had found its way home. "I want to thank you for letting me stay here. I'd rather be with you than anywhere else in the world."

"Oh, Dandi, you're welcome," Lucas's hand shook as he spread ointment on her skin. "I'm glad you're here, too." He wanted to say more, but there was a knot in his throat the size of an orange.

She lay very still, waiting for him to finish. From out of nowhere, the warm sensation of a touch in the middle of her back made her jump. A hint of a breath caressed her skin. Had he just kissed her? Immediately, millions of tiny pinpoints of excitement flashed over her skin.

"I'm putting a bandage on it; this will do until we can get you into town. We'll go after lunch and pick up some supplies and whatever you might need." Patting her back, he inspected his work. It would do. "There you go, Pretty Girl, you're all fixed up."

"Thank you, I guess I need to wash the other parts of me, I want to get rid of the club smells."

"Okay, I'll be waiting in the den if you need anything." He got up from the bed, holding his hand out to her. She took it. Such a small hand – he closed his fingers over hers and braced her while she stood up, catching her breath a bit as her sore muscles protested.

"I'm getting a bit stiff, I guess."

"You don't have to hide your pain from me," he crooned as he reached out and pushed a strand of hair behind one small, shell pink ear. When she didn't flinch away, he claimed it as a small victory. "I think you're beautiful." Would she mention the stolen kiss? Kissing her sweet back had been too tempting to resist. He was paying a dear price for the impulse, now – every cell in his body was demanding more.

"I'll hurry." Dandi climbed off the bed, a little self-conscious about her state of undress, which was dumb, considering what she had been doing for the past few weeks. It was just different with Lucas – everything was different.

"I'll fix us some sandwiches while you freshen up." Thinking about the contents of his refrigerator, he knew exactly what he'd fix - grilled cheese, tomato soup and a cold, sweet orange.

"Okay, but this is the last meal you cook – from now on, it's my turn. I want to spoil you while I'm here," she stopped in front of him, not touching, but close.

She was looking down, as if in deep thought, long lashes lay like fine lace against her velvet skin. Lucas couldn't help but think that her trust was one of the greatest gifts he had ever received. Just being this near to her almost caused his heart to stop beating. His cock had twitched to life the first moment he had seen her, and now it began to fill with a slow, sweet ache. "I look forward to the spoiling."

With a wink, he left her alone. Dandi slumped in relief, he was so intense. All kinds of unfamiliar thoughts and feelings were running through her mind. She could picture herself being held in his arms, surrounded by hard muscle. It was strange to welcome male attention. She had been in the company of men in the restaurants and the club – even church - but none had ever made her quake with desire as this one did.

Going to the bathroom, she inspected everything with awe. She'd never been in such a nice place. It was much bigger than she had first thought. L shaped, most of the room was hidden from view of the bed. There was a water closet where the toilet was and a shower big enough for two or more. Everything was white; it looked like a Roman spa.

After relieving herself, she ran water in the sink, took a washcloth and scrubbed herself hard. Lucas had taken such good care of her back that she didn't want to rinse off the medicine in the shower. It felt good to rid her body of the evidence of the club. After she dried off, she hunted in the cabinet until she found some shampoo so she could wash her hair. When she was through, she fluffed the long tresses and changed into a fresh pair of jeans and a long sleeved pink sweater. Her wardrobe left a lot to be desired. Glancing at herself in the mirror, she realized she had no make-up; she had left all of that stuff behind. Oh well. Hopefully, Lucas liked the natural look. Now to find him, her stomach was growling.

He was probably in the kitchen. Last night Dandi hadn't taken time to truly appreciate this beautiful house. As she wandered into the living room, she ran an appreciative hand over the huge fireplace and took a moment to test out the deep, overstuffed couch. She loved the colors; they were just to her taste. Dandi loved earth tones and everywhere she looked there were warm browns and cool blues with a bit of forest green mixed in.

Making her way through, she passed a formal dining room decorated in jewel tones before arriving in the kitchen she had admired last night. All of the appliances were stainless steel, the countertops were granite and the floor was Mexican tile. But what stood by the stove was breathtaking, indeed – Lucas.

Lucas worked mechanically, thinking about Dandi. He loved all types of women – blondes, redheads, brunettes. Usually he preferred the tall, willowy long drinks of water, but now he found his preference was running to the smaller, curvier siren type. There were always women he could date, but this woman's allure was off the charts. How was he going to resist her until she was ready? Chivalry was heroic, but he didn't know if he would survive the sacrifice. God, he needed his head examined. Dandi was the strangest mix of courage and fragility he had ever seen. She was sexy, smart and when she licked her lips, running that sensuous little tongue over her pink mouth, he wanted to kiss her till her knees buckled. The lady had a mouth made for loving. And her body! Without a doubt, the woman was built for a man's pleasure. Damn, just the thought made him stone hard.

"Something smells good." She padded up to him on bare feet.

"Where are your shoes, Midget?" He forced himself not to react to her nearness.

"By the bed," she walked behind him, patting his arm as she went by. "Can I help?"

"No, it's all ready. How's your back?" To Dandi's surprise, he lifted up her shirt and looked.

"It feels much better, thank you." When he had examined her injury to his satisfaction, he let her go.

"We'll put more ointment on it before we go into Hot Springs. Sit with me."

Lucas enjoyed watching her eat. Long, curly hair framed her angelic face - wispy, cascading strands of fudge colored silk fell over her shoulders and teased the tops of exquisitely shaped breasts. Since the first time he had discovered women, he had never seen a more perfect face. He couldn't quit looking at the delicate features, huge dark blue eyes framed with long, full lashes and a nose that turned up on the end just a tiny bit. What would it be like to suck on that pouty, full lower lip? Damn! He lifted up from the chair a fraction, trying to rearrange his package without her knowing what he was up to. "Here, have some milk." He held the glass for her. When she had taken a sip, she was left with the cutest milk moustache. "Look up." When she did, he kissed it away. At her gasp and widened eyes, he explained. "You had milk on your upper lip. I'm just helping you clean up."

"You want some?" She held out the glass, mischievously. "I could return the favor." Dandi couldn't help but feel happy.

"Don't tempt me." He was being honest. He wanted kisses and a whole lot more. But not till she was ready and he could explain his position. Lucas had one unbreakable rule with his women – honesty. Telling them upfront that he wasn't ready to commit had always worked for the most part. Oh sure, some of them did their dead level best to change his mind, but Lucas was focused. He knew the type of woman he wanted to marry and he did not intend to veer from his course.

Lucas drank some of his coffee, and she relished the opportunity to really look at him. When he leaned his head back to swallow, she hungrily watched his throat muscles work, and it dawned on her, anew, the wondrous differences between a man and a woman. "How old are you?"

Lucas looked at her and smiled. "Twenty-eight." He had this slow, lazy way of smiling that just made her toes curl. "I'm getting to be an old man."

"That's not old." With appreciation, he finished his meal. And while he did, she memorized his face. When his wide, firm mouth tipped into a grin, it deepened creases in the side of his face – laugh lines that she longed to lick.

The fact that he was going to be a doctor unnerved her somewhat, there seemed to be such a gulf between them – socially. "You must be very smart."

"I hope I'm a bit above average."

"I didn't graduate high school," Dandi confessed, a bit embarrassed, but she was anxious to see how he would react to what she said. "I have my GED, though and I love to read. Just before my diagnosis with diabetes, I had enrolled in some community college classes. I didn't get to go because of what happened at the club, but I will go back someday."

He loved her optimism. "I'm sure you will and for the record, I admire your courage."

"So, what are we going to do today?" She wanted to suggest they spend the day in bed together, but she was too shy.

'We' - that had a good ring to it. "I need to get your antibiotics before this storm gets any worse." Taking his phone out of his back pocket, Lucas went to his contacts and found one of his doctor friends who could help. After a few moments, he had told Rob the problem. "Yes, she's diabetic. Her name is Dandi Alexander." He listened. "Great, thanks. I'll pick them up." He folded the phone. "Do you want to go with me?"

Dandi considered it. Looking out the window, she saw that snow was still falling. She didn't have a coat, and her clothes were very casual. There was no use making Lucas uncomfortable. "Would it be okay if I stayed here and cooked the roast? If you'd let me use the laptop, I could start my job hunt."

"Okay, if you'd rather." He got up and fetched the computer for her. He didn't want to think about her planning to leave him so soon, but it couldn't be helped.

"I'll just access the internet, I promise."

"I trust you," he smiled at her. "While I'm out, I'll pick up some bread and milk, maybe some fresh fruits and vegetables."

"How long will you be gone? Is it a long way into town?"

"I'll only be gone a couple of hours. I think I'll get some boxes at the grocery store. There's a few here, but I'm going to need more for packing." He knew he could hire someone to do it, but he didn't really want anyone barging in during their private time, nor did he want strangers in his home when he wasn't there. For now, he'd pack what he could and come back after the rest when he got settled. Retrieving his coat, he got ready to leave.

"I'll be here waiting."

"Lock the door." Almost – almost he kissed her.

"Be careful." Almost – almost she hugged him.

*****

"Boss, I found where the doc lives, but no one's here." Cahill stood in the parking lot of the upscale apartment. "What do I do next?"

"Find him," Romero barked. "I would bet every dime I had that Angel Bitch is with him. It was just too much of a coincidence that she disappeared about the time he left. They had the hots for one another; everybody saw that. He was stupid enough to give Jane his card. It's a good thing Patty saw them talking or we wouldn't have known."

"He gave his cell phone number to dispatch."

"Well, Idiot, why didn't you tell me?"

"I didn't think about it."

"You'd better start thinking. If you fuck this up, you'll be sorry."

"What's going on with the detective? Is he still on your case?" The rotund cop wadded up a candy wrapper and tossed it to one side.

"He's come in almost every day, so I know he'll be back. But with no murder weapon and no witness, they're going to have a hard time proving anything. That's why I have to make sure the little slut doesn't resurface."

Cahill stepped back in the shadows. "So, what do I do now?"

Romero snarled, "Idiot. You're a damn cop, use your head. One of his neighbor's will know something about where he is. Ask them! Tell them you need to get in contact with him – there's some family emergency."

"I can do that."

"You'd better – or else." Cahill's blood ran cold. He didn't want to be on Romero's bad side.

Methodically, the cop went door to door, asking for information on Lucas Wagner. Finally he hit the jackpot.

"You might try his parent's cabin up on Pine Ridge." Lorraine Burris stood there in her bathrobe and curlers.

"Where would Pine Ridge be, Ma'am?" Cahill asked making notes on a coffee-stained pad.

"I believe its north of Hot Springs, but I'm not sure. You could check a map."

"Will do, and thank you for your help."

"Bingo," Cahill muttered as he pulled his cell from his pocket to give Romero the good news.

*****

While Lucas was gone, Dandi put the roast and vegetables in a crock pot with a can of cream of mushroom soup. In about three or four hours, the meat would be tender and the flavors would be melded together perfectly. Rummaging through the freezer she found a package of blackberries. In a few minutes she had whipped up a homemade cobbler.

After she had it cooling on top of the stove, Dandi sat with the laptop and started a search for jobs. Even with her GED, her options were few and far between, but she did find a couple of promising leads. She looked for a land-line phone, but didn't find one. Not having a cell, she wrote down the numbers so she could borrow Lucas's phone and call later. The ones that had email addresses and online applications, she took care of, the others would have to wait.

Checking the clock, she saw that only an hour had passed. What else could she do to pass the time? Looking around, she saw the boxes. She could pack! Lucas had left a couple by the hutch in the dining room and a couple by the book case. First she packed his books, enjoying the feel of leather in her hands. Next, she packed fine china and fragile crystal. She knew it had to have belonged to his mother, so she was very careful, imagining that she was holding precious memories in her hand.

After she finished, she tugged the boxes out of the way, over in a corner. Dang, she needed to do the same with the books; she had left one out in the path. Taking time to check the roast and add a little liquid, she headed to the den.

And that's where Lucas found her. "Dandi! I'm home!" What met his eyes made him smile and fuss. "What are you doing?" She was trying to move a full box of books, setting back on it like a little dog with a bone.

"Almost – done," she huffed. He raced to move it for her. "Whew! Thanks. I didn't know it was so heavy. Maybe I put too many books in."

Lucas picked it up and moved it easily.

"Show-off," she crossed her arms over her breasts.

"You didn't have to do this," he marveled at all she had done. The books had been packed and when he went through to the kitchen, he saw that the dishes had been wrapped and stored for transport. Plus, the kitchen smelled like heaven.

"I was bored."

He was touched. "Thank you. Come on, you need to take your antibiotic." He poured some juice and handed her a pill.

"Thank you. How much do I owe you?"

"Not a thing," he stated flatly. She saw there was no use to press the point – not till later. "I bought you a surprise."

Her eyes widened. "Really?" she started looking at the packages. Most of them were food, but there was a box. "For me? Are you sure?"

"Yes, open it." He enjoyed the pleasure on her face. Every woman liked to receive gifts. When she pulled the lid off, she gasped.

"You bought me a coat!?" In a blur, she was in his arms, the coat squished between them. "Thank you, Lucas. I can't believe you thought of me. I love it!" He hugged her back, her appreciation made his heart ache. You'd have thought he had bought her diamonds instead of a cherry-red wool coat. "Can we go walking later?"

"If the weather allows, yes, we can." He held her till she pulled back; he'd have held her longer given the opportunity.

"Are you hungry? I cooked for you."

He was, and the roast was delicious. How long had it been since someone cooked for him? All of his dates expected to be taken out on the town. Sitting across from her, he found himself truly enjoying the food and the company. "This is incredible. You are an amazing cook."

She grinned at him. "Wait till you taste my blackberry cobbler."

"You made dessert?" The wonder in his voice made all the work worthwhile.

"Yes, I did." She got it from the counter and placed it on the table, along with some homemade whipped cream. "The cream was about to expire, so I whipped it."

"God," Lucas groaned. "Right now you could ask me for anything and it would be yours."

Good to know, she'd shelve that information till later. "Could we play a board game after I clean the kitchen? When I was packing for you, I saw your stash."

"How about I help you clean and then we play. What did you have in mind? I have several games." Lucas glanced out the window, the wind had picked up and the snow was falling thick and fast. They were in for bad weather. Oh well, he was inside his warm house with a beautiful woman – let it snow, let it snow.

"Bezzerwizzer," she announced.

Lucas let his gaze rove over Dandi from head to foot. She was dressed in simple jeans and a pink sweater, but she looked absolutely adorable. "That's a pretty tough game, Missy."

"I bet I win," she challenged, "I like trivia, I can't reach it though; it's high up on the book shelf."

"I'll get it Short-stuff." He went after it while she loaded the dishwasher.

"Do you want to play in front of the fireplace?"

"That would be good. How about we play strip Bezzerwizzer?"

Lucas almost choked on the coffee he was drinking. She was kidding, he knew that, but if she had any idea how much he craved to touch and kiss her, she would high-tail it out of Dodge quicker than a wink. "How would that work, exactly?"

"Every time one of us gets an answer wrong, we have to take off an article of clothing." She didn't really expect him to take her up on it, she was more or less teasing – but she was trying to give him that 'sign' he was waiting for. If they only had a few days together, Dandi wanted to make every minute count.

"I don't think we have on enough clothes to make it really interesting," he followed her – staring at her ass the whole time. God, he would give his right nut to see her completely naked.

"I guess that depends on how you define 'interesting'," she looked over her shoulder and winked at him. Lucas tripped on the carpeting, catching himself – Dandi giggled and his cock began to show an interest in the game.

"All right, Sugarbritches, let's see what you've got." After all, this was trivia and he had been in school all of his life. He wasn't saying Dandi wasn't bright, she was – incredibly so, but she hadn't had the opportunity to be introduced to as many topics and facts as he had studied.

Dandi set up the game and it was Lucas's turn to go first. "All right, I'll ask you a question, Mr. Wagner. The category is Architecture and the question is . . ." she cleared her throat and smiled at him. "Ready?"

"Yes," he answered patiently.

"Okay – "What is the particular feature of "xeriscape" landscaping?"

"Hmmmm," Lucas thought. He ought to know this. "Xeriscape is landscape that utilizes indigenous plants; you know plants that naturally grow in a certain area."

"Wrong!"

"Well, you don't have to be so happy about it," he grumbled.

"The answer was a landscape that requires very little water. Take something off," Dandi demanded. "Or do I need to show you how?" she stood up and held the back of the chair, giving him a smooth move and a wiggle of her hips. Lucas forgot his own name.

"Tease,' he stammered and took off a shoe.

"A shoe? That's all I get?" she pouted, pooching out her succulent lips.

"What did you want?"

"Your shirt," she answered honestly. "I bet your chest is magnificent." Dandi had no idea how he felt about her teasing, but she was having a good time.

"Maybe next time, Sweet Cheeks. Your turn."

She gave him the box of questions and leaned on the table, sitting on one foot. "Shoot, I'm ready."

Lucas looked at her category. "Science, hmmm." He glanced at the next card. "That question is too hard. Let's find you an easier one."

She grabbed his hand. "No, I want to play fair. Ask me the question"

So, he did. "All right — here goes. What was the first animal to be successfully cloned?"

"A sheep! Her name was Dolly."

"Correct!" He looked astounded. "How did you know that?"

"I read." It dawned on Dandi that Lucas might not have expected her to be very good at this game. After all, she only had a GED. "Your turn," she took the box, considering if she should whack him upside the head for his assumption on her lack of intelligence. "Geography — What is considered to be the smallest country in the world?"

"That's easy, the Vatican."

"Shucks. That's correct; you get to keep your shirt." She looked disappointed.

"Here's your next question, the category is Design. What fashion house is behind the fragrance called 'Envy'?"

"Hmmm," she didn't know this, so she'd have to guess. "Fabrege."

"Wrong!" he said it like she had, earlier — with great drama. She took off one tennis shoe.

"Is that all I get?"

"For now." She looked at him with heat in her eyes, she couldn't help it — being this close to Lucas made her crazy with need. "My turn to ask the question." Dandi leaned forward; this was going to be fun. She pretended to read the question. "Do you like to kiss?"

God, she was adorable. "That's an odd question." He paused to consider. "Yes, I love to kiss. One of my favorite things is sucking on pouty, plump lips."

"Good answer. Your turn." She passed him the box.

He also looked hard at the card as if hunting the question. "What's your favorite sexual position?"

Oh good gravy! Did she even know one? Aha! "Missionary?"

"Interesting. I like missionary, too. Why do you like it?"

Dandi was blushing, she could feel it. Putting her hands over her cheeks, she tried to hide the warmth. "I don't know. I bet it would feel good and I could look at your face."

She bet it would feel good? Why was she blushing and pretending she didn't have any experience? Maybe she didn't want him to think about Club Tonga and what she had done there. That was fine, if she wanted to pretend, he could play her game. "Honey, all sex feels good."

Lucas was staring at her – so hard. She wanted to reach out and touch his face, but she couldn't. She was so afraid she couldn't please him. "I guess I'll go to sleep now. I'm pretty tired."

"Okay, do you feel any better?" Dang, he had almost made a move on her. He could have sworn he had read an invitation in her eyes. But, she was probably still hurting. It would be best to give the antibiotics time to kick in. His sexual appetite could wait.

"Yes, I feel much better, thank you."

"We need to put ointment on your back before we go to bed."

"I can do it," she offered.

"No, you can't." She couldn't – and he needed to touch her. Following her into the bedroom, he retrieved the medicine and waited for her to pull her shirt up and her pants down enough for him to reach the sore places. The sweet curve of her back, the narrowness of her waist – the intoxicating smell of her hair – all of it had him aching to make love to her. "Dandi, I. . ."

Dandi waited. "What?"

Hell – he had told her he would wait for a sign. He had to keep his word. "Nothing. Goodnight." He kissed her on top of the head and walked out, shutting the door behind him. Dandi held on to the bedstead with both hands. If she hadn't, she would have run after him. Soon, Lucas – soon, she promised. All she needed was a good dose of courage.

*****

Lucas woke up hard. Rubbing his cock, he considered making himself cum. Downstairs lay the most beautiful woman in the world. Shutting his eyes, he imagined walking up to where she lay in his bed. She would be all soft and sleepy. There was nothing better in the world than cuddling a warm, sweet woman. "Christ!" He flipped the switch to listen to the news on his clock radio. What he heard wasn't encouraging. "This will be another blistery, snowy day. We also have an announcement. The bridge over the Ouachita River on Pine Ridge Road is out. We repeat. The bridge over the Ouachita River on Pine Ridge Road is closed due to damages." Well, Lucas had to smile. Not only were they isolated together, there was no way that trouble would find them here, not with the bridge out.

Getting up, he threw the covers off and went to take a shower. When he went downstairs, he couldn't find Dandi. A panic momentarily hit him until he smelled the aroma coming from the kitchen. Homemade biscuits and sausage gravy! God, she was good to him. His stomach rumbled. Now where was she?

Looking out the kitchen door, he saw that the snow was still falling, but the wind wasn't blowing as hard. This would most likely be the last big snow of the year; after all, it was almost Valentine's Day. The ground was solid white, maybe six inches or more. What? There she was! Dandi was trying to bring in a load of wood by herself. Instead of carrying it in her arms, she had filled one of the large cardboard boxes and was trying to pull it across the deep snow. Heading out to help her, he chided her. "What do you think you're doing? You have a thing about tugging stuff around. Don't you? Let me get that, Squirt!"

"I can do it," she huffed.

"I'm sure you can, but there's no use hurting yourself." He started towards her when she slipped and landed in the snow on her caboose – the powder just flew around her in a cloud. Laughing at her predicament, Lucas came and lifted the box with one hand.

"I slipped," she grumbled. He held out his hand to help her up, but she ignored it – instead, she lay back in the snow and began to move her arms up and down in the deep whiteness. "Look!" she giggled. "I'm making a snow angel." He hadn't played in the snow in years, but that day he sat his box down and lay in the snow with her. But as far as he was concerned, she was the only angel in his world.

*****

They settled into a comfortable routine, Dandi cooked for them and they talked, learning all kinds of things about one another – nothing big or important, just likes and dislikes and funny stories from their past. Dandi didn't know if Lucas realized it, but they were bonding – becoming friends, exactly like she had wanted. He was teaching her that there were people in the world that one could trust and rely on and she was teaching him that you couldn't judge a book by its cover - hopefully. Every minute with Lucas was precious. She was truly happy for the first time since childhood.

"Let's go for a walk. Please?"

He couldn't resist her. Every day he had checked for tracks, no one lived up on this part of the ridge but him, so he was confident that no one had invaded their sanctuary. A walk would do them good. "Put on your new coat and we will." She sprinted to get it and came back looking like a Valentine. Lucas took his phone with him; he wanted to get pictures of everything they did together. He loved pictures. He was making memories.

"You're cute," There was nothing showing but fingers, the top of her head and her nose. Together, they left the house and walked to the back of the property. "Be careful, the ground's a little slippery." He looked up at the sky. There was a mass of snow clouds to the north. He'd have to check the weather report when he went back to the cabin.

Dandi was so happy she could almost burst. Moving along beside Lucas, she bounced and danced along the path. "I've never been able to spend time in the mountains before." She looked around her. Bright red cardinals were flitting through the trees and snow was falling, a gentle dusting of big, fat flakes. Cedars and other evergreens colored the woods which were laced with bare hardwoods that had lost their brightly colored leaves with the first frost.

"I haven't been able to spend as much time here as I would have liked to either. I've been busy with school and my residency."

Reaching for his hand, Dandi stopped Lucas in his tracks. ""Look, Lucas! Is that what I think it is?"

Ahead of them, clearly visible through the trees was a small round hill. It was approximately forty feet in diameter and rose about eight feet into the air. He had seen it so often that he didn't really notice it anymore. "The mound?"

"Yes, is it an Indian Burial mound? It looks like it."

"I think so; at least that's what my Dad said." He was about to tell her the little he knew about it when she took off ahead of him – chattering all the way.

"I'm interested in Native American Burial Mounds. I knew there were many in Arkansas, but I didn't know about this one. Not all of them have been documented. Do you know if this one has a name?"

"We always called it Ridge Mound, but I'm not sure where the name came from."

"I shall have to research this area," she said very solemnly. Dandi walked around the perimeter of the mound, almost reverently. "Did you ever see any arrowheads or shards of pottery nearby?"

Lucas followed her, totally mesmerized by this new confident Dandi. "Yes, I have a box of things up in my room. Would you like to see them?"

"Yes, I would," holding out her hands for balance, she climbed the mound and stood on top, surveying the countryside. "There is a mound near the town of Benton called the Hughes Mound. This area was visited by the explorer, DeSoto, in 1541. Near Little Rock, there are the Toltec Mounds. Only three of them have survived, but there used to be eighteen."

To say he was surprised at the whole conversation was putting it mildly. "How did you become interested in burial mounds?"

"Actually, we're not sure if all the mounds were funerary, some of them could have been used in rituals or even places of refuge." Stopping herself before she began telling him more than he wanted to know, she answered his original question. "I grew up near Monroe, Louisiana. Remember me telling you about Miss

Etta?" Lucas nodded. "Well, Miss Etta knew everything." Lucas was listening to her, really he was. But the sight of her talking so animatedly, waving her hands around, obviously enjoying herself, touched his heart. He made himself listen – "I learned about the mounds from her. She also encouraged my drawing. I have some examples of my sketches in my bag, if you'd like to see."

Lucas was fascinated. Dandi was a total enigma to him. There was so much more going on in that beautiful little head than he had ever suspected. "I would love to see anything you want to show me." At that particular moment, his mind wasn't on sex, but when he saw a rosy glow creep up her neck, he wondered if it were due to the cold or if she was thinking of more sensual things.

"I'm coming down." He moved to the edge of the mound to help her, and when she got close enough, she held out her arms so he could pick her up. He did. No other woman had ever felt so right in his arms. "Go ahead, I want to hear more."

"Okay," Dandi smiled at him. "Miss Etta was the most important person in my life other than my parents. When she found out that I was interested in archaeology and history, she drove me around the area to look at Mounds. I fell in love with all of it. Did you know that there are 700 Native American mounds in Louisiana alone?"

"No, I didn't."

"This is probably boring to you, but some of them date back to 4000 B.C. and one of my fondest dreams is to one day excavate near St. Louis in the Cahokia ruins."

"What is Cahokia?"

"It was a prehistoric city, the main dwelling place of the Mississippian tribes. The base of the main mound there was larger than the Great Pyramid of Egypt. The city was home to anywhere from thirty to forty-five thousand people. No one knows what happened to them, Cahokia was a ghost town by the time Columbus came."

"I'm speechless," he admitted. "I didn't know any of this. So you want to be an archaeologist?" He started to say, 'when you grow up' but thank goodness she was fully grown and ready to be loved on.

"Yes, I would love to study archaeology if I get to go back to school."

"You will," he spoke with absolute certainty. "There's no doubt in my mind that you can do anything you set your mind to. I've never known anyone brighter or more courageous than you." It was true – she had totally baffled him. He had not been expecting her intelligence to challenge his own – and for that he ought to be ashamed. The more time he spent with Dandi, the more he realized that she was an incredible woman, one that any man would be proud to call his own.

"Can we come back here again? Maybe when the weather clears? I know I have to leave, but I would love to see the mound bare of snow."

"Sure, we can do that." Lucas didn't want to think about either of them leaving – not right now.

They walked on, deeper into the woods, the depth of the snow made traveling a bit difficult for Dandi. Her legs were shorter than Lucas's and snow was getting down in her boots. But looking at the abundance of the fluffy white stuff made her realize she was missing a golden opportunity.

"I think I heard a buck grunt." He stopped and cocked his head to one side to listen.

"You heard what?" she laughed.

"Shhh," he tried to make her be quiet. "I think I heard a deer blow."

The whole thing struck Dandi funny and she began to giggle in earnest.

"If I were trying to hunt, Young Lady, you'd be in big trouble." He made a face at her, which didn't scare Dandi at all.

As Lucas searched through the trees, keeping his eye open for a grunting, blowing whitetail deer - Dandi dropped back. Reaching down, she gathered a handful of snow and quickly formed it into a ball, "Hey, Handsome!" she called out.

Lucas turned. Splat!

His face was covered with white powder.

"Why, you little. . ." He made a grab for her, but Dandi took off, ran a few yards and gathered up more snow. Lucas was not to be outdone; he armed himself with snowballs and began to pelt, making sure not to hit her in the face. She wasn't so caring, but returned fire with surprising accuracy. Rapturous giggles filled the air. Dandi was having so much fun and Lucas's heart swelled to bursting. Suddenly it hit him – slammed into him like a freight train – he was very close to falling in love with Dandi Alexander.

"Are you ready to go back to the house?" Their eyes were locked and Dandi was breathing hard. She wanted more of Lucas, preferably in a bed. It was time that she learned how to be a woman. His woman. It was time to give him a sign.

"Yes, but first, I want to show you a surprise." Lucas needed a moment, anything to give him time to process his emotions. This was turning into much more than he had bargained for. He desired Dandi, he ached for Dandi. He had been prepared to like her and enjoy her, but he had not intended to fall for her.

"Okay." She had waited this long, she could wait a few minutes more. He took her by the hand and led her a little deeper in the forest. They were walking uphill, and at times, he had to tug her to help her make the steep climb. Soon they could hear rushing water.

"Is that a waterfall?"

Lucas had gone so quiet. Was something wrong?

"Yea, wait till you see it, when I would come home from school. This was my special place." He picked up the pace, seemingly anxious to get there.

"Not so fast, I can't keep up," she laughed breathlessly, following him through the deep snow as best she could.

"You don't need to." He swept her up, cradling her in his arms. "Better?" It sure as hell felt better to him. He needed to talk to her, but first he had to decide what he was going to say.

"Much," the snow was still falling, a gentle drifting of flakes. Dandi entranced him by trying to catch a few of the flakes on her tongue. She didn't have any luck, but she did earn a hug from him for her trouble. He couldn't help it; there was no way he could keep his hands off of her. It amazed Lucas to learn how much had been missing from his life until she came into it – tenderness, laughter, and an incredible desire to be close to one small, adorable woman.

As they drew closer, the roar grew louder and when he finally sat her down on the top of a high bluff, Dandi gasped with awe. "It's breathtaking!" A thirty foot wall of water poured down over moss covered boulders which were now decorated with snow.

"There's a cave behind the fall. That's where I found some of the arrowheads. I'll take you there . . ." Someday. He didn't say it out loud, because he couldn't make any promises – not yet. God, what was he thinking? He tried to hold on to his dreams. He tried to picture the face of his perfect woman, that elusive paragon of virtue. She was gone. Now, he could see no one but Dandi.

"Someday." She said it for him. Laying her head on his shoulder, she asked. "Can I tell you something?"

"Anything."

"I'm so happy," Dandi confessed, turning in his arms to face him. She cupped his cheek with her hand. "Thank you for giving me this time with you. I don't know how to make you understand how wonderful you are. I'll never forget how good you've been to me. If you hadn't shown up at the club, I might not have gotten away. Romero had plans for me, plans to make me do things I would have never survived."

Her poignant little speech made a knot form in Lucas's throat. Whatever she had been through or what she had escaped, none of it mattered – only she mattered. "I'm the one who should be thanking you. I wouldn't have traded this time together with you for anything."

CHAPTER SIX

"Angel Baby is still missing. We don't know what happened to her," a stammering young college student chimed in. He was a regular customer at Club Tonga and was enjoying being questioned. "It's all over the news. Everyone is talking about her."

Detective Grimes made notes. He had meticulously gone over the scene of the crime several times. Forensics had turned up a few clues, but not enough to build a case. What he needed was a witness. He'd have to question the strippers one by one. One of them was hiding something.

Dismissing the group of regulars, he gathered the employees as a group before he split them off from one another. "So, no one has seen Miss Alexander since the night of the murder?"

"No," one of the strippers popped up. "We think she might have been murdered too. We saw this really big guy hanging around her."

"He didn't murder Dandi," Jane piped up.

Grimes knew who they were talking about, Lucas Wagner. He was the man who had initially reported the crime. "I'll give him a call." He had already looked into Wagner's background, but another conversation might be in order. The older stripper looked pensive, perhaps she was the key.

Romero stank to high heaven. The detective had no real doubt that the club owner was as guilty as sin, he just needed to prove it.

*****

When they returned to the house, Dandi warmed up their breakfast. "I think it's still good."

"It's perfect." Lucas ate with relish, consuming four biscuits and a slew of gravy. "This is so good. Thank you." Dandi was quiet – chewing slowly, looking at him with a strange expression. "What are you thinking?" he asked, wondering if he had said something wrong. Was she as confused as he was?

Taking a big bite of orange, her choice of breakfast, she enjoyed the burst of flavor in her mouth. When she could answer, she did – "I'm thinking that I need some paper and a pen."

He reached behind him and took out a tablet and something to write with from a drawer and laid them in front of her. She bent over it and started drawing.

Dandi was nervous; she was doing what he asked in a teasing, flirtatious way. Laying the pen down, she picked the tablet up and turned it around toward him. "Here's your sign. I would have put it on the front page of The Times Picayune, if I could have."

Lucas stared – and stared. Dandi had written in big, bold letters. I WANT YOU.

"Damn, Baby," Lucas put his cup down, pushed his chair back and took the sign from her hand. "Are you sure?" It didn't matter if the words were written on paper, stone, or a billboard, it was, undoubtedly, the very best news he had ever read.

He didn't look entirely comfortable; perhaps she'd better try to explain a little better. "Yes, I know we're not talking about forever, but I would love to belong to you for a little while." He was a man of substance, with a bright future – while she was – just Dandi. "You haven't changed your mind, have you? You do want me, don't you?"

She had said what he had not been able to. She had given him an out. She had given him an incredible gift with no strings and no expectations. How he felt about that, he was afraid to analyze. But the answer to her question, that he knew. "Angel, there's not a man alive who wouldn't want you."

Their chairs were side by side, but he had turned in his, facing her. She stood up, needing his touch, but she had to make certain she was welcome, so she asked – flatly. "Would you like to kiss me?" It was strange to think they had shared an orgasm, but not a real kiss. Dandi hadn't had many opportunities to kiss anyone, and she felt the need to make up for lost time.

Lucas looked her straight in the eye, never moving a muscle. "More than anything, I'm more attracted to you than you could possibly know."

She didn't need to hear anything else. He wanted her. Without warning – Dandi pounced. She launched herself into his arms and he caught her easily.

"Gotcha!" he laughed with joy. He was holding her! Heaven – absolute heaven. He arranged her sitting astraddle of his lap, much like she had during the lap dance.

For a few seconds, Dandi just rested in his embrace, enjoying his arms around her. Being held by Lucas was like being branded by pure temptation. Her mouth went completely dry, and every place where their bodies touched tingled and throbbed. His heartbeat pounded against her breasts, and there was a ridge of hardness pressing against her bottom. "Kiss me, Lucas. Please? Don't make me wait any longer."

"You don't have to beg, Baby." Being careful to avoid the sore places on her lower back, Lucas wrapped one muscular arm around her middle and tugged her up tighter against him.

Dandi became aware of her body in ways she had never paid notice of before; the shape and weight of her breasts as they molded against his chest, the sensitivity of her nipples as they swelled and grew hard from the drag of her lace bra as it scraped over the stiff little peaks. Both of these sensations were sending darts of hunger deep into her vagina. A soft, wetness grew between her thighs. It was as if her body was reshaping itself to meet his needs.

"You feel so good," she groaned, running her palms over the muscles of his arms and shoulders. This is what she had dreamed of. She wrapped both arms around his neck, rubbing her breasts against his chest. Heat suffused her skin with erotic sensitivity.

Lucas was ablaze with need. God, she was sweet and so responsive. He sucked at that lower lip, just as he had promised himself he would. He nibbled at the top one, licked at the corners and rubbed his tongue along hers, seeking to memorize her taste. With a primal instinct, he wanted to mark her, make her forget every other man who had ever touched her.

Liquid lightning danced over her skin; everywhere he touched she came to life. Dandi could imagine being Lucas' woman; she could imagine him doing wild and wonderful things to her, teaching her how to please him, to be exactly the kind of woman he wanted.

When he would have pulled back, she stopped him, twisting her fingers in his hair, seeking more of the pleasure he could give. "Please don't stop. I need you so much. I didn't know kissing could be so good."

Good – he wanted his kisses to be special. The unwanted thought whirled through his mind – strippers and hookers wouldn't kiss . . . . Stop, he ordered himself, don't even go there. "I'll give you what you need." Lucas's cock swelled. Never had he wanted a woman more. Just kissing Dandi was more sinfully decadent and lushly erotic than any other experience he could remember. Cradling her head, he kissed her hard and deep, cupping her ass with the other hand and pulled her forward so his cock was cradled against her mons.

"I love this."

"I don't want to be like the other men." Lucas muttered against her face.

"What other men?" Dandi was too lost in pleasure to care or comprehend exactly what he was saying. She was in Lucas' arms and there was nowhere else she would rather be.

"It doesn't matter to me what you've done in the past. I want to make you forget everyone else." Merciful heavens, he wanted to make love to her.

Dandi was overwhelmed. Things were moving very fast. Pushing back a bit, she took a few deep breaths. "There has been no one else, Lucas."

"I understand," he said. She wanted to forget her past. That was okay, he'd help her forget. "I've wanted to kiss you from the moment I first saw you." Lucas rubbed his face against her hair, kissing the silken strands. "I want to make love to you, but remember - this time the choice is yours, not someone else's."

"I choose you." She kissed his chin, relishing the feel of his whiskers against her skin. "Make love to me, Lucas. Please?"

"God, yes," he groaned. "Are you on the pill?"

"Yes," she was a bit embarrassed to say so, but considering the dangerous place she had worked, it had just seemed wise. "I got them at the same time I filled the insulin prescription."

"Let's go to my bed." He swung her up in his arms like a bride. She squealed and laughed throwing her head back. He bent and kissed her throat, rubbing his face in the opening of her shirt.

God Have Mercy - he knew he was going to love her tits. He had fantasized about those luscious mounds for days.

"I'm nervous," she admitted.

"No, need to be," he assured her. "I'm going to enjoy you so much," His lips formed the words, as silky as a caress.

"I hope so." She wanted to please him. When he looked at her with those smoldering sky blue eyes, Dandi felt weak and wanton. She laid her head on his shoulder, knowing this was a momentous event – a step that she could never take back, nor repeat.

Her first time.

"I'm glad it's you." Lucas was her hero, he'd make it special. He would make her first time something she would always remember.

He carried her up the stairs, down the hall and into a large, masculine bedroom. Reverently, it seemed, he placed her on the bed. In Dandi's adolescent dreams, she had thought to save herself for marriage. Today she wore no wedding band, but it didn't matter. She had waited for true love. It had been quick, but her heart told her that Lucas was the one she wanted to give the gift of her virginity.

"Are you in pain? Can you lie on your back?"

How considerate he was, "It's not hurting," she assured him.

"Good," he put one knee on the bed, coming closer. She reached out to touch him, cupping one cheek, then sliding her palm down his throat, to cup behind his neck. Dandi felt lightning arc between their bodies with a brilliant flare of heat. "Give me your lips," he instructed as he captured her mouth in a whisper of a kiss. A whimper of sweet surrender escaped her throat as his head tilted to one side and he began to devour her lips, licking and nibbling, his tongue teasing hers to come out and play.

Pure pleasure washed over her body. "What are you doing to me?" she moaned. Her heart rate had gone wild, and it wasn't just because of how he was making her feel – it was him. He was so dominant; his lips were hot, determined – making demands of her that she was entirely willing to meet.

"Can I love on you? We can take it as slow as you want." He curled long, strong fingers around her neck and his breath caressed her cheek.

"Only if I get equal time, I want to love on you too." She pressed her face against his chest. He was so contradictory – such power mixed with such gentleness. Not being able to resist, she pressed a kiss over his heart and to her surprise and wonder, she found it was racing as hard and fast as her own. "Would you take off your shirt? I'd love to run my hands over your chest. I've fantasized about that."

Lord, she was potent. The little vixen knew exactly what she was doing. "You take it off of me." He wanted the full benefit of her sensual expertise.

"Okay," Dandi sat up and went to work, unbuttoning the material – one button at a time.

The look of concentration on her face made Lucas bend down and steal kisses while she worked.

"You're making this very hard."

Lucas chuckled, "You're making something else very hard." Even though the light wasn't the brightest in the world, he could see her cheeks turn rosy. Dandi was endlessly fascinating - seemingly so innocent, yet so seductive.

"Now," she opened the edges of a shirt as if she were unveiling a masterpiece. "Oh, yeah," she breathed and set about to drive Lucas stark raving mad as she peppered his chest with kisses.

"My turn," he growled. "I want to see you." He tugged at the bottom of her shirt. "Lift your arms."

Dandi held her hands over her head, the position making her feel deliciously vulnerable. She wanted him so much; she had to bite her lip to keep from mewling in need. A hungry, emptiness pounded between her legs, her sex actually ached needing to be touched. Lucas lifted the shirt, letting it capture her arms for a few long moments. "Please, Lucas," she begged. Dandi wanted to rub against him, feel his skin slide against hers.

"My God, you're beautiful." She could feel his eyes caress her breasts, making them swell, her nipples growing puffy. One of the things she had fantasized about most was a man sucking her nipples. Dandi wanted it all – she had abstained from life and happiness long enough. "Touch me, Lucas," she took one of his hands and brought it to her chest.

Reverently, he cupped her breasts. "Exquisite. You are absolutely perfect."

"It feels good."

"God, I want you," he ground out. "I'm literally shaking with need."

But when he began to palm her eager flesh, plumping the mounds, teasing the nipples – it was Dandi who shook. "Do something," she urged. When his thumbs raked across her nipples, she closed her eyes and sighed – and when he pulled on them, her whole body trembled. "I can't wait."

"You don't have to, Baby." Lucas picked her up in his arms and placed her back down on the soft mattress. Quickly shedding his clothes, he reveled in the way she stared up at him, her hunger as obvious as his own. When she lifted a hand, beckoning him to come to her – he sank to his knees, grateful for the turn of events that had brought them together. What if he hadn't gone to the bachelor party? What if she had chosen some other car to hide away in, instead of his? Unthinkable.

Together they removed her clothes, and he ran his hands over her beautiful legs, kissing her ankles, her knees – tracing a pattern over her shapely thighs with his tongue. "You are absolutely luscious, Dandi."

Covering her body with his own; Lucas encased her in safety and warmth. She rose up and met his kiss, drawing him down. Between them, his hand went to her breast again – rubbing, shaping, milking the nipples. "I want to kiss you."

"Yes," she ate at his lips, unashamedly taking what she had dreamed about for days.

"No, I want to kiss your nipples."

"Oh," was all she could say. God yes, please. She didn't know how it would feel, but she expected it would be wonderful. Lucas used both hands to hold her breasts, pushing them together – molding and plumping, Dandi watched in awe as he readied the nipples for his pleasure. But when his mouth covered her and he began to suck, the ecstasy was so intense that she cried out his name, "Lucas!"

The taste of her, the feel of her – the privilege of touching, kissing and sucking at her breasts was absolutely incredible. Lucas hips were moving, helplessly, he was desperate to push his aching, swollen cock deep within her wet heat. She arched beneath him, pushing more of her amazing tits into his face and he wondered how in the hell he had lived without this bliss for so long. "I can't wait, I need you, now. Okay?"

She didn't answer – she couldn't think. He was kissing a line down her stomach, opening her thighs and Dandi raised her hips, needing more.

When she didn't answer, Lucas grabbed his pants and pulled a condom from his wallet and put it on. "I'll take care of you." Never had he felt such desperation to get inside a woman. "I've got to have you now." Spreading her thighs, he took one long look at her perfect body quivering beneath his - positioned himself at the opening of her vagina – and plunged deep.

Paradise. Absolute paradise.

Dandi didn't get a chance to say anything, not that she would have stopped him, but the pain that knifed through her body was totally unexpected. "No," was all she could manage to whisper.

His cock was so engorged, she was so amazingly tight – and it felt so damn good that it took a moment for Lucas to realize he had broken through a fragile barrier. Dandi was writhing beneath him, whimpering his name – but it was in pain, not pleasure,

"Damn! What the hell is going on?"

Why was he cursing at her? "I need to get up," she put her palms on his chest.

Lucas was dazed. It was hard to think. "You were a virgin? How can that be?" Pulling out of her, he sat back. Sure enough, there were traces of blood on his still hard cock.

His voice was incredulous, Dandi was confused. "I was a virgin for the same reason any woman is a virgin. I had never had sex with a man – until you."

Dandi scooted back from him. Lucas stopped her, holding one leg just above the knee. "Wait, let me see."

"No." She pressed her knees together. "I'm okay."

Nothing was okay. God, she was little and delicate and he had ploughed hard into her, taking no care at all. "I can't believe you were a virgin," He repeated himself again, not realizing how it sounded. .

"Yea, I get that," she almost snarled at him. "You can't believe I was a virgin. You thought I was a . . ." she couldn't finish. Dandi's heart was hurting worse than her privates. It was the same as with the drugs, no matter what she had told him, he considered

her to be the same as all of the other employees of Club Tonga —
tainted. "I need to get off your bed. I'm bleeding."

Lucas was devastated. He wouldn't have hurt her for the
world. "Don't worry about the damn bed. Let me get a warm cloth
and clean you up."

"No!" she was emphatic and scooted back farther away. "I
can wash myself."

"Damn!" Lucas roared. Dandi flinched. "Shit," he reached for
her. "Baby, I'm not yelling at you. I messed up, it's my fault". She
had been aroused, he knew that much. But he had taken no time
with her. Their foreplay had been minimal. He hadn't played with
her to make sure she was wet; he hadn't stretched her with his
fingers. He hadn't given her oral sex, or pleasured her in any way. In
his damn lust induced state, Lucas hadn't done any of the things
that a man did to make sure his woman was ready to make love.
And he knew better!

While he was castigating himself, she had scrambled off the
far side of the bed, put on her shirt and was wiping between her
legs with a tissue. "It's nobody's fault," she said quietly.

Lucas pulled on his pants and went to the bath for a warm
cloth. He was thoroughly disgusted with himself. "Dandi, I'm so
damn sorry. What makes this totally unbelievable is that I'm a sex
therapist, I teach men how to help their women enjoy sex."

"Don't worry about it, Lucas." Dandi was humiliated and
furious. She just wanted this to be over. The pain wasn't as bad as it
was at first; maybe she had overreacted. Still, she wasn't clamoring
for a repeat performance.

"Lay down, please? Let me make sure I didn't tear you." He
waited, unmoving.

Seeing he wasn't going to let it go without a fight, Dandi did
as he asked. "Can you imagine how embarrassed I am?" she
grumbled as he followed her back to the bed. She placed a couple
of tissues on the bed where her bottom would go, just in case she
was still bleeding. "Have you ever been with a virgin before? Maybe
this is normal. If I'd been more relaxed or used a lubricant, it might
have been better. You have to remember, I didn't really know what
I was doing."

Listening to her make excuses made him feel like the biggest
heel in the world. "A woman's first time can be beautiful and

pleasurable, if they are with a man who cares enough to make it good for them."

"Oh." Was that supposed to make her feel better? Putting her arm up over her face, she opened her thighs for him to see. "I'm okay, huh? Everything is still there, isn't it?"

Lucas had to smile, "Yes, it's all still here – sweet, pink and pretty." He examined her tender pussy. There was redness; but no tearing. Before she could move, he leaned over and placed a kiss right on top of her clitoris. Dandi jumped.

"I kissed it and made it better."

"Oh my goodness," she fussed and sat up, feeling like a fool. "Lucas, this is no big deal. Let's just put it behind us. Okay?"

With an unsteady hand, Lucas ruffled his hair. "If I had known – if I had any idea, I would have done it so differently." He got up and paced around, "How did I miss that you were untouched?"

"I don't know how you missed it, I told you over and over again." Facing the truth, she admitted it. "Lucas, it wouldn't have mattered how many times I said I was innocent. You just didn't think it was possible, As far as you are concerned, I'm just a stripper or worse." She replaced her panties.

"As far as I'm concerned you are perfect," he spit out the words. "You were a victim." Yea, she was a victim of circumstances, a victim of Romero's, and a victim of Lucas Bonehead Wagner. As he watched this beautiful woman distance herself from him – his mind raced. Thinking back over everything they had said to one another during the last week, he had to admit that she had told him – over and over. She said there were no other men; she had even told him she escaped Romero before he had forced her to do something that would destroy her – God, why hadn't he understood?

"It doesn't matter, Lucas. I'm just glad I don't have to do that for a living."

She laughed softly, but he didn't find it funny at all. She was glad she didn't have to have sex for a living. Dandi was making fun of herself. "Don't say that." Lucas was thoroughly disgusted with himself. "Let me make it up to you. Let me show you how good it can be." He walked up behind her and rubbed her shoulders.

"No, I don't think so." Dandi eased out from under his hand. "Look, I'm sure you are a wonderful lover. I know you have pleased many women. I'm just not very good at this. Can we just forget it ever happened?"

Lucas felt like she was putting a world between them. "That's not going to be easy." Lucas wanted to plead with her. "I've tasted your kiss. How am I supposed to forget that?"

The pain was about gone, but she still felt very vulnerable. "Lucas, you can have any woman you want."

"I want you." He stood before her, hands on his hips, looking like a Greek god.

"I wanted you, too," she whispered remembering the excitement she had felt as his hands and lips had moved over her body.

Wanted not want. "Are you afraid of me now?" He had to know.

"No, I'm not afraid of you." He would never hurt her on purpose, but if she didn't put some distance between them, he was going to break her heart.

Lucas sighed and sought the right words. "It was my responsibility to make it good for you." Her little face looked so sad. How was he supposed to make this right?

"Don't feel bad, I enjoyed what we did except for the very last part." What he didn't understand was the pain she had experienced from the sex was secondary. Looking back, she probably should have just gritted her teeth and let it happen. That's what most women would have done. Surely, it got better. No, what had hurt her the most was the fact he couldn't get past his first impression of her. After everything she had shared, after explaining about her past and her circumstances, he still had tarred her with the same brush as any of the other women he had met that night.

"Let's think about something else." She was tired of dwelling on her disastrous first attempt at sex. "Can we watch a movie instead? Maybe we could check the news and see if the bridge might be passable."

"We'll do whatever you want." Lucas felt like she had kicked him. Hell, she wanted to leave.

*****

While he redressed, she went to the bathroom and locked the door. After he had finished, he went to the laptop and checked the site for the local new station. Breathing a sigh of relief, he saw that the bridge wasn't fixed, but it was still scheduled to be completed before Thursday. He had worried about that. There was one more way off the mountain, but they'd have to go down the back side on a four wheeler. And he had been right earlier, there was one more wave of storms scheduled to hit, in fact they were blowing in now. He could hear the wind picking up outside.

Lucas listened for Dandi, but he heard nothing. She was still in the bathroom; he guessed she was taking a shower, washing his touch from her body. Fuck! He hit the table with his fist. What could he do? Was he ready to throw his hands up and just quit? Hell, no. No, his heart wouldn't let him do that.

So, Lucas made a decision. From this moment on, Lucas he was on a mission. He was going to woo, court, seduce and tempt Dandi until he was back in her good graces and she was back into his bed.

Before he could get up from the table to go see about her, his cell phone buzzed. Glancing at the caller ID, he saw it was the Shreveport police department. "Wagner." Damn, he wasn't in the mood.

"Mr. Wagner, this is Detective Grimes. I'm calling to ask you a few questions concerning the murder you reported at Club Tonga in Shreveport, Louisiana."

"Murder, I didn't know. So the victim died?" The connection was terrible; he could barely hear the man.

"Yes, he did. Are you sure you didn't see who shot Mr. Durango?"

"No, I did not. I didn't even know his name." He said something else, but Lucas missed it. "You're breaking up. Would you repeat that please?"

"I said, did you happen to see Miss Dandi Alexander, or Angel Baby as she is called?"

"Yes, I did."

"Well, she is missing, also. Can you tell me the last time you saw her and where you saw her? The media is having a hey-day with this. They're much more concerned with Miss Alexander than they are with the murder."

Lucas almost smiled. "She's with me. Safe with me."

"Good, well that's one question answered. I would like for the two of you to come into the station. We need for you both to make a statement."

"Not possible," Lucas didn't hesitate to answer. "Dandi didn't see anything; she was running from Romero for other reasons. He was blackmailing her and trying to get her to turn tricks. She refused."

"Be that as it may, Mr. Wagner. I still need to talk to the two of you."

Lucas calmed himself. This man wasn't threatening Dandi; he didn't know why he felt so ferocious. "At the moment, we're snowed in, and the only access road to my home is impassable due to a bridge being out. You can call the county and check, if you don't believe me. I don't know what the weather is expected to do tonight; it looks like we're in for another storm. However, we will be in Little Rock next Thursday – that's a week away." God, he hoped she was still with him by then. "The bridge is scheduled to be repaired by Wednesday, I hope. I have a meeting that I cannot miss. But if you'd like to send someone to speak to us, I'd welcome that. I'll be at the Peabody Hotel at two in the afternoon on the fourteenth." Maybe he sounded reasonable.

"Very well, Mr. Wagner. I'll be in touch." Grimes didn't sound happy.

"Oh, by the way, Dandi says that Romero's right hand man is a dirty cop."

"What did you say? Now you're breaking up."

"I said that Miss Alexander informed me that Romero has a dirty cop on his payroll."

"Shit! Do you know a name?"

"I can find out, hold on. Dandi?" he called. No answer. "Dandi?" He walked into the living room, she wasn't there. "I'll have to call you back." The phone crackled and buzzed. It was dead. "Damn, there went the cell phone tower."

"Did you call me?" Dandi walked into the room. Her eyes were puffy, she'd been crying.

"Yes, I did." She wasn't going to be happy about this, but he had to tell her. "I just spoke to the detective who is investigating the murder at Club Tonga. I told him you were safe with me."

She looked down at the floor. God, he had royally fucked this up. He might as well tell her everything. "The fact that you went missing the same night as the murder is all over the media. Speculation about you is running rampant."

"I'll never escape this, will I?" She looked defeated.

"Of course, you will. After Romero is caught and prosecuted, the truth will come out about how he was abusing you."

"I doubt that."

Actually, he did too. Good news or fair news was not the most popular story. People and the media thrived on the sensational and the scandalous. "There's more, something I need to ask you." She looked up at him, her expression uncertain and cautious. Hell, he'd make this right or die trying.

"What?"

"You said that Romero had a dirty cop on the payroll. What was his name?"

"Cahill."

"Good, I'll let the detective know." He didn't figure it would work, but he tried the phone anyway. "Phone's dead. And the bridge is still out, Dandi. We're stuck together for a little while longer."

"Yea, I figured. I looked out the window." She went to the couch and sat at the very opposite end of the couch from where he usually sat.

"Still up for a movie?"

"Sure." While she had showered, Dandi had given everything a lot of thought. She had made a few decisions. Lucas had been good to her. He couldn't help how he felt, and most any other man would have reacted the same way he had. It was up to her to rebuild her life. All she could do now was make the best of a bad situation. "I'd love to. Whatchagot?" She smiled at him tentatively, determined to enjoy what time they had left together. The pitiful thing was — she could change her mind about all of this, but changing her heart was going to take some time.

"I have all kinds." He went to the entertainment center and grabbed two handfuls. "I have a big selection of blu-rays. Take your pick." It didn't matter to him what she selected, he was more interested in making sure she forgave him and gave him a second chance.

Much to his surprise, she chose a scary movie. "Are you sure you wouldn't rather see The Proposal?" He held up the romantic comedy.

"No, I like ghost stories."

"Okay," he smirked, putting the movie in and pressing play.

"I don't get jumpy, if that's what you're thinking. I enjoy suspense."

"I didn't say anything."

During the first ten minutes of the movie, he sat on the far end of the couch, about five and half feet from her. Lucas wasn't paying a whole lot of attention to the show. As much as he could, he kept his eyes on her and he began to move. Stretching, he leaned forward as if to get a better look at the screen and when he leaned back, he moved over an inch or two.

She didn't make a move.

Eerie music filled the air and a central character was slashed into smithereens – Lucas waited for her to show a sign of unease – but she didn't. Nothing. After another short span of time, he did the leaning and stretching again, moving over toward her another few inches.

Could he be more obvious? If she hadn't been so put out with him, Dandi would have laughed. Lucas was no more subtle than a teenager. In a moment, he would stretch and yawn and have his arm around her shoulders. It only took a couple of more not-so-stealthy moves on his part till he was sitting right next to her. "Hello," he whispered. "I was a little nervous."

"Ahem. I bet you were."

"Do you want me to move?"

Pause. Pause. "No, you can stay."

"Will you hold my hand?"

"Lucas," she said with a cautionary tone.

"I just want to hold your hand – that's all. Please? We'll pretend we're in Junior High."

Heck, anything to make him hush. "Okay," she held her hand up and he took it.

And Lord Have Mercy on Her Soul! She never knew holding hands could be so erotic. Thoughts of the movie flew right out the window, because Lucas didn't just hold her hand – his hand made love to hers.

His palm slid over her palm. He rubbed each finger, traced her life-line with his thumb – wove their fingers together – even made suggestive little pushs and pulls that she could feel between her legs. And when he had picked up her hand, kissed the back and the tip of each finger, Dandi almost melted. Almost.

But, she couldn't. She didn't think her heart could take another let down. "I think I'll call it a night." Without words, she showed him how she felt. Taking his hand in hers, she tenderly kissed his palm, then jumped up and ran to the safety of her room before she did something else she might regret.

Lucas watched her go. He didn't blame her for leaving. Twice he had misjudged her. Twice he'd let her down. He didn't really deserve another shot. She was delicate of body, heart and spirit. How had he misread the situation so completely? Would she grant him another opportunity? God, he'd give anything to turn back the clock and try again. This time he would treat her with the gentleness and care she deserved.

Lucas stayed behind, but Dandi didn't leave empty handed. It was finally time to admit it. In Dandi's small, delicate hands, she held a piece of his heart.

*****

Like the reports had warned, the bad weather intensified and the next day they lost electricity. Dandi decided to make a celebration of their misfortune. She gathered all the makings for s'mores and laid a pallet on the floor in front of the fireplace. Lucas had broken limbs off of a peach tree, which they could use to roast marshmallows. It had been a horrible night and an awkward day. She was determined to make things better.

Watching Lucas settle himself in front of the fire, she had to admit she had been wrong. Last night when he had held hands with her, he had been trying to apologize, to get them back to the place they had been. It just wasn't in her to hold a grudge, so she had decided to make the best of their time together. "Are you hungry?"

They hadn't shared lunch, he had been cutting firewood and she had been doing some housecleaning. Earlier she had prepared a pot of soup and they had both eaten, but at different times. Lucas was giving her space.

"I am hungry, yes." He let his gaze meander over her body, letting her know what he was hungry for.

She chose not to react to his hot glance. Instead, she held out two marshmallows so he could load them on his homemade skewer. She did the same. In companionable silence, they held them over the crackling fire, deep in thought.

When they put the melted marshmallow and a small piece of chocolate candy between a couple of graham crackers – it was decadent. He laughed when she got the gooey concoction all over her mouth, but he didn't try to kiss it away. She seemed happy right now and he didn't want to do anything to spoil the mood. Not that he was giving up, far from it. He was just waiting for the right time. After they had their fill, she picked up the left-overs and took them to the kitchen. Upon her return, she plopped down beside him. "Tell me a ghost story," she urged him.

"Really?" He'd much rather watch her face; the firelight dancing over her skin was a beautiful sight.

"Please. It's the perfect night for it."

"Okay," he considered what to tell her. Perhaps he could use this scenario to his advantage. "The last time I was here at the cabin, I looked out the window and saw something or someone moving across the front, down by the trees. I thought it was a girl, but when I went outside, she was gone. I don't know what it was, but it reminded me of a local legend about a young woman who endlessly makes a trek across these mountains looking for her lost love."

"So you think you might have seen her?"

Now, he knew one of her weaknesses. Dandi loved ghost stories. She was leaning forward, ready to hang on his every word. "I don't know, but I know someone who has."

"Really?" she drawled out the word. "Tell me."

Lucas took advantage of the situation and leaned a bit closer. She smelled so good, like wild honey. And her lips – he would give five years of his life if she would let him kiss her again. "Up higher in the mountains, down this narrow dirt road, there's a house. It's an old house, a run-down house and everyone says it's haunted. And it may be. Grandma Beauchamp lives up there and she is as old as the hills. Everyone knows her and she has quite the reputation.

"What kind of reputation?"

"Grandma Beauchamp has second sight. Locals go to her when they need answers. She can tell you where to find something you lost. If there is a question about which man a woman should marry, she has the answer. They say Grandma knows when someone is going to die, but she doesn't tell that very often. I can remember when she did call up one teenager and told him not to go on a boating trip. He listened and stayed at home and the others that went on the trip capsized their boat and two of them drowned. Mrs. Beauchamp says she doesn't like to alter the future by telling what she knows, but sometimes she is compelled to warn her neighbors."

"Wow," Dandi whispered. Lucas knew he was milking this for all it was worth, but he was enjoying himself. "Tell me more."

"Second sight isn't Grandma Beauchamp's only gift. She can also see the dead."

Dandi inched over a little closer to him. "Has she seen the woman you were talking about?"

"Yes, she's seen her many times. Grandma says that she comes walking along the ridge this time of year, always looking for her lover, but never finding him. He was lost in the Civil War."

"What does the ghost look like?"

"They say she's pretty, has long hair that she wears in a braid. She's dressed in a simple brown dress."

"Has anyone ever heard her speak?"

"No, not that I've ever been told."

Lucas loved this, and he was about to take a gamble. If it paid off, he'd be a lucky man. Instead of looking at Dandi, he looked past her, like he was looking out the window.

"When was the last time anyone saw her?"

He let his stare freeze toward the window, his eyes got big and he made a little grab at her – "Dandi, she's looking at you through the window right now!"

"WHAT!?!?!" Dandi didn't look back over her shoulder; instead she just catapulted herself through the air and landed right on top of him.

Her bounding little body pushed Lucas back against the floor and he clasped her tenderly to him – laughing all the while. "I'll protect you."

When Dandi saw he was laughing, she realized she had been punked. "Did you think that was funny?" He was lying flat and she was sitting on top of him.

Lucas knew she had no clue how erotic their positions were. The fright had jacked her heart rate so high she was panting, her little bosoms were heaving and all he could do was lay there and stare. "I think it was one of the smartest things I ever did," he chuckled.

"I can't believe you told me that yarn!" Where she was perched on top of his thighs, her hands resting on his broad chest made Dandi uneasy.

"I wouldn't tell you a yarn, Baby." He brushed her hair of her face. "The ghost of that poor woman does wonder these hills. She's not the only scary thing around here, there's also the Fouke Monster."

"Monster? There's a monster?"

God, he loved to tease her. She was apprehensive, but she was still on top of him – that had to mean something. "Not far from here, over in Miller County, there's a Bigfoot creature."

"Oh, there's not," she chided him.

"I tell you the truth. He's been seen many times. They say he's nine foot tall and covered in dark brown hair."

"Foot! I wouldn't believe that unless I read it on the front page of the Times Picayune!"

"Pic-a-what?" Lucas snorted.

Dandi crossed her arms over her chest, pushing those darling little tits up – his mouth began to water.

"The Times Picayune is the big newspaper in New Orleans. My dad grew up there and he believed whatever the Picayune said – if it wasn't in the Picayune – it wasn't true."

"Would you believe I want to kiss you, Dandi?"

"No," she whispered.

"Yes, you do. And you want to kiss me, too. Don't you?" He wrapped a strand of her long hair and around his hand and tugged – ever so gently. "Come here."

"Lucas. . ." she said, warily.

"I just want to kiss – let's neck."

As if drawn by a magnet, Dandi lowered her body – just a fraction.

That was all the encouragement Lucas needed. He rose to meet her, capturing her lips in a soft, gentle kiss. "That's my baby."

Dandi was awash in sensation. They had kissed before, but it was nothing like this. Tiny nibbles and smooches were joined by sweet licks of his tongue. Lucas was asking, not demanding and she felt her heart flutter in her chest like a small caged bird. Unable to stay upright, Dandi sank down with him. Their bodies molded together as if they had been lonely apart. With a slight twist, Lucas turned on his side, letting her body rest on his arm. He took one long leg and fitted it over both of hers, holding her close. "Now - you're in my arms where you belong."

She wasn't so sure about belonging anywhere. "I'm nervous."

"Just kissing, Baby, that's all we're going do."

Lucas coaxed her, he cherished her. With a moan of delight, Dandi opened her mouth and let him in, thrilling to the rasp of his tongue against hers. And kissing wasn't all he did – Lucas petted her. Light caresses to her forehead, strokes to her cheek, his thumb trailing down her neck leaving a little path of fire. With a whimper, Dandi wrapped her arm around his neck and ate at his lips. It was so good!

She was responding to him. Thank God! He had been so afraid she wouldn't. When she grasped the collar of his shirt to tug him nearer, he almost moaned his relief. This was the way it was supposed to be. For the first time he was kissing for the sheer wonder of it – giving pleasure and receiving it with no expectations of taking it farther. They were sharing kisses for the pure joy of being together. This wasn't foreplay, this was delight.

With barely restrained passion, he mapped the inside of her mouth, relishing her taste. And Lord Almighty, he loved to touch her skin. She was so soft. The last time he had her in his arms, he had let lust override his good sense – but this time he was keeping a tight rein on his desire. Tenderly, he rubbed her shoulders and arms, attempting to convey adoration with every caress – every kiss.

Dandi was amazed. No fantasy had prepared her for this. Lucas was giving her deep, drugging kisses and she was inhaling them as if they were life giving sustenance. He shifted his body so he could frame her face, holding her still – and she surrendered willingly to his possession. Like fire, his lips branded hers with an all-consuming, overwhelming bliss. Her whole body tingled, excitement bubbling through her veins like carbonated water.

They lay before the fire and made out like teenagers. Lucas knew if he pushed her, she would allow him to make love to her. But it was too soon, he wanted her to come to him. So gradually – little by little, he brought them down, making the kisses sweeter, rather than erotic. Finally, he rubbed his mouth on her forehead and pulled her on top of him. "Sleep with me tonight – here by the fire. I don't think I can let you go."

"You know all the right things to say," she soothed his shirt, right over his heart.

"I wish. All I want to do is hold you and make you feel safe and. . ." he almost said loved. He almost said loved.

"Happy," she finished for him, with a sigh. "You make me feel safe and happy." As she nestled against him, he threw an afghan over them both and held her till her breathing evened out. The last thought he had before sleep claimed him was that he was happy, too.

Lucas smiled.

But when he awoke the next morning, the fire had died down, Dandi had gone back to her bed and he was cold.

CHAPTER SEVEN

"I found her."

"Are you sure?" Romero was skeptical of Cahill's abilities.

"Alexander is definitely with Wagner. Grimes talked to him." He laid the binoculars on the car seat. "They're holed up in a cabin, I can't get across the river, but I know their schedule. The detective is interviewing them in Little Rock on Valentines's Day. I even have the time and the place, all we'll have to do is intercept them. So, we wait. I bet he's fuckin' her brains out."

"Your job is to keep an eye on them, not worry about their sex life. Listen, I'm sending Marx up to do the job. He's a better shot than you, and we need you to preserve your cover. If you're spotted, it's all over for you and me."

Cahill was glad; he didn't really have the stomach for the job. Killing a woman like Angel Baby seemed such a waste of good pussy.

"Where should I meet Marx?"

"We'll be in touch. In the meantime, hang loose and keep close to the cabin in case the bridge gets fixed and they head out somewhere else, but don't let them see you. Wagner will be tough, if we can separate them; that would be best. He's known, and his testimony would just be hearsay. She's nobody. No one will miss her."

*****

"Can I get you a cup of coffee?"

Lucas had been working on the couch, catching up with some paperwork. "I'd love that."

"What do you take in it?"

"I warn you, I'm picky."

She put her hand on her hip. "Tell me, I think I can handle it."

"Okay, I like one and a half teaspoons of sugar and a half teaspoon of cream. I've been known to count the grains."

"Good grief," she laughed, returning to the kitchen, ready to tackle the hard task of getting his coffee the way he wanted it.

Lucas liked it strong; she had watched him brew it. When she poured the steaming liquid into a mug, she measured the sugar and cream the way he had specified. Taking it to him, she held it out. "See if I got it right."

Lucas didn't tell her he would've drunk a cup of muddy water to please her, instead he took the cup and sipped, determined to like it no matter if it was right or not, But to his surprise, it was perfect. "Thank you. You got it in one."

"It wasn't rocket science," she drawled.

"All right, Miss Smarty," he was tired of walking around on eggshells with her. Dandi felt something for him, he could tell. "Come sit with me," he patted the couch, "I think we need to talk."

Talk? Uh-oh. "What about?" Dandi did, going to her familiar seat on the couch. The house was becoming like a home to her and that made her a bit sad. Their time together was drawing to a close. Dandi hadn't asked many questions. It wasn't that she didn't care; it was because she cared too much.

"Nothing in particular, I just want to spend some time with you."

Dandi wasn't touching him, but she was ultra-aware of his nearness just the same. Spending last night sleeping in his arms had made her realize just what she was missing. She wanted to mend the disagreement between them before it was too late. Searching for something to say, she thought about their conversation at the Indian mound. "I'd still like to see your box of arrowheads. Do you want to see some of my sketches?"

"You want to show me your etchings?" He made reference to the classic French come-on.

Dandi rolled her eyes. "Oh, yeah – I'm going to seduce you with pictures of wildlife and ancient artifacts," she spoke a tad sarcastically.

It amused him that she understood his reference. Dandi was so smart. Any idea he had ever entertained that she was less than brilliant had faded long ago. "Baby, I'm already seduced, I'm just waiting for you to ravish me."

"I wouldn't believe that unless I read it on the front page of the Times Picayune", she threw back at him as she headed to her room to get her pad.

The Picayune again. "I'll get you a copy of the damn paper, because it's headline news. Lucas Dane Wagner Seduced by Sexy Dandi Alexander - Hopelessly At Her Mercy."

"Yea, right. I believe you," she said teasingly, but they took off like children, anxious to share their treasures with one another. She beat him back since her room was merely steps away.

"Here it is," he said upon return, plopping down on the couch so hard that he bounced her a little. With a giggle, she took the old shoe box from his hand and opened it reverently. In her mind's eye she could see a small golden haired boy holding one of these arrowheads in his hand, imagining the glint of sun catching on the water as a bronzed warrior drew back his bow to shoot at a doe drinking from the stream. "Lucas, oh my gosh! Do you know what you have here?"

"What?" he nestled against her, using their camaraderie as an excuse to get closer.

Holding up a small arrowhead, she explained. "This is a dovetail point made from pink flint. It could date as far back as 8000 B. C.

"Let me see," he took it from her and turned it over in his hand. "I found this one on Easter break when I was about fifteen, down by the pond behind the house. Of course it will be frozen over right now, but I used to fish in it. I'll take you there tomorrow, if you'd like"

"Please, I'd love to see where you played as a child." She took the dovetail point and returned it to the box and picked up a pottery shard. "This terra-cotta colored piece is from a Mississippian Caddo clay bowl, most probably."

One by one she removed the pieces and told him details about how old they were and who would have used them and for what – he listened until he could stand it no longer. Clasping her chin, he turned her head and kissed her full on the lips – right in the middle of a word.

"What was that for?" she asked, caught by surprise.

"I'm proud of you. You are so smart – and passably cute."

"Passably?" she whacked him with the lid from the shoebox. "Just passably?"

"Okay, you're gorgeous. Satisfied?" He knew he wasn't. He wanted her. "Can I see your etchings now?"

"Sketches, and yes."

She handed him the pad and he began to flip through it. When he started he was slouched back, totally relaxed. But as he looked at what she had created – he sat up, totally focused. The drawings were exceptional. Full of emotion and exquisite detail, each one transported Lucas to a place and time he never would have seen otherwise. Dandi had drawn the mounds she had visited, but she had filled the present with what had existed in the past. Ancient people worked the land, fished in the rivers and hunted game. The faces she had sketched seemed so full of life that he expected them to speak. "You're amazing," he whispered. "I had no idea you were this good. Why don't you have these in a gallery?"

Dandi looked at him like he had lost his mind. "They're just drawings, just my imagination."

"No, you are talented. I've seen enough art to know."

She waited till he was finished looking, then took the pad and laid it to one side. Now, she knew what she'd give him for Valentine's Day. "Tell me about your work. I'd love to know some of the cases you've worked on, if you could tell me without breaking any rules." His satisfied expression told her that he appreciated her interest in him.

"Okay, if you're sure you want to hear?"

"I do," she crossed her legs under her and nested her bottom back and forth, getting comfortable.

Lucas smiled at her antics. "Well, I told you that I'm a psychiatrist specializing in intimacy issues."

"Like what?"

He decided to dive right in. "I will be dealing with every type of personal problem you can think of. One quite common issue men seek help with is sexual inadequacy. Some don't feel they can satisfy a woman because their penis is too small."

"That's sad. I feel inadequate about some things, too." She didn't elaborate. "How would you help these men?"

"You have no reason to feel that way," he knew exactly what she was referring to, her self-esteem. If he had his way, she'd soon realize her true worth. "But to answer your question, I can help them in several ways. If the man is married, I meet with them both so they can discuss the issue. Most of the time, his wife isn't unhappy with his organ size. There are also positions that can prove to be more satisfying to both of them, where she will get the maximum amount of pleasure from penetration."

"You know a lot about sex, don't you?" His knowledge intimidated her. When she had awakened this morning, he had been hard. Her first inclination had been to touch him, to awaken him and let him make love to her. She knew that was what he wanted. But she was so afraid she'd fail. Even though he had taken her virginity roughly, she knew his skill as a lover was probably unsurpassed – while hers was nonexistent.

"Sweetheart, I know a great deal, yes. But I lost my head with you the other night; I did not put into practice what I preach." He put a hand on her back and began to rub. "I wish you could relax around me." When she bent over a bit to give him a little more room to work, he sat about in earnest to stroke and massage her muscles. "One thing that I intend to try for myself is a penis enlargement device."

"What?" Dandi was taken aback. "You don't need a penis enlargement device, Lucas. You are huge!" Just the thought of his cock made her feel empty and achy. "And how would that work?"

He got amused at her adamancy. "Yes, I am above average, but I want to wear the Andro Penis for a period of time and see if I grow a half inch, maybe. If I do, I would be able to recommend the device for my patient's use. Can you imagine how relieved a man would be to find out there actually was an answer to his problem?"

"Yes," Dandi could see that. "Hopefully, you'll have more luck than I did. When I was a teenager, I bought some type of ointment that was supposed to make my breasts grow. Every night I would rub it on and massage them for ten minutes. It felt good, but they didn't get any bigger."

Lucas groaned. Just the thought of her massaging some type of lotion or oil into her breasts made him as hard as steel.

She was getting mellow, Lucas was rubbing her back and it felt so good. Finally, she relaxed and let him have full access to her body.

"Here, lay in my lap so I can do this right."

He pulled her over and she went – she was both excited and leery. "Tell me more." Actually, she wanted to prolong the amazing way he was making her feel for as long as possible.

Her shirt was thin and he could feel the heat of her skin. Muscles that were tight with stress began to respond to his touch. And the soft little moans she was making sounded like music to his ears. "I have been working with one man, his name is Troy. Of all the cases that I have been overseeing, his is the one I hate to leave the most."

The mention of his relocation bothered Dandi. What if she never saw him again? "What's wrong with Troy?"

"He's a paraplegic, a polio victim. Until a few weeks ago, he had never had sex."

"He had sex? How?"

"Many men who have lost the ability to walk or move can still feel arousal and even become erect. It's different for all of them, but Troy could become erect. Other than that, he was trapped in his own body. But he wanted to know the joy of intimacy and that's where I came in. I was able to find a sexual surrogate who would help him."

Dandi thought for a moment. She knew what Romero had wanted her to do. "How is that different than a prostitute?" She hoped her bold question didn't make Lucas mad, but the comparison was the first thing that came to her mind.

Her enquiry didn't surprise him. "I won't lie to you and tell you that there are not similarities, but Alyssa enjoys her job, she's protected and she is performing an invaluable service."

"What is your involvement?"

"Good question," he admired the way Dandi thought. "I met with Troy for many weeks and listened to him. It was my job to determine how he felt about his limitations, what he needed in order to feel fulfilled and if he could handle the reality of the surrogate relationship."

"What do you mean?" A few seconds ago, he had edged her shirt up and he was now stroking her bare back. She forced herself not to react. It felt so good; she didn't want him to stop.

"Alyssa would be spending hours with him over a period of a few weeks. The minimum session would be about two hours and they would meet two or three times a week. It would be normal that they develop friendship, and he might find himself beginning to feel more. I had to make sure he was strong enough to deal with the knowledge that their association was a professional one."

"In other words, he shouldn't fall in love with her." His petting and stroking was making her feel as limp and relaxed as a boneless cat.

"Correct."

"Falling in love with the person you make love with seems like the most natural thing in the world to me. That's why you need to be careful who you sleep with." Whoops. Dandi could have bitten her tongue. Talk about a self-revealing statement! How would he react to what she had said? Dandi didn't really want to know. Abruptly, she sat up. "I need to go fix supper."

Reluctantly, he let her go. "Dandi, this isn't over with." He didn't explain and she didn't have to ask – she knew exactly what he meant. And he was right.

Leaving him to his paperwork, she went to the kitchen and prepared an old stand-by, Mexican Lasagna. It called for diced chicken, so she could use the left-overs from the roast chicken she had made the night before. When the fragrant dish was in the oven, she felt inspired to take out her sketch pad and draw Lucas. Once she began, her fingers flew. The features of his face were firmly etched in her memory, and she lovingly traced his form – highlighting the strength of his jaw, the piercing gleam in his eye and the kissable line of his mouth. On a whim, she drew herself into the picture – just from the back in that white outfit she had been wearing when they first met and – just for fun – she drew a pair of angel wings on her back. Finishing, she signed just the letter 'D' with a flourish in the corner.

"Dandi?"

"Yes?" Turning the pad over, she looked up to see Lucas standing in the doorway.

"I'm going outside to check the roof and make sure the snow isn't piling up. We don't want a roof cave in."

"No, we don't. Be careful."

"Whatever you're cooking smell's good enough to eat." He winked at her.

"Get out of here," she threw a dish towel at him. As he walked away, she realized how much like a married couple they must be acting. Except for the sex part.

*****

"Can you believe the media?" Romero stood looking out the front of the club at the vans and reporters clogging the parking lot.

"It's not the murder they're asking about anymore, it's that woman. They're making this whole thing into a romantic comedy. Where is 'Angel Baby'? Is 'Angel Baby' in love? Someone at the police station let it slip that she was with that doctor fellow and now they're more infamous than Brad and Angelina. But don't worry; at least it's taking the heat off of you." Marx knew Romero was feeling like a caged animal.

The media might not be focusing on the shooting, but Grimes was breathing down his neck. Romero was nervous. "Where did Cahill dump the gun?"

"In the river."

Romero sighed. "That's good. Why don't you head on to Little Rock and get set up? Cahill has to come back to work. He's made two trips up there, already, but the target hasn't moved. I'll be more comfortable with you up there, anyway. You are a lot less of a bumbling idiot. If he wasn't on the force, I'd have iced him a long time ago."

"He has his uses. Let's just hope he's never discovered, because he'd squeal like a stuck pig."

*****

After supper, both Dandi and Lucas were quiet. Dandi felt torn, the feelings she had for Lucas might not come along again. Would sampling joy really hurt anything? He might not want her forever, but he wanted her now. What was she going to do?

Lucas sat and gazed at the fire. He needed Dandi, and their time together was running out. Frankly, he didn't know what else to do. His mission hadn't gone as planned. He had held her hand, spent time with her – kissed her sweet lips, even caressed her – all with the greatest show of love and respect. Now, the ball was in her court. Lucas needed for her to come to him.

"Goodnight, I guess I'll go to bed."

He hadn't even heard her approach. "Sorry, I was thinking." As she walked by him, he couldn't help himself, he caught her hand.

"Can I have a goodnight kiss? Please?" She came to him, and he pulled her down for a gentle joining of their lips. He waited for her to give him any indication she wanted more. But she didn't, so he let her go. And as she walked into the bedroom, he felt more alone than he ever had at any time in his life.

After a quick shower, Dandi readied herself for bed. She turned back the silky sheet, crawling inside. Once she was there, she realized that she hadn't shut the door. She could see Lucas, plainly. He was sitting in the wide leather chair, staring into the flames. Bowing his head, he ruffled his hair and sighed. He looked sad and alone.

Her room was in darkness, he couldn't see her, but he looked up – right at her. The same feeling of longing and desperation that she felt was mirrored in his eyes. Dandi felt like a giant clock was ticking. He might get up and move any second. It was now or never. Slipping from the bed, she padded across the floor. When she emerged from the darkness – he saw her and his eyes blazed with a flame that had nothing to do with the firelight they reflected. Lucas didn't say a word, he waited.

Boldly, Dandi came to him and without saying a word, she went into his arms.

"What's wrong?" He made a place for her, cradling her against his body.

"I want to try again, if you would like to."

"Try again?" He awaited her answer, his sanity hinged on what she would say.

"Would you give me another chance? Would you make love to me?" Dandi knew he was all she had ever wanted in a man. She couldn't blame him for her mistakes. Lucas was handsome, hard-working, kind and sexy as hell. And he was here – now. Tomorrow would take care of itself.

Relief flooded his whole soul and body. "Thank God," he stood and carried her back to the bed. Tenderly, he placed her on the mattress. "I want to see you." He flipped on the bed side lamp. "Have you been crying?"

"No," she brushed tears from her eyes. "I'm just excited and unsure."

"Unsure of me wanting you or unsure you should come to me?" Stripping off his clothes, he tossed them to the right and to the left.

"Both."

"My wanting you is a given, and this time I will show how beautiful lovemaking can be. I promise." His voice vibrated with emotion and need.

"I trust you, Lucas."

"You are just so damned beautiful my teeth ache." Stretching out beside her, he brushed her tears away with a gentle finger and kissed her solemnly on each eyelid. "Thank you for giving me a second chance."

"It's my second chance, too." She rolled over to face him; they were both lying on their sides.

"I love being with you, Dandi."

His phrasing, the first two words - 'I love'– had nearly given her a stroke. She would have given anything in the world if he could love her.

"The reality of being with you like this, just takes my breath away. I fell under your spell the first moment I saw your face, it was just meant to be."

Dandi couldn't believe what he was saying. What should her response be? "When I saw you out in the club watching me, I felt the most irresistible urge to run to you. It was like I had been waiting for you." Had she said too much?

"I wish you had, it would have saved us both some time."

Wrapping her arms around his neck, she pressed her face into the hard muscle of his shoulder. "We're together tonight, that's all that matters."

"You are all that matters." Burying his face in the softness of her hair, he inhaled Dandi's scent – baby powder and honey. He'd never forget it. She smelled like love to him.

She quivered with joy when he nuzzled her neck.

"Let's get this gown off of you. I want to feel every inch of your soft skin on mine."

She sat up and he skimmed it off of her. "Turn around and let me see your back." Dandi felt cherished. With no inhibitions, she sat before him unclothed. "It looks better." Sliding a hand under her hair, he moved it over her shoulder. Dandi felt a light touch – one finger — skim down her spine. God, then his lips followed the same path. "Lay down, Baby." When she did, he kissed every ridge and every mark. He was healing her body and her spirit with love.

"I still may not be very good at this, you know."

"You let me worry about that, I won't fail you a second time." He eased her over on her back and lay down beside her, his big body half covering hers. With the tips of his fingers, he soothed the curve of her shoulder and the swell of her breast. "Dandi, you're my Angel."

"I don't want to be . . ."

"Don't say that," Lucas placed heated kisses on her cheek and neck. "Put Romero and that hell out of your mind. If anyone in the world is worthy to be called an Angel, it's you."

"I need you," she couldn't think of anything more appropriate to say. Her heart felt like it was about to burst. 'Steady — steady', she told herself. Her breath was coming in short pants; she couldn't bear to disappoint him again.

Lucas stared at her, so afraid she would disappear. "You're almost too beautiful to be real." He lifted his head and placed his lips against hers. Her mouth was so soft — tender and inviting. "Kiss me, Dandi."

Dandi surrendered to him. Opening her mouth, she gave him permission to invade and conquer. But he didn't — instead he tempted and tantalized — enticed and seduced. As his kiss worshiped her mouth, Dandi realized he was putting her first. With everything in him, Lucas was showing her she mattered. When she felt his hand on her waist, fitting his body to hers, she became aware of how aroused he was — how big — and she hesitated. But only for a moment. She was virgin no longer. There would be no barrier to their passion. So, she let her tongue dance with his — she even nipped his lip in her excitement.

"Oh yeah, that's my girl," he praised her.

Dandi wanted more. She wanted it all. Cupping his jaw, she pulled her lips from his and kissed his chin and cheek and brow. "I can't believe I'm here with you like this."

"Believe it, it's real. I was so afraid you would never allow me to make love to you again."

"I'm sorry I waited so long. I wasted too much of our time, we only have a couple more days." She wove her fingers in his long, soft hair. She loved how it felt; she loved how it looked – like strands of pure gold. "You are so perfect." With awe she caressed his body – his wide shoulders, his bulging biceps, the pads of his pecs and the flat ridge of his abs. Was this man hers to love, for a time; hers to please, for a season? If he was, then Dandi, of all women, was blessed.

Lucas wasn't rushing; he was going to take his time if it killed him. "I want you on top," he rolled to his back and took her with him. "I can see you better this way."

"I know," she held her hands up as if to cover her breasts.

"Please don't," he caught her wrists. "Looking at you is like seeing sunshine for the first time. You're glorious." He felt her tremble in his grasp. "Are you nervous?"

"A little."

"You don't have to be, you know. I will never, ever hurt you again."

His promise seemed like a gospel had been proclaimed. And she believed.

His big hands settled on her thighs and he began to caress her soft skin. "I love the way you look. You're golden, it's like you have a tan all the time."

"Creole," she explained.

"Perfect, everything about you is perfect."

The pads of his fingers made caressing circles on the sensitive skin of her thighs. Dandi became aware her vulnerable, warm sex was splayed over his bare, hard stomach. "I'm wet." She tried to scoot off of him.

"Yes, you are." He cupped her bare bottom. "Don't you dare move an inch." His appreciation was thrilling. Despite her apprehension, Dandi felt her tits begin to swell. Her nipples grew firm and her areolas blossomed. "Let's see if I can make you hungry."

Dandi didn't know exactly what he meant, but she would soon find out. He cupped both breasts and began to lift them and play with them. Lucas palmed her tits and rubbed her nipples between his fingers. A sizzling electric pleasure throbbed in the stiff peaks and the place between her legs began to pulse. "Hmmm, Lucas, please," she whispered.

"I intend to please you. Nothing else will do." Lucas stared at the softness between her legs, a downy patch of sable curls. This time he would not rush, he would appreciate every facet of her beauty. So with focused intent, he set out to drive them both insane with desire.

"My God, Lucas!" Dandi whimpered as he pulled at her nipples, setting a rhythm that directly corresponded to the throb in her clit. Helplessly, her hips began to move. She knew she would undoubtedly leave traces of her arousal on his flesh. Heat suffused her skin – partly from embarrassment and partly from sheer pleasure.

"Feel good?"

"Oh, yes."

"Look into my eyes," he prompted.

She locked her gaze with his. One hand left her breast and skimmed over her stomach on its way – lower. "Yes," she sighed as he parted her folds and lightly caressed the swollen nubbin of her sex. Dandi gasped. Covering the hand that toyed with her breast – Dandi trapped it there, so afraid he would stop.

"More?"

"Please."

Lucas chuckled. "See, this is what I should have done before, drive you mindless with need." He continued to touch her, relishing the ecstasy on her face. It was no hardship. Sliding his fingers up and down her slit, he spread the cream of her arousal, knowing that she would soon welcome him inside of her.

Dandi was amazed. She had never known it could be like this. When he sat up suddenly, she gasped. The hard muscles of his stomach gave welcome pressure against her sensitive clit. Framing her face, he ate at her lips. "God, I am so damn lucky." Pulling her back with him, he held the kiss as he rolled her over till they lay – her on bottom, him on top. Lucas covered her, sheltering her – making her feel both safe and more vulnerable than ever before. She spread her legs in welcome.

"No, not yet – I'm not near through. We're doing this right." He lowered his head and kissed her again – devouring her. Then he slid down and kissed her neck and shoulders, nibbling at the sensitive skin covering her collarbone. With determined ardor, he loved on her breasts, suckling at her tits till she was bucking beneath him.

"Lucas!" she sobbed as he tongued the tips, licked at the thrusting peaks, then opened his mouth wide and drew as much of her breast into his mouth as he could – drawing hard on silky firm flesh. "Yes!" she cried out as a climax shook her.

"Damn," Lucas muttered – totally entranced. "I want you to do that again."

Capturing her hands, he held them over her head, returning to pay homage to her tits. He suckled at the tender flesh till she was writhing in exquisite abandon.

It was hard to think, Lucas was wringing passion from her very soul. She felt calloused fingertips brush over her belly as he made his way south, kneading the flesh of her mons before dipping between her legs to find that sensitive place that begged for his attention.

"Please!" she entreated. Lucas persisted in his petting, knowing the bliss that she would feel as he began to circle and rub – massage and caress, pushing his fingers deep inside of her – stretching the place that was created to give him heaven on earth. "Oh God!" she lifted her hips, spreading her legs wide, begging for him to give her more and more and more. . .

"Oh yeah, that's my Baby," he crooned. "Cum for me, Dandi. Give me all your little cries." She bowed in his arms. Lucas held her down, making her feel everything. "Take it, Sweetheart. Take your pleasure. It belongs to you. Everything I have belongs to you."

Need consumed her. Her heart was racing – her pulse rate skyrocketing. "God!" she wailed as an explosion of complete rapture sent white hot ecstasy flooding from her head to her toes. Nothing else could feel better than this – nothing! But she was wrong. Lucas held her while she throbbed and pulsed, bringing her down with gentle kisses and tender words.

"Thank you," she whispered.

"Oh, you haven't seen anything yet, my little walking wet dream." Lucas kissed her – kisses dreams were made of. His long golden hair draped around their faces, shutting out the world – it was just them in their own private paradise.

Dandi didn't think she could feel more, but Lucas was insatiable – a powerful man intent on making her feel cherished. His mouth blazed a trail over flesh sensitized by an orgasm that had rocked her world. He licked a path around her breast, reawakening her need – nipping at the upper swell, cupping the mound, molding it as he suckled her back to full arousal. "I can't . . . . . .

"Oh yes, you can," he assured her. "Spread your legs."

"What?"

He slid down till his face was between her legs. "Oh, God!" How much more could she endure? Rising up, she watched Lucas as he nuzzled her pussy. He licked and kissed her till she was dizzy with lust. Dandi had no concept of such euphoria. But when he took her clitoris between his lips and began to suck on it, she almost levitated from the bed. "Lucas, I want – I want."

He knew what she wanted, and it was something he ached to give her. But she wasn't quite ready yet. Lucas wanted her so hot for him that she begged. Holding her thighs apart, he lapped at the cream, the pure evidence of her arousal.

"Please, please, please," she chanted.

"Give it to me, Treasure," he murmured before he upped the ante and used his tongue to spear inside her tender little channel. This was his woman – his to protect, his to pleasure. God, she tasted good. Her fingers were knotted in his hair, and she bucked helplessly, pushing herself into his face. Almost. Almost. "Come on, Baby," he urged her as he returned to her clit and took the little cherry between his lips and sucked, using his tongue to swirl around and around.

"Lucas, make love to me, please, please," she begged.

Victory.

Dandi watched him rise over her – her golden god, muscles rippling with strength and power. He took his shaft in hand, pumping it – once, twice. Do you want me, Dandi?"

"God, yes," she panted. Spreading her legs like the wings of a butterfly, she raised her hips, inviting his invasion. "Please, I need you so much."

Lucas was so turned-on; he was nearly blind with need. Taking his cock in hand, he slid it in her cream, rubbing the sensitive head over her pearl. She jerked, moaning. "Do you want me, Dandi?" he asked again.

"I beg you," she whimpered. "Put him in." The look on his face was one of triumph. She felt the head of his shaft enter her – she felt a momentary wariness.

Apparently he read it on her face because he bent to kiss her. "I won't hurt you, I promise."

She believed him. Her apprehension was overruled by a desperate hunger. Slowly, he pushed in. Dandi felt full – gloriously full. She grasped on to his shoulders and held on. "Oh, my Lord," she breathed. The sensation of him inside of her was incredible. He touched her so deep, gliding over nerve endings that sizzled with sensation. In and out. In and out. Every time he thrust a little deeper, soon he was buried to the hilt.

"Does it feel good? Am I hurting you?" Lucas had to know. "Should I stop?"

"Don't you dare stop, don't ever stop!" Dandi stared at his face and just felt. Each time he thrust in, she tried to hold on to him. He was magnificent. Watching his face was better than all the orgasms she had enjoyed – combined.

He threw his head back, his eyes closed, his neck was corded – and he growled, moaned, groaned her name. "Dandi – my Dandi."

It felt good – God, it felt good. But the more he thrust, the more Dandi wanted. She wrapped her legs around his waist and canted her hips to accept every powerful pump.

Damn, Dandi was making the sexiest, sweetest noises. Little mewls and whimpers; whispers and pleas for more *of him*! "One more time, Baby. Kiss me and I'll fly you to the gates of glory."

Lucas placed his hands on either side of her face, leaning near to her. She raised her lips for a kiss and he kept his promise – pistoning deep within her, transporting her far beyond the stars.

For long minutes, Dandi quivered, she couldn't stop shaking. The pleasure had been unbelievable. Lucas held her, rubbing her arms, bringing her down. "Dandi?"

"Yes?"

"Thank you for giving yourself to me."

Dandi rolled over in his arms so she could see his face. "There is no one else, there never had been – only you. I'm sorry I waited so long."

"Love," he took her small chin between his thumb and first finger. "I am just grateful you allowed me to touch you again. I hurt you, in more ways than one – I can admit that."

"Don't," she placed two fingers over his mouth. "It doesn't matter."

"Yes, it does." He kissed her fingers. "With all of my knowledge and all of my training – when the most important test came, I failed. I knew you were special, but I got carried away." He kissed her forehead. "I almost lost something very precious."

Dandi wanted to ask a lot of questions. He hadn't mentioned her greatest pain. What she really wanted to know was if he could get past Club Tonga. But she didn't have the courage to ask. So, she gave him a gift instead. "I have no experience," she laughed, "obviously. But, I want you know that you are a wonderful lover. You gave me so much pleasure. The first orgasm was wonderful – and so was the second."

"How about the third?" He was teasing.

"The best one, the very best one was when you were inside of me. I had no idea I could ever feel anything like that." She pressed her lips to his – solemnly. "And I want to feel it again and again." There – that was Dandi telling Lucas that she wanted forever.

"I'll take vitamins." He pulled the covers over them. "I'm so glad I found you, Dandi. I wouldn't have missed this for the world."

CHAPTER EIGHT

When Officer Cahill read the words 'Internal Affairs' on his phone display, he knew his gig was up, it was over. Should he run? He stood up, gathered his things and prepared to just walk off. Would Romero help him? He'd better.

"Not so fast, Cahill. I figured you would try to disappear."

"I was just stepping out for a breath of air."

"Mexican air?"

"I don't know what you mean, Detective Grimes."

"Internal Affairs is waiting. Would you come with me?"

"What's this about?" Cahill knew, but every second he could stall was one second he didn't have to admit defeat.

"A dirty cop begins to stink after a while. And you never exactly hid your penchant for the strip clubs. That and your overinflated bank account did you in."

"Who ratted me out?"

"No one, really. Angel Baby said Romero's right hand was a dirty cop. And while she didn't give us your name, we started looking. We didn't have to look far."

Cahill prayed the bitch died a slow painful death. "I'll tell you anything you want to know. Can we cut a deal? I know plenty."

*****

Dandi had slipped from his bed before dawn. She couldn't sleep for wondering what the future held for her and Lucas "Foot!" she threw up her hands in exasperation. Maybe, she should just ask him the question that was burning in her mind. She laughed to herself. Opening the pantry door, she stared at its contents. Ah, Lucas had bought potatoes. She would make a frittata.

Quickly, she peeled the potatoes, whisked the eggs and chopped up some ham, peppers and onions. Combining it all together, she seasoned the mix with salt and pepper, poured it into a large skillet and slipped it into the oven. Yes, she should just ask him. Dandi imagined his reaction if she just popped up and said, "What are your intentions, Mr. Wagner?"

"Did you say something?"

The voice behind her made her jump two feet in the air. "Lord, you scared me!" He stood there – so big and dear and better-looking than any man had the right to be. It took a couple of seconds for Dandi to regain her composure. "I was just messing around."

"Sit down, let's talk." He pulled a chair out for her and she eased down into it. Talk? That didn't sound good.

"Okay. Breakfast will be done in about twenty minutes. Can we walk down to the pond later?"

"I'm not worried about breakfast or going down to the pond, I'm worried about you." When he had awoken this morning, he had reached for her. It had been the most natural reaction in the world. When he had found his bed empty of Dandi, a wave of loss had hit him. If he let her walk out of his life, this is what all of his mornings would be like. Something had changed, he had changed. Dandi wasn't like other women, she was more. Making love to her had been different than all the other women in his past. With them he had found release, but it was still just sex.

"I'm fine, just a little thirsty." She had been about to pour herself some juice and check her blood sugar.

"Dang, you might need a shot and something in your stomach." He hurried to get her water, and some orange juice. "Take your antibiotic, too." He handed her the small pill. While she drank, thirstily, he went to her room and got her supplies. When he returned he knelt at her feet. Picking up her hand, he pricked her finger, then cradled it to his face while he read the result. "Shit, Baby." It was low.

While she watched, he readied her shot. "You like me a little bit, don't you?"

He glanced up at her. "Yes, I do." He smiled. "After last night, you shouldn't really have any doubt." With care, he gave her the much needed injection.

Dandi tangled her hand in his sexy mane. "I have a present for you."

In an unexpected move, Lucas laid his head in her lap. "You gave me you, what more could I want?"

"This is something you can keep forever. It's not much, but I want you to have it, think of it as an early Valentine present. Let me get it."

'This is something you can keep forever.' He wanted to keep her forever. Why was she so content to let him go? Lucas didn't know what to think.

He let her up and she went to the kitchen drawer where she had hidden her sketch pad. "I wish I could have gotten it framed." Holding the photograph out to him, "It's me and you."

"Here, sit back down. You're pale." She did and he knelt at her feet, holding the piece of paper as if it were spun glass. "Dandi, I don't know what to say." He was blown away. The likeness was uncanny, and while he admired her sketch of him, what meant the most to him was the angel who guarded his footsteps. "I love it. I'll cherish it forever."

"You're welcome. I'm glad. "

He kissed her leg, rubbing his face on her jeans. "I want to talk about what's going to happen after Valentine's Day."

Oh, no. Dandi braced herself. Not knowing what he was about to say, she covered herself just in case he was ready to say goodbye. "Okay. I think I found a few places in Little Rock where I can get a job. I sent a few emails, one or two sounded promising. And I located a women's shelter there and it will be a good place for me to stay until I can find an apartment."

Lucas stood up and pulled his chair around so he could face her. "I have another idea." He searched her face, watching for her reaction. "I'm not ready for our time to be over. I don't think I can move to Atlanta without you."

"What do you mean?" Dandi's heart was turning somersaults.

"I've always thought I had my life mapped out," he began slowly. "Since I was young, I knew I wanted to be a doctor and have a home and respectability."

Respectability.

Dandi swallowed hard. "Of course, you deserve those things."

"I had a timetable of how it would all work – residency, starting my own practice, finding a suitable woman to marry and have children."

Suitable.

Miss Etta's words came back to her. 'You have great value, Dandi. You are worthy to be loved.'

"Your wife will be the luckiest woman in the world."

Lucas cupped the back of her neck, leaning forward till his forehead touched hers. "Marriage is a long way off, what I'm concerned about is today – with you. I don't want to lose you, Dandi. I don't know what the future holds, but I don't think I can tell you good-bye – not yet."

Dandi tamped down her disappointment. He wasn't proposing. She was only nineteen; it was too early to think about marriage anyway. She wanted a career; she needed to go back to school. But she also wanted to be near this man for as long as possible. Was it wrong? She didn't know. "What do you have in mind?" Was he suggesting they live together or what?

"When I go to Atlanta, I want you to go with me. You can take classes and I'll take care of you. We will have to start slow. I have some student loans, but you'll be comfortable. This house could always be sold."

"No," she disagreed. "I don't want you to sell your home. Where we live is unimportant, being with you – that is what's important. Besides, I can get a job, I can help out."

"So, you'll do it?" He faced her. Lucas's mind was whirling with what this all meant, he felt out of control and desperate. His two selves were warring with one another; it was like trying to pull the east to meet the west. Was he strong enough?

"Yes, I'll come with you and live with you."

And be my love. He almost added.

"Great. Let's celebrate." Lucas bent over and took her face in his hands and kissed her – hard. There was so much he wanted to say to her, but he was going to take his time. He wanted to get it right.

"How? Are we going on a date?" She sounded so hopeful, he kicked himself for not doing more to show her how much he cared.

"You bet your sweet ass we're going on a date, but not right this second."

"How are we gonna celebrate?"

"By making love, how does that sound?"

Immediately, she reached for his belt buckle. "Perfect, a practice session."

Lucas chuckled. "Do you think I need practice in bed?"

"No, but I do."

Damn. She was sweet.

Lucas pulled her up from the chair, cradling her in his arms. She wished she was more experienced, but what she was lacking in expertise, she'd make up for with zeal. He reached to pull her in for a kiss, and she let him. The meeting of their mouths was explosive – not like the kisses they had shared before. There was a confident passion in their joining, no tentativeness. Lucas wanted to spend more time with her, he felt something for her – and that made all the difference. That fact gave Dandi the confidence to take what she wanted. She stood on tiptoe, with hands on his shoulders and pushed her tongue into the welcoming heat of his mouth. God, she was ravenous! Her tongue sought his – branding, marking, tasting – possessing. Her whole body vibrated with excitement. "I want you, Lucas." While he ate at her lips, she ran her hands over his body, massaging his muscles through his shirt, skimming her hand down to cup his bulge.

"Oh, God," he groaned, hardening beneath her touch. When she went to her knees in front of him, he knew he was the luckiest damn man in the world.

Unzipping his fly, she smiled up at him. "You may have to give me a bit of direction, but I want to do this. I need to do this."

"Anything you do will be appreciated," he muttered. Having her kneeling at his feet almost made his heart stop.

Dandi loosened his pants and opened them, her eyes bright with excitement. She couldn't keep her hands and mouth off of him, the sexy line of soft hair that trailed from his belly button south drew her kiss.

Her attention made him shiver with lust and something that felt a whole lot like love.

"You are so big." She palmed his erection, molding it in her small hand. "This is what brought me so much pleasure." Leaning in, she kissed the thick rod through his white underwear.

"Jesus, Dandi," he hissed as she pulled him free.

Taking his cock in hand, she squeezed it, giving a few tentative strokes. "Am I doing it right? Show me what you like."

"You – I like you," but he did as she asked – fisting his own dick, the rhythm and movement as familiar as breathing.

"Okay, let me try." He handled his penis rougher than she would have; she had always thought men were so tender here. Following his example, she pumped him.

He burned at her touch — it was like a thousand volts of electricity coursed through his body. Lucas couldn't' take his eyes off of her, she was his. Gently he grasped a few locks of her hair, wrapping it twice around his hand.

"Do you like what I'm doing?" She looked at him hopefully.

"Yea, now suck me."

Leaning in closer, she licked the sensitive head with the flat of her tongue. The friction was incredible, but the sight of her enjoying him was a thousand times better.

"Suck me," he directed, his voice taking on a commanding tone.

"Yes, Sir," she gave him a cheeky little grin and a wink.

Drawing a bit closer, she got in just the right position. Holding him still, she kissed the very tip of his cock. Then in a move that courtesans throughout the ages had used to wield power over kings, she opened her mouth slightly and slid her lips slowly over the head. The exquisite pressure — the gentle sucking — the lap of her tongue on the glans underneath the head almost caused the top of his head to blow off. "Shit," he growled.

Dandi reveled in his pleasure. He held her head, and even though he was being gentle, his hips began to buck. She felt a momentary panic — he was big and he was pressing deep. Despite her best intention, Dandi gagged. Lucas backed off a bit, letting her take a breath.

"It's okay, Treasure. This is good so good." He caressed the side of her face. "Do you want me to stop?"

She shook her head, taking hold of his thighs to hold him in place. "Never." Dandi began to suck him in earnest, laving the length of him with her tongue, swiping the head like an ice cream cone. Lucas widened his stance, and when he did she slid her hand down and began to fondle his balls.

"God, yes," he groaned as she cradled his cock with her tongue, humming her pleasure. The vibrations emanating from her sweet lips sent him almost to the edge. "Up!" he ordered. He wanted more — he wanted her pleasure before his own.

Dandi was throbbing with arousal. She needed more of what he had given her the night before. Now, she recognized the ache – the hunger in her pussy only he could assuage. Her whole body was prickly with need. Licking her lips, she tasted him on her tongue; the flavor of his essence was intoxicating. Without a doubt she was putty in his hands.

"Turn around," he moved her to face the cabinets, drawing her back against his chest. She moaned – wanting more contact, wanting more of him. "I've got you, Baby," heated kisses on her neck distracted her while he grasped the collars of her shirt and ripped.

"Lucas!" The tearing of the fabric made her even wetter. "I want you."

"You'll have me," he unbuttoned her jeans and pushed them down. "Step out." She did. His fingers danced on the taut skin of her abdomen. The tiny pair of white panties she wore was no hindrance to him – he pushed his fingers down behind the elastic and cupped her vulva – rubbing and massaging, parting her slit to spread the warm slick juices all around. Lucas knew he had her when she began pressing her hips back against his stiff cock, lifting her pelvis to give him more room to work. "That's my Dandi," he crooned in her ear as he swirled the pads of his fingers around her hot button.

"God!" she wailed. Lucas knew just what to do to make her his slave. She could feel her pussy open and shut – begging to be filled and stretched. When he sucked at the base of her neck, she turned her head, blindly seeking his lips with her own.

"Bend over the counter," he dispensed with the panties the same way he did with the shirt – with one forceful tear. "I'll buy you a closet full of new clothes," he promised. "Now spread yourself," he watched her get into position. The sight of her round, firm ass – heart-shaped perfection – tilted up for his pleasure made his cock ache. No matter his desperation, he took time to cup and fondle all of that smooth, silky flesh. "How bad do you want me?" he asked.

"More than food or water or air," she groaned.

Lucas rewarded himself by rubbing his cockhead over that delectable bottom of hers, then letting it slide between her cheeks. "You are so tight; I can't wait to be inside of you."

Dandi wiggled her bottom at him, trying to entice Lucas to get on with it. "Take me, please," she whimpered.

"Gladly," he guided the head of his cock into her tight little hole. At this angle, he could enjoy long, deep thrusts. "God, you are an absolute delight to fuck." Sex had never been so good – ever. Dandi put her whole heart and soul into everything she did – even now she was milking his cock, her enjoyment evident in every move she made.

Tightening his hands around her waist, he began to pump – never had he seen a sight more erotic than his cock emerging from her body all coated with her cream.

"Faster," she urged.

"You want more, Sugar?" she nodded her head and he slid his hands up her body – over her breasts, teasing the nipples. One hand reached up to collar her and then he slipped down to play with her clit.

"Oh, God – Oh, God – Oh, God," she moaned as he let his teeth scrape her neck. The fluttering of her little pussy told him she was cumming – and cumming hard. Her entire body jerked in his arms and he held her tight, his body becoming a battering ram as he slammed into her sweet, hot depths.

"Dandi!" he bellowed. Jets of semen ejected into her, staking his claim, filling her up with evidence of his devotion.

He held her as she shook – her little pussy muscles still working his cock, squeezing and grasping – milking every drop of his essence from him. "You'll stay with me. Promise?" he murmured in her hair.

"I promise," Dandi vowed. "Nothing in this world will ever come between us."

Speaking of something between them, Lucas realized he had made love to Dandi without a condom. He waited for the spears of panic to strike, but they didn't. Instead, he smiled. She was on the pill, and even if she wasn't – he didn't care.

*****

"Why didn't you tell me, you sly ole' dog?" Tim's private message popped up on his social media site.

"What are you talking about?" he responded. He hadn't really expected to hear from his friend. "I thought you'd be getting ready for your wedding. Isn't it this weekend?" he typed and hit enter.

In a few moments there was a reply. "Yes, it is. And I'm glad to know that I'm not the only one having fun."

Lucas wondered what Tim was getting at. Thinking of how to reply, he stared out the kitchen window. Was that a glint he saw? Probably nothing, but he had a tendency to worry about everything. The bridge was finally open, a day or two ahead of schedule. That had to be a good omen. "Just tell me what you're talking about so we can both enjoy it." He clicked the reply button. Lucas wasn't in the mood for games.

"You mean you don't know?" It seemed like Tim was playing with him.

"Know what? I've been snowbound in Pine Ridge with no access to the outside world and no electricity. The United States could have been invaded by Canada and I wouldn't know it." Click.

"Damn, you're all over the news, Wagner."

What the hell?

"Why?" Click.

When Tim's answer came, it wasn't what Lucas wanted to read. "Angel Baby's disappearance went viral, just like her dance video. The gossip is that she's with you. The doctor and the stripper, it's caught everyone's imagination. Every woman wants to be Angel and every man is jealous of you."

"Crap," Lucas said out loud. He shut his eyes. Dammit! "How bad is it?" he typed. It couldn't be too bad. The news cycles were too fast and he and Dandi weren't really newsworthy.

"I'm sure TMZ will be getting in touch with you."

Tim was exaggerating, he had to be. "Well, thanks for the heads up."

"So, it's true? You have that stripper with you? You're banging her?"

Fury rolled up in Lucas like a flood. "Watch it." His fingers hit the keys hard. "You've stepped over the line."

"Sorry, Lucas." This reply came quick. "I didn't mean to make you mad."

"Gossip about my private life is something I can't tolerate. My reputation as a doctor is too important to risk. Whatever my relationship is with Dandi, it's nobody's business but ours. Do you understand?" The flat black words on the white screen could not adequately convey his displeasure.

"Hell, Wagner. Don't shoot the messenger, I'm just telling you what's going on. The cat is out of the bag and what you do with the stray pussy is up to you."

Lucas slammed the lid down on his computer.

Dandi walked up behind him and kissed his back. "What's wrong? Were you chatting with someone?"

"Tim, it was nothing." He didn't repeat anything he'd been told. Whatever was going on wasn't her fault. God, he just hoped none of the partners saw this shit.

"Are you sure?" She wanted nothing to mar their time together. So far, the day had been a good one. Even though she wouldn't be accepting it, she had received an offer from The City Diner and that made her feel good. "So where are we going on our date?"

"Actually, it's a double date, now." He gave one last hard look toward the stand of bushes where he had seen the anomaly. In a few minutes, he'd take a walk down to the pond and check everything out.

"A double date?" Dang. She wanted him all to herself. With whom?

"My mentor, Dr. Solomon texted me. He's in town and even though I saw him a few days ago, he says he wants to see me before the meeting with the partners." Now, Lucas wondered if it was good news or something about this mess.

"Does he have a wife?" Dandi was mentally reviewing her wardrobe; she had nothing to wear that would be suitable.

"Yes, Maria is a very nice woman. You'll like her."

"Can we go early? I need to buy a dress."

Lucas held her by the shoulders and looked her up and down. "We'll get you whatever your little heart desires, but know this – you could go to a ball dressed in a garbage bag and still be the most beautiful woman in the room."

"Thank you, but I still want to be properly dressed for you. I want you to be proud of me."

Her sentiment stabbed him in the gut. "I'll be the envy of every man we meet. Now, go get pretty," he kissed her on the forehead. "We'll leave as soon as you're dressed and go clothes shopping. We don't meet the Solomons until seven."

"I'll hurry," the excitement in her voice warmed his heart. She took off, and he watched her go. How full of life she was. He'd never tire of just watching her walk.

While she took a shower, he walked around outside. What he saw disturbed him. There were footprints in the snow, coming from the woods and returning. They had stopped underneath her bedroom window. Apprehension coiled in his mind like a snake. It could have been just a curious hunter, but that was unlikely. Ways to protect her and options to consider clamored in his head. Maybe they should get a hotel room in the city and not come home. Should he call Grimes? Most likely. He had phone service again and he had promised.

Heading back in the house, he called out. "Dandi, bring your bag, I think we'll spend the night in town." He'd explain everything to her when he had her in a safe place. There was no reason to scare her. He'd take care of her. Lucas walked around and checked the windows and doors, looking for signs of tampering. He lowered shades and pulled curtains.

"I'm excited, Lucas!" she called back to him. "I haven't been on many dates."

He had already had a shower, so it didn't take him long to dress. Throwing a few things in an overnight bag, he hauled ass downstairs. The sooner they were out of these woods, the better.

"Ready?" She stood in his living room wearing a clean pair of jeans and a bright red sweater than molded every curve to perfection. "You look beautiful."

"Thanks, and yes," she held up her bag. "I'm ready."

"Good, we may not come back here. I think we'll just stay in town until my meeting Thursday."

"Really?" Dandi looked around the house that had come to mean so much to her. "I hate to go. I have everything, though." She held up her bag. "It will be like I was never here."

"Not true at all." Lucas wrapped his arm around her shoulders as he led her to the door. "You have put your mark on this place, and you've put your mark on me. The imprint of you will never leave my mind."

She prayed what he said was true.

When they were pulling out of the garage, Lucas decided to be cautious. "Dandi, bend over and see if you can find my sunglasses. I think I dropped them under the seat." She unfastened her seat belt and looked. This was his way of getting her out of the line of fire. Dang! Maybe he had been watching too many cop shows.

"I don't see them."

"Keep looking." As she did, he sped down the driveway and out to the main road.

"Sorry, they aren't down there." She raised up, a little flushed.

"That's okay, they'll turn up."

Dandi couldn't help but compare the way they were dressed. He looked so sharp in a pair of grey dress pants and a form-fitting white shirt and tie. She, on the other hand, looked like she was dressed in discards from the Goodwill store. How would she ever fit into his world? She didn't know, but she'd do her dead level best to try. "Could we get my insulin filled soon?"

"Sure," he had already thought of that. "We'll do that first, then we'll go buy you a few outfits."

"No, we'll just get the one dress and maybe some shoes." Dandi was adamant. "I can wear what I have until we can get settled and I can get a job." He narrowed his eyes and looked like he was about to say something. Then it occurred to her, "Will there be other people I have to meet and places we have to go for your work?" She was so unprepared for this.

"Not a lot; quit worrying." Lucas intended to see that she had what she needed, but even in jeans and a sweater, she looked just right to him.

His assurance didn't stop her from worrying, but she hushed about it. They pulled into a pharmacy and got out. "I think I'll get a few make-up items while I'm here."

"Get whatever your heart desires." She looked good au naturale to him. "Give me your insulin and I'll pick it up and wait for you at the counter." She handed the empty box to him and thought how lucky she was. Several women were watching them and the envy on their faces was unmistakable. Lucas was a hunk and a half.

Hurrying to the make-up aisle, she began picking up some foundation and lipstick. Dandi debated about eye liner and blush, but she decided to try some.

"Angel Baby, is that you?"

A voice behind her caused her to whirl around. "What?"

A man stood behind her; a middle-aged, heavy-set man. "Aren't you the stripper, Angel Baby?"

"How did . . . ." Dandi bit her tongue.

"It is you! I knew it!" The man was ecstatic. "Frank! Come over here!" he yelled. "That stripper from Club Tonga is over here!"

"Shush, please," Dandi begged.

Lucas heard the commotion. Leaving his items at the counter, he went to find Dandi. It wasn't hard to locate her, because she was surrounded by four men and backed into a corner.

"Show us one of your moves," one guy reached out and grabbed at her chest.

"I've watched that you-tube video of you a thousand times." Another said as they inched a little closer to her.

"Please, just let me get by," she begged. "I don't do that anymore."

"You should, I'd pay a big price to see you naked right now. How about you come home with us?"

"That's enough." Lucas growled. At his harsh words, the wad of assholes parted. "Come here, Dandi." He held out his hand and she rushed toward him.

"I can do without the make-up."

"You don't have to." He gave the men one last hard look. "Can't you idiots recognize a lady when you see one?"

He was furious. She had never asked for any of this. Dandi had only been trying to survive. She had come to his bed as pure as the driven snow, but no one would believe it if he told them. He didn't care. It didn't matter. She was his only concern.

"Thank you," she whispered. "I'm sorry about that. I forgot about the stupid video and the news reports. Spending time with you pushed the rest of the world away."

Lucas kissed her on the forehead. "Forget about it, I've seen the video and you were beautiful." He didn't mention the television and news reports.

"You think so?"

When she tried to give him money, he ignored her. "Yea, let's get out of here."

She walked out beside him, it was like standing in the shadow of a rock – he was twice the size of the sniveling men who had been harassing her.

Dandi was quiet when she went back to his car. Lucas didn't say much, either. He seemed to be deep in thought. They only traveled a couple of blocks before they came to a trendy looking boutique. "This place looks expensive."

"I think it's reasonable. I know the owner." More correctly, he used to date the owner, but they had parted amicably and were still very good friends.

"I'm paying for this," she grumbled.

"I don't think so," he stated calmly, as he pulled her from the car. "This is my treat."

"I thought I was your treat," she came back at him flirtatiously.

Dandi had been about to step up on the sidewalk when he stopped her, turned her around and kissed her soundly. "You are definitely my treat, and I'll enjoy tasting and licking and kissing and sucking. . ." his voice got lower with each word, until he was whispering in her ear, "your sweet little pussy tonight."

Zing! Her clit vibrated at the thought. Dandi entered the boutique very subdued.

"Lucas!" a very sultry feminine voice hailed him. Dandi looked up and saw this Nordic goddess walking toward them. She was tall, elegant, dressed to the nines and wore a smile that announced she knew just how perfect she was.

"Monique, how are you?" He kissed her on her cheek. Dandi took one step backward, but Lucas stopped her retreat. "We're here to find Dandi something to wear tonight. Could you help us?"

"Certainly," Monique looked Dandi up and down. "Where are you taking her, Lucas?"

"We're meeting friends at the Peabody."

"My, we must hunt something extravagant."

"No," Dandi protested.

Monique laughed. "I have just the thing. Come with me, Dandi. I like your name."

Lucas gave her a little push and Dandi followed the intimidating woman to the back. "Thank you, I like yours too. It's very sophisticated."

"Actually my girlfriends call me Moni Faye," she laughed. "Relax, Lucas and I are friends, although I have to admit, I have very fond memories of him."

In a few minutes, Moni Faye – as she insisted on being called – had her dressed in an off the shoulder burgundy gown with a filmy wrap and a pair of four inch pumps that made Dandi swoon. "This is so gorgeous," she breathed with she looked in the mirror.

"Where's your make-up? Let's get you all fixed up."

"Lucas has it," she no sooner got the words out of her mouth than Moni/Monique was hightailing it to where Lucas was waiting patiently. She could hear them talking. Dandi was so nervous. She stared at herself in the mirror and wondered how little Dandi LeBlanc had managed to wind up in a place like this.

Monique was very talented. After a few minutes of applying and concealing and brushing and curling, Dandi didn't recognize herself. The look wasn't anything to compare with the brazenness of her Club Tonga look, she was expertly made up to the point where she didn't look like she was wearing anything – she just looked – flawless.

"My God," Lucas breathed.

Dandi didn't realize he had been standing there. Watching.

"You take my breath away." He moved closer to her, handed Monique his credit card and shooed her away. "I can't believe you're real." He pushed a lock of hair from near her eye. "I'd kiss you but I don't want to muss you up."

"Muss me," Dandi whispered. "I would never want to be so fixed up I couldn't afford to be mussed."

Lucas chuckled. "I agree."

Framing her face, he rubbed his lips across hers, "Tonight, when we get to our hotel room. I want you to ride me. Will you do that for me?"

She was taller in the heels, it gave her a leverage she hadn't had before, so she tangled her fingers in his hair and took what she wanted. Her mouth met his in a gasp, she whimpered as he fused their lips together, giving her a blistering kiss.

"Bravo," Moni Faye clapped her hands once – then twice. "I'm glad to see the Master has not lost his touch."

"Damn," Lucas breathed. "Let's get out of here. I want this night over with so we can be alone."

Dandi blushed as they made their way out of the boutique. He carried the clothes she had worn into the store out in a bag. "Red is definitely your color. I knew that when I brought you the coat home, though." Helping her back into the car, he tucked her dress in before he shut the door. Dandi had never felt so cared for in her life.

The Peabody Hotel was amazing. Dandi loved the ducks that it was so famous for! Lucas held her hand while they paraded out of their cage to plop into their fabulous fountain. He explained to her the tradition of the spoiled fowl that resided in this five star establishment. "In the morning, I'll bring you back down and we'll watch them come out. They walk on a red carpet to special music. It's fun." She agreed.

He led her to the Capricio Italian Steakhouse, Dandi was in awe of the luxurious furnishings and the decadent ambiance. She hadn't been in very many nice restaurants. Actually, she hadn't been in any. 'God, don't let me embarrass Lucas'. Would she know which fork to use? At least she wouldn't chew with her mouth open.

"Lucas!" A voice hailed them from the foyer.

"That's Dr. Solomon." A waiter led them to a table next to the window. A beautiful view of the river caught her eye. "Dr. and Maria, it's so good to see you both." Lucas's friend was tall and grey-haired, very distinguished, while his wife was a lovely Hispanic woman – petite and darkhaired. "This is my date, Dandi Alexander. Dandi these are my friends Fredrich and Maria Solomon."

"Hello, I'm honored to meet you both."

She offered her hand and they were very kind.

Dandi made small talk with Maria as the men conferred together. "Where did you go to school?" Maria asked. It was a harmless question.

"I didn't . . ."

"Dandi is going to enroll in college, just as soon as we get settled, Maria."

"How wonderful." Dandi let out a breath and met Lucas's eyes. He had saved her, but he had also felt the need to cover for her, too. She didn't know how she felt about that.

The waiter came and brought their drinks and took their orders. She let Lucas order for her, and he chose prime rib for both of them. Dandi couldn't remember the last time she had eaten steak. "Save room for dessert, their cheesecake is out of the world here," Maria interjected.

"Isn't that a friend of yours?" Dr. Solomon pointed to the entrance. "He seems to be trying to get your attention. I think he's coming this way."

Lucas glanced over his shoulder. "Tracy."

Taking a quick look at Dandi, he stood quickly. "I'll go talk to him; I wouldn't want him to interrupt our meal."

"It would be no interruption," Dr. Solomon spoke, but Lucas was already on his way.

Tracy. Dandi thought. Tracy was the friend who had come after Lucas when he had been with her after the lap dance. She wouldn't look back.

"Dandi, where did you meet Lucas?" Dr. Solomon asked.

Great. For a moment Dandi didn't know what to say, finally she just lied – sort of. "I met him in Shreveport, at a club." There, that was close to being true." She tried to continue eating, but her hand was shaking like a leaf. The expression on Lucas's face had been painfully obvious, it had been panic. He had not wanted Tracy to see her because Tracy would have recognized her.

Dandi felt nauseous.

"Do you still see them?" She asked Maria.

If Maria found the question strange, she didn't let on. "No, they went to the bar, I think."

"Is something wrong, Dandi?" Dr. Solomon was watching her carefully. "You are very pale."

"Oh, I'm fine," she assured him. "I need a little sugar, if you don't mind, I'm hypoglycemic."

Maria and Fredrich hustled around and found her a packet of sugar. "Do you need to go to the doctor?"

"No, I don't," she tore open the packet and wet her finger to get some of the fine powder on her tongue.

"I see Lucas heading this way," Maria announced.

"Don't say anything, please," she looked from one to the other. She was afraid Lucas would insist she go to the restroom for a shot and they would run into Tracy. Dandi thought she might die if he were to be embarrassed by who she was and what she had been. The men at the pharmacy who had seen the video had been horrible enough – and now this. All of sudden Dandi was aware that being with Lucas was going to be much harder than she thought.

It might just be impossible.

CHAPTER NINE

Lucas got rid of Tracy as quickly as he could. He had been shocked to see his friend. The Peabody Hotel was not the type of place he would have expected to run into him, but he had been there for his parents' anniversary.

Heading back to the table where Dandi and the Solomons sat, he wondered what they had thought about his odd behavior. Hopefully he had put on a pretty good front. The idea that Tracy would have recognized Dandi and embarrassed her in front of Maria and Fredrich had scared the shit out of him. She had already been through enough and he would not allow her to be hurt any more than necessary.

"How was Tracy?" Dr. Solomon had taught at the University of Arkansas and knew most of Lucas's friends. When he had taken an interest in Lucas, he had made it his business to learn all about his past and his family.

"He was great," Lucas smiled and spoke with an upbeat tone. "I'm ready for dessert, how about it?" His host and hostess agreed, but Dandi didn't say anything. "How about it, Doll? They have a really beautiful fruit cup."

"I think I'd like that," she spoke tremulously, but she wouldn't meet his eyes. Lucas realized at that moment, that none of this had escaped her. She knew exactly what was going on.

Fredrich took charge of ordering sweets for them all and while they were waiting, he gave Lucas the news he had been saving for the most opportune time. "I wanted to talk to you before Thursday, Lucas."

"Really?" He tried to read Dr. Solomon's tone, it was hard; the old man was a consummate communicator. He only gave exactly the impression he intended to give.

"The partners have reviewed your information and my recommendation. They are very impressed with you. Our meeting with them on the fourteenth was just a formality."

'Was?' Now, he was getting paranoid. "I don't know what to say. That's wonderful news."

"Congratulations!" Maria patted his hand. "He didn't even tell me."

"Congratulations," Dandi added, but in a much softer voice.

"I had hoped to discuss some things with you tonight," Dr. Solomon continued with an unusual twist to his voice. "When you told me you were bringing Dandi along, I knew business would be better left to a more appropriate time."

"I agree." Lucas nodded his head. His imagination was working overtime. There was no way Dr. Solomon would stand in judgment over someone like Dandi. Would he?

The meal couldn't get over fast enough to please Lucas. "I can't thank the two of you enough," he began, trying to bring the evening to a close. "This has been wonderful." With a gracious smile, the Solomons took the hint.

"When I got the call from the partners, I knew we had to come and be with you. Working with you through the years has brought me great satisfaction. And I want it to continue," he said pointedly.

"Your support has meant the world to me," Lucas hugged Fredrich and Maria, and as they rose from the table, he helped Maria with her coat.

Fredrich took the opportunity to put his arm around Dandi. He had a very gracious smile on his face, but his words didn't match his demeanor. "If you have affection for Lucas and wish for him to succeed, consider carefully what getting involved with you will do to his career. Sometimes the greatest gift we can give someone is to let them go. I know you have no intention of doing him harm, but a doctor's reputation is everything."

Dandi's blood turned to ice. She looked up in the older man's face. He knew. He knew who she was. It didn't matter if he had been to the club or if he had seen the video, she had been weighed in the balance and found wanting.

"I would never hurt Lucas."

"You will, without even trying."

As Lucas turned, Dr. Solomon stepped away from her and they moved out of the restaurant. Dandi had to concentrate on each step. It was like she wasn't really there. She felt as if she was floating above her body, watching the two couples move across the sumptuous lobby.

Lucas said his goodbyes, and they stood on the front until the Solomon's had received their car from the valet. Lucas's hand had been firmly planted in the small of her back, but Dandi managed to stay a few inches away from him. Every time he tried to draw her close, she eased away. As their visitors sped out of sight, he grabbed her hand. "Let's go upstairs to our room."

Dandi didn't want to make a scene, but she didn't think she could continue with their plans. "All right." They made their way to the elevator.

Lucas had reserved a room for two nights. It was expensive, but he knew the security in the hotel was adequate. Earlier that afternoon, while Dandi had been under Monique's care, Lucas had touched base with Detective Grimes and had been gratified to find out that Officer Cahill had been taken into custody. Apparently progress was being made on the case. He was relieved; maybe he could let down his guard. The detective or his representative was still planning on meeting with him on Thursday, however. And Lucas had no problem with that. He wanted all of this cleared up so he and Dandi could begin afresh.

As soon as they were behind closed doors, Lucas reached for her hand. "Come here, I need to hold you."

She let him wrap his arms around her. Lord, how she wished all of this could have been different. This wasn't going to work, and the sooner she put an end to it, the better off he'd be. "I think I'm going to go."

"Go where? Do you need something? Ice? Some juice? Have you checked your blood sugar recently?"

Dandi place her hands on his forearms and pushed out of his grasp. "No, I'm going to a motel. This isn't going to work."

Lucas blinked. "What?" He stopped breathing. "What isn't going to work?"

"Us. I'm hurting you." She pulled the red wrap tightly around her shoulders. Dandi was cold.

Spikes of pain sank into his chest. "Hurting me?" He grasped her upper arms, not hard – but she wasn't going anywhere. "The only thing that would hurt me is your leaving."

"Lucas," she bowed her head in defeat. "Don't you see? It's obvious that I can't overcome who I am or where I came from."

"Is this about those stupid men at the pharmacy?"

"Not entirely. It's everything." Her voice faded to nothing.

There were tears streaming down her cheeks and he kissed them away. "Tell me. Is it about Tracy? I didn't want him embarrassing you in front of the Solomon's, not before I could explain everything to him, and I did."

That surprised Dandi a bit. "What did you say to him?"

"I told him that you were with me and that you were safe."

"What else?"

He placed a finger under her chin and forced her head up to look at him. "I told him you were mine."

Dandi ached. She wanted to be his. More than anything. "I don't want to hurt your reputation."

"You're not going to hurt my reputation," he ground out.

"I will, I already have. Your Dr. Solomon warned me tonight."

"He warned you? What . . . Did . . . He . . . Say?"

A flash of anger lit up his eyes. Dandi sought to explain without crying or sounding pathetic. "He said that he knew I wouldn't mean to harm you, but I would. He said your reputation was everything and the kindest thing I could do for you was let you go."

Lucas turned her loose and paced across the room. "That. . . interfering old bastard." How dare he try to undermine his and Dandi's relationship? "I can't believe he said that to you."

"It's true," she whispered. "Everywhere you turn, my past will surface. I was a stripper. I'm a liability."

"You weren't a stripper. You were a young girl that unscrupulous men took advantage of." Lucas jerked his tie off, popping it between both fists. "I know the truth."

Dandi couldn't help it; she let a small hint of accusation enter her voice. "Yes, but what did it take to convince you of the truth? At first, you thought I was capable of doing drugs. You assumed I had slept around. The only thing that managed to convince you of my innocence was my virginity. And I don't have that commodity to bargain with any longer. How will I convince people of my innocence now?" She started by him, heading for the closet to get her things.

Lucas grabbed her as she went by, engulfing her in his embrace. "This is private. This is between me and you. And the only person you have to convince of anything is me - and I'm already convinced." He ground his mouth against hers, kissing her with pent-up desperation. At first, she tried to fight him. But, he pulled her tight against him, willing her to understand. So, she accepted his kiss, but she didn't return it.

"Please," he whispered, kissing her all over her face. "Don't leave me."

"I don't know what to do," her voice shook with emotion.

He knew. Going to his knees in front of her, he pressed his face to her middle. "Love me. That's what you need to do. Just love me. Because I love you with all my heart."

Dandi's hands came up to touch his head. She stopped, they patted the air; she wanted to touch him – so much. "You do?"

"God, yes." He pressed kisses to her body through her dress. When faced with the prospect of losing her, his feelings had crystalized. He adored this woman. There was no way he wanted to live one day without her. "I love you so much."

She sank down with him. "I love you, too. I've loved you from the first moment I saw you. But I will never, ever willingly hurt you. Do you understand?"

"Don't put conditions on our love, Dandi. Please." He sought to connect with her. "Look at me." His eyes flared as he took her by the shoulders and kissed her as if nothing in the world would ever mean more to him than she did.

Not accepting him was impossible. He placed one big hand on each side of her neck, and sank deep within her; the ache and burn he invoked had become his trademark. She would recognize the feel and taste of his lips anywhere – she would never require sight or voice – her body recognized his. "I need you," she gasped.

"You have me, you have me forever."

Dandi felt her heart contract as Lucas worshiped her with his lips. She would remember this moment forever. Nothing could ever take this treasure from her. She was loved. What more could any woman ever want than to be loved by a man like this one?

Lifting his head from hers, he removed her wrap. "I need you now. Lie with me, please. I need to make love to you. I need to know you belong to me."

Fitting his mouth to hers, he picked her up, never breaking the connection. Walking across the room, he placed her on the bed and began undressing her with great care. "Is this what you want?"

"Yes." Yes. Yes. "I want you." She helped him with her clothes, then they started on his. Soon they were both naked and he stretched out next to her.

Carefully he traced her features, his eyes full of devotion. "I want to show you how much I desire you. Come." He rolled on his back and brought her with him. Lucas's body was so big and broad that she could lay comfortably on top of him with plenty of room to spare. Dandi sighed and relaxed, feeling safe and cherished.

He ran his hands over her body, soothing and rubbing, massaging and caressing. "Can we work this out, Lucas?" She felt compelled to touch him in return. Sitting up, straddling him, she began to knead his chest, teasing his nipples, raking her nails gently over his skin, watching the goose bumps rise on his flesh.

"As far as I'm concerned, it is worked out. The partners will offer me the job. Smart people don't fall for such foolish manipulation." Pushing her hair over her shoulder, he enjoyed looking at his woman. "Do you remember what I wanted you to do in bed tonight?"

Dandi smiled, running her fingers through his hair. "Ride you," she said it with a wicked little grin. "It sounds like fun. I have a request though."

"Oh really, and what would that be?" He was so thankful she was smiling. Hurting her or allowing her to be hurt was not acceptable.

"There's a number that's begun to intrigue me." She was tracing patterns on his skin, writing with her finger.

"And what would that number be? He thought he knew, but he wanted to be sure. "13? 666?" Lucas weighed her breasts in his palms, tweaking the nipples, loving how they responded to his touch.

"No," she playfully slapped him. "I want you to teach me 69."

"Gladly," placing his hands at her waist, he helped her turn over. "Now scoot your bottom toward my face." She did. "Farther. I want you to be practically sitting on my face."

Dandi trembled. Even though this had been her idea, the thought of him staring at her hoo-hoo made her feel funny. The notion didn't stay in her head very long, due to his hard, imposing cock standing proudly before her like it was begging for attention.

"Any words of wisdom?" she asked, shivering as her mouth watered at the prospect of what she was about to do.

"It's all about making one another feel good. Double the pleasure." Lucas intended to do just that. Her delicate, tender pussy would be too tempting to resist.

Pushing her hair over one shoulder, Dandi bent to her task. Curling her tongue around the head of his cock, she reacquainted herself with his heady, male flavor. "Hmmm," she moaned, loving how he felt in her mouth. Bobbing her head up and down, she began to suck in earnest – until – she felt his tongue swipe between her legs.

Lucas separated her sweet folds, studying how perfectly she was made. "So sweet," he crooned as he licked – up, up, up – from the cherry of her clit to the small, tight opening that could drive him insane. "How does this feel?" He pushed a finger deep inside of her and began rubbing, rubbing, rubbing the spongy little area that vibrated just for him.

"Oh, my, Lord," Dandi just stopped. She stopped sucking him. She shut her eyes. She laid her head on his stomach and just quivered in delight.

Lucas chuckled. "Hey, why did you stop?"

"I can't concentrate, it feels too good." Feeling a mite guilty – just a mite – she grasped his cock and held on; all she was able to do was rub her thumb on the shaft. The rest of her mind and body was totally focused on what Lucas was doing between her thighs.

"Relax, Sugar, ladies first."

Dandi didn't quibble. She was in paradise. He was giving her pure, unadulterated pleasure. Being still was impossible; she grasped the sheet with one hand and twisted it in her fingers. Unmercifully, he plied her with his tongue, holding her still while she pushed backwards against his face. "I'm failing the 69 course, I'll make it up to you," she mumbled between pants.

"You can get away with it; you're the teacher's pet."

A choked giggle escaped her lips as she wailed, "Don't make me laugh at a time like this." She could feel Lucas's hot breath on her wet flesh as he lapped at her clit.

"What better time? Lovemaking should be the most fun two people can have together."

Dandi giggled again. "I'm seriously gonna hit you if you don't get on with it back there." Lucas spanked her ass, one sweet pop. "You're a demanding little cuss."
But what she demanded, he gladly delivered.

Long languorous, liquid swipes of his tongue hyped up her need to a fever pitch. "Oh, God, I may pass out." She loved this man so much. As he ate at her pussy, she bit his thigh — took a bit of his hard flesh in her mouth and sucked. He would bear her mark.

Lucas answered her passion with his own, taking her clit between his lips, he began to suck. Dandi's whole body went into overdrive — she bucked and arched, screamed and begged — then she imploded in a perfect storm of pleasure.

"God, you're sexy," he ran his hands up her back as her little body trembled on top of his. He loved the way it felt, her resting on top of him. It made him feel complete. Lucas hadn't realized how empty his life had been until Dandi had brightened his days with her smile.

As Dandi floated to earth, she became aware of what still throbbed in her hand. He was engorged, strutted with desire — for her. She took him in both hands and rose up to give him the same gift he had given her. First, she clasped the tip and ran the pad of her thumb over the head. Lucas groaned so loud, she could feel the rumbling of his chest beneath her. Next, she stroked him, long strokes where she marveled at how firm and hard he was in her hand. "I can barely get my hand around you. You're beautiful."

Lucas closed his eyes as brilliant sensations radiated from his cock to his balls. Dandi was pumping him with vigor now, and when he felt the enveloping heat of her mouth as she closed her lips over the sensitive head, he moaned aloud. "Suck hard, Baby. I like it hard."

"Ha! Me too," she teased. But then she got down to business and Lucas had to bite the inside of his cheek to keep from blowing. Dandi was getting to him fast, usually he could go for a half hour in a woman's mouth — but the old rules didn't apply with Dandi.

Since she had been taken care of so well, Dandi had her wits about her. He was amazing. As she licked and sucked, she studied him — the sexy veins that ribbed the smooth rock-hard flesh, the mushroom head that was shaped so perfectly for her lips, the tiny slit that beckoned her tongue – she was enthralled with everything about this man. Even his balls. It was a surprise to her that she craved to touch him, roll them between her fingers, massage and fondle their firm resiliency.

His thighs twitched, his toes curled – his whole body moved beneath hers as if am earthquake was rumbling up from the depths of the earth. "Enough!"

One minute she was facing south, the next she was spun around. Lucas was so strong, he moved her as if she were a doll. "Sit up, Sugar." He arranged her the way he wanted. "Lift up," Dandi thought he was about to enter her. Instead he fit himself inside the valley of her pussy lips, sandwiched tight in her labia with the head of his cock notched right up against her clit.

"Oh, I like this," she smiled at him.

"Do you? Show me?"

He was giving her control. Dandi felt feminine and powerful. Lacing her fingers with his, she began to move, sliding her vulva back and forth over the steel ridge of his cock. God, this was intimate. He wasn't inside of her, but he was bathed in her cream – enveloped in her heat and the friction was deliciously decadent. But it wasn't enough, her pussy felt so empty; it ached, begging to be filled. "Help me," she went to her knees, needing him to take control.

Lucas took his cock in hand and sought her tight, swollen opening. He didn't know which was best – the ecstasy of feeling the tip of his shaft slide up in inside of her or watching her face as she stared at him with adoration and wonder in her eyes. "Feel good?"

"Oh, yeah," she breathed. Her skin was rosy with arousal and when she bit her lower lip and moaned, he felt his cock twitch in response.

"It's all up to you, take as much of me as you want, as deep as you want. All of it feels like heaven to me."

Dandi reached for his hands once more, just wanting to hold on to him. She was on her knees, and he was there for the taking – all eight, thick inches of him. Slowly, she lowered, impaling herself. The fit was so exquisitely tight that she swore she could feel his heartbeat deep in her vagina. Never breaking eye contact with him, she began to move – rising and falling – the pleasure so intense that she felt faint. "Touch me," she implored as she brought both of his hands to her breasts.

Fuck, yeah. Lucas palmed her tits, lifting the round, firm globes and rubbing the pads of his thumbs over the lush nipples. No woman had ever felt so perfect – being inside of Dandi was like a homecoming. With awe, he watched her throw her head back, that beautiful mane of hair cascading down her back like an ebony waterfall. She arched her back, thrusting her tits forward, her neck smooth and exposed as she worked her body up and down on his rod. "Ride me, Dandi."

God, she was beautiful. He tried to memorize every detail of her features – the elegant arch of her neck, the gentle slope of her shoulder. Despite the lure of face and form, the feeling of her pussy gripping his cock, milking him in a steady mind-blowing rhythm stole his concentration and self-control. Cum was boiling in his balls and he had to tense up to keep his orgasm at bay. She had to find release first, nothing else would do.

Gone were her troubles, gone were her doubts – the only thing that remained was Lucas and how he made her feel. "I need to hold you," she held out her arms.

Her wish was his command, sitting up he grasped her sweet ass and pulled her closer, his cock serving as an anchor to keep her fast to him. "Hold as tight as you want." She took him at his word and wrapped her legs around his waist and her arms around his neck.

"I can't move much like this."

"Yes, you can. Just move back and forth instead of up and down." Bless her heart; she followed his directions to a tee. And all the time she was kissing him – deep, passionate kisses. He would never get enough of this woman. She had not been experienced, but she was a natural, sensual woman who did not try to hide her enjoyment of him or her hunger for more. As she moved, he could feel her breasts massage his chest – God! He wasn't going to last. Intent on seeing to her needs, he slid his hand between them and began to play with her clit – swirling his fingers around the center of her pleasure.

"What you do to me!" she scraped her teeth on his neck, nipping him like a sexy little wildcat. Lucas was a goner – head over heels. He could feel her everywhere – deep in his soul, under his skin, wrapped securely around his heart. When her pussy gripped him and began to quiver against his cock, he nearly went cross-eyed with the pleasure.

"That's it, Dandi, cum for me," he urged. He kissed her sweat-dampened cheek, pushed a strand of hair off her face and buried his head in her neck as she rippled around him, her whole body jerking in his arms. "You are my Treasure. You are precious to me."

"Love you," was all she could whimper.

Lucas was desperate to pound into her. "Hold the headboard," he directed. She did. He held her hips and bucked up, sliding in and out, driving as deep up into her as he could. With every thrust, his dick bumped up against her cervix and rubbed against her spongy little G-spot. Could he make her explode again? Hell, yeah! He slammed into her again and again, every time he pushed in, she squeezed as if trying to keep him there. The friction was incredible. "My God, Dandi," he groaned.

Dandi screamed his name. "Lucas!" Heat flashed. Hearts pounded. Blood thrummed through their veins. Blissful pleasure roared up from within him as he explosively ejaculated, spilling his seed, bathing her womb with his cum. For long moments, they panted, she leaning over him, her breasts dangling in his face. Lucas kissed and licked the tips, nuzzling his face in her cleavage.

"Slide down, let me hold you." He helped her. "No, I don't want to pull out. I want to stay inside of you for a little while. Is that okay?"

Dandi's heart swelled. "Please, I'd love that." She made herself at home on top of him. Her Viking. Her Hero. Her Beloved.

*****

All during the night, he never let her go, it seemed imperative that he keep her in his arms. Sleep did not come easy, nor did it last long. As the rays of the sun broke through the filmy white curtains, Lucas could see her face. Her dear face. God, he loved her. Several times during the dark hours, his cock had hardened; just the feel of her naked breasts on his chest and her curves in his hands had kept him in a constant aroused, aching state. If he didn't find release soon, his dick was going to explode.

"Baby, I need you." She stretched in his arms – sleepy, cuddly, warm and oh, so desirable.

"K."

Lucas eased her over on her back and she held out her arms to him. Never had he felt as welcome. Feeling between her legs, he found her slippery and ready for him.

"You want me." It wasn't a question, thank God.

"I was dreaming about you," she kissed his cheek. "Come inside me, don't make me wait."

God, could she be more perfect? He rose over her, and she opened her thighs, reaching up to take his cock in hand and guide him home.

Ecstasy. Dandi groaned as he pushed in. "I love how it feels when you're inside of me. You ease the ache and the hunger."

Lucas found it hard to talk. "So good." He worked his way inside of her, the walls of her pussy caressed the full length of his cock. She wrapped her legs around his hips and lifted up to meet him. He couldn't resist kissing some part of her face or neck with every stroke. Pulling all the way out and sliding in – slowly – he set a rhythm to dazzle. He longed to please her more than she would ever know.

"Damn, damn," he chanted. The beauty of it was that the more he pleased her – eliciting those little whimpers and purrs – the more ramped up his own excitement became. Lucas thrust and pumped, undulating his hips in a lazy figure eight that ensured his cock caressed every centimeter of her tight channel. Dandi writhed, arching her back, exposing the vulnerable line of her neck. Her legs were spread wide enough to accommodate him so he rested some of his weight on her body, letting his groin drag across her sensitive clit with ever piston of his hips.

"I can't take it," she wailed. Every pass of his body over hers, every measured stroke caused a lightning flash of electricity to blaze over her body. She tightened her sheath around him, trying to capture and hold him. She wanted this feeling to last and last. "God, Lucas!"

Her name on his lips was like a litany of praise, an affirmation of their bond. Dandi's climax hit her hard and she clamped down him, squeezing him till he felt he would burst. He couldn't hold back – all of the passion boiled up and burst forth in an eruption of bliss. She milked him, and he fed her sex with great pulses of semen.

The rapture was so intense that he was amazed. Intimacy and sex with other women had always been pleasurable, but this – this wasn't even in the same universe. Lucas was floundered by ecstasy. All he could do was collapse, taking her with him, cradling her close while she quavered against him. If he had been looking for a sign – this was it. What they had just experienced together was something he wanted again and again. And not just the sex, he enjoyed being with her, talking to her, sharing with her. He wanted it all. Lucas wanted to build a life with her.

There was no one else for him but Dandi. Somehow, he had to settle this. There could be no room for doubt. All of his goals and dreams were hollow compared to how he felt about this woman. During the night, he had held her tight, letting the events of the prior evening swarm through his head. Lucas could not conceive of a future apart from her. "Dandi?"

"Yes?" she sounded content.

"The partners will hire me. I have no doubt."

"I hope so."

"Getting that job will be the fulfillment of a lifelong quest."

He felt her body stiffen. "I realize how much it means to you."

"No, I don't think you do." He took her chin in his hand and tilted her face up to look at him. "I want the job, and I'll get it. But that's not all I want."

"What do you mean?" She searched his face for answers.

"I want you."

"You've got me," she didn't even hesitate.

"Okay, prove it." His tone was adamant.

"What?"

"Prove to me that you are mine."

"How?" Dandi rubbed her hand on his chest, giving him assurance, kissing him right over his heart.

"Marry me."

Marry Lucas?

Dandi went completely still, she didn't even dare breathe. Knowing he loved her was miracle enough, but that a man like

Lucas would want to marry her was the epitome of her dearest dreams.

Lucas waited for her to say something; it seemed as if he could hear the ticking of a billion clocks. "Don't break my heart, Dandi."

Love is the strongest human emotion, it is stronger than fear or anger or joy. Dandi couldn't have hidden her love from him, even if she tried. Hugging him as tight as she could, her heart pounding in her chest she confessed. "I would never want to break your heart."

"Marry me, Dandi." He repeated.

CHAPTER TEN

Marry him?

Instead of answering him, she sat up, pulling out of his arms. He felt bereft.

"I need you to hear me, Lucas."

Lucas shut his eyes, not really wanting to hear what she had to say. "I'm listening."

"I want to marry you more than any woman has ever wanted to marry any man"

A smile lit up his face. He reached for her, she pulled back.

"But if there is any chance that I will damage your reputation, cause you pain, disrupt your life - I couldn't handle that."

"It's not going to happen." Lucas shook his head in denial. "I can have it all." He petted her face and arms, trying to imprint himself upon her. "There isn't a man on the face of the earth who wouldn't trade places with me. You are the complete package – you are smart, kind, beautiful and absolutely amazing in bed." She started to speak, but he put a finger over her lips, stopping the flow of words. "Most importantly, you are mine. I choose you." His image of the ideal woman had morphed into Dandi. No one else would do.

"Lucas," Dandi almost sobbed his name." Yes, I'll marry you – but never forget – I put you first. Protecting and loving you has to be my priority."

"What does that mean?" Lucas held both of her hands in his, not letting her move.

Dandi held his gaze, tears blurring her vision. She couldn't tell him the truth. He wouldn't ever let her leave the bed if she did. What she said aloud was, "it means that I will do everything in my power to make you happy and never regret that you loved me." What she said in her heart was entirely different, "it means that I will know when it's time for me to go.'

$$\star\;\star\;\star\;\star\;\star$$

"Where are we going?" Dandi dressed quickly. Lucas was already ready and standing by the door. It was a good thing she wasn't a typical female who stood in front of the mirror for an hour applying eyeliner.

"We're going down to the courthouse and get our marriage license."

"We're going to get married now?" Her voice came out as a squeak. "I'm not getting married in blue jeans!" She pooched her lips out, demanding he listen to her protest.

Lucas chuckled. "No, we're just getting the license. Come on, I promise you we'll find the perfect dress."

The next twenty-four hours were a whirlwind for Dandi. Lucas swept her out to the car and drove her around town, showing her all the sights. They went by the Clinton Library and the River Center and he promised to bring her back soon and show her the town that meant so much to him. The courthouse was their destination and she had to pinch herself when she signed the document that declared his intentions to take her as his wife. When they left, she insisted on holding the envelope that held the precious piece of paper. He loved her – she had the proof right in her hand.

Next they went window shopping until a simple lace sheath dress caught her eye. "Let's see how much it is," she pointed.

Lucas could tell from the storefront that it wasn't an exclusive boutique, but the dress was perfect – it was elegant and understated. Since their wedding would be in front of a Justice of the Peace, they didn't need yards and yards of satin and chiffon. "It doesn't matter how much the dress is, not if you want it."

Dandi was relieved that it fit and the price was reasonable. While she was trying it on, he slipped a few doors down and bought her a big, beautiful diamond ring. When they left the store, she clutched the bag to her breast.

"Aren't you going to let me carry something for you?" The sight of her holding her wedding dress and marriage license like they were the most precious things in the world made a knot come in his throat.

"No, but I like when you put your hand on my back."

He did, too. Touching her, connecting with her was imperative — so he did. "My pleasure."

They returned to the hotel and put up her dress and Lucas made a few phone calls. One of them was to an apartment complex in Atlanta, he had already put the deposit down, but since Dandi was coming, he wanted to upgrade to a larger floor plan. She listened in wonder; her future had taken such an amazing turn. He winked to her as he talked, patting his knee, inviting her to sit in his lap. Such an opportunity was impossible to resist. The next phone call was to the Arlington Hotel in Hot Springs, and as he booked the honeymoon suite for Thursday night, she almost creamed her panties. When he put the phone down, she pressed her lips with absolute devotion. He was so big and so invincible, yet when he looked at her with his heart in his eyes, she melted like warm honey.

The hours passed in a blur — they laughed and planned and shared and made love. He told her about the job offer and what he envisioned for their future. "I have it all mapped out, we're going to be so happy"

"I'd be happy anywhere with you," she assured him. She wasn't marrying him for a job, or status or even security. Dandi was marrying for love.

*****

"I'm here," Marx whispered into the phone. "All I have to do now is watch for them. Don't worry; Miss Alexander will be dead in a matter of hours."

"You'd better make damn sure she is. Cahill is behind bars, and I don't plan on joining him. It doesn't matter if the Detective says she isn't a witness, I know she saw me. I looked right in her eyes. They're lying, they're all lying."

"That may be," Marx agreed. "Now, do I have my times right? Go over it again with me one more time." The big bouncer flexed his muscles. "I don't want to run into Grimes. All I want is for him and the Doc to find a dead woman in her bed. You have an alibi and I have a ticket to Mexico and my money will be waiting for me there. Right?"

"Right," Romero agreed. "If you pull this off, I'll deposit a quarter of a mil in the account you gave me."

"You better, or I'll be back." Marx hung up the phone and Romero shivered. It was as if someone walked across his grave.

*****

"Wish me luck," Lucas kissed her tenderly.

"You know I do," she hugged him hard. "I wish you every happiness."

Lucas didn't doubt it. What she couldn't seem to get through her head was that she was his happiness - all of the rest of it – the career and the money and the prestige – that was just icing.

"You wait right here in this lounge and have coffee. Just as soon as I get through, we'll come back up here and dress you up in that pretty lace gown and head to the courthouse to tie the knot. After that, I'm going to love you all night long. I promise you a honeymoon you'll never forget."

"Tell me again where you'll be." Dandi wanted to go with him, but she knew it wasn't possible.

"I'll be in that conference room right around the corner if you need me."

"Okay." She kissed him again and watched him walk out the door. He was dressed in a dark brown suit and he looked like a movie star. "I'll be waiting."

"You better," he gave her a mock stern look. And then he was gone.

*****

"Lucas," Proctor Renfro took his hand. The man was the spitting image of Mitt Romney – handsome, smooth and self-confident. "Solomon has sung your praises for years."

"It's an honor, Sir."

"You'll love Atlanta," Charlotte Simmons gave him a big smile. The only female partner, she gave the group a softer side. Even though she was in her fifties, Miss Simmons was still attractive.

"Yes, he will." Chas Tonahill interjected. "All we have to do is work out a few issues."

With that statement, the meeting took a slightly different tone.

"Come sit down," Fredrich Solomon guided his protégé into a seat. "Let me outline what we're offering before we go any farther."

Lucas had known the offer, but just hearing it again made his stomach clench. "Starting salary will be ten grand a month. You'll also have an assistant, a car and an expense account equal to half your salary. Three conferences a year are subsidized and encouraged. We also have a housing allowance and a country club for you."

He had made it. Years of scrimping and studying and dreaming had finally paid off. "I'm ready. Where do I sign?" Lucas looked at them one by one.

"There's just one thing . . . ." When Proctor held up a hand, a sliver of doubt edged its way into Lucas's mind.

"What thing?"

Charlotte looked out the window. Fredrich Solomon bowed his head. Chas Tonahill fumbled through some papers. But Renfro faced him head on. "It's come to our attention that you are involved with a stripper."

"She's not a stripper."

"Is a stripper, was a stripper – hell what's the difference," Renfro threw some papers on the table. "Tense doesn't really matter, to the rest of the world Dandi Alexander is a stripper or worse. This is our position." He went on.

Dandi stood outside the door. It was cracked open about an inch and she could see Lucas sitting with the woman and the three men. As she listened to their ringing judgment of her, she felt splinters of agony pierce her heart. The more his words echoed in the small room, the more cold chills ran down her spine. All of her hopes and dreams began to crumble.

"You have three days, Mr. Wagner, before our offer is rescinded. Think long and hard. Miss Alexander is a liability. Your future is at stake. We cannot allow our sterling reputation to be dragged through a scandal like this. We want you in our organization, but we can't abide gossip, innuendo and bad publicity."

Dandi slumped against the wall. This was her greatest fear come true. She stood between Lucas and his dreams. It didn't matter what the mistakes were or how innocent she'd been, to the world at large she was trash. She knew Lucas; she worshiped him. He wouldn't turn her aside. He was a man of honor and principals. They were engaged, they had a marriage license. He'd stand by her for the rest of his days. But at what cost? She wiped tears from her eyes. It was time to go.

She peeped in, took one long, last look at the man she adored and whispered, "I love you, Lucas. Goodbye." Then she ran to the elevator as hard as she could. She didn't want anyone to hear her cry.

*****

Lucas wouldn't stand for it – literally. He stood and paced, enraged at the audacity of these pompous, third-rate assholes. "Let me tell you something, Dr. Renfro and other members of this so-called board. I love Dandi. I worship the ground she walks on. There is not another woman in this world as perfect and good as she. She came to my bed as pure and innocent as the driven snow. And if I have to choose between her and this two-bit job that you are offering me – there is no choice. I choose her. And you can take this job and shove it up your ass."

Lucas walked. He headed to the lounge and back to the woman he loved. There would be other jobs. Hell, he could start his own firm. None of it mattered – only she mattered.

He was furious.

"Dandi?!?" The room was empty. Where was she? She was supposed to wait right here. Damn! He hurried to the elevators and up to the sixth floor. Pushing the button never makes the elevator go faster, but he was still so mad he couldn't see straight. When the doors opened, he barreled out into the hall and what he saw chilled him to the bone. A man was walking ahead of him down the hall with a gun in hand. He stopped right at the door to his and Dandi's room. When he turned his head sideways Lucas recognized him. He was one of the bouncers from Tonga.

Every nightmare he had ever imagined stood before him, Dandi's safety was paramount. This was not going down. "Hey, Asshole." The man wheeled around, took one look at him – and pulled the trigger.

The gunshot rang out. Lucas jerked. He had been hit, but he was not down. A searing hot pain slashed across the right side of his head. He felt in his hair, and when he looked at his hand, it was red with blood. It was just a graze – he hoped. The man was at the door. He pulled on the doorknob, then prepared to shoot the lock. "No!" Lucas ran at him like a rampaging bull. Shouts from down the hall pierced the haze of pain and fury that clouded his mind.

The bouncer turned to shoot at him again, but someone grabbed him from behind. Hotel security had arrived. One spoke into a radio. The police were being called. "You're hurt, Mr." Lucas pushed them away.

"Dandi, I have to get to Dandi." Lucas was dizzy.

"Hey man, you're bleeding, you need a doctor."

"I have to check on my fiancé." Pushing the man aside, he inserted the key card and fell into the room. The empty room. Frantically, he checked the closet. She was gone. There was nothing left in the closet but her wedding dress and the red coat. Staggering to the bed he picked up a note that was lying across their marriage license.

My Dearest Lucas

"I love you. Don't ever doubt that. But, I can't stay. Please, don't try to find me. I wish you every happiness and success in the world."

Dandi

Gone.

She was gone.

Blackness enfolded Lucas and he escaped the searing pain in his heart.

*****

Mechanically, Dandi fled. She didn't know which way to turn or what to do. She just knew she had to get out of town and as far away from Lucas as she could get. She was poison for him. With head down, she walked until she came to a bus station. A big white, smoke chugging bus rumbled in place. She didn't have much money, but she would go as far as she could. Glancing at the board, she laid down enough money for Alexandria, Louisiana. Taking the ticket, she boarded the bus and moved to the rear.

Would he look for her? Yes, he would.

Did he love her? Yes, he did.

Did that make any difference? No, it didn't.

She was doing what was best for Lucas, he would realize it someday.

As the bus pulled away, she buried her head in her lap and cried. If she could have taken a magic pill and forget the last few months, it would be for the best. Except that she didn't want to forget Lucas. Her memories of him would be all she had.

*****

Dr. Solomon stood over him. "Calm down, Lucas. We'll find her." The emergency room was crowded. The professor had been shocked to learn the whole story from the detective's point of view.

"I want out of here!" Lucas demanded. "This is a flesh wound. I have to find her!"

"We just have a few more questions, and then I'll help you find her," the police detective shut the door.

"I've told you all I know about the shooting." Lucas sat up on the side of the bed. "Romero was a crook. He killed another crook, aided by a dirty cop. Dandi didn't see anything, she was a victim. The asshole blackmailed her, abused her, and forced her to perform. If she hadn't ran when she did, he would have had her turning tricks."

"We know all of that," Grimes waved his hand dismissively. "Miss Alexander is of interest to the media, not to us. Your story has been all over the news, but it was a distraction to us, nothing more. Cahill has been arrested, and now thanks to you, we have a man who is willing to give us information on the murder in exchange for a reduced sentence. Romero and his whole organization is going down."

"Good," at the moment, Lucas didn't care. "When can I get out of here?"

After what seemed like hours, he was a free man. But with his freedom, came no relief. Dandi was nowhere. She wasn't at the house, she wasn't at the hotel, she wasn't at the courthouse – all he could do was stand on the sidewalk and bellow his frustration. He didn't know what to do – literally, he didn't know what to do. Trying to get a handle on his nerves, he went to a coffee shop and started checking hotels and motels – one by one. He called every restaurant she had mentioned, even the shelters – but nothing. Dandi was gone.

When he returned to Pine Ridge, it was an empty lonely place. Lucas recalled her saying that it would be as if she had never been there. Even though he knew she was gone, he went from room to room – seeing her – remembering. And when he found the sketch she had made for him, he broke down and cried.

* * * * *

Dandi stared out the bus window at the passing scenery without really seeing anything. Her arms were empty, her hands were shaking and her heart felt like it had been crushed between two rocks. Had she done the right thing? Would he be happier without her? Maybe she ought to call him, just to let him know she was all right. She had his cell phone number; she could go to a pay phone and place a call. Yea, that's what she would do.

As the bus moved up the ramp to cross over I-20, a semi came out of nowhere and hit the bus broadside. CRASH! Dandi was thrown out of her seat. People were yelling and metal was screeching. The bus lurched to one side and Dandi tried to grab hold of – anything. The last thing she heard was her own terror filled scream as the bus plunged headfirst off the side of the overpass.

* * * * *

"Miss? Miss?" A light shining directly in her eyes made Dandi cringe. It hurt.

"What?" Where was she?

"Do you know your name?"

"Yes," she groaned. "It's Dandi, Dandi Alexander." Dandi LeBlanc was more correct, and as soon as she got enough money together to change her name, she would.

"What year is it? Who is President?" Dandi tried to think. "Barack Obama."

"Very good. And the year?"

"Uh," God, her head was throbbing. "The year is 2009."

"What month is it?" The doctor sounded concerned.

"Uh, I don't know. October?" She shook her head, something wasn't right.

"No, it's Valentine's Day, 2010."

"What? I don't understand." A wave of panic swept over her. What was going on? What had happened? Heck, she couldn't remember.

"Do you know why you're here?"

"No," she stared at the kind faced man in the white coat. "I don't have any idea."

"You're in the hospital. There was a bus crash. We've done some preliminary testing, there doesn't seem to be anything wrong with you, other than a gash on your head, a slight concussion and some memory loss." The doctor looked at a bump on her head. He laughed a little, "That sounded like a lot wrong with you, didn't it. Actually, you are very lucky. It could have been much worse. Several people died. Is there anyone we can call for you?"

Dandi knew the answer to that question. "No, there's no one." A sense of loss that had nothing to do with the past haunted her mind. "Do I have stitches?" She felt of her head, there was a thick bandage over her right eye.

The doctor stepped back and looked at her, steadily. "Yes, you have eight stiches. Look, I'm going to call in a specialist. Your memory loss worries me more than anything. What I'm about to tell you may come as a surprise, or it might jog your memory." He paused, as if for effect. "The baby is fine."

Dandi didn't say a word. She just looked at the doctor blankly.

"Did you understand me? You're pregnant."

Dandi shook her head. "No, I'm a virgin."

"No," the doctor patted her knee. "You're going to be a mother. Do you know who the father is?"

Dandi felt nauseous. She let out a shaky breath. "I don't have a clue."

*****

"How are you feeling, Sweetie?" The older nurse tucked the covers up around her. "Can I get you anything? Do you want some Jell-O?"

"No, I'm not hungry." Dandi's hands were shaking. She didn't know what she was going to do. How was she going to support her baby? "I'm thirsty, though."

The nurse handed her some water. "Here drink this."

She tried, but a sudden pain in her stomach caused her to jerk, spilling water everywhere.

"What's wrong?"

"I hurt," Dandi was scared. "What if it's the baby? What if something's wrong?"

The nurse leaned over her and pressed the call button. "I need help in 201," she called out. As she passed near to Dandi's face, she stopped and sniffed. "Your breath smells fruity. Are you a diabetic?"

"No," Dandi cried. But then, what did she know? She hadn't even known she was pregnant. "I don't know," she confessed. "I'm lost."

"I'll be right back." She left and returned with two others and a lab kit. "Give me your finger." She held Dandi's hand and took some blood. In a few minutes, they had ascertained she might be diabetic. "Here suck on this candy," the nurse handed her a peppermint. "We'll get this blood work processed as quickly as possible."

One of the nurses pushed her damp hair off her forehead. "Poor girl. Would you like something to read or the TV on?"

"I like to read," she admitted. Lying back, she took deep breaths trying to calm down. Dandi felt like everything was out of control. She had no money, no insurance, no family and she had lost part of her life.

"Let me get you something," the nurse left and was gone for a few minutes. When she returned she had some magazines. "I picked up some of everything."

"Good, thanks," she held them to her chest, wishing she had someone's hand to hold.

"You rest and we'll be back as soon as we know what to do for you."

"Thanks." Dandi closed her eyes and let the sugar get into her system. Finally, she felt a little better, so she thumbed through the magazines. There was a cooking one, a gossip rag and one about guns. She flipped through the more feminine ones first, but then she picked the other one up and the cover photo caught her eye. "Beau!" Dandi couldn't believe it. Her first cousin Beau LeBlanc was on the cover. Quickly, she leafed through till she found the article on Firepower Munitions. Apparently, Beau had done well for himself. She scanned the page until she found a number. Reaching for the phone, Dandi prayed someone would answer. For the first time since she had opened her eyes in the hospital, she felt hope.

One ring. Two rings.

"Firepower Munitions. May I help you?"

"Could I speak to Beau LeBlanc?"

"Speaking."

His voice had changed so much, he didn't sound like himself. Oh well, she had to try. "Beau, this is Dandi. Your cousin, Dandi." She began to cry. "I'm in trouble. I need help."

"Tell me where you are. I'll be right there."

CHAPTER ELEVEN

THREE YEARS LATER

Lucas Dane Wagner rubbed his eyes. It had been a long day. "Joyce, could you come in here, please?"

"Yes, Doctor." In a bit, the boss of his domain swept in, all two hundred and fifty pounds of her. His secretary ruled the roost, he just worked there. "I brought you a muffin, you missed lunch," she looked at him accusingly.

The Touch Institute was an undeniable success. Dane had all the work he could handle. "Am I through for the day?"

"No," she pulled up a chair and joined him. "You have a 'low libido' in ten minutes."

"Joyce, I told you not to refer to the patients by their condition. That could be construed as unfeeling." He knew that wasn't the case, Joyce was everyone's grandmother.

"Very well," she didn't let his suggestion phase her. "I have the report from the PI, too." She laid a file on his desk and patted it, a sad smile on her face.

"Nothing?"

"No, nothing."

"Hell!" He got up and stalked across the room. "Maybe I should get a new firm to help me."

"Maybe you should get on with your life."

The flat harsh words coming from the soft little woman almost caused him to reel backwards. "Never." His answer was short, hard and emphatic.

"You can't spend the rest of your life hunting someone who doesn't want to be found."

"I don't believe that." Lucas stared out at Jefferson Street in downtown Lafayette. "I will find her, I have to." In the three years since Dandi had walked away from him, Lucas had not missed one day praying for her. He had not missed one day looking for her. He had not missed one day longing for her. Oh, he had tried to move on – but his heart wouldn't let him. When his body demanded sex, he dealt with it alone, like he dealt with most other things. He didn't want another woman. He only wanted Dandi.

"I wish you'd talk to someone about this," Joyce urged. "You know the value of therapy and you need therapy."

The bell over the front door sounded.

"You need to see to the front desk," he pointed to the door, not wanting to hear her logical argument. "The 'low libido' is here."

She gave him a sweet smile and went to take care of business. Lucas sat down and arranged his papers, reviewing the patient's history. Sylvester Booth was married, but he and his wife had not enjoyed sexual relations in almost three years. The first thing he had done was rule out any medical issues. He had Sylvester checked out until he could make sure that low testosterone or prostate trouble was not a factor. Apparently, he was as healthy as a horse, so today they would proceed to the next step. Later, he would interview the wife, but today it would just be the men.

"Dane, Mr. Booth is here," Joyce gave him a sly smile.

"Thanks," a slightly overweight man came into the room. He was balding and looked extremely uncomfortable, but he was there.

"Come in, Sylvester. Have a seat."

"All right." He sat and straightened his pants, then straightened them again.

"How long have you and Candace been married?"

"Twelve years," this information was given with a sigh.

"Do you still love her?"

"Yes," when he answered he did so with raised chin, as if he was offended at the question.

"Does she still turn you on?"

Sylvester looked surprised at the question. He didn't answer right away. When he did, he looked over Lucas's head instead of right at him. "She doesn't try."

"What do you mean?"

"She's let herself go."

Lucas hid a smile, the wife wasn't the only one who had let herself go, but now wasn't the time to deflate his ego. "How so?"

"She's gained a few pounds, she doesn't wear any make-up unless we're going out and the clothes she wears aren't sexy."

"So, if she fixed herself up, would you want to have sex with her again?"

The man leaned over and put his head in his hands. "I don't know."

"Do you want to divorce your wife?"

"No!" again Sylvester answered adamantly.

"How old are you?"

"Forty-two."

"Have you ever cheated on your wife?"

"Shit. Once."

"Only once?"

"Yea, the guilt got the best of me."

"Okay, so you've had sex once in three years. Right?"

"Hell. Right."

"Are you ready to be celibate for the rest of your life?"

"God, no. I miss sex."

"Fine. That's what I needed to know."

"So, what's the next step?"

Lucas made some notes. "I want to have a session with your wife and ascertain how she feels about these same issues. After that, we'll all sit down and have a conversation. How does that sound?"

"Good, I guess." Mr. Booth looked embarrassed. "Is this normal?"

"Much more normal than you would think." He stood and walked around to shake the man's hand. "I can help you, Sylvester. If you and your wife will follow my advice, you'll be enjoying the marital bed again very soon."

Joyce made cards for the next two appointments. Lucas returned to his desk to get his coat. Going home wasn't the most appealing idea, but he didn't feel like going out tonight. Maybe he'd go by the stables and check on the horses. "Joyce, I think I'll drive out to the tracks."

"Wait, you've got a phone call."

"Who is it?"

"Beau LeBlanc, Line 2."

A smile lit up his face as he picked up the phone. "Beau, how are you? How's Harley?"

"Excellent, Dane. How are you?"

The Cajun's deep voice was a welcome sound. He had grown fond of the couple. "I'm good. What can I do for you?" He didn't think they needed his professional services, but he wasn't going to assume.

"I'm calling to invite you to a party. Harley and I are engaged. We want you to celebrate with us."

"Ha! Excellent! I'd love, too." This couple would have made it, either way, but he liked to think his therapy had played a role in their happiness.

"Great, bring a date if you'd like, Dane."

"I don't date. Look, my friends call me Lucas. I go by Dane because of the other Dr. Lucas Wagner who practices in town."

"Okay, Lucas. I can do that. You don't date? Lord, you sound like my cousin. She's a beautiful woman, but she has closed herself off to all possibility of a relationship."

"Really? Has she had some type of a traumatic event in her life?"

Beau hesitated. "Maybe. I've been thinking about suggesting she come see you."

"I'd be honored to help you both. What's your cousin's name?"

"Dandi."

Lucas dropped the phone.

*****

Beau LeBlanc surveyed his domain. Today, he celebrated his engagement to Harley Montoya. He was surrounded by family and friends. Life was good. "Look at that gator!" a woman squealed. Beau laughed. Indy had brought a new woman into the fold.

"Relax, Pamela, Amos Moses is toothless."

His friend and co-worker didn't have the best taste in women. This one was a radio news woman, but she looked a little high strung to Beau. Not like his Harley. He let his gaze stray across the yard until he found her – ah, there she was. The most beautiful woman in the world – she was exquisite. The bravest woman in the world – she was the premier bomb tech in the south. And the smartest woman in the world – she was with him, after all.

"Ragin' Cajun, how's it hangin?"

He looked over his shoulder. "Joseph McCoy, good to see you, Man." He stood up and hugged his best friend. "Where's our Cady?"

"She's talking to Dandi. How do you feel?"

"I feel great, you?" Since Harley had turned over the day to day operations to Waco, he could breathe easier. Just knowing his fiancé wouldn't be called in to diffuse a bomb, did wonders for his ability to sleep at night.

"My life is as good as it gets," his eyes moved to Cady. "I have two babies on the way and the love of an angel."

"How's the rest of the McCoy clan?" He had seen them just a few days before when he and Harley had attended Libby and Aron's wedding.

"Good, Aron and Libby left on their honeymoon and the rest of us are holding down the fort," the two men overlooked the looks of lust they were receiving from the single women at the party. They were taken. "Not much has happened since we saw you at the wedding a few days ago except I saw something on the internet that I think you should see." Joseph looked serious.

"What do you mean?"

"It's about Dandi." Joseph looked over to where his Cady was talking animatedly with Beau's cousin.

Beau looked too. The women in question were such a contrast, both beautiful in their own way; Cady possessed an ethereal beauty while Dandi seemed to take pleasure in trying to give off a tomboyish air. She failed miserably, but no one had the heart to tell her. Dressed all in black leather, she thought she looked tough, instead she looked fragile. "What about Dandi?" he growled a little. Dandi had been through a lot. He was protective.

"Here, let me show you." Joseph motioned for him to move away from the rest of the crowd. They stood next to the still waters of the bayou.

His friend held out his phone. "It's a video of an exotic dancer called Angel Baby."

Beau frowned and took the phone. "What has that got to do with Dandi?" He only had to watch a few frames to realize what he was seeing – this was Dandi. "My God."

"You told me she had some memory loss."

"Yea, she lost this, apparently."

"I can't say I blame her." He took his phone back. "I remember a little bit about the scandal, it had to do with a murder investigation, but I don't watch too much television. Besides, I have a special dislike for investigative reporters."

"I remember, that Warner girl did a number on you, didn't she?"

Joseph grimaced in memory. "Yes, she did."

Beau looked over at his younger cousin. "I'm not telling her about this, she may have blocked it for some reason. The human mind has ways of protecting itself. Right now, she's safe and happy. She'll remember on her own when the time is right."

"I agree, but I wanted you to know."

"Not everybody would recognize her, she looks different," Beau crossed his arms over his chest. "It's as if she wanted to change."

"Her hair's shorter, and she works hard at pushing people away."

"Men, she works hard at pushing men away." He provided a safe haven for Dandi, and a strong arm if she needed it. "Of course, we know she didn't push one away."

"Lucy." Joseph named Dandi's little girl. "McCoy's produce male babies; thank goodness. I'd hate to think I had to raise a little girl."

"I may have found her some help," he pointed at a man who was walking across the lawn. "I'll have to introduce you to Dane."

"Joseph!"

"Excuse me, Beau. I'm being paged." Cady was motioning him to come and dance with her.

"I'm just glad you can dance." Both of them thought back to the time when Joseph had been paralyzed. "Will you sing for us before you go?"

Joseph hesitated, then threw up his hands. "Hell, yeah, I guess so. Make sure you find me a guitar, I don't like to sing without music."

A gentle kiss on his cheek almost brought Beau to his knees. "Hey, Darlin'," he pulled Harley close. "How's the pig coming?" They were roasting a whole pig in a pit in the ground and the aroma was out of this world.

"Almost done. What was that all about?"

"Dandi, I'll tell you later. Look who's coming?" He nodded his head toward the parking area.

"Waco!" She took off at a dead run.

"That's right – run after another man!" He yelled and chuckled. As far as he was concerned, Waco had saved his life. He had taken on Socorro, freeing up Harley to marry and have his babies. He owed Waco – big time. Scanning the crowd, Beau looked at the people he loved. Everybody from Firepower Munitions had arrived. Dandi's girlfriends, Deb and Cindi – the Wild Bunch, as he called them had arrived. Joseph and Cady were here as well as a few other friends that he wouldn't trade for love or money. Only Savannah was missing, but she was busy with Patrick and all was well.

Finally, his eyes settled on Dane/Lucas who was standing on the periphery of the party like a child peeking in the window of the candy store. "Come on over, Dane. Don't be a stranger."

Dandi looked up when Beau yelled and her eyes gravitated to the man he was talking to. Wow! What a man! Not that she was in the market for one, but if she ever did – this would be the type of man she would want. Ripples of excitement coursed through her body as she looked at him. He was big and blonde and built like a Viking. But he wore sunglasses, so she had no way of knowing if he was seeing her or not.

Covertly, she stole glances at him. So, this was Dr. Dane Wagner. Dandi didn't have to be told because he was the only one invited that she did not already know. The man was definitely out of her league. Not that it mattered; she wasn't cut out for men and relationships. Dandi knew that. She wasn't sure how she knew it, but she did.

Since coming to live with Beau, Dandi had struggled with the missing chunk of time. What all had transpired during those missing months, she didn't know. Something big had happened, something she didn't really want to remember. What she did know was momentous enough. She had developed diabetes and gotten pregnant. Night after night, she had lain in bed and tried to recall the face of Lucy's father. But she couldn't. She couldn't even remember the bus crash that had stolen her memory. Whatever had happened, she had been given a gift – her Lucy. She wouldn't trade Lucy for anything.

"Wow, would you look at him?" Cindi elbowed Dandi. "God, he's scrumptious."

"Damn, he's fine." Deb pushed both of them out of the way to get a better view.

"Do you mind?" Dandi laughed. "He's not on the menu, so you can quit drooling over him like a T-Bone steak."

"Who is he?" Cindi asked, her brown eyes twinkling.

"I think that's a friend of Harley and Beau's, a doctor."

Cindi placed the back of her hand on her forehead. "Call him over, I feel faint."

"Will not. Stop it." Dandi whispered out the side of her mouth. "Let's try to be dignified."

"We'll try to be dignified," Deb giggled. "If you'll try to remember you're a woman."

*****

Lucas stood his ground. It was her. He forced himself to stand still. God, he was shaking. It was Dandi. His Dandi. The woman he had been searching for every day for the last three years. Every cell of his body ached to hold her again.

She looked at him.

He stopped breathing.

He halfway expected her to run toward him – arms outstretched. And if she had, he would have caught her and welcomed her home.

But her gaze slid over him, entirely too easily.

Was she planning on ignoring him? Damn! He had rehearsed this day a thousand times in his mind. Lucas had a speech all rehearsed, but now he couldn't think of the first word.

Did she not see him? Maybe she was embarrassed. Yea, that had to be it. Didn't she realize they could work through anything? Didn't she know he would move heaven and earth to be with her?

No, apparently she didn't. From where he was standing, she was paying no more attention to him than if he were a bug in the grass.

Dandi poured glass after glass of iced tea. "You two could help, you know?" Grumbling they began to pitch in. Deb and Cindi had become her best friends. Lucy was her life, but these two had given her companionship. They had made it their mission in life to make her laugh and smile as much as possible.

"Hey, Dandi," Rick held out his glass. "Could I have a refill?"

"Sure," she poured the amber liquid, loving the sound of the clinking cubes against the crystal. "Did you finish rebuilding that zombie gun?"

"I did, I sure would like to show you how it turned out. How about going back over to the shop with me after the party?"

Dandi laughed. "It's a Wednesday night, Rick. We work together tomorrow. Won't that be soon enough?"

Rick's face fell. "Yea, I guess so." He moved on, taking his tea glass with him.

"How can you be so cruel?" Deb chided her. "The guy is smitten with you. And he's cute in an Ashton Kutcher kinda way. Why won't you go out with him?"

"I don't date," Dandi explained for the millionth time.

"She doesn't date," Cindi spread her arms out wide, giving Deb a gesture of resignation. "You don't even know why you don't date, do you?" Deb asked. The beer in her hand was giving her extra courage.

Dandi tugged at the hem of her short, sleeveless leather vest. She was glad Lucy was at a play-day, she didn't want her to see her Mom lose her cool. "I do know why I don't date, Miss Buttinsky. I don't have anything to offer a relationship, that's why."

"I beg to differ."

Dandi froze. That voice! It was a deep, husky, commanding voice. She was afraid if that voice told her to jump, she'd just ask – 'How high?' "What?" She turned around to look at the bigger-than-life hunk who was standing over her like the mountain who had come to Mohammed.

"I've been looking for you."

"Oh, you must be thirsty. Let me get you some tea." Her hand shook as she poured it and held it out to him. "I'm glad you could come for Beau and Harley. I hope you have a good time."

"No, I don't want tea." Lucas didn't know whether to be angry at her, or go to his knees at her feet. "I'm just thankful I found you."

"Why don't you go with this nice man and get a plate of food, Dandi." Cindi took the iced tea pitcher away from her and gave her a nudge in the man's direction.

"No, thanks," Dandi stood her ground. "He's thirsty, not looking for a dinner companion," she smiled at her friend with a hint of warning. "How about lemonade instead?" She reached for another beverage.

"Are you going to pretend you don't know who I am?"

"Oh, I know who you are." She gave him a sweet smile. "You're the doctor who helped Beau and Harley."

"Is this a game, Dandi?"

Deb and Cindi froze beside her. Dandi didn't know what he meant. "No, I don't play games," she answered coolly. Then she felt guilty. He wasn't speaking personally, she must have misunderstood. "If you're interested, we are going to be having some target practice after the meal. You know us, any excuse to shoot a gun." Her body was drawn to his; she could feel the pull like a giant magnet. Dandi had to fight the impulse; it would have been the most natural thing in the world to move into his arms.

To her surprise, he reached across the table and touched her face. "Are you telling me that you don't remember me?"

His touch made her tremble. "No, sorry." She wished she could say otherwise. Could this be someone from her past? She guessed it could be possible, but forgetting this man seemed unlikely. "You must be confusing me with someone else. I have one of those ordinary faces."

Lucas looked like he was about to argue, but he let his hand drop.

"Dandi! Where is that pot of BBQ sauce you made? I can't seem to find it." Harley was calling her from the backdoor of the house.

"Excuse me, it was nice meeting you." She made her escape, leaving her two dumb-founded friends standing in front of the most compelling man she had ever met. Was it possible she knew him? As she had so often done, she probed her memory – but the hazy images of leering faces and snarling voices only made her push the thoughts away. No, he wasn't a part of that pain.

Lucas was stunned. What was going on? His whole body was in turmoil – his heart was pounding and his gut was clenched up as tight as a drum. Unable to do anything else at the moment, he stepped back into the crowd and bided his time. Willowbend was a beautiful place. The house was a typical antebellum home with the wide verandah and graceful white columns. A rolling green lawn filled with crepe myrtles, stately oak trees and azaleas spread out to the banks of Bayou Teche. Beau's toothless alligator basked on a sundappled log. He didn't know anyone but Beau and Harley – and Dandi. So, Lucas decided to mingle. Maybe he could find out what was going on.

*****

Dandi played hostess. She dished up salads and carved meats. She brought out loaf after loaf of buttered French bread. She cut cakes and sliced pies. Anyone who needed help, she did her best to aid them and make them feel welcome.

"You look familiar to me." Pamela Morrisey stared at her from over a plate of BBQ.

"You're the second person who mentioned that to me today."

"Hmmmm, it will come to me, I never turn loose of an idea. When something puzzles me, I'll dig at it until I figure it out."

Dandi nodded at the woman, politely. "Okay, well if I can help, let me know." After what seemed like forever, she was able to get her own plate and settle down. Beau and Harley stepped up in front of everyone and thanked them for coming. She was so happy for them. No one deserved the good life more than they did. Next, Joseph McCoy sang a song, 'She Cranks My Tractor' and many people got up to dance.

"May I join you?"

It was Dr. Wagner.

"Of course," she sat up a little straighter as he took the seat next to hers. They needed bigger chairs; he dwarfed the one he was sitting in.

Dandi was so aware of him; her appetite left her high and dry. She laid down her fork. Looking around, she sought out Deb and Cindi for moral support, but they were nowhere to be found.

"So, tell me about yourself, Dandi." Lucas managed to keep his voice on an even keel. He couldn't stop looking at her – she was the same, yet she wasn't. Her hair was a lot shorter; it just danced on the tops of her shoulders now. Her body was the same sweet luscious curves, but she held herself more aloof now. And what was with the all-black? Dandi looked like a fairy queen masquerading as a biker chick.

"Oh my, there's not much to tell." She shifted in her seat and cleared her throat. "I help out at Beau's, as you know. I've learned a lot about guns and cars. The guys are good to me."

Lucas felt his hackles rise. He wanted to be the one who was good to her. "You are easy to be good to, I'm sure."

"I'm even rebuilding a motorcycle. Can you imagine that?" she grinned at him mischievously.

Actually, no – he couldn't. "It's hard to imagine you with a streak of motor oil on that cute upturned nose. And I see no hint of grease under these fingernails."

He took her hand and Dandi felt a warm sizzle travel up her arm all the way to her nipples. "It's a Sportster."

"An 883 or a 1288?" Lucas was still baffled about how she was acting. If she was faking not knowing him, it was a class act.

She was impressed. "An 883."

"What else?" He wanted to know everything. He was so hungry for information about her – hell, he was hungry for her. Period.

"I paint and sketch."

"That's wonderful. Do you dance?"

"I used to when I was younger, but not in a long time."

He watched her face; there wasn't a hint of subterfuge. "That's a shame, I bet you dance beautifully."

"I don't seem to want to anymore. I guess our focus changes." She played with her potato salad. "I'm getting a degree. I only have another semester to go."

A thrill shot through Lucas. He was so proud. "What will your degree be in?"

"Archaeology and Anthropology from LSU, I'm focusing on Native American studies and specific Louisiana history and culture."

And he was missing all of this; a pang of longing almost split his chest in two.

Several people were milling around the dessert table. "Excuse me, I better see to the coffee. Thank you for talking to me. I enjoyed it very much."

Lucas didn't want her to leave. "I enjoyed learning more about you."

"Me too," she was about to walk off. "Oh, and the most important thing," she placed a delicate hand on her chest. "I have a beautiful daughter."

Lucas almost bit his tongue. "You have a child? How wonderful! How old?"

"She's almost three."

CHAPTER TWELVE

Lucas watched her every move. She still had that cute little walk, where when she stopped, she'd bounce in place. He knew it was a way she dealt with nervousness. Hell, he hoped it was him that made her quiver and wiggle. How was he supposed to leave her today? Just the thought that she could have borne his child made him want to hoist her over his shoulder and take her home with him.

When everyone walked down to the shooting range, he followed. Beau had a major set up here. Firepower Munitions built custom guns and had many government and private contracts to upgrade or perfect gun designs. All of his employees were crack shots. But the sight of his Dandi holding a rifle almost did him in. Trying to be casual, he wandered up to stand next to her.

"Hey, Dane. I'm glad you decided to join us." Actually, she had been looking for him. Despite her stance to keep herself out of the romantic fray, just standing near to him made her wet.

"I couldn't stay away from you." He said the words as casually as if he had commented on the weather.

Hitting any target would be difficult today, her hands were shaking. "Well, here." She handed him a gun. "Let's see if you're any good."

"I'm good at lots of things." To his disappointment, she didn't even react to his flirting.

"Excellent, you can be on my team. Maybe we'll win."

Damn, he had gone hunting, but shooting at a bull's eye from half a world away was something altogether different. "Hmmm, I'll give it a shot." He smiled at his own pun.

"Good one," she said dryly. "You first."

Before he took aim, he glanced over at Beau and the McCoy man who were shooting very well, almost as good as Beau's fiancé, but she was ex-Navy Special Ops. Lucas chuckled, that just blew his mind. Harley was so feminine and beautiful; it was hard to imagine how capable she was. At another target Indy, Rick and Waco were making great headway. The other women were watching from the sidelines, but Dandi seemed as much at home with a gun as Harley did.

Taking aim, he prayed he wouldn't miss the target entirely. Slowly, he pulled the trigger. Crack! He squinted at the target, then breathed a sigh of relief. It wasn't a bull's eye, but at least he hadn't disgraced himself.

"My turn," she felt in her back pocket and took out a barrette – pulled her hair up and put it in a high pony tail. The familiar little phoenix that he had kissed so often came into view.

"Nice tat."

She jerked a bit, turning to look at him. He wondered if what he said sounded familiar. He had said it before.

"Thank you." She pushed her bangs out of her eyes. "It's a little warm out here, isn't it?"

When she moved a lock of her dark hair a scar came into view on her forehead. "What happened?" He couldn't have kept his hands off her if he tried. Lucas ran a gentle thumb over the raised scar. "What hurt you?"

"I was in a bus crash on the Valentine's Day before Lucy was born." Taking aim, she shot twice in quick succession. Both of them were very near the bull's eye. "I got this," she rubbed the scar, "and I lost about six months of my life."

"What do you mean?" he almost took her in his arms. "What did you lose? Lucy was okay. Were you in the hospital for six months?" The name wasn't lost on him. He hoped, subconsciously, she had named the baby after him. God, he didn't even know if the baby was his, maybe he was putting the cart before the horse. No, that wasn't true, he knew Lucy was his. Dandi loved him. She hadn't slept with anyone else. Still, he ached to see the child.

"I lost time. I lost my memory. I don't remember anything that happened in the months before the bus crash."

Lucas almost staggered under the weight of what had happened. She didn't remember him, it wasn't a game. "You could have been killed," his words came out in a harsh whisper. "What happened?"

"They said an eighteen wheeler hit us broadside at a stoplight on an overpass. At the angle it hit the bus, both vehicles crashed and fell off the overpass. Several people were killed. I was tossed around, but I was lucky."

Lucas paced about three or four feet away, then came back. She probably thought he was crazy, and maybe he was. "You don't remember anything that happened before the crash? Why were you on the bus? Where had you been?"

Dandi didn't understand. "I don't know. All of that information is gone, Dane. It's like smoke that drifted away on an evening breeze."

"Don't call me, Dane. Call me Lucas." He had to hear her say his name. Oh, his excuse to use his middle name was a viable one. There was another Dr. Lucas Wagner, but he was a General Practitioner. The real reason was that it had been almost impossible for him to hear others say his name, when all he could hear was her voice. For weeks, every time he had shut his eyes, he could hear her say, 'Lucas, my Lucas.'

"Lucas?" she tested the sound. A flash of something illuminated her mind. Lucas. It sounded familiar. "Why not Dane?"

"My friends call my Lucas, Dane is my middle name." All of that was true.

"Okay," she smiled. "Lucas fits you much better." To his delight, she pushed his hair out of his face, caressing his cheek as she did so. "You have beautiful hair. I like blonde hair."

"Can I see you again?" The others were still doing their target practice, but they were lost in their own world, and there was no where he'd rather be.

"Thank you, but no."

His heart sank.

"I don't date."

Lucas pressed her. "But why? You are a delectable woman and I want to spend as much time with you as possible."

She shook her head. "I can't really explain it, there's just something holding me back. I don't want to date."

"Are you afraid of men?" He wanted to ask. 'Are you afraid of me?' but he didn't. "I could help you if you'd let me."

Dandi shook her head and smiled. "No, I don't really want you psychoanalyzing me. I'm busy with school and Lucy and work. I don't have time for men. But I do appreciate you inviting me."

Lucas refused to give up, it was just too important. "It's not right, Dandi. A woman like you shouldn't be alone."

"Ha! I think I'd be more trouble than I'm worth." At his puzzled expression, Dandi tried to explain. "My mom always cautioned me. She said, 'Dandi, never be more trouble than your worth, if you are, people will be sorry they wasted their time with you.'"

Lucas just stared at her. He could remember holding her body as she came. He could remember taking her sweet gasps into his mouth as he kissed her, how it felt to be buried deep inside of her. She might be trouble, but it was trouble of the very best kind. "Foot," was all he could think to say. "That's ridiculous. I wouldn't believe that unless I read it on the front page of the Times Picayune."

Dandi burst out laughing. "Hey, I say that. My Dad used to say it all the time." She looked at him. Time seemed frozen. An odd sense of déjà vu swamped her senses. "I like you, Lucas."

Thank God. "I like you, too, Dandi."

"We're playing paintball tomorrow, if you'd like to come. It's a group activity, but you're welcome."

Paintball? He'd never played, but that wouldn't stop him. Her presence was the only incentive he required. "I'll be here."

*****

At home, Lucas lay in his bed and shook with need. He relived every moment they had spent together. Just seeing her today, being near to her was paradise. There was so much he needed to think about, but his erection was enormous and he needed relief. For the first time in a long time he had hope. Closing his eyes, he imagined kissing her lips, nuzzling his face between her breasts, sinking balls deep inside of her sweet heat. "God!" Taking his cock in hand he stroked his own flesh in a hard fist. "Dandi, my Dandi!" He wanted to wrap himself around her, bury his head between her thighs, take her higher and harder than any man had ever taken a woman. "I love you!" he shouted to the empty room as he pumped his cock, his hips lifting from the bed in supplication. Lucas's whole body went tense as he threw his head back and roared loud enough to be heard in the next county. Hot jets of cum arched up and fell on the skin of his belly and thighs. "Please God, let her love me back, let her remember me." Grabbing a towel from the bedside table, he wiped himself clean, rolled over and clasped the pillow to his face. He was tired of being alone.

The next morning, Lucas had two priorities. First he had to see to his will. He had responsibilities, he had a child. And he wanted no possibility that Dandi and Lucy wouldn't be taken care of if something happened to him. His lawyer tried to give him a hard time, asked if he wanted to have a paternity test. Hell, he hadn't even seen his baby, but he didn't have to. He was a father; he knew it as well as he knew his own name.

Second, he had to learn how to play paintball. After checking it out on the internet, he concluded that it was simple warfare, except he'd be armed with a gun that shot water soluble dye. Knowing Beau and Firepower Munitions, they would have a world class game field and take their play very, very seriously.

Taking a break between patients, he drove to the sports shop and bought everything he'd need. If Dandi wouldn't come to him, he'd go to her – anywhere, anytime. As he drove back to the Touch Institute, he let it sink into his mind, body and soul that he had found Dandi. She was safe and – thank God – she was still single. He had his work cut out for him, for he had to win her love for the second time around.

His afternoon appointment was one he dreaded. Kevin Young was being a first class bastard to his wife. But at least he was seeking help. Sandra Young was pregnant – for the fourth time. Plus, she was on the pill. At first Kevin had accused her of infidelity, but she had gone along with his demand and had a paternity test. After verifying that the child was his, he started on her about failing to take her birth control regularly. The poor wife was at her wit's end and Lucas was tempted to tell Sandra she'd be better off without the scoundrel. But she wouldn't – not really, they had 3 other children and if he could counsel Kevin and his young wife, maybe he could save their family.

Joyce buzzed him when they arrived. As much as he tried, Lucas had a hard time keeping his mind on business. Just the knowledge that he would see Dandi that afternoon had him as jacked up as a teenager. He couldn't quit smiling to save his life, and he didn't want to give his patients the idea that he was enjoying their trouble.

"I went to the Doctor, Kevin. He said it wasn't my fault." Sandra wailed.

"Of course it wasn't your fault." Lucas interjected. "It takes two to make a baby." Lucy. He had a child. Her name was Lucy. He couldn't get the thought out of his head.

"We didn't need another child. And birth control is your responsibility." The man was getting red faced.

"Do you want me to have an abortion?"

The stark question shocked both Lucas and the husband. Lucas didn't speak. He waited to see what Kevin would say.

"No," he hung his head. "No, I don't want you to have an abortion." He looked up at Lucas. "I love my kids. It just makes me angry that we didn't get a chance to plan. The doctor should have told us that those antibiotics negated the birth control pill."

Lucas almost fell off his chair. Bam! Dandi had been on antibiotics when they were having sex. No wonder.

"Can't you love this baby?" Sandra asked as she wiped the tears from her eyes. "It won't be her fault we didn't want her?"

"Stop," Lucas had to stop them. "Think about this. You have a precious child on the way. Five years from now, hell, a year from now when you look into her face, this will seem absolutely ludicrous. You will be holding and loving your daughter and whether or not you had followed a schedule or set the date for her birth will be meaningless. Think of the children you have, could you imagine life without them?" He had raised his voice, but all he could see was Dandi's face and imagine what their child looked like. Did she look like him or her? Or was she a little diplomat who displayed both of their characteristics? What if Dandi hadn't taken the antibiotics? What if he hadn't went to the club? What if? What if? God, he was going crazy thinking what might have been.

"You're right." Kevin stood up and knelt by his wife. "I'm sorry. We'll make it somehow." He leaned up and kissed her.

Lucas leaned back and ran his hand through his hair. His outburst had not been normal therapy. He owed them an apology. "Look, I'm sorry. I shouldn't have raised my voice. Both of you have legitimate concerns that we need to work . . ."

Kevin and Sandra were kissing. "Huh." Lucas smiled.

After he had seen them out, he came to a decision. Lucas needed to talk to somebody. And he might end up getting his ass kicked, but Beau LeBlanc was the obvious conclusion.

Confession time.

*****

She couldn't get him off her mind. Lucas Wagner. Dandi stared into the mirror for long minutes trying to picture them together. She couldn't. Was it possible that a man like him could want her? Since coming to live with Beau and giving birth to Lucy, she had pushed her past out of her mind. Arlon and Sam were a distant memory. Her days on the street and working at fast food jobs seemed like someone else's life. Even the happy days she had spent with Miss Etta didn't seem quite real. It was like a fog had settled over her former life and only now – today – was important.

"AHHHH!" she let out a little yell, not loud enough to wake her baby, but loud enough to echo in the small bathroom. Her tiny apartment was located in the back of Firepower Munitions warehouse. Beau had built her and Lucy a thousand square foot sanctuary of their very own. Harley had helped her decorate and Rick and Indy made sure she had everything she needed. Between her family, her coworkers and her friends, Dandi's life was full.

Almost.

She could remember her youthful dreams. She could remember wanting someone to hold and love. Life had thrown her a curve when her mom had died, a blow she had never fully recovered from. And since the bus crash, she had known – without a shadow of a doubt – that there was some barrier standing between her and love. It was an oppressive feeling, a certainty that she couldn't shake or substantiate. The worst part was that she was afraid to analyze it very closely. Whatever the root of her fear was, it was a reality she wasn't ready to face.

Dandi put on a load of laundry and did the dishes. Lucy was already in bed and as she put up her toys, she couldn't help but steal kisses and marvel at her blessings. Who was Lucy's father? She didn't know, but she was thankful for him. He had given her a great gift.

Ding! Her front door bell pealed. Putting the last stuffed toy in the storage box, she padded barefoot to see who was there. Standing on tiptoe to look through the peephole, she saw it was Deb. Dandi breathed a sigh of relief. Deb Schultz was a lifesaver. Throwing up the door, she hugged her friend. "Hey, Deb."

They were so much alike, it was scary. Oh, not physically. Deb had beautiful blonde hair and dark brown eyes. But like Dandi, she was a tomboy. She loved sports as much as Dandi did, a fact that she attributed to her brothers – two of which were professional water skiers with a huge water park. It wasn't all fun and games, Deb had lost a sister to a violent crime and she devoted a great deal of her life to organizations that supported the families of victims. Dandi loved Deb.

"Hey, Girl. Do you have anything to eat? I'm starving."

"Always." Dandi loved to cook, so she led her friend to the kitchen and warmed up her a bowl of jambalaya.

"Oh, yum, thanks," the blonde settled down to inhale the Cajun food.

"What's up?" something told Dandi that her friend hadn't come just for the food.

"It's Rick."

"I'm sorry, Deb. I just don't like him the way he likes me."

Deb eyed her hard. "Are you sure?"

"Yes, I am." If she were going to like someone it would be Lucas.

"Good."

"Good?"

"Yes, I want him. I'm going to ask him out, but I wanted to make sure how you felt before I did."

Dandi laughed out loud. "Go, girl! Are you really going to make the first move?"

"You darn tootin, he's too cute to pass up. And the worst he can say is 'no'" She said flatly, then collapsed on the table. "If he says 'no' I will just die."

"He won't." Dandi was sure of it. "How could he turn you down?"

"I hope you're right." Deb dug in to her food with new vigor. "So, what's up with you and the hunk doctor?"

"Nothing," Dandi said, not knowing if that was the truth or a lie.

"I saw you two shooting together."

"Yea, and he's coming to paintball too. He's Beau and Harley's friend, not mine."

"Do tell," Deb said in a sing-song voice. "I think you protest a little too much."

Later that night, as she lay in bed, she abandoned all of her protests and allowed her imagination to soar. Lucas called her up on the phone and asked her out again, this time he wouldn't take 'no' for an answer. When he called for her, he had flowers and he took her to the show and out to eat. Dandi wondered if she had ever been on a real date. The youth trips at church didn't count. After she had run away from home, there had been no opportunities. Most importantly, she had never met anyone she wanted to date. What had happened during her lost days, she had no way of knowing. Had she dated Lucy's father? She hoped so.

Yawning, she shut her eyes and wondered if she liked sex. What did it feel like? What would it be like with Lucas? Oh my goodness! She felt her cheeks grown warm. He was an expert at it. "No, no," that was reason enough to avoid him. How embarrassing it would be to have to admit she knew nothing about sex other than what she had read in a book or watched on regular television. Pulling up her dress, she felt for the Cesarean scar from when she had delivered Lucy. Then she felt for the stretch marks that were still on her tummy. None of those things were very attractive. No, it would be better if she didn't get involved with the sexy sex doctor.

But as she drifted off to sleep, her body had other ideas. "Harder, Lucas." Oh, she loved having her nipples sucked. He was bent over her and she twined her fingers in that glorious mane of his and held his head to her breast, so afraid he'd stop. Eagerness sizzled through her veins like a burning fuse.

"Do you want me, Dandi?" He whispered in her ear.

"God, yes," she intoned as she went to her knees in front of him, her hands on his zipper.

"Give me what I need, Sugar."

Dandi licked her lips. She needed what he needed – her lips on his cock. Pinching her thighs together, she tried to give her clit just a bit of relief. Her pussy was so hungry, she needed Lucas to stretch her – fill her – fu. . . . ." A tremor of arousal caused Dandi to jerk so hard she woke herself up. "My God!" Enough of the dream remained to answer one very particular question.

She was pretty sure she liked sex.

* * * * *

Cindi sidled up to Dandi and put her arm around her neck. "I like Dane Wagner. I think I'll make a play for him."

Dandi didn't see her wink at Deb.

"I don't think so." After her dream last night, she was feeling a bit territorial. Oh, she had no reason to be – but she couldn't shake the possessiveness she felt toward him. Her body wanted Lucas, even if her mind knew she couldn't have him.

"And why is that?" Cindi was a teaser. She loved to give Dandi a hard time. With hair the color of chestnuts and a cover model's body, Cindi could have any man she wanted.

"Cause I have guns and I know how to use them."

"Hahaha!" Cindi loved it. She knew all about guns too. Her family was military, and she had her eye set on one of Patrick's buddies. Dandi knew this, but she still didn't enjoy the idea of her and Lucas.

"Well, if you want him, you had better get after it. Someone else will grab him up if you don't."

Dandi might not be able to grab him, but she sure as heck could shoot him. Splat!

"Gotcha!" She laughed. Dandi loved paintball!

Her happiness was catching. Lucas wasn't complaining. Having Dandi capture him was exactly what he had intended. Beau wouldn't be happy, he liked to win, but right now – it was more important to win the hand of fair maiden than a paintball war.

"Yes, you have me." He agreed.

Or he had her, she didn't know which. Before she could react, he took her by the shoulders and pushed her behind a big oak tree and covered her body with his. "Lucas," she breathed his name like a prayer.

This time he wasn't asking. He had stood it as long as he could. "I have to do this," he whispered, "don't hate me, please." Lucas brushed his thigh against hers, and lifted her chin with his finger.

Dandi melted. "I won't hate you," of that she was certain.

Slanting his mouth over hers, he caressed her lips with his own. Slowly Dandi softened, opening to him; her hesitant acceptance had him burning with need. The familiar taste of her kiss was almost his undoing. Lucas wanted to ravish her, consume her, grind his cock against her softness and let her know exactly what she was doing to him.

But he didn't.

She didn't remember him. To her – this was a first kiss. So, he ramped himself down to a controllable level and set out to woo and seduce. With great care he took her bottom lip between his and sucked on it, laving it with his tongue. How he had fantasized about kissing her again, and now she was here in his arms, and he was almost shaking with the wonder of it. A tender smooch, a sweep of his tongue between her lips, and finally – God, Finally! – she began to tentatively kiss him back. Her sweet little tongue darted out to mate with his and the significance of her small gesture wasn't lost on him. There was no way he could contain the growl of triumph that rumbled up deep from his throat. Wanting more, he framed her face, eating at her lips, tempting her to open her mouth wider and let him in.

Lucas put everything he had into the kiss, to him this was a test – a test he either passed or failed. But when he felt her little hands touch his arms and she clasped onto his shoulders, he knew he had gained major ground. Shifting his body, he wrapped his arms around her waist and hauled her closer. There was no way he could hide his arousal from her and maybe it was good that she realize how utterly affected by her he was. Sinking deeper into the kiss, Lucas devoured her, relishing the sugary sweetness he had missed so much.

"Lucas?" Beau's voice broke through their passion. "Can I talk to you a minute?"

Hell.

He didn't just turn her loose like some untried boy, he kissed her once more tenderly on the lips and once on each eyelid, and loved that she trembled in his arms. "It's okay," he assured her. "I've got you."

"Sure, friend." He didn't turn all the way around, no use advertising how big his cock was. "Can you give us a second?"

To Dandi's dismay, Beau chuckled.

"I'll never hear the end of this," she sighed.

"There won't be an end to this if I have my way. Have dinner with me."

"I. . .I . . .can't." Could she?

Nope. Not happening. "It's just dinner, no pressure, I promise. We'll just talk." Yea, talk. Like they had been talking for the past five minutes. "Don't you like me, Dandi?"

Like? Yes – too much – "I don't understand why you would want to, Lucas. You're so sophisticated and I'm just Dandi."

Just Dandi.

She had no idea what she meant to him. "I want, hell, I need to spend time with you." He wondered if it would help if he went to his knees and begged.

"Look at your career, what you do for a living, don't you know how intimidating that is for me. You are rich and sophisticated, things that I am not. You are society, I'm not. Plus, you're an expert on lovemaking. Apparently I had sex at least once, I have a daughter, but I don't even remember it,"

"Is that what this is about?" Lucas was flabbergasted. "Do you think I expect some level of expertise or a receipt for a country club membership?"

"I don't know," Dandi muttered. "I really don't know. I'm confused."

God, nothing had really changed. She didn't remember him, but she seemed to remember her insecurities. "All I can tell you is that I am so interested – damn that doesn't even come close – I am totally bewitched by you. I can't think of anything else."

Dandi swallowed nervously, "I'll cook for you, if you'd like. You can meet my daughter. How about Saturday?"

Lucas put a hand on either side of her head, enclosing her completely between his body and the tree. "I'd love to spend time with you and your daughter. I'll count the seconds." Stealing one more kiss, he pushed away to go find Beau. He couldn't have hid the smile on his face if he'd tried.

Beau waited for him a discreet distance away. "What's up, Bro? I know I asked you to chat with Dandi and see if you might help her, but I was a little surprised to see you making out with her here in the woods."

"I had already decided to talk with you about it. There are some things you need to know." Beau didn't intimidate Lucas at all. But he was his friend. Frankly, Lucas was grateful that Beau was protective of Dandi. He knew he sure as hell was.

"Are you planning to state your intentions?"

"Among other things." Now, wasn't the time to go into it. There were too many other people milling around. "How about if we meet for a drink tomorrow night?"

"Sounds good to me."

The big Cajun slapped him on the shoulder. "Who tagged you?" He pointed to the big red splat right over his heart.

"Dandi."

Beau threw his head back and laughed. "Why am I not surprised?"

*****

"Can I talk to you?" Dandi shuffled through the paperwork in her hand. Beau's office was always filled with catalogs and magazines and handbooks. She could barely see the wood on his desk. They had just received a big contract to supply cases of AR-15s to a nationwide sporting goods store and her cousin was trying to juggle employee and supplier schedules and he wasn't having much luck.

"Yes, of course." He pulled three books out of a chair and turned it around so she could sit down. "What's the problem, Darlin'?"

"Tell me about Lucas Wagner."

"Hmmm," Beau leaned back in his chair. "What do you want to know?"

"What kind of person is he?" She didn't really know what to ask, she just yearned to know more about him.

"Well, he's a good man." Beau was sure of this. "He's respectable and dependable. His practice is successful. He serves on a lot of boards and works with charities. He's written books. He owns race horses."

"What about women?"

"Well, he's not gay." Beau teased.

Dandi blushed. "I figured that."

"I don't know a lot about his personal life. He's not married. He doesn't date much, if any. I've seen him with a few women at charity events, and as far as I can tell, he has very high standards."

Beau didn't realize his remark about high standards cut her in a way she couldn't even explain. Miss Etta's words kept floundering in her head. She was worthwhile. She was valuable. Now, if she could just convince herself of that fact. "Lord, I'm going crazy."

Beau continued. "Boy crazy? I'd say it's about time. I've been worried about you, Munchkin." Seeing her look of exasperation, he summed up his thoughts on the good Doctor. "Shoot. What can I tell you? The man is well-liked in the state. Hell, he could run for governor and get elected."

Great. That answered her question. Lucas Wagner was clearly out of her league.

"Why?"

"Just curious."

"Yeah." He didn't believe her for a minute.

Dandi got up to go. "Thanks."

"Where are you off to?"

"I have class."

"Guess what I heard?"

"What?"

"Rick has a date with your friend Deb"

Dandi smiled. "I'm glad." At least someone had a chance at being happy.

Indy came barreling in. "Boss, we got a call. They've spotted a gator over in Bourg Louisiana in the Intercostal Canal. He's estimated at 800 pounds. We need to go move him before some redneck shoots him. The sheriff is afraid he'll crawl out into one of the residential communities."

"Sure thing," Beau stood and pocketed his phone and keys.

"Hey, Dandi," Indy smiled. "Pamela sure enjoyed meeting you. She can't stop talking about you."

"I can't imagine why." Dandi hadn't even spoken to the woman but once.

"She thinks you're a celebrity in disguise or something. I don't know, she won't tell me, I guess she's embarrassed."

Beau's ears perked up. "Pamela needs to hunt some real news to report, like this monster gator."

"I agree, but once she gets her nose into a story, she's like a bloodhound." Indy followed his boss out the door.

"Well, she won't sniff anything out on me. I'm nobody," Dandi couldn't imagine anyone being more boring than she was.

"No squirt," Beau called over his shoulder. "You're somebody who needs to get to work. We'll be back in a while. Call Dunbar's and tell them we'll need to push our order up by two weeks if we're going to get those conversions done in time."

"Yes, Boss." She stuck her tongue out at her cousin. Time to go to work; she could worry about Lucas later.

*****

"Alyssa, this isn't your fault." Lucas placed his hand on the crying woman's shoulder.

"I hurt him."

"No, you healed him." He pulled a chair up beside of her. "Ron Comeaux had never known a gentle touch from a woman or shared a kiss or found any type of sexual release until you came along."

"This was different, Dane. He's different than Troy," she spoke of the last case they had worked on together.

Lucas chose his words carefully. "I know you've thought about this, but can you imagine being unable to even touch yourself or self-pleasure yourself in any way? Ron is paralyzed and he just longed to know what it felt like to be a man."

Alyssa cried harder. "You don't understand."

Maybe he didn't. "Explain." These two people were under his charge. He had been the one to bring them together. Sexual surrogacy was something he believed in with all of his heart. A successful and compassionate surrogate could give a patient an amazingly powerful therapeutic support system. It could be used to not only heal sexual trauma but provide a way for patients to grow their sexual confidence and skills.

"It's not just Ron who got attached. It's me."

"Ah," now he saw the big picture. Well, damn. Obvious question. "What do you want to do about it?"

"I don't know." She wiped her face with a tissue that Lucas had provided.

"Well, I think you need to think on it long and hard. Your final session has been completed, any contact that you have with

Ron now, will be up to you. But I advise that you are cautious, you are dealing with someone who is vulnerable and hopeful." When Lucas had set up his practice here in Lafayette, he had contacted her and she had seen fit to move to Louisiana from Arkansas. Lucas had made it worth her while, financially. She was good, but he got a sneaky suspicion he was about to lose her to another man.

"I would never hurt him," she almost spit out the words.

"Not intentionally," he was beginning to understand that maybe Alyssa was the one who had been pushed away. "How did you leave things between you?"

"He told me not to come back."

"Do you think he meant it?"

"No, I don't."

"Do you want me to talk to him?"

"Yes, I do."

'Another job for Superman,' Lucas smiled to himself. "I'll be glad to." Now, if he could just solve his own problems.

*****

After talking to Ron, Lucas was determined to play matchmaker. This was a highly unusual situation, but lately he was a big believer in love. His love-life was looking up and he wanted everybody to know the same happiness he hoped for.

He and Beau had decided to meet at a sports bar, SCORE, located across from the street from the campus. "What's your poison?" the Cajun asked.

"I'll take a draft beer," Lucas had worried all afternoon about what to say to Dandi's cousin. He had come up with the only answer as far as he was concerned – the whole truth.

Beau got them drinks and they settled into a semi-private booth at the back of the club. "So, tell me what's going on with you and Dandi."

"It's serious, on my part."

Beau looked skeptical. "Serious? I'm not doubting Dandi's charms, but you just met the girl."

Lucas started to explain, but Beau didn't give him time to talk.

"She's been through a lot, and you've got a hard row to hoe. Since she came to me three years ago, I've never known her to give another man the time of day. To say I was surprised to see her kissing you is an understatement. Plus, there are some things you don't know about her past."

Lucas stopped him with a raised hand. "That's where you're wrong. I know about her past."

"What do you mean?"

"I am her past." Lucas stated simply.

"Dehelyoussaye?!?" Beau was all ears. "I can't say I didn't wonder after seeing you in that lip-lock."

"She doesn't remember me, not yet."

"So, you know about her time in Shreveport?" Beau approached the subject cautiously. He hadn't had time to delve into what Joseph McCoy had told him, but he intended to.

"I met her in Shreveport when she was dancing at Club Tonga."

"Damn!" Beau didn't like to think about it. "I saw that stupid ass video someone made. How in the world did someone like Dandi end up in a place like that?"

"She was just waiting tables; Dandi had no intention of ever stripping." Lucas explained about her diabetes and how Romero had blackmailed her. "The night I walked into the club she was ready to run because he had plans to start making her work for him, if you know what I mean – prostituting"

Beau cursed. "What happened?" Lucas explained about the shooting and how she had escaped and he had looked for her. "I was so relieved to find her hiding in my back seat. A lot of other stuff transpired, but to make a long story short, she ended up going home with me. I just couldn't let her go. We fell in love. But that stupid video and the hoopla of her going missing after the murder made her name and face too recognizable. People gave her a hard time. Men would come on to her. The straw that broke the camel's back was when some idiots who were about to offer me a job backed out because of her. She ran. We were about to get married – I had the damn license and she ran."

"Hell, I'm sorry you two had to go through all of that."

"Oh, that's not all. She had a narrow escape. That snake from the club was convinced she was a witness and had sent a hitman after her. Thank God, Dandi got away, but I wasn't as lucky." Lucas showed Beau the scar on his forehead – almost a matching scar to the one Dandi had received in the bus crash.

"My God, I had no idea." Beau was flabbergasted. "So, Dandi ran from you because she thought she was bad for you? That's when she was in the bus crash?"

"Yes, she left a note and disappeared on Valentine's three years ago. Not a day has passed that I didn't look for her."

"So, you're Lucy's father?"

"Yes, I am. I haven't seen her, yet, but I don't have to. There's no way I'm not the father. Can you see any resemblance?"

Now, that he mentioned it, Beau realized Lucy was the spitting image of Lucas. Beau decided not to spoil the surprise. "A little bit maybe, around the eyes."

That was enough for Lucas. "I want my family back."

"I want you to have them back," Beau agreed.

"What are we going to do?" Lucas wanted his help and his support.

"Well, you're the Doctor, but I say we don't tell her."

"Not an option, she's got to know who I am."

"No, I think you should tell her you know her and love her and all that – but don't tell her the hard stuff about her stripping and Angel Baby. Let her remember that on her own."

"It's going to be difficult," Lucas mused. "Do you think she has blocked this on purpose?"

"I thought about that," Beau took a sip of beer. "There may be some part of her that doesn't want to remember."

"Do I have your blessing?"

"Yes – but you'd damn well better not hurt her, or you'll answer to me. She's been through enough."

"I'd rather die." And Lucas meant it.

204

CHAPTER THIRTEEN

"Mama, what are you doing?"

"I'm cooking a pork roast and sweet potatoes; we have company coming for supper."

Lucy caught on to Dandi's skirt and swung around her mama's legs. "Is Aunt Harley coming?"

Harley wouldn't be her aunt when she and Beau married, but that didn't really matter. "No, we have a gentleman caller."

Her cell phone buzzed, causing her to jump. "We're on our way over. I have a pitcher of margaritas. You make the nachos."

Cindi and Deb.

"No, no, you two stay right where you are."

"Why?" Cindi sounded affronted.

"Cause, Cindi Mitchell, I have a date – sorta."

"Aha! With who? Dr. Delicious?"

"God, please don't call him that." Dandi blushed as she scurried around the kitchen putting a finishing touch on the pork roast and sweet potatoes.

"What kind of doctor is he? A brain surgeon?"

Before Dandi could curb her tongue, she answered. "No, he's a sex therapist."

"Mu-wah-ha-ha-ha!" Cindi cackled. Her other best friend's sense of humor was legendary. She shared Dandi and Deb's love for the outside and anything competitive, plus she could cuss like a sailor if the cause warranted, but Cindi was beautiful. Dandi just wished she had Cindi's looks. Men were absolutely crazy about her.

"Stop it, Cindi!" She could hear Deb laughing equally loud in the background.

"Sorry, but you're priceless. No dates, no men, no relationships – you have been so straight laced and puritanical and now you're dating a sex doctor?"

"That's right," she mumbled. "Deal with it."

"Mama? Where's my doll?"

"In the sunroom, Precious."

Knock. Knock. Knock."

"Look, he's here. I gotta go. You can torture me later." She put the phone down and went to let Lucas in.

He stood before her, bigger than life and so handsome he made her heart pound. That wasn't all that was responding, her stomach was upside down and her nipples were tight and achy. "Come in."

Lucas felt like a creature of the night who had been granted entrance. Without the invitation, he would have had to stand outside her world and only wish for acceptance. "Thank you. I brought you these." He stooped to pick up packages from the floor.

"Oh, my goodness!" He had brought candy, wine and four bouquets of roses. "I wasn't sure which you'd prefer, so I bought them all." And he had - red ones, pink ones, coral ones and roses so white they almost put your eyes out.

"This is too much."

"No, it could never be enough and I brought this for Lucy." He held out an expensive computer game.

"Way too much." But she couldn't help but smile. "I've never received flowers before, or at least I don't remember any."

Instantly, Lucas regretted never giving her any. Maybe if he'd made her feel more loved – she wouldn't have left. "I'll make it up to you."

"Mama!" Her daughter's mad entrance caused them both to look her way.

Lucas felt like he had been hit by a Mack truck. DAMN! Beau had been right; there was a resemblance, but more than just around the eyes. There was no denying it, the child before him was ethereally feminine, a little blonde angel with a rosebud mouth, blue eyes and hair so blonde it looked like spun gold. She had his eyes and hair and nose and smile – God, she was his, and there was no denying it.

For the first time, the obvious hit Dandi like a freight train. She couldn't quit staring at her child and this man she barely knew. She stared and stared, her heart in her throat.

Lucas knelt in front of Lucy.

"Look, Mommy. He has yeller hair just like me." Making herself at home, she began climbing up in his lap, perching on his knee.

Dandi felt like a bomb had been dropped into her world.

"Who are you?" she asked Lucas Dane Wagner.

He didn't even hesitate, but answered calmly, holding her gaze as surely as one would hold a frightened bird who had fell from its nest. "I'm Lucas, the man who loves you more with every breath I take."

Emotion swamped Dandi. She wanted to run, but she couldn't leave her child, so she hugged herself as tightly as she could. "Lucy, honey, will go check on your kitten in the sunroom? See, if it's still asleep."

"Yes, Mama." She patted her new friend on the cheek. "I'll be back"

"I'll be waiting," he assured the little angel. As she moved from the room, he followed her every step. So many wasted days. How would he ever get them back?

When Lucy was out of earshot, she said almost accusingly. "You are Lucy's father."

"Yes." He stood before her.

"How? Where? When?" She covered her face with her hands. "I don't remember. I don't remember anything." Dandi was panicking. "I have impressions."

"What kind?" Lucas moved a step closer to her.

"Leering faces, shouting, a feeling of being dirty, I don't know. My impressions are enough to make me know that I don't want to remember." A sob caught in her throat. "I don't know who I was. I don't even know if I want to know who I was." Lucas had moved closer, even as she was backing away. "Was I bad?"

"Oh, God no." He tried to take her in his arms.

Dandi avoided him, staying just out of reach.

"Mama isn't bad." Bad was a word that Lucy understood. Lucas turned to look at the pixie who was holding a kitten over her arm like a purse.

"No, you're right. She's the best mama in the world, the most precious woman in the world to me."

"Take your kitten and go play now," Dandi desperately wanted Lucy out of the room, she didn't want her to be scared by her mother's tears. "I'll see to the food and we'll call you when dinner's ready."

"Okay, Mama." She skipped away.

Dandi turned into the kitchen and began mechanically taking care of the meal.

"I'll help." Lucas stepped right in, determined to make himself indispensable in her life. "It all smells wonderful." He handed her a hot pad so she could remove the meat from the oven.

"Thank you," Dandi whispered, but she was shaking so hard she couldn't do it. "Here, you get it."

Lucas took care of it for her. "Let's let the pork rest, it's always good to let the juices settle."

Dandi sat down at the dining table. "Okay."

"How's your blood sugar?"

"You know about that?"

"Yes, I know everything." She showed him where the testing kit was and he sat her down in a chair and took care of her, even giving her a dose of insulin.

"God, Lucas. What else do you know?" She was afraid of the answer.

Kneeling at her feet, he answered, never taking his eyes off of her face. "I know how your nipples taste and I know they're puffy and the prettiest coral pink. I know the sounds you make when you cum, when you fly apart in my arms."

"STOP!" She got up and left the kitchen – he followed.

"What's the last thing you remember?" He had to know.

She went to a corner of the couch and sat down, pulling her feet under her, making herself as small as possible. "I remember living in northwest Shreveport. I was working at a fast food restaurant and getting arrested," she finished with a bite in her voice.

"You say that like you think it will put me off, make me want you less. I already know all about it, your roommate put the watch in your pocket and you took the fall for her."

Okay, so he did know. "Where did we meet?"

Lucas sat down by her, and it pained him in his heart when she drew even further into the corner. Carefully, he answered. "We met in a club."

"Tell me everything."

So, he does. A sanitized version. "I came into the club and saw you dancing. You stole my breath and my heart. A man was giving you a hard time and I intervened. One thing led to another and we ended up leaving together."

"Why?"

Lucas agreed with Beau, it would be best to let her remember the difficult stuff on her own. Right now, the important thing was that she understand he loved her.

"We recognized one another. It was an instant attraction – like now."

"Wrong."

"I'm Lucy's father." He stated what he thought was the obvious and a damn good reason for them to be more than friends.

"Are you?" It seemed undeniable to her, but she couldn't remember. It was driving her mad. "How can you be sure?"

"I think the fact that she looks identical to me is pretty convincing, don't you think?" At her frown, he stated the rest of his case. "I can also be sure because you've never slept with anyone but me; you love me too much to sleep with anyone else." She closed her eyes as if in pain, but she listened. "You were a virgin when you came to my bed. We used protection, but you were taking antibiotics for those stripes on your back."

She jerked her head up to look at him. "What are those stripes? How did I get them?"

"You were hurt." He sought the words to explain without giving everything away. Luckily, he was saved by a small, sweet belle.

"Mama, who is this man?"

She couldn't deny them. "This is your father."

Standing about three feet from him, a vision in baby pink, she put her hands on her hips and glared at her father. "Where have you been? I've been waiting on you."

Love swelled up in like a spring. "I've been looking for your mama."

That answer seemed to satisfy Lucy, but it only created a maelstrom of mixed emotions in Dandi.

She managed to get off the couch and kiss her daughter soundly. "Why don't you help your Daddy to a seat at the table? He looks hungry."

Lucas agreed. She was right about that. He was hungry for his family – for her and for this nightmare he had been living the past three years to be over. He stayed and they ate and they laughed. He was relieved to notice that Dandi began to relax. Looking at his daughter, he asked. "When's your birthday?" He knew it ought to be coming up soon.

The little girl looked to be in deep thought; she glanced at her mom for help. Dandi held up ten fingers. "Oh, yeah! In that many days, I'll be free." He understood 'free' was three.

"Officially, we've been telling everyone she was three for six months. She thought two sounded too much like a baby."

"Are you going to have a party?"

Lucy nodded in the affirmative and Dandi clarified. "Just a small gathering for family."

"I am family." Lucas would not be denied.

"Yes, you are." She admitted. His approval showed on his face, it made her smile back at him.

Together they gave Lucy a bath and put her to bed and Lucas was privileged to read her a bedtime story and kiss her goodnight. They stood by her bed till she drifted off, then he took Dandi's hand and led her back to the couch. "Sit with me."

"Okay, if you'll tell me more."

He wanted too, so he steeled himself to say just the right thing. "There was a huge storm the night we met. Arkansas got more snow during that week that we had in decades. Because of the storm and because we couldn't bear to be apart, I took you to my cabin."

"I went home with you, the first night we met?" She was appalled.

"We were cautious," he smiled at her. "But it was love at first sight."

"God, I must be cheap." She looked dismayed.

Lucas grabbed her hands. "No, no, you were pure and perfect. You needed me, but not nearly as much as I need you." Tense was important, he still needed her.

"You rescued me," she didn't exactly know from what, but she was sure of the feeling. Dandi could almost grasp it. It was like reaching for the string of a balloon that danced just above her head, a little out of reach in the wind.

She listened as his words shone a light into the darkness of her mind. She could hear them, she could understand them, but it was as if he were talking about someone else. "We were together for two glorious weeks. We fell in love."

"What happened?" she asked without emotion.

He hesitated. "We had a misunderstanding."

"What kind of misunderstanding?"

From out of nowhere, her phone rang. This time it was Dandi who fussed under her breath, but it was Beau. She listened.

From the remarks Lucas could hear, he could tell something was wrong.

When she hung up, Dandi had a dazed look on her face. "Beau and Harley were attending a party celebrating Patrick and Savannah's wedding. Do you know them?"

Lucas shook his head, no.

"It's a long story, but Savannah is a friend of Harley's and she was engaged to be married to a soldier, Patrick O'Rourke. About the time I moved here, Patrick was reported killed in action, Savannah went through hell. But she is a great believer in miracles and the afterlife and although it seems unbelievable, it wasn't true. Patrick had been a POW. There was more to it than that, but he returned and they are married now. Beau and Harley were with them when Beau got a call that another friend of theirs Aron McCoy. . . "

"Joseph's brother?" Lucas interrupted.

"Yes, Aron has just been reported missing on his honeymoon. He was diving and didn't come up."

"Damn, God, I'm sorry." Lucas thought how awful it would be to have the world by the tail — be on your honeymoon with the one you love and disaster strike. "What can I do?"

"Beau and Harley are going to Texas to Tebow Ranch and probably on down to the island where it happened. Beau is really close to the McCoy family. I've got to go pick up some papers and the keys to the shop and I'll have to feed that damn alligator every day." She got up. "I have to get Lucy up."

"No, let me stay with her and you go deal with whatever you have to do. I'll take care of our daughter."

Dandi only paused a moment, he was right. Their relationship was unusual, to say the least, but she trusted Lucas. "Okay, I'll be back as soon as I can."

While she was gone, he had a look around her living room, he didn't snoop, but it bothered him that there was nothing personal to speak of, there was nothing that defined Dandi. It was like she existed in a shell, afraid to look out and see what was around her. Sadly, Lucas knew it wasn't the world she was afraid of, she was afraid of knowing the truth of who she was.

Dr. Solomon's words came back to him, again. He and the professor had reconciled, to a degree. Their relationship would never be what it used to be, but at least they were speaking. The idea of being two people — the idea that he had clung to, was a total pile of shit. He had longed for respectability, never realizing that what gave him his value wasn't his station in life, but what he was made of — what kind of man he was. And Dandi. . .Dandi thought she was less than perfect. She longed for who she used to be, instead of what she feared she had become. But Dandi hadn't changed, she was still the same beautiful, kind, loving person she had always been.

Lucas's past had shaped him, but it had made him a better man. Dandi's past could be the same, and he'd convince her of that if it was the last thing he ever did.

He stood at the window till he saw her lights, and he had the door open for her when she arrived. "Everything okay?"

Dandi was glad to see him. She hugged him. Almost. "They are pretty upset, I don't know if there's a reason to hope or not. Harley seems to think so, and she's psychic. Damn! I haven't thought of that — now what she has been telling me makes sense." Dandi chunked her purse on the couch.

"Tell me," Lucas was bemused and a little perplexed. He didn't know anything about Harley being psychic, he didn't know if he believed any such thing.

"Harley looks at me oddly sometimes, and she told me this the other day. 'Your secret is safe with me, until you're ready to hear it. Then she almost repeated Miss Etta's words to me verbatim, that I was valuable and worthy to be loved." She was conscious of Lucas's eyes on her. He made her feel warm.

"You are valuable and you are loved." Lucas ached to show her just how much.

"Stop," she held up her hand. "She also told me love would be the hardest thing I ever tried to accept. She must have been talking about you."

"I don't know about that," Lucas pulled her close. "I think it would be easy to accept, all you'd have to do is. . ."

She pushed on his chest, stopping his flow of words. "I think you'd better go, Lucas. I don't think I can take anymore right now."

Disappointment and sexual frustration frustrated him. "All right, but before I do," he cupped the back of her head underneath that beautiful bounty of dark chocolate hair. "I need to know how you feel about me."

"What do you mean?" Dandi attempted to move, but he held her fast. She wasn't fighting him, she was fighting the familiarity she felt in his arms – it scared her.

"I need to know if you're attracted to me. Are you interested in me?"

"I feel. . ." she tried to put it into words. He deserved the truth. "I want to feel . . ." breaking down she bowed her head. "I don't know you."

"You've forgotten me. But I know you." She was his heart.

"Who am I?" she asked in desperation.

"You're my Dandi."

"No, no," that wasn't what she wanted to hear.

Lucas realized he was pushing her too hard. He stepped back. "Look, I understand. This is all just too much, too soon." He wiped a tear from her cheek. "Thank you for my daughter. I look forward to a lifetime of loving her and you, if you'll let me."

"Oh, Lucas."

"God, I love to hear my name on your lips."

Leaning forward, he placed a chaste kiss on her forehead. "Find me Dandi – please, look in your heart and mind and find me."

*****

Over the next twenty-four hours, Lucas devised a new plan. He was going to tempt and tantalize Dandi right back where she belonged, with him. He made a point of dropping by Firepower Munitions at lunch, delivering her favorite vegetable pizza and he was also there after work to escort her to daycare to pick up Lucy, then he took his girls home. When he got them safely to their doorsteps, he kissed his sweet little girl and her mother and excused himself - - hopefully, they would miss him.

And miss him they did, Dandi was beside herself wanting and wishing he would call. Lucas didn't disappoint, and she was beginning to believe he never would.

"Hello?"

"I wanted to talk to you before you went to bed."

"I'm glad you called," she spoke tremulously.

"Are you?" there was a lilt to his voice.

"I missed you."

Hell, he had to hold the table to keep from sprinting out the door. "I'm glad, I miss you, too. Would you and Lucy do me the honor of having dinner with me tomorrow evening, here in my home?" He was so afraid she'd say no.

"Yes."

Yes! "Excellent, I'll pick you up from work."

He did as he promised, even having a car seat in his car this time, so they wouldn't have to drive Dandi's small SUV. When they left the daycare, Dandi was curious as to where Lucas lived. When they turned toward Gumbo Road, she knew he lived in a mansion. What else had she expected? Lucas knew what he wanted and he went after it. Now, how did she know that? Dandi shook her head. Was her memory returning? Or was she just forming an opinion of him now. Knowing he went after what he wanted was comforting, because it seemed as if he wanted her.

She was right about the house. "I love it." And what was there not to love? It was a villa with a wide verandah, a red tile roof, and vast green grounds with a flowing stream in front of it. "I don't think Lucy and I are dressed for this." She looked at their blue jeans and simple shirts.

"Nonsense, this is my home and you are the most important people who have ever visited me. What you have on is immaterial. Actually, I'd rather you had on less," he winked at her.

Dandi couldn't help but smile.

To say she was impressed, was putting it mildly. There was an outdoor kitchen and a pool. The back porch with its sumptuous, deep, comfortable furniture was bigger than her whole house. There were rose gardens, a grand staircase, a formal dining room and a wine cellar. The media room was huge and the bathtub was big enough to swim in - - Dandi was overwhelmed, but Lucy was in hog heaven. She raced about and squealed and picked her out a room and informed her mother that she thought they ought to live with her Dad.

"I agree. Families are supposed to live together. Aren't they Lucy?"

"Yes, especially when they have horses!" She pointed out in the pasture with big, blue eyes.

He took them for a walk around the grounds and introduced them to his Quarter Horse race horses. "This is Sugarcane and this is Southern Comfort and this little beauty is Red Hot Chile Pepper." Lucy begged to pet them and he held her up to do so.

"Do they win a lot of races for you?"

"Southern Comfort has the best record, but they're all young."

"You must be very successful," Dandi said without a hint of a smile in her voice.

"Is that a bad thing?"

"No, it just makes it harder."

"Harder to tell me 'no'?"

She just shook her head.

He led them in the house and hoped they liked his surprise. To the best of his ability he had tried to recreate one of the more special evenings he had spent with Dandi. "We're going to eat in front of the fireplace. I have trays of sandwiches and pitchers of lemonade and then we're going to make s'mores."

Lucy knew what a s'more was and Dandi did too. He watched her face carefully but she didn't really react like she remembered anything. They sat cross legged in front of the fire and ate their fill. The sticky marshmallow treat made Lucy laugh and Lucas kissed the white goo from his baby's fingers and chocolate from Dandi's lips. After Lucy had worn herself and them out, she lay with her head in Lucas's lap and her feet in Dandi's. "I love this," he whispered. "I love having the two of you here."

Dandi made sure Lucy's eyes were closed. "We don't fit in," she worried.

"Hold on," he stood up, picked his small child up and carried her to the couch in the adjoining room.

It was time to get serious.

"I'll be right back," he went to retrieve some items. When he returned, she had laid down flat of her back and he couldn't any more resist her than he could stop his next breath. Going down to the rug with her, he was stretched out next to her and had his arm around her before she knew what had happened. "Don't ever tell me that you don't fit into my world." She turned her face away, but he cupped her cheek and made her look at him. "My world was created with you in mind."

"Really?"

"Really," he dusted her face with butterfly kisses. "Let me show you something." He pulled her up. "I took these while we were together. After I lost you," he stopped and took a breath. "I had them printed out so I could look at them somewhere besides my phone and my computer."

Dandi took pictures from his hands. They were of her, some with him, but countless of her alone. She was laughing and playing in the snow or cooking or just fooling around – but in every one of them, she had her heart in her eyes. "I loved you."

"Yes," the past tense she used almost killed him. "You loved me."

"And this, you made this for me as a gift." He gave her the sketch, the one where she had the angel wings.

"Angel wings? What was I thinking?" She looked at Lucas, but he was staring at her solemnly, as if he were gauging her reactions. So she studied it, trying to see what he saw. Dandi knew her own work, she recognized it. Gazing at his beautiful face on the sketch pad, she could tell it was drawn with a powerful emotion. Her heart ached to remember that feeling.

"The angel wings were very fitting. Give me your hand." She laid the sketch down and placed her hand in his. He enclosed it in his big warm hand. "Do you trust me?"

"Yes," there was no question of that.

"Do you want me?"

"Yes," there was no question of that. She might not remember her former love, but a new tenderness and deep affection was growing.

"One night, I held your hand like this." He wove their fingers together, rubbing her palm with his. One would think the contact would be comforting, but Dandi found herself thinking erotic thoughts. This mountain of a man made her ache between the legs; he made her breasts throb. And he hadn't even touched her yet, nothing beyond a kiss and holding hands. Well, he had – according to him they had made love, repeatedly, and he had fathered her child. But Dandi couldn't remember those encounters. No, she was lying. Her body seemed to remember.

Lucas turned her hand over, cradling it. What was he doing? "Lucas?"

"I teach people how to communicate in the bedroom. How to tempt or tease one another until surrendering to the pleasure is the only thing they can think of." He lifted her hand and kissed the soft center of her palm, she could feel the tip of his tongue touching her sensitive skin.

"Holy Dickens," she moaned.

"I want to make love to you. I want to show you how I feel. Would you let me?"

She bit her lip. He was waiting. Is that was she wanted? Yes, it was. She was undeniably attracted to him. Just being this close to Lucas made her wet. "Alright. I want to be with you." Suddenly she grabbed his hand and held it to her heart. "There's just one thing you should know."

He loved the way she cradled his hand next to her body, she had done this before. "What should I know?"

"Lucy is yours. I would never keep her from you. You can see her as much as you want, anytime you want. So, I just wanted to tell you that – in case."

"In case what?" He didn't like where this was going.

"You don't have to make time with me in order to have her in your life."

One moment she was sitting up, the next she was flat of her back and covered by Lucas's body. He wasn't weighing her down, but she could feel him from the tips of her breasts all the way down to the tips of her toes. "Let's get one thing straight – right now. I already love our daughter; I would die for her at any moment. I had my will changed the morning after I knew she existed." Lucas further anchored her by taking one of her hands in each of his and holding them over her head. "But I would want you in my life, in my bed, in my heart even if there was no child. Do you understand me?"

"Yes." Dandi's body was enflamed. Even though the move was strange to her, she pushed her hips up against him, begging for a more intimate touch.

"Daddy?"

Lucas groaned. Dandi groaned. Then he smiled. This was the first time he had ever heard his daughter call for him. Perfect. "Daddy. Could there be a better word in the English language?"

"Yes, Dumpling?"

"I'm thirsty."

"Be right there." He got up and held his hand out for Dandi. "I'm going to tend to my darling daughter, but I want you to think about something while I'm gone. I want to see you alone. I love Lucy, but I need some time alone with you. There will come a time when we will lock our bedroom door and I will love you till you can't wiggle, but the first time – I want you all to myself with no chance of interruption. Think about how we can make that happen."

When he rose, taking the heat of his body with him, she felt exposed and alone. She wanted him back. Hell, she wanted him – bottom line. A vibrating in her pocket felt sorta good, till she realized it was her own phone. "Perv," she said to herself and smiled. Glancing at the readout, she saw Harley's name. "Have they found Aron?"

"I wanted you to know we're in the Cayman's. We came to be with Libby."

"What do they know? What do they think?"

"No one knows anything for sure. A search is being made of the island and of course divers and boats have been combing the bay."

"I don't know Aron and Libby, but I will pray for them." Harley asked more questions about what was going on at home, and Dandi assured her all was well.

"Who was that?" Lucas came back in and she told him about Aron and what Harley had said.

Just thinking about Aron and Libby's tragedy made Lucas want to repair the breach between he and Dandi even more. "What did you come up with for us? When can we be together?"

She had an answer. "If you can get away, we're doing a Gun and Reptile Show at Beau's wildlife preserve. Cindi said she would keep Lucy. I have keys to Beau's tree-house. We could spend the night there and maybe go down to New Orleans for a night too, if you'd like."

Lucas smiled. "I can't wait to chase you around in a tree house. I'm going to show you how it feels to be loved."

"I can't wait." She got up, "I guess we'd better be going. Do you want to take us home or should I call a cab?"

"Do you think I'd send the two of you home in a cab?" Lucas realized that Dandi had no memory of him caring for her. She had been on her own before they met and on her own since they had parted.

"No?"

"Hell, no!"

"Come on," he put his hand on the small of her back. "Let's get our baby and I'll take the two of you back to your apartment.

He toted Lucy outside to the garage and Dandi followed. She couldn't help but watch the movement of the powerful muscles of his back, his legs long and sturdy. Obviously, he was more man than she had ever imagined dealing with. Yet she had – damn!

She opened the door of his Mercedes and he placed Lucy in the car seat, fastening her securely. Before he backed up, he kissed her forehead. Her chubby cheeks quivered as she let out a sweet baby sigh.

"I don't know why I didn't see the resemblance between the two of you right off; it's uncanny."

"You weren't expecting it, I'm sure it's difficult to deal with lost memory. At some point you have to just go on and build a new life for yourself." As a psychiatrist, he could state the accepted theory, but this was personal. He wanted Dandi to remember him. But he'd take what he could get. If he had to make her fall in love with him all over again, that's what he would do. "We did good though. She's the most beautiful little girl in the world."

Dandi had to cover her mouth, laughter just burst out. "I think you're a bit prejudiced, Lucas."

"Every parent should be," he put an arm around her waist. "Here, now let me fasten you in. I used to do this for you." He opened the door, helped her and took her breath away as he reached across her to insert the seat belt. There was no way he could miss how her nipples hardened. "You want me, don't you?"

"Yes, I do."

"Good. Tomorrow, we make love."

*****

"I don't like this; I don't like it at all." Dandi had no more than stepped out of the crocodile enclosure than he had nabbed her.

"What? I had to put the baby back," she had been introducing a group of fifth graders to their newest edition to the Gharial family. The endangered species was one Beau was breeding for preserves around the world. "Indy had the parents distracted with some chicken carcasses."

Lucas fumed; his whole body seemed to be expanding with each breath. "How do you think I feel watching you risk life and limb over and over? You are my soft, precious woman and I'd much rather you were at home planning parties or baking cookies where it's safe."

He did not just say that?!? Dandi wheeled on him and got right in his face. She glanced around to make sure no one noticed, but she could not let this pass. "I have a job. I'm good at my job. I do not take risks. I'm not the society type, and if that's what you're looking for, then you might as well look elsewhere."

To hell with that, "I don't have to look elsewhere. You're exactly what I need."

Dandi snorted. "I wouldn't believe that unless I read it on the front pages of the Times Picayune."

"One of these days, you just might." Lucas wasn't mad, but he was frustrated. What did he have to do to convince her? She acted like part of her remembered the past. Maybe what they went through was so traumatic to her that it had bruised her soul.

Dandi wasn't through. "I appreciate your concern, but if you think you're going to keep me at home barefoot and pregnant, then you are in for a surprise!"

The fire in her eyes didn't make him angry, it just turned him on. Yea, he was overreacting, but he couldn't help it. So far today, he had watched her handle a python about the same size as she was. He had watched her climb on the back of an alligator and hold its snout down while Rick had taped its mouth and now, she had ventured into the enclosure with a pair of man-eating crocodiles who looked big enough to swallow a small car. What she said did give him hope, however. "Barefoot and pregnant? Does that mean you're considering moving in with me?"

Realizing what she had assumed, she blushed. "I don't recall being asked, and I'm not sure what my answer would be if I were," she pushed on his big mountain of a body. But he didn't budge.

"You have an open invitation. What did you think I meant when I told you I had created my world for you? I picked that house out for you. I chose the colors of the carpet and the walls and the furniture based on what you had told me you preferred. I changed my will to make you and Lucy beneficiaries. I have lived the life of a damn monk in the hope that I would find you again. Do you know I haven't had sex since the last time I slept with you?"

Dandi was floored. "I had no idea." How do you respond to something like that? He had prepared a home for her? She knew he had put Lucy in his will, but he had included her also? But both of those things together weren't as surprising as the fact he had not made love with anyone – he was waiting for her. She gave the only response she could. She threw herself in his arms and wrapped herself so tightly around him he couldn't breathe. "You don't have to wait any longer. I'm ready. Love me."

CHAPTER FOURTEEN

Lucas twirled her around. "It's about damn time," he snarled, playfully. "I do love you, and I'd be more than happy to illustrate that concept when we can sneak away to somewhere private."

"I'm through for the day; let's go to the tree house." She grabbed his hand and started pulling.

"You don't have to work so hard, I'm very willing," he laughed, picking up his pace to keep up with her.

"Sorry, I'm nervous, but you'll help me."

Her confidence touched him. "Help you? Baby, I'd turn the world upside down for you." Beau's wildlife compound was filled with people, and she wound in between them, leading him just like she had through the crowd at Tonga. That seemed like a lifetime ago, and their circumstances had completely changed. Yet Lucas knew this was meant to be – there wasn't a shadow of doubt in his mind. Their destinies were intertwined. When he considered the way they met – the way she came back into his life – none of it was by chance. Someone, somewhere was looking out for them.

He paid no attention to the scenery, the calls of the wild birds did not draw his gaze, when an acquaintance called his name he did not even acknowledge them. His entire being was zeroed in on this small woman who not only led him by the hand, but also with an invisible string she had tied around his heart.

They left the compound proper and started down a narrow path toward the bayou. He wondered if they were headed the right way, until he saw the house peeping through the trees. "Christ!" LeBlanc had built an amazing structure. It seemed to be a natural part of the landscape. The house looked like it had taken root and grown in the bayou. Made of cypress, it was constructed high on stilts, hugging the massive trees with decks and stairways and docks that meandered around the trees and down to the water. "I can't wait to see the inside. Especially the bed."

"We're using the guestroom; it's where I stay when I come over. I think it's better than the master bedroom."

"Does Beau have any resident reptiles that I need to know about?"

"No, it's safe, but you don't have to worry. I'll protect you," she teased. He swatted her playfully on the butt, and thanked God for all one hundred ten pounds of her. They walked up the stairs and onto the front gallery, she unlocked the door but they didn't go in. Instead they stood for a few moments and took in the bayou, the dark green waters that moved lazily by. Cranes swooped in and fish jumped. The view was out of this world. "There's nothing more beautiful than the swamp. Some people are afraid of it, but I find it to be a sanctuary."

Lucas drew her back against him. "I want to be your sanctuary. Make love with me." He picked her up and she directed him to their hideaway. Dandi's room was something out of a fantasy. "Did you design this?"

"Yes, I stayed here with Beau when I first came back, before he built my little apartment." A queen size canopy bed stood in the center of a room done all in white. It looked to be constructed of mahogany and was covered with silken drapes that created a private haven for them. "I'm scared," she confessed, cupping the side of his dear face. "I'm going to disappoint you."

"Let me tell you something," he placed her on the bed and sat down beside her, pushing her hair over her shoulders, caressing the skin of her neck. "We've had this conversation before, but I will tell you again. Your pleasure is my responsibility and when you receive pleasure, so do I. So, all I ask is that you place yourself in my hands and let me love on you."

Her answer was to unbutton her shirt. "This feels like my first time."

"It will be better than our first time, I promise you." Slowly, he began to undress her, skimming her jeans down her curvaceous legs. Nothing would do but that he had to stop and pay homage to the silken skin on the back of her knees. He held her leg up and kissed the curve of her calf and licked the tiny beauty mark next to her knee. "I've missed you, so." His body was throbbing; it had been so damn long.

"I think I've missed you, too. Sometimes in the night, I would reach out for someone – I didn't know who, but I was always disappointed that you weren't there."

"Sit up; let me get this shirt off." He peeled away the layers, unfastening her bra. Hot Damn! "You're bigger." He feasted his eyes on her delectable tits. "Did you breast-feed?" The reality of what he had missed hit him.

Dandi tried to cover herself with her hands, but he was right, she was bigger. "Yes, I have stretch marks."

"I don't care, you're perfect." He pushed her hands away, "I want to see all of you. Any evidence that you have borne my child would be precious to me." The tight peaks of her nipples made his mouth water.

As he eased down next to her, she cuddled into him. God, he smelled good – all woodsy and male. She splayed her fingers across his chest, letting her fingertips dance over the hard planes and the smattering of soft hair around his nipples. "You are so sexy."

"Ha!" he laughed, "I'm glad you think so."

Dandi felt emboldened. "You are," she laid her head on his chest, loving the steady beating of his heart. Could this man belong to her? The thought made her shiver, and when she did, he cradled her closer. Wanting to touch him, she let her fingers dance over his abdomen as she draped one of her thighs over his, showing him, without words, her willingness to be vulnerable to him.

"Do you know what you're doing to me?" His voice had dropped an octave, husky with emotion and need.

Looking up at him with a twinkle in her eye, she admitted. "Not really, I'm sorta winging it."

"I am yours, I always have been." The look in his face, the love in his voice – it was her undoing. He caressed her arm, seeming to wait for some type of a signal from her.

"It seems impossible," but she wanted it to be true. Her body quivered, waiting for his touch. Her clit pulsed and cream began to gather in her throbbing pussy as her body made itself ready for him. Years had come and gone since she had known his touch, but now her whole being clamored to be possessed by his – to remember.

"We'll go slow, and you can tell me when something feels good." Dandi held on to his shoulders as he kissed her collarbone. Butterflies fluttered in her stomach as his tongue traced the underside of her breast. "Velvet, you are soft as velvet," he whispered sweet words that made her quiver. When his warm mouth enclosed her nipple and began to suck, she whimpered a moan of gratitude. She pushed the curtain of blonde hair back from his face so she could watch him suckle hungrily at her flesh. Seeing the ecstasy on his face was almost as erotic as the pleasure he was giving her.

Dandi caressed his head, working her fingers through his hair as he made his tantalizing journey from one nipple to the next. "This feels amazing," her whole body was in tune with every pull of his lips, her pussy was opening and closing, her hips were dipping into the mattress as she simulated the movements they would make if he were making love to her. Lucas plumped her breasts, pushing them together, molding them, rubbing one nipple as he sucked the other. She tried to isolate each gift he gave her – the deep draws, the nips, swirling his tongue round and around her areola – all of it was so good it made her body weep. She was more than ready to be taken.

As his lips left her breasts to feather their way up to her collarbone, he talked to her. His words were as satisfying as his loving. "You'll never know how much I've longed for you. I don't regret one day I've waited for you; there is no one in this world that I love as much as you. If I had to wait an eternity for you, it would have been worth it." It began to dawn on Dandi exactly what their relationship was – it was serious. Lucas wasn't playing with her, he was devoted to her.

"Lucas, I didn't realize. I didn't understand." She would have continued her explanation, but what he was doing didn't allow for something so mundane as thinking. He settled between her thighs and began slide his lips down from her breasts, past her belly button, and Dandi began to pant as she saw where he was headed. Her whole body seemed to sing with anticipation.

"Do you want this? Do you want me to kiss your pussy?" His hand caressed her body, wandering from her waist to her breast – playing with her nipple as he licked and nipped on her lower abdomen – just hinting at the joy to come.

"Yes, I want it – I want you." She lifted her hips, trying to get him to move faster, but he took his time, licking the top of her thigh – staying just inches away from where she needed him most. Dandi was panting, her clit was throbbing and she was afraid she might cum before she ever got to feel the heaven of him kissing her pussy. "Lucas, please!"

One lick – one touch – one lap – that was all it would take and she would explode in a firestorm of bliss. "Watch me, Dandi. Watch me love you. Look into my eyes, let me see everything you're feeling." Soft kisses, tiny licks – he teased her, staying just above her wet slit. His warm breath provided a little relief, but not enough. She shuddered, she writhed, she strained to open as wide for him as possible. His fingers gently soothed over her mons, appreciating the bare flesh she had prepared for him in hopes he would do exactly what he was doing.

At last. Lucas took his fingers and opened her up, as if for his delectation. He groaned. "You are so beautiful, so soft and pink. I love that you're swollen and wet. That means you want me. Don't you?"

"Yes, damn you!" She ran her fingers through his hair, which hung like a silken curtain across her thighs.

He smiled; he had her right where he wanted her – on the edge. Pushing one finger into her tender little hole, he gloried when she bucked off the bed. Splaying his hand over her middle, he held her down and gave her what they both needed. Lucas began to kiss and lick, pressing his tongue inside of her, mimicking the movements his cock was demanding. Sliding upward, he tickled her clit, tonguing the little nubbin until Dandi was thrashing her head, the tension in her body rising to a crisis level. Cream began to flow from her body and he lapped it up. She sobbed and begged, "Lucas, my God, please, please!"

With all the skill he possessed, he ate at her pussy, sucking her clit, worshiping her in the most intimate way a man can. Dandi wailed as her climax came, she arched her back almost double, but Lucas held her down and continued to lave and suck, ensuring that she rode the crest of ecstasy just as long as possible. When it was over, he kissed her tenderly all along the crease of her thighs, all along the faint mark of her C-section, bringing her down until she was a sated and soft armful for him to hold.

He moved up and lay down beside her, stroking her waist and pressing soft kisses on her face. "Does any of that bring back memories?"

She wished she could tell him that it did, but she couldn't. Instead, she offered him something better. "You're making me love you. I tried to hold out because I wanted to recall the old feelings, but I don't have to, what I feel now is just as powerful and just as good."

"I agree," he collared her neck; she knew he could feel her heartbeat under his palm.

When he kissed her deeply, Dandi could taste herself on his lips and tongue and excitement began to build again. Feeling between them, she stroked his hot, huge cock through his pants. "Can I see you, now?"

"Yes, but I have to be honest. If I don't get inside of you soon, it'll all be over with." Lucas was desperate to cum inside of her. He had been waiting too long. Quickly, he shed his pants and underwear and lay back for her to look her fill.

Dandi sat up and stared at him in wonder. With a gentle tentative touch, she grazed his steel-hard shaft with her fingers, even skating down to cup and weigh his balls. When he shut his eyes and moaned, she smiled. His response to her made her feel powerful. That she could cause this magnificent man to shudder was a dream come true. "You are impressive," she admitted as she stroked him, passing her thumb over the leaking tip end. "I know this all fits inside of me, but I don't see how."

"I'll be glad to show you." Knowing he couldn't wait any longer, he pulled her down and drank from her lips, working her breast in his palm.

Dandi was ready; she wanted to know what it was like to take him inside of her body. She wrapped her arm around his shoulder and hooked a leg over his waist, trying to rub her pussy on his cock.

"Are you still on the pill?"

"Just got back on it last week."

He snorted. "I'll take that as a compliment."

"You do that. It is."

"So, I don't have to wear a condom?"

"No, no, I want to feel you – all of you."

"Damn, yes," he rose over her and she ate him up with her eyes, he was larger than life and all hers. Hooking her knees over his arms, he opened her up and pulled her to him. Dandi was trembling with need, she couldn't take her eyes off his face and the love she could see shining in his eyes was the icing on the cake for her.

When she felt the head of his cock probe at the gate of her pussy, she lifted her ass and tried to impale herself.

"Easy, baby, easy," Lucas had to maintain control; he was just too near to exploding. Pushing into her, he flexed his hips, working his way into her tight channel. Merciful Heaven! It was like nothing he had ever felt. Maybe it was the endless longing, the months of aching, the nights of dreaming of this moment — but as he slid his cock into her wet heat, Lucas gasped. "God, you are so tight, so lush."

Dandi whimpered. "It's so good."

Good was an understatement, it was heaven. Trying to make the rapture last as long as possible, he rocked his hips with a gentle thrusting motion. Beneath him, Dandi wasn't still, she met his thrusts, her sheath holding his cock tightly as a glove.

Lucas's cock was unbelievably thick and there was no part of her that was not caressed and rubbed. She had no idea she could feel so full, or that full could be so wonderful. With every push into her, he tilted his pelvis and the friction was out of this world. She held on to his forearms, her nails raking into his skin. "Harder, baby!" she begged. "Give it to me harder!"

Lucas pushed her legs back against her body — opening her up even farther. Angling his hips, he searched for that one spot guaranteed to make her scream. Pulling all the way out, he slid back in — again and again — hammering into her until she clamped down on him, keening her pleasure as her control shattered and a zillion points of light flashed through her mind and body. "LUCAS!!"

Holding her sweet ass, he didn't let up, but continued to pound until he came, his whole body vibrating with pure ecstasy. His cock pulsed with her, but still he ground his hips against her loving the way his cum shot out of his cock and bathed her in his seed.

Dandi kept cumming, she couldn't stop, the aftershocks persistent and powerful. All she could do was hold on to him and enjoy. A sense of complete bliss and awe washed over her. "Hold me," she requested.

"Gladly," he rolled onto his back and took her with him. "Are you all right?"

"Better," was all she had the strength to say.

He'd take that. It was a damn good start.

*****

"Get up, sleepy head. It's time to let the good times roll," Lucas popped her on the ass with a towel.

"What the heck?" Dandi opened her eyes. He had kept her up half the night; they had made love three times. "How can you be so energetic? You've worn me out!"

"I'm happy." That was his explanation, and it was a good one. Dandi smiled.

She got up and showered while he made coffee. "Let me call Lucy before we go."

"You can, but I already called and checked on her, she's fine." His thoughtfulness made her smile. But she called her baby, anyway, just to tell her she was loved. As soon as they were ready, they headed out, traveling over the long Atchafalaya Bridge that spanned the largest swamp in the United States.

While they drove, they took the opportunity to share and relearn more about one another. "What has been your favorite class so far?"

She was thinking, but she was also mesmerized by the sight of his hands on the steering wheel. They were broad and strong, the veins on the back a perfect place to lick. Dandi had done that last night, she had kissed him from his lips to his toes, giving him a blow job that had him bellowing like one of the bull alligators in the swamp.

"Dandi? What are you thinking?" Lucas asked with amusement in his voice.

"Huh?" She giggled. "Last night, I was remembering how those big strong hands of yours felt on my body."

The Mercedes swerved, "Don't say things like that while I'm driving," he teased. "Now answer the question and get your mind out of the bedroom before we have to pull over so I can ravish you on the side of the road."

"Hmmm, that's not exactly motivation for me to talk about college. I'd rather be ravished." His look of mock warning made her smile. "I enjoyed the classes on Indian Burial Mounds the most."

"Did you ever get to excavate at Cahokia?"

"No," Dandi looked at him in wonder. "It always amazes me that you know me so well."

"I don't know why it should, I love you."

His simple explanation made goosebumps appear on her arms. "Do you have any partners in your practice?"

"No, I'm on my own." He couldn't tell her about the job he lost or that missing out on that opportunity was probably the best thing that could have happened to him. The Solomon Group had been hit by a huge scandal, much worse than anything sweet Dandi could have ever done to the sanctimonious bastards. Chas Tonahill had not only been embezzling from the company but he had been caught molesting his patients while they had been under hypnosis. The company had gone bankrupt. While he and The Touch Institute had flourished. Lucas had achieved his goals of respectability and community status. He was involved, plugged in, lauded and sought out. But none of it – none of it – had satisfied him. Without Dandi all of the accolades and accomplishments were hollow and meaningless.

"I read an article you wrote in the newspaper."

"What newspaper?"

"The Times Picayune."

"Your favorite newspaper," he grinned.

"Yes, it said that you were heading up the Global Study on Sexual Attitudes and Behavior." She was beyond impressed.

"I am, it's a universal problem. The study focuses on almost thirty thousand people and over three quarters of them have had at least one sexual problem, but only eighteen percent had sought medical help. We are trying to educate people on the ways that modern therapy can alleviate some of their problems. I think it's tragic that people don't feel like they can be honest and ask for aid in achieving what I consider every human being's right – to enjoy intimacy and find solace in companionship."

When Lucas had lapsed into professor-speak, she had almost felt intimidated. "I am sure it's hard to admit your personal problems and failings to a stranger. People are so quick to judge, even when they have problems or faults equal to or worse than the person they are judging. Sex and sexual issues are gossip fodder and some folks thrive on sensationalism. A perfect world would be where everyone could realize that no one is perfect and that we all want the same thing — to be accepted. Doctors like yourself can provide people with a safe place to express those doubts and insecurities."

Lucas was amazed at her insight. She had no idea that she had just pinpointed the very issue that had torn them apart. He only hoped when her memory did return, she would turn to him instead of worrying about what the rest of the world thought about her. "Very true, you said it well." Wanting to get on a happier subject, he turned to his daughter. "What was Lucy's first word? Mama, I bet."

"No, banana."

Lucas laughed. "Banana?"

"Yes, she loves fruit, especially bananas."

"Did you have hard labor? I saw the C-section scar."

Dandi hung her head. "Yes, I couldn't have her, she was breech. I almost didn't make it. Beau and Harley were out of town and I was by myself. Lucy was early, and I was young and thought the contractions were too far apart to go to the hospital. But they started coming harder and faster than I expected and I couldn't drive myself. My phone was dead and I couldn't find the charger, I messed up."

Lucas groaned, "God, I should have been with you."

"I know, I was wishing for someone about that time, I'm surprised I didn't contact you telepathically. I begged for her Daddy to come, whoever he was."

What they had lost was magnified in his mind. "I'm so sorry about everything." He wished he could just pour his heart out and get it all out in the open.

"Did you really look for me — every day?"

"Yes," Lucas covered her hand. It was so tiny and fragile, yet more capable than anyone could imagine. He had seen her prepare a meal, paint a portrait, shoot a gun, control a wild animal and weave those same sweet hands in a dance so artistic it could bring tears to your eyes. "I hired a team of private investigators to find you, but we were looking for Dandi Alexander, not Dandi LeBlanc. When you disappeared, you vanished."

"I couldn't wait to get rid of Arlon's name, I wanted my Dad's name back."

"I can understand that, I don't blame you, but it made finding you impossible. You had no credit cards to trace, no insurance, no family that I knew the name of – you never mentioned LeBlanc to me, I didn't even know your parent's names."

Dandi smiled sadly, "We must not have talked much, I guess we just had sex." She was teasing, but the remorse for lost time was there.

"We did share, but - we were battling our own demons, I guess."

"What do you mean?" she wanted to know.

The miles were passing quickly; Lucas could see the Crescent City spread out before them. What should he say? "I was trying to get my career started and you were trying to deal with school and diabetes. We were both struggling."

"I still don't understand why we broke up."

There was that question again, and this time he answered as honestly as he could.

"I don't either, Dandi. It wasn't my decision."

"Oh." Dandi couldn't help but imagine the worst. Had he been unfaithful? She couldn't imagine that. Had she been unfaithful? No, she wasn't crazy. Was it money problems? Did she want to know? Yes, she did. "Lucas, do you think I should get therapy? Would hypnosis help? You can tell me all the details you know, but I'll never understand me or why I did what I did or how I felt about you and our relationship unless I regain my memory."

Lucas pulled under a huge pecan next to the beautiful Maison Perrier, a luxury B&B just off St. Charles in the Garden District. "Let's don't worry about it today, Let's concentrate on enjoying ourselves. I still believe it will all come back to you when you're ready, but like you – I'm impatient." Frankly, Lucas was torn. He wanted her to remember, but he didn't want her to be hurt by her past any more than she had already been. Hell, he couldn't have it both ways, he knew that.

A bell-hop came to help them with their luggage and Lucas led her into the lobby. He couldn't wait to make Dandi feel pampered and special. He had several things planned for them to do and she said she had a couple of surprises for him, he couldn't imagine what they could be, but he looked forward to finding out. Their room was on the second floor, complete with a balcony. "We'll have to come back and watch the Mardi Gras parade from here."

"This is beautiful, thank you." Dandi inspected their room. It had a private bath, a sleigh bed and a fireplace. "You know, we could cancel all of our excursions and just stay here and make love if you want."

Lucas snagged her as she walked past. "Temptress! Don't worry, I'm going to fuck you till you can't walk, but I want our relationship to be based on more than just sex. I want you to love me for my mind as well as my body."

He was teasing, she knew, but she played along. "You do have a beautiful mind," she took hold of the bed post and swung back, letting her hair dangle toward the ground. "But I am equally enraptured with your sexy physique. I mean - you are hot, hard and hung." As she talked, she shimmed on the post, wiggled her ass at him and tried her dead-level best to turn him on.

She was succeeding. Dandi was working the post like a stripper pole and he knew it was pure instinct; she had no memory of Tonga or Angel Baby.

"To hell with the street car ride, we'll do that later. Show me what you got, Angel." The name slipped out before he could call it back, but she just threw her head back and laughed.

"It's nothing you haven't seen before, but I do enjoy you looking."

"I think you enjoy me touching you the most."

"You might be right. Let's test it and see."

She picked up her simple red sheathe dress and skimmed it over her head.

"Lord Have Mercy. Where did you get those?" Her magnificent body was showcased in a tiny red lace bra and a matching red thong. "God, I love you in red." Her ass cheeks looked like the most perfect Valentine he'd ever envisioned.

"I went to that Secret store and I bought several surprises for you."

"I love surprises," he unzipped his pants and took out his rock-hard cock.

Dandi was feeling daring, Lucas loved her body and it made her want to tease him. "Do you see anything you like?" She bent over and spread her legs, what you might call an open invitation.

"Shit," Lucas walked up to her and palmed her round, firm derriere, rubbing his hands all around and down, lifting the cheeks a little. She pushed back against him, indicating she wanted more. He looked up to find that Dandi was watching him over her shoulder, and when she touched the tip of her tongue to her lip and winked, his cock jumped.

This wasn't going to take long, Lucas hadn't realized this was a fantasy of his, but he was beyond aroused. He pulled her thong to one side, and dipped his fingers into her creamy, hot center. "Oh yea, you're so wet for me."

"I ache," she laid her head on the bed, presenting her ass for his pleasure. "Touch me some more," she purred.

"How hard do you want me to touch you?" Playing with her, he gave her a gentle pop on one cheek.

A sweet heat radiated out from her clit. "Harder." This was crazy. She didn't want to be spanked did she? He accommodated her, popping her a little harder on the other side of her ass. Erotic fire began to build between her legs. "Do it harder, Lucas," she challenged him.

He couldn't believe it. Did he know this woman? He ran a hand over the spectacular curve of her back, letting her think he was just petting her, then when she least suspected, he spanked her twice and damn if she didn't groan. "Fuck, you are so sexy." He took his cock in hand and rubbed it between her legs, massaging her vulva and clit with the wide head.

"Mmmmm," she moaned. "Mount me, please." She spread her legs wider, enticing him to bury himself balls deep.

"You are amazing. I'll never get tired of you as long as I live." Placing one hand on her back, he braced her as he pushed in. They both groaned. God, the pleasure was fantastic. There was no holding back this time, he had to have her.

Dandi gasped as his long, thick cock slid inside of her. Ecstasy. She couldn't help herself, she reached down to rub her own clit.

Lucas looked down and watch his cock disappear inside of her, watched it emerge coated in her cream. He groaned at the absolute mind-blowing sensation of his cock sliding in and out of her tight, tight pussy.

"God, this is heaven," Dandi groaned as she clawed at the bedspread, squeezing him just as hard as she could.

"When you cum, say my name. I need to hear you say my name," he demanded. Leaning over, he reached around her waist and pushed her hand away so he could massage her clit. He wanted to take his time, take her in an achingly slow rhythm, but he couldn't. Instead he wrapped his fingers in her hair and pulled back, and when he did, she gave him what he needed – "Lucas! My God! Lucas!"

Her cry was all it took, he plunged into her deeply – taking her in several hard, fast thrusts, his cum pulsed into her in hot, creamy jets. Dandi relaxed on the bed, trembling. "You are so perfect, I'm so glad I found you." He rested his head in the middle of her back, rubbing his cheek on her smooth skin.

"That was fun," she giggled beneath him, "I think I'm gonna like it here. New Orleans brings out my wild side."

"I can see that," he chuckled along with her, kissing a line from her shoulder blade down her back, ending with a nip on her rear.

"Hey!" she yelped, and he gave her a warm pop.

"Let's go have some fun, the Big Easy awaits!"

And so they did. They did it all. The first thing they shared was the street car that ran the length of St Charles. Dandi loved the clickety-clack and listening to the conversations of the other passengers. She pointed out the sights to him that were special to her, the mansion owned by Anne Rice where she had set her famous "Witching Hour" novel, one of Dandi's favorites – Tulane and Loyola University and the Audubon Zoo. "If you don't mind, we're coming back to Tulane tomorrow, Savannah and Patrick O'Rourke will be here. Savannah is speaking at a culture symposium and I think I might get a job offer."

"Congratulations!" Lucas kissed her right there. "Tell me about this job and how far away from me would you be?" He hadn't meant to interject negativity, but it was the first thing he thought of, he couldn't help it.

Dandi looked at him sorta funny, as if she didn't get his point. Then it dawned on her, "Oh, no. I wouldn't be going anywhere. The Louisiana Cultural Center has a Lafayette branch, that's where Savannah works and I'd be sent on day trips, maybe a day or two more, but there isn't anywhere in Louisiana that you can't get there and back in a few hours." She put a hand on his arm. "I'm not going anywhere, Lucas."

He believed her, but the agony of losing her once made him so very vulnerable. "I know, and I'm so proud of you. I'll be honored to meet your friends."

They traveled to the Quarter and dined at Gallatoire's on redfish and crabmeat; they visited the Jax Brewery and walked on the Moonwalk. As evening drew near, they rented one of the horse drawn carriages and held hands as they were carried from street to street, listening to jazz musicians serenading on street corners and the whisper of the wind as it wound its way among the narrow, historic street.

The whole time, Lucas kept his arms wrapped around her, and not just because there was a nip in the air, he just loved to hold her. "Thanks for coming with me, I've been here countless times, but it's all new with you."

She rested her head on his shoulder, for once in complete contentment. "Everything is going to be all right, isn't it?"

"I'll do everything in my power to make you happy." Lucas prayed he could keep his promise.

That night, their lovemaking was different – more intense – they both felt an urgency to become one with the other. Lucas had pulled her in the shower, "Wanna play some more."

"Always," she was becoming addicted to this man.

While the warm waters had washed over them, Lucas had taken control and unleashed his power in a kiss, tangling his tongue with hers, in a sensuous dance of seduction. He was masterful. Dominating. He took. He possessed and she surrendered. Oh, not that she didn't have power, Dandi had power. Lucas followed every clue her body offered, every whimper, every shiver – whatever she wanted – Lucas delivered.

"Take me," she urged, already so turned on she couldn't think straight.

"Soon," he promised, as he held her hands over her head, bracketing her thighs with his own, rubbing his body against her from chest to hips. She was held immobile – between the proverbial rock and the hard place.

"What are you waiting for?" she gasped and he swallowed her words with another kiss.

Lucas's whole being vibrated with a desperate need to brand her as his, mark his territory, claim his prize. "The right time," he growled,

"The right time for what?" she thought now was just fine. Dandi needed to be filled, she pulled one hand free and slid it down between their wet bodies and found his cock, wrapping her fingers around his thickness.

"Not yet," he moved her hand back over her head, capturing both of them with one of his own.

Her breasts felt heavy, sensitive, she needed for them to be sucked – God, she just needed. "Lucas, do something," she pleased.

"What do you want?" he asked between kisses, as he rubbed his mouth down her neck and across her shoulder. "Could this be it?" he cupped her breast, thumbing the nipple, readying it for his lips.

"I think you got it," she arched her back, offering her tits to him. He did not disappoint, bending a little to reach her, he opened his mouth wide and enveloped her whole areola in his mouth. He didn't just suck, he consumed – laving and chewing, sucking and suckling – Dandi stood on tiptoe, wanting everything he could give.

"What else do you want?" he asked as he rubbed a teasing path over the top of her pussy. "After I satisfy you, I'll tell you what I need."

"Touch me, damn you," Dandi nipped him on the shoulder, so overwhelmed with desire that she longed to just crawl under his skin and stay there.

"Patience, patience," he chanted as he dipped into her folds, teasing her slit, but keeping away from that hard knot of nerves that was singing his praises. "You're so creamy, so ready for me. How much do you want me, Dandi?"

"Grrrrr," Dandi snarled, just about ready to either bite him or beg him to get what she wanted.

"Tell me." He let his thumb graze her clit, one brief pass that made her jerk.

"You know," she tried to let that suffice.

"Honesty is the best policy," he chuckled.

Dandi was about to pass out, her knees were weak, but just before she was about to collapse, Lucas pushed two fingers up inside her and her whole body stiffened in grateful surprise. "Oh, yeah."

"Is that what you want?" he began to finger-fuck her, rhythmic come-hither motions that pin-pointed that magical hot spot that could bring her to her knees.

A wail broke from her lips. "Yes! No!" she clamped her thighs around his wrist, trying to trap him between her legs.

"Which is it?" he asked, but she shook her head, not able to say. "Open your legs and I'll give you what you need." She did, and he rubbed her clit, massaged her vulva until she cried out and gushed, gifting him with the undeniable evidence of her capitulation to his plan.

"Was that it? Are you satisfied?"

"No!" she was emphatic. "I want you."

"All right," he agreed. "Put your hands on me." He released his hold on her and she hungrily sought him out, enclosing his cock in both of her hands.

"I love the way you're made," she rubbed him, one fist over the other. He was big, velvet over steel, alive and pulsing in her hands.

"What else do you love?" he pushed her.

"How you feel inside of me," she wrapped one leg around his hip, offering herself to him.

"Like this?" he picked her up, easily, her legs draped over his forearms, her ass cupped in his hands and pushed his cock in — slowly — reigniting her desperation.

"That's a start," she was playing with fire, even in her lust-dazed state, she was aware of the game they were playing. Her fingers grasped his shoulders and tightened as he pistoned his hips working his dick further up into her with each jab. "I think you got it," she whispered against his shoulder.

"Almost," he agreed as he shoved his way on home, Dandi's heels dug into his ass in appreciation. "Now, for the good part."

The good part was very good. Dandi was grateful for the support of the shower as he swiveled, undulated, and flexed his hips, making sure that no part of her was untouched or untested. All she could do was hold on as he tunneled deep within her, fulfilling all the fantasies she had ever had, giving her exactly what she needed.

Lucas was a force of nature, as he fucked her, he kissed her and in between kisses he praised her, telling her how beautiful and perfect and wonderful she was. Both of them were damp with perspiration, this was not a gentle joining. They were mating. It was primal. It was real. And when their worlds exploded, they exploded together. White hot streams of pleasure swept them out in the deep and they rolled with the waves of ecstasy, crashing back against the shore only to settle into the sea of contentment.

"Was that what you needed?" He asked as he held her close, loving the way her body felt against his.

"Yes, you knew exactly what I needed." She sighed as he set her on her feet and turned off the now cool water. "How about you? You said you'd tell me. Did you get what you needed?"

"Not yet," he admitted, as he dried her body with a soft, warm towel. "I want you and my little girl to move in with me."

CHAPTER FIFTEEN

The soft Louisiana moonlight bathed him in a silvery glow. She lay with her pillow tucked under her chin and studied his face. He had asked her to move in with him. His asking for something more permanent didn't come as a huge surprise, but Dandi found her own reaction to his suggestion revealing. Like a typical woman, she wasn't quite satisfied. Didn't he want to marry her?

Oh, he had been so excited and his enthusiasm was contagious. But now, in the dark of night, she wondered if agreeing to leave her apartment and move Lucy and her meager belongings into his mammoth mansion was the right thing to do. People lived together before marrying these days, she knew that. But it wasn't something she had ever seen herself doing. Come to think of it, she hadn't ever thought she would be a single mother either, but Lucy was the best thing that could ever happen to anyone and she wouldn't have traded her for love or money.

Still, as she gazed at the man she loved, she wanted more. Reaching out, she placed her hand on his forearm, soothing the muscle and hair roughened skin. How excited he had been when she agreed, he had lifted her high in the air, then let her slide her down his body, kissing her all along the way. For hours, they had whispered plans and words of love. Dandi hadn't been able to sleep, her mind had been racing making plans and lists of things to do. Lucy would be crazy happy and Beau would understand – maybe.

"Morning, my love," his deep, sleepy voice caused her heart to race.

"I woke you, I'm sorry, I just had to touch you."

He rolled over and snuggled against her. "I'm glad you did."

She put her arm over his shoulder and kissed his neck. It wasn't but a second till it registered with her what she felt nudging against her leg. He was hard. So hard. Smiling a secret smile, she lifted the covers and slipped beneath them.

"Hey, where are you going?"

"Down here." They had slept naked so there was no hindrance to her goal. All of a sudden he whipped back the cover, it was still pretty dark, but she could see him clearly enough to know where to put her mouth.

"What a way to start the day," he groaned as she reached for him, grabbed his thick cock and licked her lips on her way down. Running her tongue over the swollen head of his erection, his fingers threaded through her hair and tightened. "Damn, so good. Open your mouth, wide. Oh yeah. Suck me, baby." The intense pleasure in his voice caused her shudder. She held him with one hand, wrapped the other around his thigh and took him deep. God, it was good. Closing her eyes, she just let herself enjoy being with him – his silky hardness, his clean-musky smell, his tangy taste – she lapped at the little slit at the tip of his dick and relished the way he groaned her name. "Dandi, my Dandi."

His hand cupped the back of her head as he flexed his hips and began to stroke into her mouth. Pleasing him was her only thought. She sucked hard, pumping his shaft close to the root. He groaned his approval. Drawing him from her mouth, she licked and lapped at the head, cradling him with her tongue. Feeling adventurous, she drug her teeth over his sensitive flesh, smiling around his girth when he responded. "I love your mouth on me," his praise just made her want to give him more. When he threw his head back and growled, her body responded and she felt herself begin to ache and tingle.

She used to think that oral sex would be distasteful or something you just did to make your man happy, not something that a woman would enjoy doing, But, she was wrong. Dandi loved the feel of him in her mouth, she loved the power it gave her – the power to give him untold pleasure. Hollowing her cheeks, she sucked harder, swirling her tongue all around the head. Then taking him deep, she bobbed her head up and down, moving her lips up and down his shaft – faster and faster. "Mmmm," she hummed her satisfaction.

Lucas was lost in the pleasure. He closed his eyes and let the ecstasy spread out over his body. His hips bucked sympathetically, his thighs were tense, his balls heavy – his toes curled. Nothing was better than this. With a shout, he emptied himself into her mouth.

"Come up here," Lucas was euphoric and his cock was spent. He tried to pull her up, but Dandi wouldn't come.

She wanted more. Her breasts were heavy, her pussy was throbbing and she needed him. Taking his now flaccid member in her hand, she began nuzzling her face against it, kissing it tenderly.

"What are you doing, Baby?"

This was one morning Lucas would not forget. Dandi had given him an incredible blow job, swallowing every drop. But she wasn't through. In a scene other men would have died for, she licked him clean, sucked him hard and rode him until they both came, trembling and crying out their love.

Laissez le bon temp rouler.

Let the good times roll.

*****

It had rained during the night. The streets of New Orleans were clean and almost empty; very few people were out milling around. Lucas and Dandi rode the street car to Canal and then walked through the Quarter to have coffee and beignets at Café du Monde.

They walked down Royal Street where he stopped at a jewelry store and bought her a beautiful necklace, a fleur de lis to commemorate their trip. Dandi was happier than she had ever been.

But when they walked down Bourbon, Lucas nearly had a stroke. In the window of one of the clubs, there were posters of women in different states of dishabille. Perhaps some of them were current performers, or notable ones from the past, but one was familiar – too familiar. It was a poster of Angel Baby, one apparently made as she danced at Tonga in the familiar white outfit made famous from the viral video. Lucas held his breath. Dandi had been laughing and joking, "I've never been in a place like this, Lucas. Have you?" When he didn't answer right away, she giggled. "Of course you have, you're a man."

"Yes, I have in my bachelor days."

She wondered at his phrasing. Did meeting her put an end to his bachelor days?

Her gaze wandered over the poster and Lucas stopped breathing.

But she kept walking.

Dandi hadn't recognized herself.

Lucas knew then that something was going to have to be done, he couldn't keep living like this, waiting for the other shoe to drop. It was time Dandi knew the truth about herself and realize her past had no power over her. She was still the same person – the woman he loved.

They visited a few esoteric stores and the Voodoo museum and ended up at K-Paul's for lunch. "What looks good?" he asked as they studied the menu.

She was dressed in a simple black dress and a pair of flats. They wouldn't be going back to the room before attending the lecture. "I love my necklace," she patted it against her throat. It dresses up my outfit."

"You look beautiful," he complimented her. And she did. He was aware of the glances she received from other men. Their appreciation of her and envy of him was apparent. Asking her to move in with him last night was just the first step. He was getting ready to propose, but he had decided to go big. Lucas was going to make a grand gesture, one that she could not possibly misinterpret.

They placed their order. Dandi wanted to try the crawfish primavera and Lucas got a shrimp po-boy. "Give me your hand," he held his out.

"You've made me very happy," she put her hand in his.

"This is just the beginning, I can't wait to get you and Lucy moved in."

"Wagner? Is that you?" A man's voice hailed him from across the room. He looked over to see the mayor of Lafayette coming toward him with a big grin on his face. "You're coming to the banquet aren't you?"

Lucas had to think a minute. Banquet. Oh, the Chamber banquet. "Actually, I hadn't made up my mind." Actually, he hadn't given it any thought. He had more important things on his mind.

"You have to," the Mayor stood by his chair and held his hand out to Dandi. "Don Simpson."

"Don, this is Dandi LeBlanc," he had to bite his tongue. He wanted to say 'my fiancé so bad he could taste it.

"Hello, it's nice to meet you."

"You need to talk this guy into coming to that banquet and bringing you with him." He glared at Lucas. "I can't overemphasize that you need to come. I hate to ruin the surprise, but didn't you get a certified letter?"

It dawned on Lucas that more was going on than a simple chamber banquet. "No, but I have been distracted lately," he winked at Dandi. "What was it about?"

The mayor slapped him on the back. "You're our 'Man of the Year'."

Lucas was surprised and honored. "Well, heck. Thank you, Don. I appreciate it."

"How well do you know this guy?" Don aimed his question at Dandi.

"Pretty well, I guess." She knew enough, she knew she adored him.

"He's done more for our little neck of the woods than most anybody. Dane serves on bank boards, hospital boards, charity board – you name it, he's done it. Those articles that he writes for the newspapers have put our little area on the map. And what he did for me and the wife – well, we're grateful for that, too."

Lucas wished Don wouldn't keep extolling his supposed virtues, and all he did for him and his wife was suggest they listen to one another and he take something for his erectile dysfunction. "Okay, we'll be there. When is it?"

"Tomorrow night. You can see why I was worried. Haven't you been checking your emails?"

Lucas confessed that he hadn't. Since he had upped his efforts on winning Dandi, he had ignored other parts of his life. "I apologize, as you can see, I have a beautiful distraction."

"Yes, you do." The Mayor agreed.

After he had departed, Dandi leaned over and kissed Lucas on the cheek. "Congratulations."

"You will go with me, won't you?" He had planned on proposing tomorrow. The surprise he had planned would be hot off the press and Lucas was more than anxious to see how she reacted. After that, he planned on telling her the truth about their past and hold her tightly until she came to terms with it.

"Yes, I would love to go with you." She was feeling good about herself. After talking to Savannah, and hearing about the possibility of a job offer, she felt like she had something to offer Lucas. Dandi had worked hard at building a life for she and Lucy.

And she felt she had. She had a job, almost had a degree, and had the respect of all who knew her. "I'll be proud to be sitting with the Man of the Year."

After lunch, they rode the streetcar back to Tulane. "This is my alma mater," he didn't know if he had ever told her.

"Really? It is a very prestigious university. I took most of my classes online so I wouldn't have to leave Lucy at night."

He squeezed her tight, "Thank you for taking such good care of our daughter."

As they made their way into the auditorium, Dandi was surprised to see several hundred people attending. She glanced to the front and saw Patrick O'Rourke standing by his petite wife. The ex-Marine stood head and shoulders above everyone else and was easy to spot. "There they are, come on and I'll introduce you."

They made their way through the crowd, "Savannah!" Dandi called out.

"Dandi! How good to see you!" She hugged both of them and introduced Lucas.

"Lucas?" Savannah questioned. "I thought your name was Dane."

"Lucas to my friends," was the only explanation he gave and they accepted it graciously.

"I'm looking forward to your presentation," Dandi offered.

Savannah leaned on her husband's shoulder. "I think you'll enjoy it more when you find out who the author of the paper is that I'll be citing as back-up for my findings."

"Who?" Dandi was interested. Louisiana folkore and history was one of her greatest loves.

"You," was the simple answer.

"Me?" She was flabbergasted. "You mean the one on the Pointe Coupee Parish?"

"Yes, and I'm also citing your work on the LSU Campus Mounds."

Dandi held her chest; her breath was coming in small pants. "I can't believe it."

"Well, believe it." Savannah was ecstatic for her friend. "When I'm through, Patrick and I would love to take you two to dinner. I have a formal offer to make, if you're interested."

"I'm shocked," was all she could say. "Can I ask you a few questions?"

"Hey man," Patrick nodded at Lucas. "Why don't we go get a cup of coffee and let these two plot?"

"Sounds good to me," Lucas kissed Dandi on the forehead. "I'll be back."

"Thank you," she threw her arms around him and hugged him. "For everthing."

Patrick stole a kiss from his own wife, then led Lucas to the back where coffee and cookies had been laid out for the attenders. "Your wife has done well for herself," Lucas knew of Savannah's work with the Cultural Center.

"Yes, she has." Patrick agreed. "She speaks highly of Dandi."

"I'm glad." Lucas wondered how to broach the subject. "I understand that you were presumed dead. That must have been hard on Savannah."

Patrick pulled out two chairs close to one another. "It was. I never want her to go through something like that again."

Lucas found himself wanting to confide in Patrick. They had something in common, a forced separation that none of them had asked for. "Our situation is not exactly the same, but Dandi and I have lost time. We were engaged to be married, and through a series of unfortunate circumstances, she and I were separated. Dandi was in a bus crash and lost her memory of me. I'm trying to win her love again."

Patrick listened sympathetically. "Has she regained her memory?"

"No, not yet." Lucas watched her speak animatedly to Savannah. "She needs to remember, but I dread it in a way."

"Did you two have a hard time?" Patrick accepted a refill from a passing waiter.

"Yes, and I don't know exactly what pushed her away. I'm a little afraid to find out." Lucas had struggled with Dandi's leaving. Had she overheard the partner's threats or had she just gotten cold feet?

"She loves you, I can tell."

"I hope you're right."

They returned to their women and found a place to sit to listen to Savannah's talk. She had prepared a slide presentation with photos of the mounds, illustrating Dandi's research. "As a Louisiana native, it fills me with great pride to share with you our ancient and rich history. We are a state whose claim to fame not only includes pirates and kings, but we have provided a safe haven for the Acadians who fled him after their diaspora, their exile. New Orleans was a viable city long before the American Revolution, yet this area has been inhabited as far back as 400 A. D."

Savannah went on to show slides of Poverty Point, Watson's Brake and other burial sites. One of the things that surprised him was the reference she made of Dandi's relationship with one of the premier archaeologist in the South. Apparently she was working with him to create an 'Ancient Mounds Trail' that would link 37 significant historical sites across the state. "We have with us, Dandi LeBlanc, who will be joining our team at the Louisiana Cultural Center. Please give her a hand."

When Dandi stood, Lucas's heart swelled. He was so proud. After the lecture, Patrick escorted them to his car and drove them to port where they boarded one of the steamboats that traversed the Mississippi and had supper under the stars.

Neither Lucas nor Patrick brought up their sad times of separation from their women, but both understood and appreciated how lucky they were to be together.

When Lucas and Dandi returned to Maison Perrier, Dandi was walking on air. "Can you believe they want me to work with them?"

"Yes, I can. You are talented, super-smart and very decorative," he teased her as he cornered her against the door for a kiss.

"Thank you, I'm relieved that you are proud of me."

"That's not the only thing I feel for you." He pushed his erection against her. "You want to help me fulfill a fantasy?"

"Of course," she rubbed her face against his, loving the feel of his five o'clock shadow. "But let's check on Lucy first and let me call Harley and ask about Aron McCoy."

"Good," he needed to get used to being a family man.

"Hold the thought about the fantasy, though. I'll be right back," she wiggled her tush at him as she dug her phone from her purse.

"I won't forget," he smiled as he envisioned Dandi tied spread eagle to the bed.

Lucy was fine and Lucas had to talk to her, too. He couldn't resist telling her than she and her Mommy would be moving to his house. Of course, Lucy was more excited about the horses than anything else. Next, Dandi called Harley and was sad to hear that Aron McCoy had not been found. The search was still ongoing, however.

"It's sad," Harley whispered. "Libby has almost made herself sick. They found his wedding ring today. And you know that I sometimes get feelings from objects?"

"Yes," Dandi had never really spoken of this with Beau's fiancé. She wasn't sure how she felt about those types of things.

"I don't think Aron is dead."

Dandi got cold chills at the conversation. "I hope you're right. Did you get any specific information from your vision?" She struggled with the words, not knowing exactly how to phrase it.

"Only that he suffered some kind of trauma, but I felt no cessation of his life force." When Dandi didn't answer right away, Harley lowered her voice. "When you need answers, when the questions get too heavy for you to bear, come to me. I know who you are."

"What do you mean?" Dandi shivered. "You know who I am. I'm Beau's cousin."

"Yes, you are. You are a valued and beloved member of his family and soon to be mine. But we're all two people, Dandi. I am a rape survivor, and a warrior; I have diffused bombs on the bottoms of ships and in terrorist strongholds. But, I'm also a woman who is very much in love with her man. It has been hard for me to reconcile all of those pieces of myself. But I have. I'm whole. I know who I am."

Dandi shook with the implications. "You know something about my past, don't you?"

"All things eventually are revealed, Dandi. Hold up your head. You are amazing." Dandi had to sit down as Harley quoted Miss Etta verbatim. "You are valuable. You are worthwhile. You are worthy to be loved."

Dandi hung up the phone, not knowing what the future held, but hoping she had the courage to see it through.

*****

Harley stood gazing out of her window. Beau came up behind her and kissed her neck. "What are you thinking?"

"I'm worrying about Dandi and Libby and Aron."

"You're a worrier all right."

Harley smiled. "Yes, I have my worry list. It' keeps me occupied."

"I have something to occupy you," he nudged her backside with his swelling cock.

"Yes, you do. And I love everything you do to me." She turned in his arms and raised her head for his kiss. But in the back of her mind was an image – it was foggy and distant, but very real. . . .

He opened his eyes and shaded them against the bright light. Where was he?

"How are you feeling, Sir?"

"My head hurts," he tried to sit up.

At first he thought the movement of the room could be attributed to his dizziness, but then he realized he was on a boat. "Where am I?"

"In the Caribbean, Sir."

"Damn, what happened to me?" He looked down to discover he was only clothed by a sheet. "Where are my clothes?"

"Don't worry; garments will be furnished for you."

He held his hand to his head. There was a knot as big as a chicken egg on his forehead. "Have I been in an accident?"

"Yes, you have. You are very lucky, Sir. We picked you up a few days ago. You almost drowned."

Looking around, he could see that he was on some type of luxury vessel. Two men in white coats were attending to a meal being laid out on a table – for two.

"Drowned?" God, why couldn't he remember? Where had he been? Damn, that wasn't the most important question.

"I hate to ask this, but – Who the hell am I?"

*****

"Here, Lucy, help Mama pack up your toys." Dandi was at the same time elated and shaking in her shoes. Moving in with Lucas was a huge step. He had dropped her off this morning with the promise he'd be back to get her in time for the Chamber of Commerce banquet where he would be named Man of the Year.

She had gone into work, but Indy had sent her home, telling her she was practically useless in her excitement. That was fine by her; it would take her a couple of days to get everything packed up. Indy had looked worried, though. Something had been bothering him. "God, I hope he didn't screw up that order with Dunbar."

A banging on her door caused her to almost drop a plate she was wrapping in newspaper. Why she was packing her dishes, she didn't know. Lucas had everything she'd need and what he didn't have, he would certainly buy for her. But she was attached to these cheap plates with their decorative butterflies flitting across their plastic surface. "Just a minute!"

When she finally had the door open, it was to find Deb and Cindi staring at her with an odd expression on their faces. "What's wrong?"

"She doesn't know," Deb spoke to Cindi, "or she wouldn't look so happy."

"Hey, I have every reason to be happy. The man I love has asked me move in with him. I'm packing now!"

When they didn't smile with her, it hit her what they had said. "What don't I know?"

"Where's Lucy?" Cindi asked.

"In her room telling her cat all about their new home."

"Well, make sure she stays there."

"She's occupied," Dandi was getting worried. "What's going on?"

"You've got to see this." They drug her to the couch and forced her down on the worn blue velvet. Deb knelt and put a CD in the player and pressed Start.

"What is it?"

"You." Deb looked at her almost accusingly. "Why didn't you tell us you were famous? And wicked?" She tempered her words with a smile, but it didn't do a thing to make Dandi feel better.

Her friends sat on either side of her as a news report came on. It was one of those Gossip Shows that air on late night cable. They were interviewing a radio reporter. "Hey, that's Nita, Indy's girlfriend."

"Yea, traitor-bitch." Cindi grumbled.

"What?"

"Just watch." In a few moments, they began showing pictures of a strip club in Shreveport and talking about a dancer who had been involved in a murder investigation. Apparently the dancer, Angel Baby, had disappeared.

"What does this have to do with me?" She didn't understand.

"Everything." Deb pointed.

Dandi refocused on the screen and saw her own face. "That's me!"

"Yes, that's you, Angel Baby!"

Dandi's body went ice-cold. They played a video of a stripper dancing to an old song that she had always loved, 'After All.' Miss Etta had taught her a modern dance routine to the tune. "What am I doing?"

"You're stripping!" Deb whacked her on the leg.

"Oh, God!" Dandi felt nauseous. The reporter had cut back and run an old interview of her and she didn't have to listen – she remembered every word. She remembered everything. It all came rushing back on her like a tsunami. She remembered Romero and Jane, Patty and Cahill. "God, I remember." She grabbed her head, tears beginning to flow. She remembered meeting Lucas for the first time. She remembered the lap dance and running from the club. She remembered waking up in Lucas's back seat and the clerks at the convenience store, how he had thought she was on drugs, and how he had talked her into going home with him."

"So, tell us!" Cindi urged her. "What happened to you?"

Dandi couldn't talk. She stood up and paced, holding herself so tight around the middle that she could barely breathe. She remembered Lucas taking her virginity and how he had presumed she was used. "I remember falling in love," she wailed. "I remember the hope and the dreams." God, she remembered her fear that she wouldn't fit into his world and how it had been confirmed by the men at the pharmacy and Dr. Solomon. "He lost his job because of me," she cried.

"What are you talking about?" they flanked her, trying to get her to calm down.

"Lucas! I remember everything!"

"Listen to me," Cindi shook her. "I don't understand everything, but there is one thing I do know. That man loves you, he doesn't just look at you, he drinks you in. He adores you."

"Yes, but . . ."

"No, buts. . ." Deb agreed. "He already knows all of this and he loves you, anyway. Right?"

Lucas did know everything. But how would he react when he found out everyone else knew the truth of who she was?

CHAPTER SIXTEEN

Lucas drove up to Firepower Munitions and pulled around to the back. He was early, but he hoped to see Lucy for a few minutes before they took her to the babysitter. Tonight, his family would be going home with him. And he had a surprise for Dandi, and a ring. "We're going to have a little talk tonight." Despite what Beau had said, Lucas thought it was time they got everything out in the open. He just couldn't take the chance she'd find out some other way. If he could tell her himself, he could make her understand that none of it mattered – not at all. She was as perfect today as she had been then – a perfect angel.

The day had been crazy. He had seen five patients and ate at his desk. After making sure his surprise for Dandi was ready, he had ran by the newspaper office and picked up his copy earlier. The article in question would run tomorrow, but he wanted Dandi to see it tonight.

Bounding from his Mercedes, he ran to the door and tapped on it. No answer. He knocked again. Twice he had tried to call her, but she hadn't answered. He had presumed she was working so hard packing that she had let her phone accidentally die down. When she didn't answer his third knock, Lucas panicked. He threw open the screen door and tried the knob to the wooden door. It was open. So he went in. "Dandi?"

He could see her. She sat on the couch. She wasn't dressed for an evening out. "What's going on?"

"I'm not going."

All right. "Are you tired? Are you sick?" He went to her. She wouldn't look at him. "What's wrong?"

"I'm Angel Baby. I remember everything," she whispered in agony.

A weakness hit Lucas like someone had let the air out of his life. "You are partially right, you are my Angel and you are my Baby." He tried to take her hand.

She moved it.

"I remember Tonga and Romero and stripping and the shame and the fear."

"Me. Do you remember me?" He took her face in his hands and held it still when she tried to get away. "Do you remember me?"

"Yes."

"If you do, you remember that I loved you then like I love you now and that I never, ever wanted you to leave me."

"I love you, too." She whispered. "I remember loving you then, and I love you now."

He let out a sigh of relief. "Thank God."

"I love you enough to give you up."

Terror slapped Lucas in the face. "no way in hell." He didn't intend to go through this again. "Please come with me. We need to talk."

She agreed with that. They had a lot to discuss, Lucy in particular.

"I'll wait for you here. This is your big night."

"Damn, my night. All I want is you."

"Nita, Indy's girlfriend, she recognized me. It's all over the news, people know. They won't give you your award!" Her voice rose with every word.

Lucas was desperate. "Listen to me. Do you think I give a flying fuck about that award? You are my reward." He pulled her to him and kissed her. He didn't stop, even when she tried to squirm out of his arms. Instead he patiently kissed her, tenderly kissed her, until she opened her lips and let him in. They kissed until he let her breathe, then he rubbed his cheek on the path of her tears.

"I'll embarrass you," she buried her head in his neck.

"No, you won't embarrass me, but you'll break my heart if you don't go."

"I don't want to hurt you. I remember what those people said who were with Dr. Solomon. I stood at the door and listened to them tell you that you had three days to make up your mind. You could either have me or the job."

"So you ran," he took her hands in his and kissed her fingertips.

"Yes, I didn't want you to have to make the decision. So, I made it for you."

"It wasn't the right decision, Dandi. If you had lingered a few more minutes, you would have heard me tell them to stick their job up their asses."

"You did?"

"Yes, and I want you to know that I made the right decision. I've never regretted it. If I had gone with the Solomon Group, my reputation would have been ruined. Not by you, by them. They were ran by crooked people, not Fredrich, he was innocent. But one of the others embezzled and abused his patients."

"Oh, my goodness."

"I came out of that room calling your name. And when you weren't there, my heart sank. I ran back upstairs to our room, and when I did, I met up with Romero's gorilla." He pulled his hair off his temple and showed her the scar. "I wasn't about to let him anywhere near you."

"Oh, God!" she threw her arms around his neck, "he hurt you."

"He didn't hurt you, that was the most important thing. Dandi, no one's opinion about any of this matters a bit to me. Only you matter."

"Are you sure?" she wanted him to be very sure.

"Positive." He kissed her once more.

"I had planned to call you, just before the bus crashed; I knew I needed to hear your voice, at least one more time"

"Oh Baby, I wish you could have. I've missed so much." Lucas picked her up and cradled her close. "Now go get ready, we have a big night ahead of us and it has nothing to do with Lafayette's Man of the Year."

Bless her heart, she went to get ready. Lucy was asleep in her bed and Lucas went and lay down beside her. His baby. He loved to watch her sleep. While he waited, he texted the editor of the Times Picayune and arranged for enough papers to be delivered to the hotel where the chamber banquet was being held. They would come in handy when he laid his heart on the line.

Dandi wished she could sink through the floor. Everyone was staring and whispering.

"Relax; they are just saying how beautiful you look." And she did. The dress she wore was simple, a long red sheathe gown with a sheer wrap, very much like the one he had bought for her in Little Rock. "You are elegant and perfect."

"I hope they aren't expecting a floor show," she said dryly, attempting a bit of humor.

"No, they're not, but I am." He winked at her. "When you did that little pole dance on the end of the bed for me in New Orleans, you got my attention."

"Stop it," she put her arm through his, seeking his protection.

They were shown to their seats — up front. And everyone who came close to them spoke as graciously to her as they did to Lucas, but she could still see questions in their eyes.

"While you were getting dressed, I watched that tape your friends had brought over."

"You did?"

"Did you watch the end of it?"

"No, I couldn't."

"You should have. They interviewed the Detective and your friend Jane. You were praised. They told how you had been abused and how innocent you were and how you had been blackmailed. Everyone knows the truth now, they know what I know, and they know you."

Dandi didn't know what to say. She hoped he was right. A server brought their food, and Lucas pulled her) close to whisper in her ear. The man nodded and smiled at him. "Eat up," Dandi tried, but the chicken while probably prepared well, tasted like cardboard.

When they called him up to the podium, Dandi clenched her fists so tight that she dug her nails into her own palm. What would they say when they introduced him? She almost fainted with trepidation.

"Tonight, I have the pleasure of introducing you to someone who well deserves the title as Lafayette's Man of the Year. This man has committed his time and money to help our city and our citizens. He always puts the welfare of others first. I know he's well known to you, he represents us well. Lucas Dane Wagner is an author, a Dr. of Psychiatry, serves on the boards of numerous companies and charities. He is a philanthropist. He raises fine horses and many of us are proud to call him friend."

Dandi clapped harder than anyone else.

"Thank you, Mayor. Thank you Ladies and Gentleman, it is an honor to be with you tonight. I had a speech all prepared. I was going to tell you how privileged I am to help people find themselves. So many times, we are afraid to be ourselves, we're afraid to show any weakness, we're afraid to ask for help when there are those out there who would love to lend a helping hand. I wanted to tell you about how important it is that we accept ourselves for who we are. I had a rough childhood. My mother and father had problems and weaknesses that I vowed I would overcome. And I did. I thought that achieving success and establishing myself as a respectable member of the community was what it was going to take to make me happy."

He had everyone's rapt attention.

"I was wrong."

People began murmuring.

"Don't get me wrong, I am grateful for what I've achieved. But I've learned some lessons along the way. We can only be who we are. We can't let other people's mistakes ruin our lives. We can't value the opinions of others more than we do the truth."

There was a smattering of applause.

Lucas held up his hands. "Let me tell you my truth. I'm in love." He smiled. Dandi blushed. Women in the audience made swooning noises. "I would like to introduce you to the most perfect and beautiful woman in the world. Dandi LeBlanc." He held his hands toward her and there was more clapping. "She means everything to me. In the midst of an ugly, hopeless world, I found the rarest and most precious of jewels. I found love. I found Dandi."

Dandi looked at him through tears.

"I lost her for a while, but she's here tonight and I want you to hear and witness as I ask her a most important question."

"Lucas?" she whispered.

"Waiters, could you give me some assistance." She watched as several men came in, all carrying stacks of something. . . . it was newspapers. And they handed them out – to everybody – including her. "This is tomorrow's edition of The Times Picayune."

The waiter had laid it upside down. With trembling fingers she turned it over and every doubt she had ever had was answered in black and white.

"My Dandi has a favorite saying. When she hears something that she doesn't quite believe, she'll say – 'Why I wouldn't believe that unless I read it off the front page of The Times Picayune.'"

"I love you." That was all she could think to say.

"Well, here it is, Darling. I'm pouring my heart out here in front of God and everybody." She looked down at the paper. The headline took her breath away. LUCAS DANE WAGNER LOVES DANDI LEBLANC. The article beneath was a marriage proposal. I love you more than life. Will you marry me? Will you walk by my side? Will you live with me and be my love? Will you give me more beautiful children? Will you be my Dandi?"

She looked up at him, and was overwhelmed and all she could to do - - was run.

"I love you." She said to him, tremulously before she took off like fire was nipping at her heels.

There was thunderous applause. "Excuse me," Lucas said. "That's my cue, wish me luck."

Dandi hadn't run far, she wasn't leaving him. She'd never leave him again.

"You'd better stop." His voice broke a little.

She did.

The applause continued.

"Do you know what that is?"

She shook her head. She knew, but she didn't know what he meant.

"That's acceptance of who you are and what we will become." He pulled her to him. "But you know what?"

"What?"

"I don't need it. I appreciate their acceptance, but I don't care. All I need is you."

"I love you." She said it again. She had said it three times.

260

"I know." And he did. He believed her with all his heart. "Will you marry me?"

"Yes, I will." She answered with a sob.

"Hot Damn!" He picked her up. "Let's go get our baby and go home. I want to make love to you in my bed."

Later, when they had Lucy tucked in for the night, he took her by the hand and led her to his room. "Sit here," he eased her to the bed. Then he knelt at her feet. "I want to show you something." He took a piece of paper from out of the nightstand drawer. "Do you remember this?"

She did. "It's our marriage license from before."

"Yes, and I want you to know that I love you so much more now that I did then. And I'll love you more next year and even more the next."

"Thank you for never giving up on me," she cupped his dear face and kissed him.

"It wasn't even a possibility; I'd have looked for you every day of my life till I found you, even if it had taken the rest of my life."

"When I think back at the near misses we had, it's a miracle we found each other," she kissed his hand.

"I prayed for you every day. I relived every moment we shared. Every step I took was part of the journey back to you."

Dandi was beyond words. All she could do was let him hold her.

"I have something I want to give you." He took a ring from his pocket and held it out. "I've carried this with me ever since Valentine's Day three years ago."

Dandi held out her hand and he slipped the ring on her finger, then she threw herself into his arms. "What did I ever do to deserve you?"

"You were created for me. Before time began, we were." He picked her up and walked over to his sound system and flipped it on. Strains of the song she had danced to, 'After All', came pouring out of the speakers.

She tensed in his arms and he tightened around her. "No, we're making new memories. Dance with me."

The music swelled around them and an overwhelming wave of love swept over her. "We have been through a lot."

He set her on her feet and they began to sway. "Yet, here we are again." He kissed her on the nose. "I guess it must be fate."

She laid her head on his chest. "After all that we've been through, I can't deny it, our love is just meant to be."

"Yes, it's you and me, Forever." Lucas backed her up to the bed, giving her a mischievous grin. "Now, strip!"

She laughed out loud. "Strip? What will you give me if I do?"

"I'll give you all the love my heart can hold." He began to undo the buttons of his shirt.

"Deal." She kicked off one shoe and then the other.

Lucas couldn't take his eyes off of her. "Best deal I ever made."

They had both found what they needed and what they wanted.

Love.

ABOUT THE AUTHOR

Sable's hometown will always be New Orleans. She loves the culture of Louisiana and it permeates everything she does. Now, she lives in the big state of Texas and like most southern women, she loves to cook southern food - especially Cajun and Tex-Mex. She also loves to research the supernatural, but shhhh don't tell anyone.

Sable writes romance novels. She lives in New Orleans. She believes that her goal as a writer is to make her readers laugh with joy, cry in sympathy and fan themselves when they read the hot parts - ha!

The worlds she creates in her books are ones where right prevails, love conquers all and holding out for a hero is not an impossible dream.

Visit Sable:

Website: http://www.sablehunter.com

Facebook: https://www.facebook.com/authorsablehunter

Amazon: http://www.amazon.com/author/sablehunter

Hell Yeah! Series Reading Order

Cowboy Heat http://amzn.to/WhY6dw
Cowboy Heat Sweeter Version http://amzn.to/11fiBVQ

Hot on Her Trail http://amzn.to/U3zpT1
Hot on Her Trail Sweeter Version http://amzn.to/19m1WHf

Her Magic Touch http://amzn.to/11b1aw6
Her Magic Touch Sweeter Version http://amzn.to/1byKNL0

A Brown Eyed Handsome Man http://amzn.to/17zmNpY
A Brown Eyed Handsome Man Sweeter Version
http://amzn.to/15oW1k9

Badass http://amzn.to/UsrJJ4
Badass Sweeter Version http://amzn.to/16TqDNX

Burning Love http://amzn.to/15Z4Lyi
Burning Love Sweeter Version http://amzn.to/1iEzOV0

Forget Me Never http://amzn.to/U3PjwK
Forget Me Never Sweeter Version – Coming Soon

I'll See You in My Dreams http://amzn.to/11nsvpg
I'll See You in My Dreams Sweeter Version – Coming Soon

Finding Dandi http://amzn.to/12kK4Kh
Finding Dandi Sweeter Version – Coming Soon

Skye Blue - Coming Soon
I'll Remember You – Coming Soon
Thunderbird – Coming Soon
*Books in the Hell Yeah! Series are grouped by Hell Yeah!,
Hell Yeah! Cajun Style AND Hell Yeah! Equalizers

Cookbook
Sable Does It IN The Kitchen http://amzn.to/VAqFo4

Available from Secret Cravings Publishing

TROUBLE - Texas Heat I
My Aliyah - Heart In Chains - Texas Heat II
A Wishing Moon - Moon Magick I
Sweet Evangeline - Moon Magick II
Unchained Melody - Hill Country Heart I
Scarlet Fever – Hill Country Heart II
Bobby Does Dallas - Hill Country Heart III
Five Hearts - Valentine Anthology - A Hot And Spicy Valentine

For more info on Sable's Up Coming Series El Camino Real – Coming
Out 2014
Check out Sable's Fan Page on Facebook
http://facebook.com/authorsablehunter